PROMISES

MADE

TABLE OF CONTENTS

Promises Made is a work of fiction.

This novel is not meant to be taken as a means
to any cures for any type of neurological injuries.

The characters in this book are not real.

No part of this book may be used or reproduced
in any manner without written consent by the author.

Chapter 1
WISH YOU WERE HERE

On calm, warm, Saturday night in June, in a middle class neighborhood, Ted Stroit sits on his porch watching his daughter Gina play hopscotch with her friend Julie Wolbach. Playing on the radio that sits on the window sill is Pink Floyd's *"Wish You Were Here"*. Ted kicks up his feet, looks up onto the starry night, and takes a long smooth drag of his cigarette. After he exhales, he looks at the smoke seemingly hover over his head as there is little wind to dissipate it. He realizes how dark it has gotten since he first came out to relax and turns his attention back to the two girls playing hopscotch. Watching Gina hop along the sidewalk, Ted notices how much his daughter reminds him of his wife Linda. She has the same olive skin and dirty-blonde hair cut just above her shoulders. As the Pink Floyd song comes to an end, Ted turns off the radio. "It's getting dark Gina, time to turn in."

"Ok, Daddy, this will be the last game, we're almost done."

Gina was on square nine of ten within the chalk-drawn hopscotch board when it was Julie's turn to throw her stone. Julie's throw landed perfectly onto square ten and she began her hop - one foot, two feet, one foot, two feet, but as she approached square nine, she lost her balance. Before Julie could let out her usual "Oh Darn", Gina let her friend off the hook. "That's Ok Julie. You can have a do-over. The wind blew hard and knocked you over. That wasn't fair."

A little surprised, Julie wasn't about to disagree. "Yeah, I would have made it if it wasn't for the wind. Let me try again." This time, Julie completed her hops and won the game.

"Good game Julie, I'll see you tomorrow Ok?"

"See you tomorrow Gina. Good night Mr. Stroit."

"Good night Julie."

Julie ran into her house which was next door to the Stroit's home. Gina ran to meet her father. "Daddy, didn't you tell Mommy you were going to stop smoking?"

"I'm trying sweetie. I only had one cigarette, so I'm doing better. By the way, there wasn't any wind that I noticed. Why did you let Julie win?"

"I had already beated her two times. I didn't want Julie to feel bad."

"That was very nice of you. Tell you what, since you were so nice, I'll get you some ice cream before you get ready for bed. How's that sound?"

"That sounds great! And with chocolate syrup?"

"Sure with chocolate syrup."

"Yay!" Gina yelled licking her lips as she ran to the kitchen. Ted followed behind. He dished out two scoops of vanilla ice cream, covering them with chocolate syrup.

"Daddy, what time are we leaving to see Mommy tomorrow?"

"I want to get there early, around 9:00, why?"

"I want to get something before we leave to bring to Mommy."

"What are you getting for her sweetie?"

"It's a surprise Daddy." Within minutes, Gina's the ice cream was gone.

"You shouldn't eat that so fast Gina. You'll get a tummy ache."

"No I won't. I could eat ice cream for breakfast, lunch, and dinner."

"Now that you've finished, why don't you get washed up for bed."

"Ok Daddy." Gina ran up the stairs. A few minutes later Ted could hear the bathroom water running. Later Ted walked up to his daughter's bedroom where Gina was already tucked in. He kissed his daughter on her forehead. "Goodnight sweetie." He walked to the bedroom door, turned on the Casper night light and turned off the bedroom light. "See you in the morning."

"Goodnight Daddy, see you in the morning."

Ted was up at 6AM. Because of his work, he had always gotten up around 6AM. Even on weekends, he couldn't sleep past seven. He made some coffee, turned on the television and watched the Morning News. Within an hour, he could hear the opening and closing of drawers as Gina got out of bed and dressed. A few minutes later Gina came down wearing jeans, and her favorite shirt - pink with a rainbow on the front. "Good morning Daddy."

"Good morning sweetie, I see you are wearing your favorite shirt."

"One day I'm gonna follow a real rainbow so I can get to the gold at the end."

"One day I'm sure you will. I believe you can do anything you set your mind to. You want some breakfast?"

"Ok, but just cereal. I want to hurry and see Mommy to give her my present."

"Cereal it is. Fruit Loops Ok?"

"Yeah, Fruit Loops are good."

As Ted got up and walked to the kitchen, Gina went outside. "Where are you going Gina?"

"I saw some pretty flowers growing and I'm gonna pick 'em to give to Mommy when I see her. That's the surprise."

"They aren't the neighbors flowers are they?"

"No, Daddy, I saw some on our lawn. They're really pretty like sunshine."

"Hurry back, you know how you hate it when your cereal gets soggy."

"I'll be fast Daddy."

Ted had Gina's cereal on the table. He didn't know what to say when he saw his daughter enter the house holding dandelions. "Aren't they beautiful Daddy? They look like little sun shines."

"Uh, why yes, yes they are sweetie, Mommy will love them."

"And they smell nice too. You want to smell them?"

"Not right now. Why don't you put them on the table by the door so you don't forget them? Come in the kitchen, wash your hands and eat your cereal. When you're finished, we'll go see Mommy."

Gina rushed through her bowl of Fruit Loops. When the last bite of cereal was gone, she tilted the bowl to her mouth to slurp down the last bit of milk. "Ok Daddy, I'm finished. Are you ready to go?"

"Sure sweetie, let me get my keys. Don't forget your flowers." Ted with his keys in his hand, Gina holding her dandelions in her hand, went off to see Linda, Ted's wife, Gina's mother.

It was almost four years ago when Ted had come home from work to find his wife lying on the kitchen floor motionless. Her skin was pale, her lips purple. Ted knew right away there was nothing he could do. His wife had passed away. Doctors told him that Linda died from an aneurism in her brain. The only comforting thought was that Linda went quickly and felt no pain. She never knew what hit her. Gina was four years old at the time and what can you tell a little girl at that age about what had happened to her Mommy? All Ted could say was that God had needed Mommy and that she would be waiting for them in heaven. Ted told his daughter that her mother was still with them in spirit and that she loved her as much as any mother could love her child.

Ted had rarely attended church since his wife had passed. He didn't consider himself to be a religious man. He certainly wasn't as religious as his wife, who dragged him to church as often as she could. Even though Ted wasn't a regular church going man, he did believe that one day he and his wife will be together again.

After Linda's passing, Ted visited her grave site every day. After a year or so, it was a couple times each week. Then, it was once a week. Now, it was the first Sunday of each month. The visits to Linda's grave every month is mostly for Gina's sake. Gina always knows her mother is around and loves her. Ted doesn't need to visit Linda's grave to think of her, which was still every day. The best times in Ted's life were the times spent with his wife. Even when Ted and Linda had little money they always enjoyed being together. To this day, four years after her passing, Ted couldn't consider seeing another woman.

On the drive to the cemetery, Ted reminisced about their time together. He thought how unfair it was for a child to lose her mother at such a young age. After the twenty minute drive, Ted and Gina got out of the car and began walking the cobbled stone path to Linda's grave. Ted held Gina's left hand. Gina's right hand was holding her dandelions. When they got to the granite stone, Gina began to speak. "Hi Mommy, I brought you these beautiful flowers and they smell really nice. I hope you like them. School will be finishing up in a couple weeks. I've gotten really good grades. I've been doing really good. Haven't I Daddy?"

"Yes you have, you would be real proud of our little girl Linda."

"Daddy has been doing great too. I know he told you he would stop smoking and he has been trying really hard. Haven't you Daddy?"

"I have, I have."

Several minutes later, from a distance, Ted could hear someone shouting – "Hey what are you doing with those weeds? Don't be putting weeds all over the grass! What do you think you are doing?"

Ted and Gina turned to see the caretaker rushing towards them – "Hey, stop that! Get those weeds out of here!"

"Stay here sweetie. Daddy needs to talk to the man."

Ted walked up to meet the caretaker. The caretaker's face was so red that he looked like he had been out in 100 degree dry heat for several days. "What the hell are you doing with those weeds? Can't you get some real flowers?"

Ted, trying to keep the hollering to a minimum, walked up close to the irate man. "Look, I know they're weeds, you know they're weeds, but that little girl thinks they are the prettiest flowers on earth. She wants to give them to her mother. Now are you going to tell her she can't give them to her mother?"

The caretaker, looking at Gina, calmed down, let out a sigh. "Uh, look, I'm sorry. The boss has been up my ass all week about getting rid of these damn weeds. On top of that, it's been a dry season, the grass has been hard to keep green and he thinks it's my fault. He thinks I've been slacking on the job. You know how it is, don't ya?"

"Sure, look, as soon as we leave, you can remove them. Ok? Just let my little girl give her mother her flowers."

The caretaker looked over towards Gina and the grave the little girl was standing next to. He now felt terrible for screaming. "I'm sorry sir. It's just well you know how it is. You look like a working man. I can tell by the calluses on your hands. You know how it is, right?" The caretaker looked back to Gina. "Hello there little darlin', those are some real pretty flowers you got there."

"Hi mister, I picked them myself. They look like little sunshine don't they? They smell good too."

"Ok hunny, it's time to go. Tell Mommy good bye and you'll be back next month."

"Bye Mommy, we'll see you next month. By then, I'll be out of school for summer. Bye mister."

"Good bye darlin'."

Ted took Gina's hand and they walked back to the car for the ride home. As Ted opened the car door to let Gina in, he looked back at Linda's grave. He could see the caretaker already removing the beautiful pieces of sunshine that his daughter had picked for her mother.

"Daddy you didn't talk to Mommy much, how come?"

"Well sweetie, I really don't have to speak out loud for Mommy to know what I'm thinking. Your Mommy and I loved each other so much we could talk without saying a word."

"You mean Mommy could read your mind?"

Ted smiled and remembered how he could never get away with anything from Linda. "Yeah Gina, your Mommy could read my mind."

"Do you think Mommy can read my mind too?"

"Eh, maybe, I know she loves you more than anything in the world."

When Ted and Gina got back to the house, Ted sat in his recliner, picked up the remote and flipped on Sports Center. Gina walked to the kitchen to pour herself some orange juice. As she finished pouring, she heard a low wailing sound coming from the back yard. Putting down the carton, she went out to the yard and saw a small black and white kitten peeking out from behind the shed. Gina stepped outside, and approached the kitten slowly, not wanting to scare it away. The kitten, hesitant as well, continued to let out a low wail. As the kitten took a step back, Gina stopped, then slowly got down on one knee and let her hand out. "Here kitty, here kitty, I won't hurt you. Come here kitty, come on."

The kitten took a couple steps towards Gina who continued to hold out her hand. "Here kitty, kitty, come one, I won't hurt you. That's it, good kitty. Come here." The kitten took a few more steps towards Gina, and, after a few minutes, and more coaxing, the kitten was now rubbing his head against Gina's hand. Gina ran her fingers through the back of the kitten's head, down its back, and could now hear the kitten purr. "You're such a pretty kitty. Where did you come from? Are you hungry? I bet you haven't had any breakfast yet did you?" After gently rubbing the kitten's head and back, Gina picked up the kitten, walked back to the house, and placed him down on the kitchen floor. "You wait here. I'll get you something to eat." Gina pushed a chair to the countertop, climbed up and grabbed a can of tuna from the cabinet. She grabbed a coffee plate, a cereal bowl and stepped down. Ted, nodding off in front of the TV didn't hear a thing. Gina opened the can of tuna, emptied it on the coffee plate, got some milk from the refrigerator and poured some into the cereal bowl.

"Here you go kitty." As soon as Gina placed the tuna on the floor, the kitten dug in.

"Daddy, Daddy, come here, come here?"

"Huh, what? What is it Gina?"

"Come in the kitchen Daddy, look what I found."

Ted, still groggy, got up from the recliner, walked to the kitchen, and saw the kitten chowing down the tuna. "What the hell is a cat doing here?" Ted hollered. The kitten stopped eating, turned to look at Ted, and raised his back.

"Daddy you scared him, and you told Mommy you would stop swearing too."

"Gina, where did that cat come from?"

"I found him."

"What do you mean you found him? Where did you find him?"

"In the yard behind the shed, he was crying because he was hungry."

"Whose cat is that? I've never seen that cat before."

"It's my kitty Daddy. I found him."

"Hunny, I'm sure he belongs to somebody. Cats just don't pop up out of nowhere." At least Ted was *hoping* the cat belonged to someone. "Have you ever seen him before?"

"No Daddy, I just found him. Can I keep him? He needs a home. Please Daddy, please?"

Ted took a deep breath before answering. "Sweetie, if nobody comes looking for him, he can stay. If someone comes looking for him, he has to go back to his owner. Ok?"

"Ok Daddy, thank you, thank you!"

"Don't thank me now. As soon as someone comes looking for him, he's going back to his owner. Instead of milk, give the cat water. The last thing I need is him throwing up all over the place. When he's done eating, let him out again. I don't want him going to the bathroom all over the house either."

"Ok Daddy." Gina took the milk away from her new friend. She was about to pour it back into the milk carton when her father stopped her.

"Gina, pour the milk down the sink."

Sensing things had calmed down the kitten went back to eating his tuna. Ted shook his head, and then walked back to the recliner. He hoped someone would come and claim the cat. He took another look into the kitchen, and saw Gina petting her new found friend. Ted knew that no one was coming to claim the cat. He had another mouth to feed.

The rest of the afternoon was uneventful, Gina stayed in the yard except to come in for dinner. Ted spent most of the day in his recliner watching TV. He made a few phone calls. One was to his friend Joe to set up the usual time and place to meet before they went to the Union Hall in the morning. Later that night Ted went out back to see Gina still playing with the cat. Gina had a string and was waving it in front of the kitten as he pawed at it. "Come inside Gina, time for bed, you have school tomorrow."

"Ok Daddy." Gina picked up her kitten, and carried him into the house.

"Gina, what are you doing with that cat?"

"He's going to sleep with me Daddy."

"Don't you think he would be better off outside?"

"No Daddy, he's just a baby kitten. He's safer with me."

"What if he needs to go to the bathroom?"

6

"He already did, and he threw dirt over it so no one would notice."

Oh, great, Ted thought. He could picture himself stepping in it the next time he cut the grass. "Wash up good before bed. I'll be up in a few minutes to tuck you in."

Gina went upstairs. Ted heard the water running for her bath. After a few minutes he heard the opening and closing of drawers as Gina put on her pajamas. Ted finished watching the local news, and then went upstairs to see Gina already fast asleep. He also saw the new addition to the family curled up in the corner of Gina's bed by her feet. As Ted began to close the door, the kitten lifted his head, looked at Ted, yawned, and then placed his head back on his paws. If Ted didn't know better he could swear the cat just told him, he was here to stay and that Ted had no say in the matter. Ted turned on the Casper night light, turned out the bedroom light, and closed the door.

Ted was up at 5:30. After thirty minutes, he was washed, dressed, and headed down to make some coffee. He was surprised to see Gina in her pajamas letting in the cat from the yard.

"Good morning Daddy. Oreo needed to go out and do his business."

"Do his business?"

"Yeah, he needed to go to the bathroom. Can you get some tuna for him for breakfast?"

"Oreo huh, how did you come up with that name?"

"I named him Oreo because he's black and white, just like an Oreo cookie."

"Oh, I see." Ted opened a can of tuna, placed some on a plate. "Here you go, breakfast for Oreo. I guess I'm going to have to get some real cat food on my way home today. How about you Gina? You ready for some breakfast?"

"Ok, after I get dressed."

"I'll make French toast. It will be ready when you come down."

"That sounds good. I'll be down in a jiffy." Gina headed back upstairs. As Ted made the French toast he looked over at Oreo. He shook his head while the cat sat there staring, observing everything Ted was doing. "Not hungry Oreo?" While the French toast was sizzling, Ted began brewing his coffee.

Gina, as she said, was back in a jiffy. "Mmmm, that smells good."

"It will be done in a minute. Would you like some orange juice?"

"Yes please." Gina ate her breakfast. Ted sipped his coffee, and Oreo, already finished his breakfast, laid next to Gina's chair. When they were finished, Ted put the dishes in the sink.

"I have to get to work sweetie. Mrs. Bachwel will be over in a few minutes to take you over to her house. You can watch cartoons until she stops by. Oreo will have to stay here."

"Alright Daddy, have fun at work."

"I'll see you later sweetie."

"Aren't you going to say goodbye to Oreo?"

"Sure, I almost forgot. Goodbye Oreo." Ted winked at his little girl who had Oreo on her lap. Gina turned her attention towards the cartoons.

Sara Bachwel was Julie's mother. After Linda had passed away, the Bachwel's were a great help to Ted. Since Julie and Gina were the same age, Sara was able to see the both of them off to school, and greet them when they came home. Julie and Gina were like sisters. Sara was a stay at home mom who loved Gina as her own. Sara's husband, Steve, was also a nice guy. While Ted was in the construction business and loved sports, Steve worked in the insurance industry and didn't know a football from a basketball. However, he too cared for Gina and offered any help he could in Ted's difficult time. Ted felt lucky and very appreciative to have the neighbors next door.

Though Ted continued to hope that someone would stop by to claim Oreo, a couple weeks had passed and no one came. Oreo was Gina's to keep and care for, and Gina really did care for the kitten. She was up every morning to feed him and let him out to "do his business". At night, Oreo took his now claimed little corner of the bed by Gina's feet.

"Well Gina, it looks like no one has come to claim Oreo."

"I knew no one would Daddy."

"We should take Oreo to the veterinarian to get checked out."

"Take him to a veteran? I thought a veteran was a soldier."

"Not a veteran sweetie, a veterinarian. A veterinarian is a doctor for animals. When you get sick, you see a doctor. Pets need to see a veterinarian."

"But Oreo isn't sick. He's fine."

"I know he looks well, but we need to get him checked out just to be sure. He can't talk like you and me so we really don't know if he is sick or not. A veterinarian will know for sure."

"Oh, where do veterinarians work?"

Ted, never needing veterinarian before, didn't know. "I'm not sure. I'll ask someone at the Hall."

The secretary at the Union Hall told Ted of the veterinarian that she uses - Karen Lindstrom. She was caring and didn't charge too much. The following Saturday, Ted, Gina, and Oreo made a visit to Dr. Lindstrom. Karen was tall, thin and not only good with animals, she was great towards Gina. Karen told Gina how much she loved being a veterinarian. She could see all kinds of pets - kittens, puppies, birds, and other animals. Gina was in awe of Karen, who checked out Oreo, and then gave him a rabies shot. Before giving the shot, Karen assured Gina that the needle would ensure that Oreo stayed healthy. When she was finished Karen told Gina how brave her little friend was and that she had nothing to worry about. Oreo would be healthy for a long time as long as Gina would care for him.

"Oh, I'll take care of him Dr. Karen, he's a good kitty. Aren't you Oreo?" On the way home, Gina asked. "Daddy, how do you become a veterinarian?"

"First, you have to do well in school. After grade school, there's high school, then after high school, you go to medical school for animals. Why are you thinking about becoming a veterinarian?"

"Yeah, I think it would be great to work with animals all day."

"If you continue to do well in school, I think you would be a great veterinarian."

"I know, I think I would too. I just love animals, don't I Oreo?"

The next morning, Ted and Gina drove off to see Linda. As Gina and Ted walked the cobbled road, the caretaker who had complained about the dandelions approached Gina with a bouquet of purple lilacs. "Hi there darlin', I know how much you love flowers, and I saw these so I thought you might want to give them to your mom."

"Oh wow mister, they are beautiful. Aren't they beautiful Daddy?"

"They sure are Gina. Sir, really you don't have to do that."

"Oh, I don't mind. I kinda felt bad the way I treated you last month, and I heard you say you'd be back the first Sunday of the month, so I thought to myself right then that I'd make it up to ya. I'm not really such a hard ass. I was just uptight over my boss complaining so much. And, we have plenty of flowers here, so it's no sweat off my back."

"Well, thank you sir."

"It's Brian, Brian Sweeney, but everyone calls me Campy. I got that name when I first started here. Being the new man on the totem pole, I had to camp out at night here to keep an eye on things. I kinda liked the peace and quiet, so when my turn was up, I asked if I could stay on the night shift for another few months. That's when they started calling me Campy."

"Thanks Brian, eh, Campy. Thank Mr. Sweeney Gina, and we'll give them to Mommy."

"Thank you Mr. Sweeney."

"Don't mention it darlin'. Call me Campy. Everybody calls me Campy. Have a nice day."

"You have a nice day too Mr. Campy. See ya."

Gina couldn't wait to give her mom the flowers and tell her about her new friend Oreo.

Chapter 2
PRISON BREAK

There were only two weeks left in Brandon Leshing's summer vacation. He didn't want to waste it staying inside the house. In a couple weeks too much time would be spent inside studying and doing homework. At 8AM Saturday, wearing his Alabama Crimson Tide football shirt, he was ready to do something fun. The sun was shining. It was a beautiful day. Brandon rushed through his cereal, went outside and sat on the lawn in front of his house. Within fifteen minutes, as Brandon knew he would, Louie Buccelli came running out of his house across the street to meet him.

The neighborhood that the boys live in is a new development of three story single homes. Houses in the neighborhood are still being developed. Behind Louie's house, which he has lived in all of his seven years, is a row of homes that are seventy-five percent complete. Brandon's family moved into their home three years ago. Brandon, eight years old, is the only child of Pat and Cindy Leshing.

"Hey Louie, here comes Frankie and Jimmy, feel like playing a prank on Frankie?" Frankie and Jimmy Grogan are twin brothers, also eight years old, who live in the corner house at the bottom of the street.

Louie, always up for some laughs, especially when it's him and Brandon teaming up, couldn't wait to hear Brandon's plan. "Sure what do you want to do?"

"Go behind my steps. I'll talk to Frankie and Jimmy and get them to face towards the street so they can't see you. Once you see them and me talking, come up slowly behind Frankie and bend down right behind him. He won't even notice you. I'll dare him into racing me to my yard. When he turns to run, he'll trip over you."

"Yeah, that'll get him for sure. You'll have to give me a signal when to come out."

"I'll scratch behind my head like this. When you see me do that, come over, but quietly."

"Ok." Off Louie went, behind the steps on the side of Brandon's house. As Frankie and Jimmy got nearer, Frankie asked – "Hey Brandon, where'd your side-kick go?"

"We're trying to get some of the guys together to see what we could do today. We saw you guys coming up, so Louie went to see if he could round up a couple more. You got any ideas Frankie?" As they talked, Brandon swayed the two brothers so they both had their backs to Louie who was crouched behind the steps. "Hey, you guys want to see something really cool?" Brandon asked.

"Sure." Jimmy said.

"I found this really old arrow head stone in my back yard." Brandon began to dig into his pockets. Frankie and Jimmy, fixated on Brandon, didn't notice Louie was peeking out from behind the steps. "Oh, man, I had it a while ago." Brandon took his right hand out of his pocket and began to scratch behind his head giving Louie the signal. Louie slowly crept up behind Frankie. Within a few seconds, Louie had quietly positioned himself right behind him. He could hardly contain himself as the anticipation of seeing Frankie's face was hard to suppress.

"Yeah, right Brandon. You had a valuable arrow head and suddenly lost it." Frankie said.

"I swear I found it in my yard. I bet I left it there, come on hurry, I'll show you." Brandon began to run to his yard, Frankie, not noticing Louie was behind him, turned to run. As soon as he took a step, he fell over Louie. Brandon and Louie busted out laughing. Even Jimmy started laughing. It was a good successful prank. Frankie though, didn't think it was so funny.

"I'm gonna get you Louie! You won't be laughing when I do." Louie started running, laughing all the way. He ran behind the car parked on the street. As small as Louie was, he could run. He was quick as a mouse. When Frankie ran to one side of the car, Louie was on the other. When Frankie ran to the front, Louie ran to the back.

"Come on Frankie, you'll never catch him. It was a joke." Jimmy said.

"Yeah Frankie." Louie was still laughing while trying to catch his breath. "It was Brandon's idea."

"Come on Frankie, it was just a prank. Don't take it so hard." Brandon said.

Frankie also was out of breath with his red face still not back to its normal color. "Fine, but you'll get yours Louie. You won't know when it's coming, but you'll get yours I swear!"

Joe Liddon and John Rapris were walking up the street. They lived around the block. Joe was the same age as Louie, seven. John was the same age as Brandon, Frankie and Jimmy, eight. "Hey guys, what's up with Frankie and Louie?" John asked.

"Ah, Louie and I just played a joke on Frankie." Brandon answered.

"He fell for it hook, line and sinker." Louie couldn't get the smile off his face.

"I told you Louie, you'll get yours!"

"What are you guys up to?" Joe asked.

"Not much, how about you?" Jimmy replied.

"You want to head to the shopping center?" Joe suggested.

"You got any money?" Frankie replied.

"I got a buck." Joe said. "How about you?"

"I don't have a dime." Louie said.

"I got a buck fifty, but I'm not wasting it on you guys, especially you squirt." Frankie said looking at Louie. Together they had three dollars and fifty cents.

"We can't do much with that." John said.

"How about we play Prison Break?" Joe suggested.

"Yeah, alright, are the rest of you up for it?" Brandon asked.

"That sounds good." Jimmy said.

"I'm up for it." Louie chimed.

"I figured you would be up for it Louie since your master was up for it."

"Ok, Frankie, let it go, will ya. Let's choose teams." Brandon said. "I'll be one captain, who wants to be the other?"

Frankie blurted out "I do" before Brandon finished his words. "Ok. Joe, take out a coin. We'll flip to see who chooses first."

"Heads or tails Frankie?"

"Tails never fails." Frankie said. Joe flipped his quarter, it landed on tails. "Ha, tails never fails. I win, I pick first. I'll take Jimmy."

"Ok, I'll take John."

"Oh, you didn't pick your side kick. Ok, I'll take the squirt." Frankie didn't want to take Louie, but he took him out of spite. He knew Louie wanted to be on Brandon's team. "And I'm the captain Louie, which means you have to do what I say."

Brandon, surprised with Frankie's pick, took Joe. Louie was disappointed that Brandon didn't pick him first. "Ok, we'll be the prisoners, you be the guards." Brandon said. "You got to give us five minutes, and then you can come looking for us."

"Fine, one minute is 60 seconds. We'll count to 300." Frankie replied.

"That sounds fair." John said.

"Since I'm the captain, I pick who counts to 300. Louie, as your captain, I command you to count. Can you count that high squirt?" Louie gave a quick glance to Brandon with a look to say, *you should have picked me*. Brandon looked back to Louie frowning, *sorry buddy*.

Louie started his count. "One, two, three, four, ..."

"Come on guys, let's hide." Brandon, Joe and John took off running. They took a left at the corner of the street and headed straight for the unfinished houses. When they got to the first house at the bottom of the street, Brandon stopped the other two. "Ok guys, they're going to try to catch us, but, we're gonna turn the screws on them and catch them."

"What do you mean Brandon?" Joe asked.

"We'll hide out in the back of the third house up there. In the middle there's a hole in the floor. The builders haven't completed it yet. We'll cover the hole with ply wood or something, so they won't notice it. Then we'll move some stuff to make a path so when they come in, they'll walk right to the hole. When they walk over it, they'll fall in and we'll have them trapped."

"Yeah, that sounds good." The three prisoners ran up to the third house on the left. When they went inside they quickly went to work. They moved trash cans. They found some boxes, two by fours, and some copper pipe. They aligned the debris to make a path up to the hole in the middle of the floor. The hole was three feet by three feet wide. It was five feet deep. "Instead of plywood, we can use this cloth." Joe said.

"Hey that's a good idea Joe. Grab one end of the cloth and go over the other side of the hole. John, get that can over there and place it on the cloth. Then grab those boxes and put them on the cloth on the other side." Joe and John did as Brandon instructed. Within minutes the trap was set, they hid in the back of the house. "Oh man, this is going to be great."

Seconds later they could see the guards, Frankie, Jimmy and Louie coming up the street. "Make some noise to lure them in. But not too loud, we don't want to make it too obvious."

"Ok Brandon." John grabbed some wood and slid it across the ground making it sound as if they were moving something to hide behind.

As the three guards got closer to the house, Jimmy said, "I hear them in that house."

"Yeah, I can hear them too." Louie began running to the house.

"Hey Louie, hold up, we'll catch them together." Frankie shouted. "Louie, hold up. I'm the captain. You have to do as I say. Hold up!" However, Louie didn't listen to Frankie. Within seconds, Louie was half way to the house where he knew the prisoners were. He wanted to be the one to catch them. Brandon didn't pick Louie to be on his team and Louie wanted to show Brandon that was a mistake. He ran up to the unfinished door, and through the path that was set up. Louie took one step onto the cloth and the trapped worked. Louie fell right in.

"Hah! We got you!" Joe shouted. They ran to the hole and saw Louie lying on his back.

"Ugh, oh man." Louie moaned.

"Louie, are you Ok?" Joe asked. By now Frankie and Jimmy had joined them. All five boys were looking down at Louie who continued to moan.

"Louie, are you Ok, come on get up." John said.

"How did he fall down there?" Frankie asked.

"Brandon had us build a trap for you guys and Louie fell right in." John replied.

"Oh, so now it's the side-kick that gets pranked. How's it feel side-kick?"

"Frankie shut up. I think Louie's hurt. Louie, you Ok?" Brandon asked.

"Everybody laughs when it's me that gets pranked."

"Frankie shut up!" Brandon yelled.

"I'm just saying that's all."

"Oh, Mommy, somebody get my Mommy. I feel kind of weird. I can't move."

"What do you mean you can't move? Does it hurt?" Jimmy asked.

"Mommy, get my Mommy."

"Louie, hold on, we'll pull you up." Jimmy suggested.

"No, I can't move, somebody get my Mommy."

"Ok, Louie, I'll get your mom." Johnny said.

"Hurry, Johnny." Brandon said. "Johnny's getting your mom Louie, hang in there."

Johnny ran out the door shouting. "Mrs. Buccelli! Mrs. Buccelli!"

"Brandon, I can't move. I feel so weird." Louie began to cry.

"Does it hurt Louie?" Frankie asked. The other four gave Frankie a shut up look. "I'm being serious. Does it hurt Louie?"

"No, but I feel really weird."

"Hold on Louie. Johnny's getting your Mom." Jimmy tried to ease Louie's mind.

Claire Buccelli was a stay at home mom and her son Louie was the world to her. Johnny banged on the door. "Mrs. Buccelli! Mrs. Buccelli!"

"Johnny, what is it? What's wrong? Where's Louie?"

"He's hurt Mrs. Buccelli, Louie's hurt."

"What do you mean? Where is he?"

"He fell in one of the new houses. We were playing Prison Break and Louie fell."

"What! Oh my God! Which house? Where is he?"

"He's in the third house."

"Wait here Johnny, let me get my keys." Claire ran to get her car keys and cell phone. When she had them, she ran to the car. "Get in the car Johnny, show me where Louie is." Claire started the car, peeled out of the drive way, and sped down the street. She made a left at the corner, down the street, and then made another left up the unpaved road, to the third house. When they stopped, Johnny ran back into the new house. "Louie, your mom's coming."

By now Louie was down to a low moan. Claire came running into the unfinished room. "Louie! Oh my God, Louie can you hear me?"

"Mommy." Louie murmured.

"Louie, talk to me! Are you hurt?"

"I can't feel anything Mommy. I can't move."

"Baby, Mommy's here. I'm calling an ambulance. Stay calm, hunny." Claire pulled out her cell phone and dialed 911. "Hello, my name is Claire Buccelli. I need an ambulance behind Lyman St. We're in one of the new houses. I think it's the third one from the bottom of the street. Hurry!"

"Claire, this is Thomas Sheldon. What exactly happened, who is hurt?"

"It's my son, he fell. He can't move."

"Is he conscious?"

"Yes, yes, please get an ambulance!"

"I've already contacted them, they're on their way. You said you are behind Lyman St. in one of the new houses. You are located at the third house from the bottom, correct?"

"Yes, hurry! Louie, can you hear me?"

"Yes." Louie faintly spoke.

"Claire, this is Thomas, can you tell if your son is bleeding?"

"Louie, are you bleeding?"

"I don't know. I don't think so."

Claire didn't noticing any blood. "No, I don't think he is bleeding."

"Good, try to stay calm. The ambulance is on its way. I'll be with you until they get there. Is there anyone else with you?"

"Yes, his friends, five of them." The other five boys were in a state of shock. Each one knew something serious had just happened to their friend Louie. Brandon was visibly shaken.

"How old is your son?"

"He's seven."

"Is he able to talk? Is he coherent?"

"Louie, can you hear me?"

"Yes Mommy, can you hurry? I'm getting cold."

"Yes baby the ambulance is on its way. Where is that damn ambulance?" Claire screamed into her cell phone.

"It's a couple miles away. You should be hearing the siren soon. If you are in the house, send one of the kids outside so they can flag down the ambulance when it arrives."

"One of you, go outside and wave when the ambulance comes to let them know where we are."

"I'll go out Mrs. Buccelli." Joey and Johnny went out to flag down the ambulance.

Within minutes, they could hear the siren. Then they saw the ambulance at the bottom of the dirt road. "Up here! Over here!" Joey and Johnny shouted. The ambulance pulled up to the house followed by a police car.

"Baby the ambulance is here. Can you hear me?"

"Yes Mommy." Louie's voice was becoming fainter.

"Oh God Louie, you're going to be Ok. Do you hear me? You're going to be Ok." Claire, seeing the ambulance, hung up the phone without acknowledging Thomas the dispatcher. Jeff O'Leary and Peggy Conrad jumped out of the ambulance followed by police officers Ed Cevalas, and Gregory Trinatti.

"Over here, Louie's in here." Johnny shouted. Johnny and Joey led the ambulance and police personnel into the house.

"I'm Jeff O'Leary, this is Peggy Conrad. You must be Claire Buccelli."

"Yes, my son, Louie, he's hurt." Jeff and Peggy ran to check on Louie.

15

"Mrs. Buccelli, I'm officer Ed Cevalas and this is officer, Gregory Trinatti." Officer Trinatti went to assist Peggy and Jeff, officer Cevalas stayed next to Claire.

"Stand aside boys. Let the people do their jobs." Officer Trinatti said.

"Hello Louie I'm Jeff, this is Peg. Can you hear me?"

"Yes, but I can't move." Louie said, but barely audible.

"We're coming down, we're gonna help you. Stay still. Don't try to move."

"Is your son allergic to anything Mrs. Buccelli?" Peg asked.

"No. He's never had any allergic reaction to anything. Is he going to be Ok?"

"That's what we're going to check. We're going to get him stable and get him to the hospital." Jeff and Peg lowered themselves next to Louie. Jeff took Louie's pulse. As Peggy checked Louie's legs, they began to shake uncontrollably.

Claire noticed Louie's legs shaking. "Louie! What's going on? What's wrong with him?"

Jeff tried to calm Claire down. "We'll get him stable Mrs. Buccelli."

Louie's five friends looked on in horror. Each had the thought Louie was leaving them. Brandon wanted to shout out to Louie to hold on, but he could barely breathe.

"Are you still with me Louie?" Louie didn't respond. "Peg, check his vitals." Louie stopped shaking and was now unconscious.

"Louie! Louie!" Claire shouted.

"Officer Trinatti, we're going to need the stretcher, and your help getting Louie out of here. We'll need four cable lines to pull him up."

"Right, I'm on it."

"Oh my God! Louie! Louie!"

"Try to stay calm Mrs. Buccelli. He's in good hands." Officer Cevalas tried to calm Claire.

"Stay calm? How can you say that? That's my baby down there, he's unconscious, he can't move and you're telling me to stay calm?"

"He's in good hands. He'll be fine. We're here with you, and we'll be with you until we can get him to the hospital."

Officer Trinatti was back. "Here comes the stretcher."

"I got it. Peg, try and straighten him out, slowly." Peg and Jeff had gotten Louie onto the stretcher and fastened the four cables to each corner. "We have him stable. I'm going to throw up each cable. One of you, catch the other end."

"Ok." Officer Trinatti replied. All four cables were now up on the floor.

"Peg, climb up and help lift the stretcher onto the floor. I'll stay here to make sure it stays balanced." Peg climbed up onto the floor. "Officer Trinatti,

Peg, you get the bottom cables. Officer Cevalas, get one of the boys to help you with the top cables."

Officer Cevalas walked up to Brandon. "What's your name son?"

"My name is Brandon sir."

"Brandon, help with this cable. We're going to pull Louie up slowly. Can you do it?"

"Yes officer." Brandon grabbed one of the cable lines.

"I can do it officer." Frankie claimed.

"That's Ok son, we only need one person. Ok Jeff, we have the lines." Officer Cevalas said. "We're ready when you are."

"On my command, I'm going to count to three. On three, slowly lift. Ready?"

"We're ready."

When they got Louie safely onto the floor, Claire rushed to her son. "Louie! Louie!" She wanted to hold Louie, but officer Trinatti grabbed her before she could.

"Mrs. Buccelli, let the people take a good look at him. I know you want to hold him, but we need to get him to the ambulance. Do you understand?"

"Yes, but my baby, my baby!"

"He's going to be ok."

Before Jeff climbed out of the hole, he could feel a pipe that was barely visible on the ground. Louie must have fallen on his back onto the pipe. He had a feeling he knew why Louie couldn't move. Jeff climbed out of the hole, went over to Peg, who was already with Louie to make sure he was stable enough to be transported to the hospital. "Can you hear me Louie?" No response. Peg lifted one eye lid, flashed a pen light into his eye. "Jeff, we need to get him to the hospital ASAP."

"I know."

Officer Cevalas gathered Louie's friends. "Boys I'm going to need your names." Each boy gave the officer his name. "Do you all live in the area?"

"Yes, we all live around the block." Jimmy replied.

"Can one of you tell me what happened?"

"It was Brandon's fault officer." Frankie blurted. "He built a trap so Louie would fall in."

"What!" Claire shouted at Brandon. "You did this on purpose? How could you do this to him Brandon! He looks up to you. How could you do this?"

"Mrs. Buccelli, I, I didn't mean to, I didn't. I swear." Brandon was visibly choked up.

"Mrs. Buccelli, let officer Cevalas do his job." Officer Trinatti was by Claire's side. "I don't think it was anyone's intention to hurt your son."

Officer Cevalas turned to the boys. "Is that right son? You built a trap and he fell in?"

"I guess. I mean me, Joe and Johnny we built it."

"Yeah, but it was Brandon's idea officer." Joe didn't want to get into any trouble. "He was the captain, he told us to do it. Frankie was the other captain."

"I didn't know they were building a trap officer. It wasn't my fault." Frankie shouted. "We were the guards. Brandon's team was the prisoners."

"Am I going to go to jail officer?" Brandon sheepishly asked.

"No son, no one is going to jail."

"If you need me to testify officer, I will." Frankie said, while sneering at Brandon.

"Shut up Frankie." Jimmy said.

"What? It *was* Brandon's fault. If Louie dies, he'll be up on murder charges."

"Frankie, shut up!" Jimmy said again.

"No one's going to die, and no one's going to jail. Ok, boys I got all I need for now. Why don't you head on home."

"Officer, Louie's gonna be Ok right?" Brandon asked.

"Sure son, he's in good hands now."

Jeff and Peg had completed their check on Louie. They radioed in to Memorial Hospital that they would be driving in shortly with an unconscious seven year old boy who was unable to move. Claire rode in with the following police car. By now, a small crowd had gathered to witness the event, including another police vehicle. Two other police officers were holding the small crowd of bystanders at bay. One of those bystanders was Cindy Leshing, Brandon's mom. When Brandon came out of the house, he ran to her. "Brandon, what happened? What happened to Louie?"

"Can we go home mom? I need to tell you at home."

"Sure, let's go."

As soon as Brandon and his mom stepped into the house Brandon blurted out with tears streaming. "I think I killed Louie mom!"

"What, they told me Louie was hurt. What do you mean? What happened?"

"I told Joey and Johnny to build a trap. Louie fell in and now he's hurt real bad. He can't move. He might die mom and it's my fault. I might go to jail for murder."

"Brandon, no one's going to jail. Calm down. From the beginning, tell me what happened."

Brandon explained what happened. As an eight year old boy seeing his best friend lying unconscious, knowing he was the cause, he felt certain he was going to jail. Cindy tried her best to calm her son down. When he seemed to settle down a little, Cindy went to the living room to call her husband. "Hello Pat."

"Hey Cindy, is everything Ok? You need me to pick something up on the way home?"

"No Pat, everything is not Ok. I need you to come home right away. There's been an accident with one of Brandon's friends."

"Oh God, is Brandon hurt?"

"Brandon's fine. It's Louie that's hurt."

"Louie? But Brandon's fine?"

"Yes, Brandon is fine! I need you to come home."

"If Brandon isn't hurt, why do you need me to come home?"

"Because your son thinks he is responsible. He thinks he might go to jail for murder."

"Jail? For murder? Why does he think he's going to jail for murder?"

"He's not going to jail Pat, but he is scared. I think you should come home right away."

"But Brandon isn't hurt right?"

"No Pat. Brandon isn't hurt, physically."

"Well, you're there with him. You can explain he's not going to jail can't you? I can't come home just yet. There's a big meeting happening in an hour. I have to attend."

"Pat, can't you get someone to cover for you? This is your son for Christ sake!"

"Cindy, you know there is talk of a buyout of our company. Right now everyone is on pins and needles. Everyone is doing everything they can to keep their job in case this buyout goes through. This is too damn important to miss."

"Is it more important than your son Patrick?"

"Cindy, you said Brandon isn't hurt. You're with him. You can calm him down. There's nothing I would actually be able to do that you're not doing anyway. Look, I'll get home as soon as I can. I promise. Then, if he needs to talk, I'm all ears."

"Fine Patrick, go to your damn meeting. We'll talk when you get home."

"Cindy, I promise, I'll be home as soon as I can." Pat Leshing was a faithful husband and a good provider for his family. He worked as a Regional Sales Manager for Virginia Cable Company. Virginia Cable was a small company serving the Virginia, Maryland, and D.C. areas. Because cable was relatively new to the area when Pat started, business was great, the money was good and the hours he worked were normal. He worked nine to five during the week, and occasionally on Saturdays. Now there was talk that the small company was going to be bought out by Universal Cable.

Universal Cable primarily handled customers from Pennsylvania, New York, Ohio, Delaware, and New Jersey. Recently, Universal expanded to Virginia, and Maryland. Thus they became a large competitor overshadowing the smaller Virginia Cable. The fear at Virginia Cable was that with the buyout, and because Universal was based out of Philadelphia with regional offices in other states, that only a handful of employees would retain their positions.

Most, would be given a severance, and let go. Pat didn't want to be one of those let go.

When Pat got home, Brandon was in his room. "How's Brandon doing Cindy?"

"He's fine Patrick. You should have come home earlier today."

"I understand he was upset. From the looks of things, you handled it fine. You did great. You're a great mom, and a terrific wife. What happened anyway?"

"From what Brandon told me they were playing some game. Brandon and a couple other kids built a trap that Louie fell into in one of the unfinished houses. Apparently Louie was hurt very badly. Brandon said he couldn't move and when I saw Louie being taken to the hospital by the ambulance, he looked unconscious."

"An ambulance came? Wow, Louie must have been hurt pretty badly then. Have you spoken to Claire or Dominic?"

"No, I haven't seen either of them. They must be at the hospital."

"What about this jail stuff?"

"Apparently Brandon was the one who told the other kids to build the trap. So, Brandon thinks he is responsible for the accident and will go to jail."

"Did you explain to him that you don't go to jail for accidents?"

"Yes Pat! I explained everything!"

"Ah, like I said a great mom and a terrific wife." Pat gave Cindy a kiss on the cheek. Cindy didn't respond in kind to his gesture. "What's for dinner? I'm starved."

"You can make your own dinner Patrick! You should have come home this afternoon."

"Cindy I would have if it was just another meeting. You know how tense things are since the buyout talk."

"Well, I'm exhausted from all the tension today as well. You're on your own for dinner."

It had been three weeks since that fateful day. No one outside of Louie's parents had seen Louie. The prognosis for Louie wasn't good, he had broken his back. He was paralyzed from the waist down. However, true to Louie's nature, he was as upbeat as any seven year-old could be. Louie's mood may have been due to the medication he was on. Or it may have been due to the fact that he didn't fully grasp the ramifications of his injury. Doctors didn't dare tell him that his prognosis wasn't good. Part of the reason was not to deepen the hardship, but also because the doctors really didn't know the true prognosis. Louie's spinal cord wasn't completely severed. So that meant his condition was incomplete, and at this time it was the best news Claire and Dominic could have.

Most of the talk at Mother Mary Catholic Elementary school was about what had happened to Louie. Some kids thought Louie was dead. Worse, some rumored that Brandon had killed Louie. All Brandon could do was tell anyone who asked, anyone who listened, that it was an accident. But few kids asked. Most just spread the rumor of the day. Although no one really picked on Brandon at school because he was bigger than most of the other kids, he could hear the whispers. Brandon killed Louie. Brandon threw Louie down a twenty foot hole. Brandon beat Louie to a pulp. Even Joe, John, Frankie, and Jimmy who knew what had happened didn't stand up for Brandon. When kids sneer, chastise, or worse, ignore a kid, it's hard for another kid to stand up for the one being chastised. Peer pressure at that age is tough. Because of the severity of Louie's injury, the other four kids didn't want to be associated, or blamed for his injury. In their young minds, they still thought Brandon could go to jail, and they didn't want to be associated to that. In Frankie's case, he hadn't forgotten the prank Brandon and Louie played on him that day.

Not being able to see Louie, or talk to him made it hard on Brandon. If he could just talk to him, tell him he didn't mean it. Tell him he was sorry. Cindy and Pat tried their best to comfort their son who was noticeably shaken over the accident. Unfortunately Cindy or Pat couldn't honestly tell Brandon that Louie would turn out fine. So, they told him to keep praying, to keep positive as best he could.

Aside from going to school, Brandon didn't venture outside. To get by each day, and sleep at night, he would somehow convince himself that Louie would be Ok. Every morning when he awoke, it was Louie that was first on his mind. Because Louie's parents lived across the street, the hardest part of Brandon's day was going to, and coming home from school. He dreaded any eye contact that might occur between him and Louie's parents. Louie's father seemed easier to take than Louie's mom. Brandon knew that Claire blamed him for her son's injury. Although Claire never said a word to Brandon, he knew what she was thinking. Dominic, on the other hand always tried to say something. "Hello Brandon. Louie told me to say Hi." Or, "Louie's doing better." It was when Dominic said this that Brandon just wanted to run over and ask for sure how Louie's doing. But, his guilt, and the guilt laid upon him by Claire always prevented Brandon from saying anything other than, "I'm praying for him."

A couple months had gone by and Brandon still hadn't seen Louie. With the holidays getting closer, most of the kids at school had forgotten about Louie, but not Brandon. Louie was still on his mind every day from the minute he awoke to the minute he fell asleep. While most kids were thinking of the holidays and what fun times and great presents they would have, all Brandon wanted for Christmas was to see Louie. Then, two weeks before Christmas, Brandon got his wish.

Dominic had told Cindy that Louie was coming home for the holidays. When Brandon heard this, he pictured Louie coming home, full of energy. It would be the old Louie running up to Brandon's house banging on the door asking him to come out and play. It was the best Christmas present Brandon could have. The closer Christmas came, the more excited he became. The thought of Louie's demise, the guilt Brandon felt was being lifted from his shoulders. With Louie coming home, Brandon was finally starting to think of other things in his life, such as school assignments, Christmas presents, especially what present to get for Louie. Brandon had more energy that was noticeable by his mom, and for this, she was grateful.

The day finally arrived, Saturday morning and Louie was on his way home. Brandon sat on the living room couch constantly looking out the window waiting to see his friend. At 1PM, Brandon finally saw Louie coming home. However, it wasn't anywhere near what Brandon had hoped. Louie came home in an ambulance. When he came out of the ambulance, he was in a wheelchair. Two people in white clothing wheeled Louie up his driveway and into the house through the garage door. Dominic was there watching, offering any assistance he could.

The guilt Brandon had felt, the thought of Louie's demise came crashing down hard on him again. Maybe that was how people always came home from the hospital. Maybe Louie was alright after all and this was just the way things were done with people who spent months in a hospital. Maybe it was just so the people at the hospital knew that their patient would make it home Ok. Brandon wanted so badly to go down and see Louie.

"I see your friend is home. Aren't you going to go and say hi?" Cindy asked.

"I will later mom. I'm sure Louie's got to get settled. Maybe he's hungry or something. I don't want to bother him right away."

"Ok hunny, but it sure is good to see that he's out of the hospital isn't it?"

"Uh, yeah, it is mom. It's good to see Louie come home." But Brandon wasn't sure. He still couldn't get by Dominic and especially Claire to go down and see Louie for himself.

The next week of school would be a short one. Only three days and then it's off for the holidays. On his way to the bus stop Monday morning, Brandon saw Dominic in his car. As Brandon walked, Dominic pulled up beside him and rolled his car window down. "Hey Brandon, Louie's been asking when you'll stop over. How about stopping over tonight?"

"I'd love to Mr. Buccelli, but I got this school project due Wednesday. I'm a little behind and I really have to finish it up tonight."

"Oh, that's too bad. How about stopping over tomorrow night?"

"I don't think that's a good idea either. I have some chores to do around the house."

"Oh, I see, and Wednesday? I know you kids will get out of school early. How about stopping over right after, around 1:00?" Brandon didn't know what to say. He was out of excuses. He really did want to see Louie. He paused, looked back at Louie's house to see if Louie's mom was watching.

Dominic knew the real reason Brandon didn't want to stop over. "Brandon, look, I know what happened was an accident. I don't blame you for what happened. Louie certainly doesn't blame you either. Claire will be over her sister's house Wednesday. They're going shopping together. Louie would really like to see you. What do you say?"

"It really was an accident. I would never do anything to hurt Louie. Kids at school are blaming me, and, Mrs. Buccelli."

"I know Brandon. It has to be hard on you as well. Louie doesn't blame you. It would really pick up his spirits if you would stop by. I think it would be good for you as well. As for my wife, well, she doesn't have to know. She'll be out with her sister, so she won't be home."

Brandon was relieved to hear Mr. Buccelli say these things. He was relieved to hear that Mr. Buccelli, and especially Louie, didn't blame him. Mr. Buccelli was right. Seeing Louie would be great for him too. "What time is Mrs. Buccelli going out?"

"She'll be going out around eleven. She won't be home until well after three."

"I get done school at noon, so I could stop over around one."

"That would be great Brandon."

"You're sure Mrs. Buccelli won't be there? It's not that I don't like her, it's just, well."

"I know, don't worry, Louie will be happy to see you. 1:00 Wednesday then?"

"Yep, I'll be there at 1:00 on Wednesday."

"Great, I'll tell Louie. I got to run off to work. You have a great day at school Brandon."

"Sure, and thanks Mr. Buccelli."

"You're welcome." Dominic rolled up his car window and drove off down the road.

Wednesday came and Brandon was home from school by 12:30. He ran in his house, put his books on the chair and looked out of the living room window. Just as Mr. Buccelli said, Louie's mom seemed to be away. Brandon kept looking out of the window. He wanted to be absolutely sure Mrs. Buccelli was gone. He was also a little nervous to see Louie. What would he say? How would Louie look? Did Louie really not blame him? Would Louie be the same happy go lucky kid he had always known? Or would Louie be angry, or worse crying about what Brandon had done to him? But, more than any of his fears, Brandon wanted to see Louie, so, he headed across the street to Louie's house.

23

Brandon opened the screen door next to the garage that led to the basement and knocked. Louie's father greeted him. "Hi Brandon, it's great to see you." Brandon hoped Louie opened the door, but was relieved it wasn't Mrs. Buccelli. "Louie, someone's here to see you."

"Is it Brandon?" Just the sound of Louie's voice was music to Brandon's ears.

"Yep, come in Brandon. We converted the basement to Louie's room. Go on in. I'll be upstairs."

"Thanks Mr. Buccelli." Brandon walked to the back room. He wanted to run, but also wanted to be sure Mr. Buccelli had gone upstairs by the time he saw Louie. Seeing Mr. Buccelli was half way up, Brandon opened the door to what used to be the game room, now Louie's bedroom. When he opened the door, there was Louie.

Louie was sitting on a sofa. To Louie's right was his bed, and next to his bed was a wheel chair. The second Brandon stepped in, Louie's eyes lit up. "Hey Brandon finally you came over! Where have you been? How have you been? How are the guys?"

Brandon didn't know what to say. It was great to see Louie. He sounded like the old Louie. His eyes were bright. His smile still there, but from the neck down, Louie looked frail. On his chest, Louie wore something that looked like a baseball umpire's chest protector, only it was plastic. Louie had a shirt over the protector, but Brandon could see the white plastic at the bottom where the shirt was too small to cover it up. Louie was always the smallest kid in the class, but now, he looked tiny, especially in that plastic armor suit.

"Louie, you look great." Brandon lied. "I'm sorry I didn't get here sooner. You know how school is and all."

"Brandon, have a seat, sit down." Louie pointed to a chair.

"Sure Louie. How have you been?"

"I'm getting better. It was tough for a while. I had three operations. They had me on this bed for a month and I couldn't move. But I made it through. I'm going to have to miss school this year, but I should be back by next year. And by then, I'll be older than the rest of the kids in my class. I won't be the smallest anymore. No one will pick on me then."

"No one will ever pick on you Louie. If anyone gives you any trouble, you tell me, ok?"

"Yeah, sure Brandon."

"Are you able to walk and stuff?"

"A little bit. I got to use this walker for short walks like from my bed to the sofa and stuff. And I can't get up and down steps yet. That's why my parents converted the game room into my bed room. Isn't this great? I got the biggest bedroom in the neighborhood. I'm getting better though. You should have seen me last month. I couldn't even stand. The doctors were all amazed at how I'm doing. They say if I keep it up, I'll be running as fast as ever in no time."

"That's great Louie. That's real…" All at once the guilt Brandon felt became overwhelming. "Oh Louie, I'm sorry." Brandon couldn't hold it any longer. Tears were pouring out of his eyes, he could hardly speak, "Louie, I'm so sorry. I never meant to hurt you. I never meant to make you like this. I never…."

"Brandon, it's Ok. I'm doing a lot better. Don't cry. I know you didn't do it on purpose."

"Louie, I didn't. I didn't mean to…."

"Brandon, it's Ok. It's Ok." Here was Brandon, the biggest kid in his class blubbering like a baby. And here was Louie, the smallest kid in his class, with every right to feel sorry, every right to be angry, and every right to be crying. Here he was comforting Brandon, telling him that everything would be Ok.

"Louie, I swear, I'll help you any way I can. If you need anything let me know."

"Ok Brandon."

"I'll do whatever it takes to get you right again. I swear, I promise, whatever it takes."

"Thanks Brandon, but I'm going to be fine. You'll see next year, I'll be the biggest kid in the class." Brandon and Louie talked for over an hour. And then, there was a knock on the door.

Brandon turned and expected to see Mr. Buccelli. Instead, it was Louie's mom. Brandon was stunned. He wanted to say something, but before anything came out, Mrs. Buccelli spoke. "What are you doing here!?"

"Hi Mom, Brandon came over to visit."

"Get out! Get out of my house! How dare you come in here!"

"Mom, Brandon didn't do anything. He just came over to say Hi."

"Get out I said!" By now Dominic had come down.

"Claire, Brandon just came over to see how Louie was doing."

"Get him out of my house! How could you let him in this house?"

"Claire, come on now."

"Out! Get him out!"

Brandon wanted to run the second he saw Louie's mom, but she was standing in the doorway. When Dominic grabbed his wife and turned her aside, Brandon dashed for the door and ran out.

"How dare you come in this house! You son of a bitch, you killed my son!"

"Claire! Get a hold of yourself. Brandon I'm sorry." Brandon was already out the door.

"Mom, why did you do that? Brandon didn't do anything. He didn't kill me. I'm right here."

"Oh Louie, I know you're right here. You'll always be here."

Brandon ran as fast as he could back to his house. When he got home, he ran straight to his bedroom. Although the visit didn't end the way Brandon had wanted, he was happy to have talked to Louie. He got to tell him how sorry he was and that he didn't mean to hurt him. He knew for sure that Louie didn't blame him. Louie wasn't angry with him. Brandon promised Louie he would make it better. He made his promise and he was going to keep it. He would always look after Louie. Whatever needed to be done to fix Louie, to get him right, Brandon was going to do it.

Even though Mrs. Buccelli didn't want Brandon around her son, Brandon would somehow look after Louie. The Christmas holiday had come and gone. Brandon had gotten to see Louie one more time. He was able to give Louie a Christmas present – it was the latest most popular game for X-BOX – Zombie Nation. Though Brandon couldn't afford it, he asked his parents to help buy it for him. To pay them back Brandon asked that they not give him any presents for Christmas. Louie loved the gift and he and Brandon played for hours as Mrs. Buccelli was out with her sister. This time Dominic was on look-out for Brandon so another encounter with Claire would not happen.

Maybe it was wishful thinking, or Brandon's mind playing tricks on him, but he really thought Louie was getting better. Things were starting to get better all around. That was until Brandon was awoken early Saturday morning to the sound of sirens. At first, he thought he was dreaming about the sirens he heard when Louie was first injured. But this was no dream. The sirens were close, Brandon ran down the steps, and looked out the living room window. He saw the ambulance in Louie's driveway. In a few minutes his heart felt as though it had stopped. He saw a gurney with someone on it. The blankets covered the whole body, even the head. Then, he saw Mrs. Buccelli crying, screaming for her baby. She was in the arms of Mr. Buccelli who was also in tears. Louie, their son, had passed away.

Dominic told Cindy and Pat that Louie had passed away during the night while he was sleeping. Louie had died as a result of an embolism which caused his heart to stop. Brandon couldn't believe it. How could this be? Just a few days ago, they were playing Zombie Nation.

Brandon told Louie he was going to make things right. He had made a promise that he now could not keep. The guilt he felt was overwhelming. He wished it was him that died instead of Louie. Cindy and Pat tried their best to help her son cope with the loss of his friend. Though Brandon was eventually able to carry on, going to school, sleeping and eating normally, the guilt he felt would never go away. Somehow, the promise Brandon made to Louie, was going to be kept.

Chapter 3
THEY GROW UP FAST

The weather was warmer than usual on this Sunday Spring morning. Ted looked at Gina and marveled at how tall his sixteen year old daughter had grown. "Are you ready to go Gina?"

"Yep, I'm ready dad."

"I guess the dandelions haven't bloomed yet, huh?"

"Oh dad that was seven years ago. You know, you could have said something instead of letting me carry those weeds to the cemetery."

"You were so happy to have them and I'm sure your mother loved them. They were from the heart, how could I tell you they were weeds?"

"That groundskeeper sure didn't like them."

"No, he didn't care too much for them. He was nice enough to give you lilacs on the next visit."

"Yeah, he turned out to be Ok. I wonder what happened to him."

"He's still there. I've seen him as I drove by on my way to a job site a few weeks back. Maybe we'll see him today." Ted and Gina went to see Linda, as they have done the first Sunday of each month.

The following morning, the temperature was cooler, but still a sunny, Spring day. Ted gathered his thermos full of coffee, his keys and was ready to go to the Union Hall. "I'll see you this afternoon sweetie."

"Ok dad. Hopefully something will come up at the hall. Good luck."

"You have a good day at school."

"I will. Aren't you going to say good bye to Oreo?"

"Of course, how could I forget? I'll see you later Oreo."

Gina no longer had to go over Mrs. Bachwel's to wait for the bus. She was older now and very mature for a girl her age. Growing up without a mother, Gina took up the responsibilities of cooking, shopping, cleaning, and occasionally nagging her father about his smoking. She was a very good student who socialized like most girls, going to parties, school dances, etc. She talked constantly about boys with her girlfriends, but Gina didn't have a steady boyfriend, at least none that Ted was aware. And, in Ted's mind, at her age, he was glad there was no steady boyfriend of whom he was aware.

For Ted, the construction business had gone through a slow winter. There wasn't much construction going on as the economy as a whole was very slow. When there was work, it usually lasted no more than a week or two. It had been over three months since Ted had been at the same job site for more than two weeks straight. He was able to scrape by for the most part, but was hoping things would pick up. For the first time in many years, Ted had to dip into his savings to keep up with the expenses. With the minimal amount of work, most of Ted's days had been spent at the Union Hall talking to other iron workers who were also looking for work. Lately, the hall was getting more and more popular as work was getting harder and harder to find. Some workers, including Ted, had to take jobs out of state in Delaware, or New Jersey.

Before heading to the Union Hall, Ted always stopped at the local WAWA to meet up with co-worker and what could be considered Ted's best friend, Joe Wolfers. Ted was always an early riser. Joe Wolfers never seemed to sleep. Anyone who met Joe for the first time would swear he was on some kind of amphetamine drug. And, occasionally Joe was, but that was only on occasion. Once you got to know Joe, you realized his bark was much worse than his bite. He wouldn't hurt a fly. Deep down Joe was a good friend. He was always on time, and if he could help a friend, Joe had no problem doing so, no questions asked.

As Ted neared the WAWA, he could tell Joe was already there by the blasting of Lynyrd Skynyrd's "Simple Man" – Joe's favorite song. It was Joe's favorite song because he said it fit him to a tee. It was 60 degrees outside and as Ted pulled into the parking lot, Joe was standing by the door of his van. He was wearing a tank top tee-shirt, with a cigarette in his mouth, staring into the side view mirror, combing back his slick greasy hair. When he was done combing back his hair, he put on his black do-rag with a white skull and cross bones. After getting his do-rag just right, Joe glanced down at the new tattoo he had on his bicep. It was the third tattoo he put on this month. The tattoos Joe wore were the children's stick-on type that washed off. For Joe, each tattoo usually lasted a week because he had some kind of aversion to washing. He did like to smell good though so when Joe was done admiring his new tattoo he put on his third splash of cologne that he bought at the dollar store. After splashing the cologne, Joe looked back into the mirror, adjusted his do-rag again, flexed his newly tattooed bicep and gave himself a wink. While grooming himself in the WAWA parking lot, Joe only took his eyes off the mirror when he went to grab a sip of coffee or when he saw a cute girl. A "cute" girl to Joe, meant any girl eighteen to eighty within shouting distance. Every time a cute girl caused Joe to look away from the mirror, the words "Hey beautiful, how you doin'?" jumped out of his mouth.

Ted pulled up next to Joe. "Hey, Teddy boy, what's going on? Did you see the way that girl was staring at me as she walked into the WAWA? I think she wants a little Joe-Joe."

"Yeah, she's probably a psychologist and finds you to be fascinating."

"You got that right Teddy boy. I am a *fascinating* man. Hold on, she's coming back out. Hey there beautiful. Are you heading off to work?" The "cute" girl was about forty years old, stood five foot eight and weighed ninety pounds soaking wet. She was wearing an expensive suit, and looked as if she was on her way to a job in a law office. Upon hearing Joe's very clever (at least to Joe) advances, the "cute" girl glanced at him, then quickly looked towards the ground and began walking faster. She tried mightily to get to her car before Joe came near, but, she lost. Joe, oblivious to the fact that this "cute" girl wanted to be as far away from him as possible, caught up to her.

"Me, I'm my own boss. If I don't feel like going to work, I take the day off. How about taking this beautiful day off and heading down the lake with me? You like to fish? We can have a picnic?" Joe wanted so desperately for the "cute" girl to notice his barbed wire tattoo. He looked her in the eyes, glanced down to his bicep and gave a little flex. But she just wanted to get the hell out of the parking lot.

"Um, I don't think so. I have to get to work." The "cute" girl was now practically running towards her car. *Why oh why was the only parking spot at the end of the lot?* As fast as she tried to walk, Joe was keeping up step by step. He was oblivious to the fact that she thought of him as psychotic. When she finally got into her car, she immediately turned on the ignition and peeled away. Joe walked back to his van shaking his head.

"Man, what a shame Ted, a girl that pretty so stuck up."

"Yeah Joe, I can't believe she wouldn't take the day off from work to go to the lake in her Madison Avenue suit with a man wearing a tank top tee-shirt, a skull and bone do-rag with a barbed wire tattoo in sixty degree weather at six thirty in the morning. What's this world coming to?"

"You got that right, that's the problem with this world Teddy boy, no one is friendly anymore. A woman wouldn't know a good man if he came up and smacked her on her head."

"You got that right Joe." Ted said sarcastically. "A man's got to slap her hard to show her how good he is."

"I know it's getting harder and harder to meet a good woman these days. Hey what do you think of the new tat?"

"It looks great Joe, is that real?" Ted knew it was a stick on.

"Nah, I'll get a real one, one of these days, but these last a week and they only cost a buck. I got ten of them. I got this one, an eagle, and a skull and bones. They look like the real thing don't they?"

"Yep, the best thing is they come off with a good wash. For you, I can see how they last a week."

Oblivious to the insult Joe just went to his next thought. "Hey speaking of women, you should have come out with me last Saturday night to The Tavern. It was packed, full of good looking chicks. I walked in and got a seat right away at the bar. As soon as I got to the bar and ordered a beer, two people got up and left. So I grabbed one of their seats. I'll tell ya Ted, I'm like a God in that place. It's like the parting of the seas when I walk in. Everybody knows me. When they see me walk in, they all step aside and let Joe-Joe get to the bar. All the people are cool there. They know a working man needs his beer so no one bothers me with any chit-chat. Its great man, you gotta come out with me."

"I got my daughter at home Joe. I don't like having her home by herself on a Saturday night."

"Let me tell you about the new bartender. Her name is Sasha. Teddy, I gotta say, I think she wants me. Every time I order a beer, she'll place it on the bar, but she'll lean forward just a bit. Just so I can get a little peek at her titties. I swear she smells like strawberries. You should smell her, man she smells good."

"I'm sure she smells nice and all women want you Joe. You know that."

"Ah, come on, not all of them. I gotta leave some for the rest of the world. A man only has so much love to give. But get this, she tells me she's single. She has five kids, but they're older. So, that's Ok. She tells me she loves fishing and camping. The best part is she can't stand the guy she's living with."

"She sounds like a winner Joe. You get her number?"

"No, I'm playing it cool. I don't want to come on too strong. I gotta play around a bit see where this goes. I want to make sure she isn't some psycho like the last one, Ginger. You remember her right?"

"I remember Ginger." Ted met Ginger one time. And that was one time too many. It was at a bar, appropriately named The Dog Pound. It was Karaoke Night and Ted got there after Joe and Ginger. Even though it was early in the night, Ginger was already three sheets to the wind. Ted had never seen a girl so drunk. Instead of a normal "Hello" with a handshake or kiss on the cheek, Ted's introduction was "Come here Joe's friend, you handsome devil." Ginger jumped into Ted's chest and would have fallen to the floor except Ted did catch her. He regretted that when Ginger began to try to stick her tongue down his throat far enough to tickle his tonsils.

Joe went right along with it. "I told you she was a great girl, didn't I Teddy boy?"

"Yes you did Joe."

"And she's friendly too huh Ted?"

"She's very friendly. If she were any friendlier, we'd be half naked."

The word naked perked Ginger right up. "Hey, I like the way you think Teddy boy. Joey, I sure like your friend."

"You hear that Teddy boy, Ginger likes you. I knew you two would hit it off."

"That makes my night Joe, if a nice classy girl like Ginger here likes me, there's hope for me yet."

Ginger had enough talk. "Come on, let's have some drinks, I'm starting to sober up. Hey Bartender! What's a girl got to do to get a couple of Tequilas and beers? Hey Joey, Teddy boy what do you want? Drinks are on me."

"Get me a Bud baby, Ted what do you want?"

"I'll take a Bud as well."

"Bartender, make that three Buds and two shots of Tequila." When the bartender came back with the drink order, he told Ginger that'll be $17.00. "Joey, hunny, give me a twenty."

So much for drinks on her Ted thought.

Ginger slammed down the two shots of Tequila, then pounded down half her beer before handing Joe and Ted their beers. The highlight of the evening was when Joe told Ginger that "Simple Man" was his favorite song. Seeing that the title was on the list of songs for karaoke, Ginger hopped up on the stage (there was no waiting in line for this princess), grabbed the microphone, and told the DJ to play "Simple Man".

"This one goes out to my two favorite guys Joey and Teddy boy." Joe gave Ted a wink of approval. Ginger didn't know the words to the song, and she was too drunk to read the words on the screen, (or maybe she couldn't read at all, Ted didn't know). She was also just a wee bit off key. And by a wee bit that was like a plane scheduled to land in New York being a wee bit off course and landing in Russia. After the first verse, people began to boo Ginger off the stage, to which this drunk delicate flower promptly grabbed her crotch and gave everyone at the bar the middle finger.

"I tell you she's got a lot of spunk doesn't she Ted?"

"She's a real go-getter! You better reel her in before she gets away."

"I'm trying man, but she's so independent. She tells me doesn't want to be tied down."

"Have you actually tried Joe? I mean actually tying her down? I think she might go for it."

"That's why I like you Teddy boy, always thinking. I might have to give that a shot."

The crowd finally had enough of the next drunken American Idol, so the DJ hopped up on stage and asked for the microphone. Ginger responded by smacking him over the head, breaking the microphone in two. She was thrown out of the bar. Joe was kicked out as well sticking up for his new found love, and Ted, well he was glad to get the hell out of there. That was the one and only memory Ted had of Joe's previous love, Ginger. Now, it was Sasha that Joe wanted Ted to meet.

"You gotta head out to The Tavern with me Teddy. You gotta tell me what you think of Sasha."

"I don't have to see her Joe, I'm sure she is much more mature than Ginger. You said Sasha has five kids, she loves fishing, camping. She can't stand the guy she's living with. What's not to like?"

"Ah, now you're just bullshitting me. I mean it man, come out and meet her. I'm sure she has a friend. You got to get back in the scene yourself."

"We'll see. Right now we got to get to the Hall."

"I wonder what Jen Jen's wearing today? I can't wait to smell her. I bet she smells great."

"I don't know Joe, but hopefully she has some work lined up for us."

Joe and Ted arrived at the Union Hall parking lot, Joe in his van, Ted in his car. "Hold on Ted, I gotta smell good for my Jen Jen." Joe splashed on more of the dollar store cologne. "You want a splash Ted? Smells just like Drakkar but only cost a buck."

"No thanks Joe. I'm here to pick up a job, not a woman."

"Hey you never know who you might meet. And Jen Jen's got a little thing for you, I know it. You should try to hit on that. You gotta get back into the action. It's been ten years since Linda passed. You gotta get back into the game before you're too old to play you know what I mean."

"Joe, I know exactly what you mean. I told you before don't talk about my wife like that. If I want to start something with a woman, I'll go for it. My wife has nothing to do with it. Office romances never turn out good for either party." Ted sounded very convincing in his argument with Joe, but in a way, Joe was right. It had been ten years since his wife had passed. Yet, he still thought of her every day. As for getting old, Ted knew he still had time. He noticed a couple times when women looked at him, or talked to him in a way that said "I'd like to get to know you better". But, Ted still couldn't picture himself falling for another woman the way he had felt about his wife Linda.

"All right Teddy, sorry man. You know how much I liked Linda."

Joe walked past Ted. "Jesus Joe, what the hell, did you swim in that shit?"

"It will wear off. It only cost a buck a bottle, so you gotta put a little extra on for it to last." When Ted and Joe walked into the Union Hall there were already over a dozen Iron Workers mingling around. As soon as they stepped inside everyone within thirty feet turned and looked at the two. Some men held their nose, some laughed. Everyone knew Joe was in the building.

"Hey Tommy, how's it going?" Ted asked. "Hey Steve, what are you doing here? I thought you were on that school job?"

"I was but got laid off. It turned out to be a three day job. Damn Joe, what did you do? You pull an all-nighter, and sleep with a couple five dollar hookers? I can smell you from a mile away."

"It's nice to see you too Stevie. As a matter of fact I did have a great weekend. And by the way, I never have to pay for it."

"Come on Joe, let's sign in. I'll catch ya later Steve."

"Alright Ted. Hey, Jen was asking about you."

"I told you Teddy, Jen Jen's got a little thing for you."

"What did I tell you Joe?" When Ted and Joe walked up to the desk to sign in, there was Jennifer Manley, talking on the phone.

Jennifer was thirty five years old. All of her life she was the one girl that every guy wanted. In grade school Jennifer needed to wear a bra earlier than any other girl in her class. This made her attractive to almost every boy in her class. To every boy, Jennifer could do no wrong, and she loved the attention. However, she wasn't stuck up about it. Jennifer was equally social to every boy she met. She didn't seem off limits to the boys who normally wouldn't approach a girl, let alone someone as attractive as her. She had a way of taking away any awkward fears that boys had with girls. While every boy wanted to be around her, nearly every girl despised her. But that was ok. Jennifer had plenty of male friends to keep her entertained.

By high school Jennifer had a beautiful smooth, slightly freckled face. She had a slim waist without needing to exercise or watch what she ate. She had naturally blonde hair and stood about five foot seven. She also had a nice rack. Even as a high school sophomore, male adults, including some of her teachers, had trouble keeping their eyes from checking her physical assets when engaged in conversation. To make it harder on the men, Jennifer did her part by wearing tight bright shirts.

Jennifer wasn't the brightest student in the classroom, but she was smart where it counted. She could always get the benefit of the doubt in receiving passing or failing grades, by having an acute awareness of the men around her, and what made them happy. Jenifer had a very high I.Q. in social interaction, especially when it came to men.

In Jennifer's junior year of high school she was dating the senior captain of the football team. During Jennifer's senior year, everything changed. It was that year when she became pregnant with her daughter. She ended up marrying the captain of the football, team right after high school graduation. Two years later she gave birth to her second child – a son.

The marriage ended a few years after Jennifer's son was born. Her high school sweetheart began to drink more and more. When he was most drunk, he started verbally abusing her. In his mind, Jennifer was the reason he couldn't make more of himself. He could have been somebody had she not gotten pregnant. Now, he was just a carpenter. When the verbal abuse turned physical, Jennifer packed up and left with the kids. The only good thing to come out of the marriage besides the children was her ability to land an administrative position within the carpenters union. Now, at thirty five, while still the girl every guy at the Hall wanted, she was well aware that her beauty wasn't going to last.

"There she is. How's my little Jen Jen?"

"Well hello there Joseph. I knew ten minutes ago you would be here."

"You did? How's that beautiful?"

"That's when I started to pick up that wonderful cologne you wear."

"Ah, aren't you cute. You see Ted, every guy gives me grief about my cologne, but the women love it." Joe, catching Jennifer's eye began to flex his bicep to try and guide her to look at his new tattoo.

"Is that a new tattoo Joseph? It makes you look tough and dangerous. That must have been painful to get." Jennifer knew it was a stick on. "I would be so afraid to get one of those."

"Nah, it's temporary. That's nice of you to notice though. What do you think?" Joe was now in full bicep flex mode.

"It looks rough. Makes you look like a real biker dude."

"Yeah, and you like that don't ya Jen Jen?"

"Oh yeah Joe that's what every girl is looking for, a guy that you can smell coming a mile away, wearing a tank top tee shirt, a skull and bone do-rag with a stick on barbed wire tattoo on his arm."

"Now you're just messing with me. You know you want some Joe Joe."

Ted finally had enough. "How bout I take over the books so you two can go somewhere private."

"That's fine with me Teddy boy, what do you say Jen Jen?"

"I don't think the boss would like that too much. How are you doing this morning Mr. Stroit? Did you have a good weekend? And your daughter Gina, I haven't seen her in a long time. How is she?"

"I'm fine Jen. Gina's doing great actually, she's finishing up her sophomore year at school, and everyone is healthy, even Oreo the cat. So, I can't complain."

"You didn't answer me about your weekend, how was your weekend?" Jennifer was curious to see if Ted was with another woman. As oblivious as Joe was to the world and the people around him, he was correct about Jennifer having a thing for Ted.

"You know me Jen, very boring. Not much happening."

"You should call me Ted. We should go out. I'm sick of these losers I keep dating. I need to go out and have some fun. You haven't had a fun weekend in a while either."

"Hey, what about Joe Joe here? I'm always having fun. I'll show you a good time Jen Jen."

"Joseph, I'll be honest. You scare the hell out of me. I'm too delicate for your idea of fun. Besides, I hear about all those women you're with."

"For you I'd tone it down a notch. You don't have to worry Jen Jen. You're safe with me."

Ted, not really in the mood for social talk, needed to get to the point for coming to the hall. "We'll see about going out Jen. Right now, I can't afford to have a fun weekend. Any work starting up?"

"Well, don't tell anyone this but the call I just was on was a foreman looking for a couple guys to help put up a hoist at the hospital at twelfth and Lucas Street. You interested?"

"Yeah, sure but I don't want to step on anyone's toes."

"Don't worry about it. You've been out as long as most. Besides, now you owe me a fun weekend. And no "I can't afford it" excuses. I'll line it up for you and Dr. Smell Good. Go down and talk to Mark Hampton. Tell him you talked to me."

"Hey thanks Jen. I mean it."

"You can thank me by taking me out for that fun weekend."

"Ok, come on Dr. Smell Good." Ted and Joe headed to the job site.

When Ted and Joe arrived at the hospital, Ted asked a construction worker where he could find Mark Hampton. Mark was the foreman on the job

34

for the iron work. The construction worker pointed to a trailer about 50 feet away. Ted and Joe made their way to the trailer.

When they got to the trailer there were three men circled around a table. "Any of you Mark Hampton?" Ted asked.

"Yeah, that's me. Are you the guys from the hall?"

"Yep, Jennifer Manley sent us. You have some work?" Joe asked.

"No, this is where we hang out for our vacation. Nice isn't it?" Mark replied.

"Jen said you need help on a hoist." Ted jumped in as Joe was about to go off on the smart-ass.

"I'm sorry, we're already two weeks behind schedule and one of the crane operators called and said he can't make it today."

"No problem." Ted said. "Where do you need us?"

"We need a couple guys to help with the equipment hoist." As Mark came closer to Ted and Joe he couldn't help but smell the cheap cologne. "Jesus, what the hell are you wearing?"

Before Joe could speak, Ted jumped in. "We hit a pot hole coming down. Joe had some cologne spill on him."

"Yeah, Ok. Well, unfortunately for you guys this is just a three day job. Maybe by then the cologne will wear off."

"We'll take what we can get. And for your information, I've been getting some good feedback from the ladies about the cologne." Joe's first impression of Mark wasn't too friendly.

Mark looked at Joe incredulously. "I've already got two guys over there, you probably know them. They're from your local – Kenny Wittle and Jake Blocher."

"Yeah, they're good guys. Let's go Joe. Thanks, we'll see you later."

"Yep." Mark and the other two were already looking over the map on the table as if they had forgotten Ted and Joe already.

As Ted and Joe got to within eye sight of Kenny Wittle, Kenny started up the conversation. "Hey Ted, and look who he brought, the lady killer himself. What's going on Mr. Wolfers?"

"Kenny, how are you doing?" Ted replied.

"Kenny, it's great to see you too. It's been awhile." Joe replied. "We just got sent down from the hall to help out. What do you guys need?"

"We've gotten the base of the hoist set. I need you two to monkey up and secure each section of the hoist to the building to the top of the eighth floor. I got Frank Thompson working the crane to lift the steel for the hoist.

"No problem." Joe said.

The work was really a two day job, but Ted and Joe could make it three. It wasn't much work, but it was something. The work they had to do was put up the skeleton steel which would be used as an elevator to hoist equipment. Anything from nails to wood, to drills would all be lifted up each floor of the building. The hoist was to be used for equipment only, no persons allowed since the hoist wasn't a permanent fixture.

Each skeletal piece of steel was a square grid about three square feet per section. Joe and Ted had to secure the corner of each section to its bottom and top square grid. On the base of each cement floor of the building, there were bolts to fasten the hoist. There were four bolts to each floor. The skeletal piece of the hoist was about four feet away from the building.

Starting mid-way to the second floor, Ted and Joe climbed up the hoist. They signaled Frank to lift up another section to secure. When that section was done, Ted and Joe climbed up the skeletal iron where Frank would send another section of the hoist to secure. At the end of the day, Joe and Ted had built the hoist to the fifth floor.

"You guys work fast." Mark, the foreman said. "At least something got done today. Good job, I'll see you in the morning."

"See you then." Ted replied as he and Joe headed for home.

"I didn't think much of that guy at first, but he seems to be Ok Ted."

"I've worked with Mark once or twice before. He can be a real ass when he wants to, but as long as work gets done on time, he's actually a good guy. I'll see you tomorrow Joe."

"Meet at WAWA?"

"Yeah, 6:30 sharp, I don't want to be late."

When Ted arrived home, Gina was in the living room typing in her lap top. He could smell something was cooking. "Hey sweetie, what's cooking?"

"Hey dad, since you weren't here when I got home I decided to make some pork chops for dinner. I have them baking in the oven and some potatoes boiling. I took out some lima beans as well."

"That sounds great. How was school?"

"It was Ok. Tommy Rubiliski got sick and threw up all over his desk in homeroom. It was gross, but funny. Wendy captured it on her cell phone and just uploaded it to Facebook. Want to see?"

"Uh, no, I think I'll just head upstairs to wash up for dinner."

"Ok, it should be ready in 20 minutes. I'll give you a yell. And by the way, I can tell you were smoking. How long have you been telling mom you would be quitting?"

"I only had a couple cigarettes today to counter the smell of that cheap cologne Joe wears."

Gina knew exactly what her dad meant. "You were with Mr. Wolfers huh?"

"Yep, I'm working with Mr. Wolfers." Ted went upstairs, undressed, put his dirty clothes in the hamper, and took a shower. When he was done, he put on some sweat pants, tee shirt, and sat on his bed. On his table he gazed at the picture of Linda and him in their wedding picture. Next to that was a picture of Linda with an inscription in the corner: "Every time you see this

36

picture you better think – *This is the love of my life!*" The inscription ended with a little smiley face. To this day, every time Ted looked at the picture he thought to himself – *This is the love of my life!*

"Dad, dinner's ready."

"I'll be down in a minute." When Ted came to the kitchen, the plates were set, the pork chops were in the center of the table, and alongside were the mashed potatoes and lima beans.

"This looks great Gina. I really appreciate it."

"No problem dad. I was in the mood for pork chops, and when you weren't home when I got in, I figured you were working. Was I right?"

"You were right. But, it's only a three day job. I'm putting up a hoist and will finish that up tomorrow. Friday, we'll just be cleaning up."

"Well, three days are better than none."

"True, but if it doesn't pick up soon, I don't know what we'll do."

"I'm sure it will pick up. It always does right?"

Ted looked across at his daughter as she once again reminded him of Linda. "I guess. Just like your mother, always looking at the positive."

The next morning Ted met Joe at the WAWA. Joe had his music blaring, wearing a tee-shirt, his trademark do-rag, smoking a cigarette, sipping coffee and checking out the "cute" girls as they passed by. "You know if you keep glaring at all the women who pass by, Amir in there is going to put a restraining order on your ass."

"No he won't Teddy boy. I'm his number on customer."

"I'm sure he can live without you buying a cup of coffee every day."

"That's right, that and a pack of smokes."

"Come on, let's get to the job. I don't want to be late."

"All right Teddy." Just then, a twenty-something year old girl, who must have weighed at least 250 pounds walked by. "Hey baby how you doin?" After no reply, they drove off to the job site.

At midday Mark Hampton came out to see how the hoist was coming along. "It looks good guys. Looks like you'll be finished by the end of the day."

"We think so. We'll have some cleanup, but we should be done by noon tomorrow."

"Well, if you guys do finish early, I'll still put you in for a full day. You guys did a real good job. I'll check on you later. I'm heading to the corner for some lunch."

"All right Mark, we'll talk to you later." See, I told you as long as work gets done on time he's actually a pretty good guy.

"Yeah, you were right Teddy. I guess first impressions really don't mean shit."

By the end of the day, the hoist was completed. All that was left was clean up which would be done tomorrow. Looking over their work, Ted noticed something. "Hey Joe, what's that hanging on the fourth floor slab?"

"Oh shit, looks like the connector bolt came loose. That's on my side. I'll climb up and tighten it."

"Nah, I got it Joe. At the pace that you climb, it will take an hour."

"Oh, fuck you Ted, you want to fix it, go ahead."

"I'll be back in five minutes." Ted climbed up the skeletal steel to the fourth floor. He secured the bolt and was getting ready to climb back down when he noticed a wooden plank. "Hey buddy, slide that plank over. I'll use it to walk onto the floor." Rather than climb back down, Ted decided to use the wooden plank as a board to walk the two steps needed to get from the hoist to the building. With the plank in place, Ted took one step onto the board. Before he took his second step, he heard the crack.

The guy who had slid the plank over tried to grab Ted's arm, but, he was too late. Ted had fallen four stories onto the ground. Joe was one of the first to get to Ted. "Teddy! Can you hear me? Teddy! Teddy!" Because they were working on a hospital building, within minutes, an ambulance was there to take Ted to the very hospital he was working.

When Gina got home from school she noticed there was a phone message waiting on the answering machine. Looking at the caller ID, she noticed the same number had called five times. She sensed right away something was not right. When she listened to the machine, it was Joe asking her to call him as soon as possible. Gina called Joe immediately. He explained to her that her father had fallen at work and that he was in the hospital. Joe was still there waiting to hear from the doctor, but none had come out since he had been there. Joe offered to come and pick up Gina.

When Gina had gotten to the hospital Joe took her right to the desk to check in and ask about her father. Gina provided the nurse with as much information as she could. "I'm Gina Stroit. My dad was brought in here a couple hours ago. Can you tell me where the doctor is?"

"Hello, yes, I am aware your father has been brought in. He is still in the operating room. The doctor will be out as soon as he can."

"Operating room? What is wrong?"

"I'm sorry Gina, I can't say for sure. Unfortunately I can't give you much information. I really don't know. I'll go to the OR and see if I can get someone to come out to explain."

"Thank you, nurse." Gina and Joe sat down next to the reception area.

"Gina I don't know what happened. We were finishing up and your dad noticed a bolt loose on the hoist so he climbed up to tighten it. When he was done, he had a wooden plank placed between the hoist and the building floor and when he took a step, it must have broken."

"Did he speak to you?"

"He was semi-conscious. He wasn't talking, he was mumbling. I couldn't really understand him. Luckily we were so close to the hospital the ambulance came literally within minutes."

At that moment, a female doctor had come to talk to Gina. "Hello, I'm doctor Pretian. I assisted on your fathers operation. You must be his daughter."

"Yes, I'm Gina. Is he alright?"

"He is stable. I'm afraid your father has broken his neck."

"Oh my God! Is he going to be Ok?"

"He is in critical but stable condition. We removed all of the bone fragments from the injured area. We stabilized his neck. That is all we can do for now. There is too much swelling for us to do any more work."

"Can I see him? Is he going to be Ok? "

"We're not sure what the prognosis is at this time. He is resting. He is not conscious. We have to keep heavily sedated. He has been given medication to help reduce the swelling. You can see him. Just don't expect him to talk."

"Where is he?"

"I'll take you to him." Doctor Pretian took Gina and Joe to the ICU room where Ted was lying. He was motionless, with tubes coming out from his arm. He also had a tube coming out from his throat.

Gina held her father's hand. "Hi Daddy, can you hear me? It's Gina. Can you hear me?" It seemed like every ten seconds someone, a nurse, or a doctor was coming in to check on Gina's father. Joe, not knowing what to say, or do, and feeling as if he was in the way, said to Gina – "I'll be outside. If you need me for anything, just yell, Ok?"

"Ok, thank you Mr. Wolfers."

Doctor Pretian came back into the room. "Gina, I'm afraid you will have to limit your time to a few minutes. For the next several hours, your father will be heavily sedated. I know this is hard, but we will have nurses and doctors constantly checking in on him. He is getting the best care possible."

"Is there anything I can do? I, I don't know what to do. I wish there was something I could do."

"Right now there is nothing you can do but pray. Hopefully tomorrow, we will have a better understanding to the extent of his injury. We expect him to be more conscious some time tomorrow as well. Is your mother with you?"

"My mom passed away several years ago. It's just my dad and me."

"I'm sorry. Is there someone who can take you home? Is the man outside a relative or friend of yours? I know this must be difficult, but you should try to get some rest and come back tomorrow?"

"How can I go home and rest not knowing how my father is?"

"Honestly Gina, we won't know anything for at least 24 hours. If anything does change, we will call you immediately. If you like, I can prescribe a sedative to help you rest."

"No, no, I don't want that. I just want to know my father is going to be Ok. Why can't I just stay here? I won't get in the way."

"Gina I know this must be very, very difficult. But as you have seen we will have many nurses and doctors coming in to constantly check on your father. Believe me your father is receiving the best care possible. With all of the medication he is on he won't be alert until at least tomorrow. Sitting here won't change anything. Tomorrow you can come back and most likely you will be able to speak to your father." Dr. Pretian motioned to Joe to come into the room.

"What if he does wake up? I want to be here when he wakes up. I want him to know that he's not alone."

"There is a very small chance that he will wake up. And if he does, we will most likely give him another sedative in order for him to sleep. Right now the best chance your father has is to rest."

"Are you sure I can't stay in another room? I'm sure you have empty rooms here don't you?"

"I'm afraid we can't do that Gina. I promise, if anything changes with your father's condition, I will call you personally."

Joe had listened to the last bit of conversation. "Gina, look, the doctor said there is nothing you can do. Let me take you home and I'll pick you up tomorrow morning and we'll stop back then. Hopefully by then your dad will be awake and can talk. You staying here won't change anything. Let these people do what they are supposed to do to help your dad."

"He's right Gina, and like I said, if anything changes I will contact you immediately."

Gina, looking at her father in what looked like a peaceful sleep, relented. She knew that no matter how much she protested, she wasn't going to win the argument. "What time can I come back?"

"Visiting hours start at eleven, I'll tell the head nurse on staff that you can come in at ten. Ok?"

"Ok. Mr. Wolfers, can you pick me up tomorrow at 9:30?"

"Sure Gina, sure, I'll pick you up at 9:30."

That night, Gina didn't sleep at all as she lay in bed holding Oreo. Gina never really knew her mother since she had passed away when she was very young. She grew up used to the fact that it was just her and her father. She didn't know what she would do if she lost him. He was the most important person in her life. He took care of her. He was the strong supportive rock that she had always depended upon. Now, he would have to depend on her. She prayed for her father to stay with her. She couldn't bear to live without him.

The next morning Joe was at the house at 9:15. They drove to the hospital, and as they pulled up, Gina looked out at the construction site where her father had fallen. Work was going on as usual. It was as if her father's fall never happened. Unknown to Gina, it was all everyone at the job talked about. When they got to the reception desk, the receptionist pointed Joe and Gina to the same room Ted was in the previous night. When they got to the room, they were both surprised to see Dr. Pretian standing by Ted. "How is he doc?" Joe asked.

"It's still too soon to tell. What we do know is that he broke his neck in the C5 and C6 regions. His neck is stable now. We will continue with the medication to reduce the swelling for at least another day. At that time, we will know a little more as to the extent of the injury."

"My dad's going to be Ok right doctor? He isn't going to die, is he?"

"His chances of making it through are very good. I know this is difficult. I really do. I can't speculate any further than that right now Gina."

"You mean he could be paralyzed?"

"I'm afraid so. However it is too early to tell. Your father kept himself in good shape, and he is relatively still young. He's going to need you to be strong for him. Can you do that?"

Gina, staring at her father, not truly believing the situation, gave a slight nod and a meek, "Yes" to Dr. Pretian. "I'll do whatever it takes doctor."

"I'll leave you three alone. I have other patients to see. There will be nurses checking in on your father throughout the day. Ok?"

"Yes doctor. Thank You."

"Yeah doc thanks."

Once the doctor left the room, Gina walked over to her father, gently took his hand. "Hi Daddy, I'm here." Ted gently squeezed his hand back at Gina. He barely opened his eyes. He gave a slight smile, and let out a dry, quiet mumbling. "Hey sweetie" was all he could muster. Ted drifted back to sleep.

A few hours later, Jennifer, from the Union Hall walked in. "Hi Joe."

"Hey, Jen."

"Hi, you must be Gina. Ted has spoken of you often. I'm Jennifer Manley. I work at the Union Hall. How is he?"

"Hi Mrs. Manley."

"Please, call me Jennifer."

"He's pretty out of it. I spoke to the doctor and she said it's too early to tell. She said he broke his neck in the C5 and C6 area, whatever that is. She said he could be paralyzed, but he's strong, so I'm praying he will be fine."

"I'll work on the insurance paperwork so you don't worry about that."

"Oh, thank you, thank you so much Jennifer. I know my dad would appreciate that."

"And don't worry about coming down to see your dad Gina. Any time you need a ride, or if you need anything you just call me."

"Thank you, Mr. Wolfers."

Chapter 4
MOVING ON UP

"Cindy, it's finally happening."

"What's happening Pat?"

"The buyout, Universal Cable has bought out Virginia Cable."

"Oh my God, when is that happening?"

"The official announcement will be on Monday."

"What are we going to do? Is your job safe? Are you being laid off?"

"What are we going to do? We're going to celebrate. I've been offered a promotion to Sr. Manager of Customer Relations."

"Are you serious? Pat, that's great news."

"All those late nights and weekends paid off. Over sixty percent of the company was let go. Most of the people who were kept were those working low level positions. I'm one of the few who actually received a promotion with the merger. Notices are being sent out today, tomorrow and Friday to those who are being laid off. But, I was told I'll be promoted within the Philadelphia office. That's Headquarters! That will give me a chance to really move up the ladder."

"Wait, what was that about Philadelphia?"

"In order to accept the Sr. Manager position, I'll have to work in Philadelphia. Actually a suburb of Philadelphia called Blue Bell."

"We've lived in Virginia all our lives? We have family here."

"Cindy what choice is there? I either take a promotion with a great chance to further advance my career in Philadelphia. Or I say, *no thanks*, and get laid off. Then what? With this economy, who knows how long it would take to find another job?"

"What about my job Pat?"

"Cindy, with my promotion you don't have to work right away. You can take some time off. Go back to school if you like. Universal offers tuition reimbursement to me and it's available for you as well. I'm telling you this is the best thing to happen since Brandon was born."

"What about Brandon? Is he supposed to pack up and leave school? Leave his friends?"

"Cindy, the move isn't immediate. We can wait until the end of the school year. Honestly, I think this would be good for Brandon."

"Good for Brandon, what does that mean?"

"Come on Cindy, Brandon's kind of been an introvert since, well, you know, since the Louie incident. You've said so yourself. He doesn't go out with friends. He keeps to himself all the time buried in his books or on the computer. I think the change will do him good. It has to be hard for him to go out and the first thing he sees is the house Louie lived in across the street."

Cindy couldn't disagree with Pat's statements. It was true. Brandon had kept to himself since Louie's death. Although Cindy and Pat had gotten Brandon counseling, it had done very little to help. As time passed Brandon immersed himself more and more into his books and his computer. He was getting straight A's in school. But his social life was sacrificed. In fact Brandon had no social life. Maybe moving away would help snap him out of it. "Ok, Pat. Maybe you're right."

"Sure, I'm right! I get my promotion, you get some time off to do what you want, and Brandon gets a fresh start. This move will be great for all of us."

"So what do we do now?"

"The move doesn't happen until June. We'll break the news to Brandon tomorrow at dinner. If you like, you can put in your notice at work. This will give you more time to get the house in order which we will have to sell. And, we'll have to look for a house in Philly. Corporate wants me to head up to the main office in a week or so to meet up with the team. It's only for a day, but we can stay another day or two to look around the neighborhoods."

"Ok, yeah, I guess so."

"What's wrong? Aren't you excited?"

"Yeah, I guess, but it's just a shock. We're packing up our lives and moving away. This isn't something you do every day."

"I know, but trust me. This will be the best thing for all of us. It's a higher profile job for me, more money for all of us. Brandon gets a start fresh. If you want, you can go back to school. It's a win for all of us. You'll wonder why you hesitated. This is going to be great!"

The following day, after Cindy finished putting dinner on the table, she yelled for Brandon. "Brandon, come on down, dinners ready."

"Alright mom, I'll be down in a minute." When Brandon saw the table, he noticed there were three plates. It was rare that Brandon saw three plates on the dinner table. "Is dad home? I didn't hear him coming in from work."

"Yep, for once your father is joining us for dinner."

"Must be a special occasion, we're having steak too."

"You're right Brandon, this is a special occasion." Brandon didn't notice that his father was behind him.

"Oh, hey dad, I didn't know you were home."

The three sat down, to a rare family dinner. "This all looks great Cindy. How's school Brandon?"

"Fine, I have some tests coming up soon. Next Wednesday starts Spring break."

"Well, you've never disappointed in the class room that's for sure. You've been working hard this year, as always. A break should be good. How would you like to spend some time in Philadelphia on your break?"

"Philadelphia? What's in Philadelphia?"

"Brandon, your father has some good news for us."

Pat was almost bursting. "Good! This is great news! Brandon, you know I've mentioned that Virginia Cable may be bought out by Universal?"

"Yeah, you've been saying that for a while. Did that happen? Is everything Ok?"

"Yes it did. The official announcement will be sent out Monday. And it isn't just Ok, it's great! Universal has given me a promotion. You're looking at the Sr. Manager of Customer Relations."

"That's great dad, congratulations."

"That's not the only news Brandon. Tell him Pat."

"Yes, well, Universal Cable's main office is in Philadelphia. That's what's up in Philadelphia. With the promotion we get to move there. What do you think? Your mother and I are excited to get a new start." Pat gave Cindy a brief look and half-smile. Cindy looked back as if to say "Don't sugar coat it".

Brandon didn't quite know what the move meant. *Fresh start?* What exactly did his dad mean by *"fresh start"* with the move to Philadelphia? Why couldn't his dad stay where he was? Were they really moving because of a promotion? Or were they moving because of what Brandon did to Louie? Were his parents were just making this up so his feelings weren't hurt. Did Louie's parents force them to move? Brandon saw the way Louie's mom looked at him whenever she made eye contact. Mrs. Buccelli hated Brandon. Louie's dad wasn't so bad, but his mom had it in for him. He just knew it. Maybe it was teachers at school asking Brandon's parents to leave. Brandon wasn't ever in any trouble, but he heard the whispers behind his back. The kids, some of them anyway, still thought Brandon was responsible for Louie's death. Maybe some of the teachers felt that way too.

"Well, what do you think?" Pat asked.

"Why move? Do we have to move? Mom, are we being forced to move?"

"Brandon, no one is forcing us to move. Your dad was one of the lucky few to keep his job. Even luckier, he received a promotion due to all of his hard work." Pat was now glowing at his wife. She really did understand his dedication to his job, the reason for his missed dinners, the missed parent-teacher meetings. "Brandon, if you have any trepidation about moving, we can discuss it. We aren't being forced to move. This is our decision, and if we are all not on board, we'll stay."

Pat's glow just took a turn towards pale. "Brandon, no one is forcing us to move. This is just an incredible opportunity for us to move up the corporate ladder. With the promotion comes more income. Your mom can take off from her job and go back to school like she's been wanting. The move won't happen until June, so you can finish out the school year here. And it's not like we're moving to Siberia. Virginia is only a few hours away and we'll come back on holidays to visit relatives. Trust me son, this is good for all of us."

The more Brandon thought about it, the more he liked the idea. Maybe no one would know him in Philadelphia. Maybe no one would know what he had done. He wouldn't have to hear the whispers anymore. "Ok mom, dad, I'm fine with the move."

"That's my boy!" Pat had everyone on board. The move up the corporate ladder was happening. "Your mother and I were planning on heading to Philly next week. I have to meet some of my new co-workers and staff. We thought it would be a great opportunity to have a look around the neighborhoods. Maybe pick out an area for us to move. Since you're off for spring break, how about coming up with us?"

"Yeah, sure dad, I'm in."

Two weeks later, Pat, Cindy and Brandon drove to the suburbs of Philadelphia. They checked into a hotel that was less than a mile from the Universal offices. While at dinner, Pat planned their itinerary. "I have to be at the Blue Bell office at 9AM. The office is only five minutes from here so we'll leave at 8:30. You can drop me off and then you two can spend the morning doing whatever you like. You can visit the mall we passed a mile back and do some shopping. I should be done by noon. I'll call you when I'm done and you can pick me up. Then we'll look around the neighborhoods to see if there is anything we like. I don't expect to find our new home, but maybe we can decide on an area we want to concentrate on when we come back. Sound good?"

"Sure Pat that's fine."

"Brandon?"

"Yeah, that sounds good."

"Ok then. Man, I'm excited. I can't wait to see the office. I'm a little nervous though. What if the meeting doesn't go well? What if I'm not what they're looking for and they decide to go in another direction?"

"Pat, you'll do fine. You got promoted for all of the hard work you have put in over the years. They won't change their mind, and go in another direction from one meeting."

"I'm sure you're right hun. It's just, well...."

"You'll do fine. If you want to make a good impression, you'll need to get a good night's sleep."

"You're right Cindy, thanks."

The next morning, Cindy dropped Pat off at the main office at 8:45AM. He opened the door and an aroma quickly caught his senses. It smelled like big company. He was on his way. Sr. Manager, just a few steps away from being on the board of one of the biggest cable companies in the world - a Fortune 500 company that was still growing. Today, Universal served the Eastern part of the U.S. tomorrow, the rest of the country. And he was going to be in the midst of its growth. Pat walked over to the receptionist. "Good morning sir, my name is Kim Kelly, how may I help you?"

45

"Hello. I have a meeting with Jim Lawry. My name is Pat Leshing."

"One moment please, I'll see if he is available." Kim picked up the phone and dialed Jim Lawry's office. Pat looked around and thought "This is where I'm supposed to be. No more small time."

When Kim hung up the phone, she tried to get Pat's attention. "Mr. Leshing." Pat was lost in his own little world thinking of his bright future, where, in a few years, he would be sitting in as one of the Board of Directors. "Mr. Leshing!" Kim spoke up a bit this time.

"Uh, yes, sorry, I'm just eh...."

"It's Ok. Mr. Lawry will be down in a moment. Please have a seat." Kim extended her hand to point to the couches and chairs.

"Thank you Miss eh, Kelly. Thank you."

"You're welcome. Mr. Lawry will be down shortly. Please, have a seat."

Pat sat down in the comfortable faux leather chair, again wondering about all the possibilities of managing such a large and prosperous company. And although he was looking forward to his start, he didn't want to be bothered as he drifted back into his imaginary Board of Directors world.

"Pat Leshing? Hi I'm Jim Lawry." Jim extended his very large arm to shake Pat's hand. Pat couldn't help notice how black Jim's hand was. Maybe it was due to the stark contrast to his white sleeved shirt, but Pat had never seen a man so black. It wasn't as if he hadn't worked with African American people, but this man was as black as night, and large enough to block out the sun. Jim's hand was almost twice the size of his. Pat extended his hand, which Jim enveloped, as they shook. "How was the trip to Blue Bell Pat?"

"Not too bad. It's my first time coming here from Virginia."

"Great. Let's head upstairs and I'll introduce you around." As Jim led the way, Pat couldn't help wonder if Jim had played some sort of professional sports. But, he didn't want to sound dumb or naïve, and worse, he didn't want to insult his new boss by not knowing if he did play professionally, so, he didn't ask. They took the elevator up to the fourth floor. When they stepped off, Pat gazed out at the number of cubicles he could see. And, past where he couldn't see, he was certain there were more. Just the cubicles he did see were more than what his entire building had in Virginia.

"This way Pat, this floor is pretty much made up of our Customer Service representatives. These are the people you will be over-seeing. We have over 200 representatives on call 24 hours per day, seven days per week."

"Wow, you get that many complaints?" Pat tried to start off with humor.

Pat's attempt at humor didn't go over too well. Jim quickly turned and said, "No. While we do get our share of complaint calls, over eighty percent of our calls are from new customers, or customers wanting to change, or upgrade their service. Universal has acquired three companies in addition to your previous employer. So, naturally customers call to inquire about what changes will be made to their channels, or what types of packages we offer or what the costs will be."

As Pat walked by the cubicles, he couldn't help but notice the many pictures the employees had on their desks. Many of them were pictures with their family. Some had different sport team logos, or high school and college logos. Pat thought the people really seemed interested in sports around here.

"We are a family oriented company Pat. When we hire someone, we not only hire that person, but we accept their family into ours. That's why you see most of the desks have family photos. We have company picnics twice per year. We also have a family Christmas party every year. Universal advocates a healthy active lifestyle for our work staff and their family. We encourage our employees and their families to get active. We especially support youth sports programs. Some of our employees have grade school, high school or college kids who play sports. Some of those kids are very good at what they do. When we see such kids excelling, we like to let that out across our Universal community. We sponsor youth camps, and we donate to Athletic Clubs. Of course as a company we aren't asking our family employees to all be stars. We just like for them to be active. Sports activities keep the kids healthy, off drugs and out of trouble. I understand you have a son, correct?"

"Yes, Brandon, he's fourteen. He'll be starting high school next fall."

"Have you decided on a school yet?"

"No, the three of us, my wife, Brandon and I, will be spending the next couple days driving around different neighborhoods looking for a home."

"Does he play any sports?"

"He does play baseball and football with the kids in the neighborhood." Pat lied. Brandon hadn't played any organized sports in the six years since Louie had died. What's a little white lie when you are trying to impress your boss?

"Football huh, that's great. I think you'll find football to be our number one sport in this area. If Brandon plans on playing high school football, we have many great choices. There's the Catholic League where La Salle has an excellent program. That's in Wyndmoor. There's the Public League where Washington and Northeast have good programs. Then there's the Academia League which is a smaller league. Conscientia is a private school. It has an outstanding academic program. Over 98% of those who graduate go on to college. My son graduated from there. His senior year he captained their undefeated, league championship football team. My daughter will be a senior this fall. She plays basketball and field hockey."

"Thanks Jim, we're just looking around at the neighborhoods for now, but I'll keep that in mind. I'm sure Brandon is planning on playing football next fall." Pat continued with the lie.

"I played football for the Eagles in 95 and 96. But, I tore up my knee and that was that. Best two years of my life though. I would go through it all over again, even knowing I'd go through most of my adult life with nagging arthritic knees. Thank goodness my parents made me concentrate on academics. Recognition alone didn't put me in this position at Universal Cable. I graduated from Boston College with a 3.8 grade point average in telecommunications. That's what got me in this company. Of course, the football didn't hurt in opening the door. But the academics, that's what got me hired."

"I remember you with the Eagles." Pat wanted so desperately to impress his new boss. "In Virginia we mostly get Ravens football, but I remember when the Eagles played us. If I recall, you had an outstanding game."

"We didn't play the Ravens in 95 or 96. It must have been someone else you are thinking."

Again, Pat's attempt to impress his new boss failed miserably. His joke didn't go over well. He lied about his son playing football, and now this. Pat's day wasn't starting off as he had hoped.

"Over here is where your office will be." Pat's office was bigger than the CEO of Virginia Cable had. He had a beautiful mahogany table with a real leather chair. "This is Judy Reinhardt. She will be your main assistant. Sam Thompson will be your assistant on weekends or when Judy is on vacation."

"Hello Judy, I'm Pat Leshing. It's nice to meet you."

"It's nice to meet you Mr. Leshing." Judy said smiling with bright white teeth and ruby red lipstick. She could have been a poster woman in a dental office. On her desk was a picture of her family - her husband, and three children, two boys and a girl. The boys wore baseball uniforms. The girl was wearing a cheerleader outfit.

"Please call me Pat. May I call you Judy?"

"Of course Pat. Welcome aboard."

"If you'll walk this way, I'll introduce you to those who will be reporting to you." Jim and Pat walked into a conference room. There were six people in the room - two women, one from India Pat assumed, the other a heavy-set Caucasian, and one man were at one end of the table. The other three men, two African American, the other Caucasian, all of whom looked very athletic, were discussing off work topics. The six people ranged in ages from early to late thirties. When they noticed Jim in the room they quieted down and turned their attention to Jim and Pat.

"Gentlemen, and ladies, please have a seat. This is Pat Leshing our new Sr. Manager from Virginia Cable. As you know, Pat will be taking over for Reggie Williams who has recently retired. Pat will be coming on board in June. You six will be reporting directly to Pat, who will report directly to me. I'll leave you all to get to know each other." Jim turned to Pat. "Pat, it was nice to finally meet face to face. I'll be in touch as we get closer to your June start date. Guys, try to make your new boss feel welcome ok?" Jim said with a smile. He gave Pat a slap on the shoulder and then left the room.

"Hello, as Jim stated, I'm Pat Leshing and I'll be starting permanently here beginning June 1st. However, between now and then, I'll be transitioning from Virginia Cable, so I'll be stopping by every so often to discuss some projects I'd like to kick off when I begin. For now, I'd just like to talk about ourselves; get to know each other. I'll go first…" Pat continued his meeting with his staff, after two hours, Pat called his wife to come pick him up.

The next two days day went according to plan. Pat, Cindy and Brandon drove through the various neighborhoods Pat had picked out, including ones mentioned by Jim. Sunday night, after the long exhaustive weekend, Pat and Cindy lay in bed, both tired from all of the travel. "You never told me how the meeting went. Everything go Ok?"

"The meeting with my staff went great. I'll have six people reporting to me, four men and two women. All of them seemed really nice. But, my meeting with my boss didn't go too well. I put my foot in my mouth when I joked about why so many customer service reps were needed. I asked if they really had that many complaints. Jim, my new boss, didn't seem to think that was too funny. Then, Jim told me that he was a football player for the Eagles. So I told him I remember him playing the Ravens and that he was a really good player. He told me he never played the Ravens."

"Well why did you say that?"

"I don't know Cindy. I was just trying to make a good impression. How was I supposed to know the Eagles didn't play the Ravens in those years?"

"Well, I don't think they will hold that against you. You've got the job and I'm sure they'll give you at least thirty days before they fire you." Cindy smiled. Pat stared into the ceiling. "Hey, come on. That was a joke. You're going to be fine. They wouldn't have given you the promotion if they didn't think you could handle the job."

"I know. I'm not worried about that."

"What are you worried about?"

"It's Brandon. Universal Cable isn't like Virginia Cable, Cindy. They really compete. Right down to the employee. That's what makes them so successful."

"What's Brandon got to do with Universal? It's not like he's going to work there."

"Universal is family oriented. Jim said - they don't just hire the person they accept the entire family. They have company picnics, family Christmas parties. They involve the whole family."

"So what are you saying? Brandon and I have to measure up to Universal?"

"Cindy, you should have seen the people there. Anyone who has a kid Brandon's age plays some kind of sport. Jim specifically said - Universal encourages sport activities for their employees and family. Sports help kids stay healthy and away from drugs."

"What's that's supposed to mean? Brandon's very healthy and he never once did drugs, which is a lot, especially after what he went through with Louie. Brandon is a straight 'A' student. He's polite, he doesn't get into trouble. You should be proud of your son. You shouldn't care what Universal thinks. Brandon is fine just the way he is."

"Cindy I love Brandon. I *am* proud of him. I know he is a straight 'A' student. But, I think he needs to be more, you know, well-rounded. He's always got his head in his books or in the computer. He doesn't go out with his friends the way he used to. He was really good at baseball and football. He's got to get back into that for his own good."

"For *his* own good, or you and Universal's own good. And how would you know how good he was at football? You hardly saw a game. You were always at work on Saturdays, remember? Brandon's fine just the way he is."

"Cindy, come on. You even said a few times that you wished Brandon would have more of a social life. What harm would it be for him to try out for football or baseball again? He doesn't have to be a star. Just so he tries. Who knows, he may even like it. I know he used to like playing sports."

"Yes, I do sometimes wish he were more social. But I'm not going to force him into something he doesn't want, or isn't ready to do. He's fine the way he is. If he wants to immerse himself in his schoolwork and studies, that's fine with me. There are a lot of other things he could have immersed himself into that would be a hell of a lot worse."

"Cindy, I'm not going to force him into anything. But it won't hurt to ask if he would want to try some sports would it?"

"Fine, but if he does play, it's because he wants to, not because Universal wants him to. Got it?"

"Yeah, he'll play only if he wants to."

"Yeah, yeah, good night, Pat." Cindy turned the light on her side out, slammed her pillow and lay on her side facing way from Pat. Pat, reached over, kissed Cindy on her neck. Cindy was having none of it.

"Good night Patrick!"

The next day Cindy had dinner on the table. "Brandon, dinner's ready."

"Alright mom, I'll be down in a minute." As Brandon approached the table he saw his father. "Slacking off at work now that you got the promotion?"

"Nah, I'll be working normal hours from now until June. Not much to do except ensure our Virginia customers that their cable packages won't change and their rates won't increase. All new customer activity is being handled in Philly."

"I was just kidding. I know you would be the last person on earth to slack off at work. Dinner smells good mom."

"Yes, Cindy, if I had known you were such a good cook, I would have tried harder to make it home for more dinners. What is this anyway?"

"Pat, I could make lobster and filet mignon every night and you still wouldn't make it home every night for dinner. This is something I wanted to try. This is ravioli stuffed with crab and feta cheese with a light cream sauce."

"Wow, you hand made this? I'm really impressed. It looks delicious!"

"Well thank you Pat. Hopefully it tastes delicious as well. You know, now that I'll have extra time on my hands, I was thinking I might look into some culinary classes, try something new."

"I'm sure it will be delicious. Speaking of trying new things, you know Brandon I've been thinking about the areas and schools around Blue Bell. Once school caught my eye, Conscientia. It's a small private school that has a great academic reputation. Over 98% of the students who graduate go onto college. It is challenging academically, but you have always been a straight 'A' student. I think you would fit in perfectly there."

"That sounds good I guess. I'm not familiar with the schools up there, but that sounds as good as any. Hopefully they have a good science program."

"I'm sure they do." Pat cleared his throat before continuing. "In addition to the academics, they require their students to participate in activities other than class work. They like their students to participate in sports activities. You used to play baseball and football. You were pretty good too. What do you think about trying out for the football team in the fall?"

At this point Cindy had stopped eating. She stared at Pat, attentively listening to every word coming out of his mouth. Although he wasn't forcing Brandon to play, he wasn't exactly giving him any alternatives either. It also would have been nice if Pat had discussed the school and its activity requirements with her before bringing it up to Brandon. "It's just one school out of many Pat. *We* can discuss what type of school he wants to attend. And besides, I'm sure Conscientia offers other activities in addition to football. There's soccer, cross country, and maybe you can participate in club activities like theater or the chess club, or…"

"Chess club? Honey, no offense, but the Chess Club isn't exactly a physical activity. Moving Queen Four to Bishop Six, or whatever the term is, isn't too active. They want their students to be fit mentally and physically."

"First of all, who are they? Universal? You? Second of all, if Brandon doesn't want to play football, I'm just suggesting some alternatives. It's up to Brandon to choose for himself what he wants to do, right?"

"Of course, I just remember how good he was when he did play football. Remember Brandon?"

Brandon was beginning to feel uncomfortable watching his parents argue, especially over him. "Yeah, football was fun, but…"

"There, you see Cindy. He enjoyed playing football. He might enjoy playing football again. That's all I'm saying."

"And what I'm saying is that it's his choice what he wants to play and I'm offering some alternatives to football." Cindy was visibly angry at her husband. She turned her attention to her son. "At any rate, Brandon, it's not like you have to decide now. School doesn't start for a few months so you think about what you want to do and decide for yourself. Agreed Pat?"

"I was just making conversation. With the move, we all have an opportunity to start fresh. You just said, with some of the extra time you will have, you thought about taking culinary classes. Although school *is* still a few months away, it will be here fast. It doesn't hurt for Brandon to start to thinking about what he needs to do."

"And what he *wants* to do."

"That's what I meant, what he wants to do at his new school." Pat didn't want to push this conversation any further. "Mmmm, I don't know how you made this honey but it sure does taste delicious. Maybe you should look into teaching culinary school. Brandon, what do you think? Your mom would make a great chef don't you think?"

"Yeah, this is great mom."

"Thank you honey."

"You're welcome." Pat replied.

"I was talking to Brandon."

During the Memorial Day weekend, Pat and Cindy threw a summer/going-away party. The people who attended were mostly Cindy's friends and family. Some of Pat's co-workers, some who were laid off, some lucky enough to keep their job, attended as well. Louie's parents, Dominic and Claire Buccelli were also invited, but they declined. Rather, it was Claire who had declined. Cindy and Pat were able to say goodbye to Dominic, but Claire did not want any part in talking to the Leshings. Dominic told Pat and Cindy that he didn't hold any grudge against Brandon. He knew Brandon would never intentionally hurt Louie. He knew Louie adored Brandon and that Brandon protected Louie like a little brother. Claire didn't see things this way. All Claire saw was that her son was dead, and that the cause of her son's death lived across the street. Claire was having such a hard time of it that she hardly ever went out unless it was out of necessity. She kept Louie's bedroom just as it was prior to his death. Pat and Cindy thanked Dominic for his understanding. They understood Claire's position as well. They couldn't imagine losing their son. All they could say was they hoped in time that Claire would be able to move on.

The beginning of June finally arrived. For the Leshing family, it was time to move. Though it was hard for Cindy to leave her home, the area she grew up, the only area she knew. It wasn't as tough for Pat and Brandon. Pat couldn't wait to start on his new career at Universal. In his mind there was no way he was going to make something of himself in a small rural town in Virginia. It wasn't that he hated Virginia as much as he felt he was being held back. He knew at some point in his career he would have to leave the small town in order to make it big. But, he never could convince Cindy to move. Now, he had her convinced.

Brandon was going to go to a place where no one knew him. He could make a new first impression without anyone knowing what he did to Louie. Every time he stepped outside he couldn't help but look across the street and see Louie's house. He never looked for long as the thought of Mrs. Buccelli coming out and catching his eye was frightening. In Philadelphia, he wouldn't have to worry about Mrs. Buccelli, or the kids at school or their whispering behind his back. One thing he would never forget is the promise he made to Louie. Somehow, some way, he was going to make it right.

The summer months at Universal Cable were generally the slowest of the year. This was the time of the year when people took vacations, or went out to the movie theater to view the latest block buster. But Pat was working ten hours a day, six days a week. Cindy thought the work week would be less of a grind for Pat now that he didn't have to worry about the company being bought out and him being laid off. Pat's reason for the long hours was that he was the new guy. He had to let his boss, the executives, and the directors know that hiring him was not a mistake. He had to set an example for those who reported to him. How could he ask someone to put in extra hours if he didn't put in extra time himself? He assured Cindy that it wouldn't be too long before he could cut the hours back. He just needed to get grounded. Two months in, and Pat was still averaging sixty hours per week.

"I see you've enrolled your son at Conscientia, excellent choice. I hope the fact that I have had both my children enrolled there didn't affect your decision." Jim stated.

"Cindy and I looked at several schools and we both thought with Brandon being new to the area and not knowing anyone, he would do better at a smaller school. As you said, they do have a great academic program. They also have programs like theater, photography, and art. They just built a multi-million dollar amp theater that looked amazing. Brandon hasn't decided yet about football though."

"Oh, I thought you said he played football back in Virginia. I would give it some thought. It's been proven that kids who are active in sports tend to do better in life in general. Universal gave a grant to a group of psychologists and social experts to perform a ten year study on the advantages and disadvantages of playing sports while in high school. The study kept tabs on the kids through high school, and college - those who went to college. It was our way to combat those who criticize us for promoting a sedentary life style. You know, us being a company that sells TV. Anyway, what the study found was that kids who play sports are more social, more apt to become leaders. They are more inclined to take risks. Whereas those who did not play sports tended to be more introverted and were physically less healthy. So we try as best we can to promote an active life style for our staff and their families, especially the kids."

"Well, school starts in a week or so, I'm sure Brandon will give it some thought."

Pat truly believed that his standing in the workplace would be a heck of a lot better if his son played football. With the start of school coming soon, Pat made one of his rare appearances at the dinner table. "School starts tomorrow, you ready Brandon?"

"Yeah, I guess. I'm ready as I'll ever be."

"How about I drive you to school tomorrow, so you won't be late? I can drop you off, and then head to work."

"Sure, I was going to take the bus, but I'll take the ride. Thanks."

Cindy was suspicious of Pat's generosity. "It's just to make sure he gets there on time, that's all."

"I didn't say a word Pat."

"You didn't have to dear."

The next morning Pat dropped Brandon off for his first day of school. "Brandon, I don't want to push you or anything, but I'd really like for you to try out for the JV football team. I remember how good you were when you played, and I think it would be a great way to meet new friends. If you don't like it, you don't have to stay on the team. You can do whatever you like. But, I think this would be a great start. You don't have to say yes or no, just think about it ok?"

"Sure dad, I'll give it some thought."

"Thanks, you have a great first day."

"Alright dad, I'll see you tonight."

"You bet. I'll see you then."

For the second day in a row, Pat made it home for dinner. "Brandon, how was the first day of school?"

"It was good. The school is very cool. There are fifteen to twenty kids in a classroom. They have all the modern computer equipment. Their science labs are unbelievable. The other kids are mostly friendly. I made a couple friends, Natalie and Allen. Natalie is from the Netherlands and is here as an exchange student."

"That sounds great. But I hope you're not planning on spending the next four years in the computer and science labs. Have you given any thought to signing up for JV football team?"

"Patrick!"

"What Cindy, I'm just asking. I know the students have to choose to participate in extracurricular activities during the year. Am I right Brandon?"

"Yeah, that's true. I did think about what you said this morning."

Cindy slammed her fork down. "I knew it!"

Brandon, not wanting to sit through another argumentative dinner, spoke before his father could. "Its ok mom, dad just asked if I would be interested in playing football."

"You see honey. So, what did you decide?"

"Allen, the guy I met in school actually plays quarterback. I went with him to see the coach of the JV team. The coach thinks I'd make a pretty good player. He actually thought I was asking about trying out for the varsity team. I guess because I'm a little bigger than most kids in my class."

"You see, even the coach thinks he would make a great player."

"How would he know Pat? He never saw Brandon play. I bet he says that to all of the kids so they sign up."

Pat didn't hear a word Cindy said. He wanted to know if Brandon decided to give football a try. "So, did you sign up?"

"Yeah, he told me first practice is a week from Wednesday. I told him I would be there."

"Fantastic! I can't wait to see you play. You'll be terrific I just know it. Congratulations son."

"Well I really haven't done anything yet so I don't know what you're congratulating me for."

"I'm just happy to see you try Brandon that's all."

"Brandon if you are doing this just for your father's sake, you don't have to. You can participate in any activity you like, even if it is a science club, or math club, or chess club, anything you like."

"Cindy, he's going to give football a try. You know Universal did a ten year study showing that kids who participate in sports tend to be more social, more of a leader, more of a risk taker. I want what's best for Brandon that's all."

"You want what's best for Brandon or what's best for you and Universal Cable?"

"I was just making a suggestion, that's all."

"Well, enough suggestions. Brandon, you sign up for what you want. You'll turn out fine whatever you decide. Ok?"

"I will mom."

"Now, no more talk about football. Let's enjoy the Moroccan chicken dinner I've prepared."

Later that night, before turning out the light, Cindy turned to talk to her husband. "Pat, what is your obsession with Brandon playing football?"

"I think athletics would be good for Brandon. You know, make him better balanced, more rounded. I'm just afraid he'll go right back into immersing himself into his books and computers again. Don't get me wrong, I'm glad Brandon gets the grades he does. I'm afraid if he applies himself solely to his studies, he'll miss out on friendships, parties, social events that normal kids his age have."

"First of all, When did you get to decide what is normal? Brandon is normal, whatever normal is. Second, you heard him at dinner, he made a couple friends his first day at school. He's doing fine if you ask me. Believe me, it could be a lot worse."

"Cindy, don't get me wrong, I'm not saying Brandon is a bad kid, or that he's going to end up bad. Jim said at work today when he played football it was the best thing he ever did. The study that Universal has done found that kids who play sports turn out better than kids who don't play sports."

"Oh, so that's what this football thing is all about. You're using Brandon to make a good impression on your boss and those at Universal! I can't believe you Pat. You know you talk about Brandon immersing himself in his books and computers. What about you? What life do you have outside the sixty hours you immerse yourself into work? You work six days a week, you rarely show up for dinner. What kind of life is that?"

"Cindy, I don't want to fight about this. I'm only making suggestions for Brandon to do things outside of school work. And to your point, yes, I do put in a lot of hours at work. I have to. If I don't someone else will and I'll be replaced. I have a family to provide for, bills to pay, and now an expensive school to pay for as well. You actually made my point. There's going to come a time when Brandon won't have a choice. There's going to come a time, very soon, when he'll be in the same position as me. There won't be a choice to play football, or baseball, or whatever other sport he may like. It's best he tries to play as much as he can now."

"Good night Patrick! If he wants to play, he'll play. If he doesn't want to play, he won't play."

Chapter 5
I WILL SURVIVE

As the van approached his house, the first thing Ted noticed was the ramp leading from the sidewalk to the front door. For now, while in a wheel chair, this would be his pathway into and out of his home. As his wheelchair was lowered from the van, Ted saw his daughter Gina, now seventeen years old walk out of the house to greet him. The driver of the van walked to the back of Ted's chair. "Ok, Mr. Stroit, hands in while I get you out of the van." This was Ted's first view of his house in over six months. The previous five months were spent at Pebble Rehabilitation Center.

"Welcome home dad. Do you like the addition? It's pretty nice huh?"

Ted gave a slight smile, and meekly nodded his head. The driver of the van pushed Ted up the ramp and into his house. Once inside, the man asked Gina to sign some papers. He looked at Ted and said "Best of luck to you."

Ted appeared to not have heard the man. He looked at the changes inside his house. Gina, after waiting for her father to acknowledge the man's gesture, finally said, "Thank you sir." The man turned and walked out the door.

"Dad, how are you feeling?"

"Fine Gina, I'm fine."

"Oreo, look who's home." Oreo came in from the kitchen to see what all the commotion was about. "Oreo missed you so much, didn't you Oreo?" Oreo sat licking his paw as he had just finished eating. "Well, as you can see we made some big changes. The first was the ramp as you saw. We converted the office room to your bedroom. A door was put in so you can have your privacy. It's just until you're strong enough to get up and down the steps safely."

"I see."

"Are you in any pain? I picked up your prescriptions. I have one for Vicodin which you are supposed to take one every four to six hours. I have a prescription for Paxil which you are supposed to take once a day. And I have one called Baclofen which you should take one in the morning and one at night before bed."

"I'm fine Gina."

"Are you sure? When did you take the Vicodin? You're supposed to…"

"I said I'm fine Gina. I'm fine."

"Ok, I'm sorry dad. I'm just trying to make sure I follow doctors' orders. Are you hungry?"

"No, not right now, maybe later. I'm a little tired. I'm gonna go lay down for a bit."

"Yeah, sure dad, do you need help getting in bed?"

"No, I can manage."

"The hospital said that the home care person will be stopping by between one and two o'clock today. Do you want me to wake you? It's 11:00 now. "

"Just give a yell when he's here."

"Will do, are you sure you don't need any help…."

"No, I'll be fine Gina, just give a yell when he shows up."

"Ok dad."

Ted rolled into his new bedroom and shut the door. He had practiced getting in and out of bed for the past several weeks while at Rehab. When he shimmied himself to the middle of the bed, he fell back to lie down. He looked over at the bureau that was brought down from his bedroom. On his bureau were the pictures of him and his wife Linda. He began to wonder where it all went so wrong. The young couple's lives weren't supposed to be like this. Linda was gone and his only child now had the burden to watch after him while he tried to regain a somewhat normal life. Ted laid there thinking of what might have been, what *should* have been.

His thoughts went from his wife, to his own life, then to Gina. She was a senior in high school. She had already lost her mother whom she had hardly known, and the father she knew was gone as well. When most kids her age are going out with friends, talking about boyfriends, and parties, Gina had to watch over her father. It was as if in some ways Gina had gone from being a child to a middle aged person with an elderly parent while skipping early adulthood. Ted decided right there that Gina wouldn't go through that. He was going to do whatever he could to make sure Gina lived her life as a normal teenager and young adult. He was determined to work as hard as possible to get to a point where he could survive on his own. Ted closed his eyes and drifted off to sleep. After what seemed like a few minutes, Ted heard his daughter yelling for him. "Dad the home nurse is here." A bit groggy, Ted answered "I'll be right there."

When Ted opened the door he saw a tall, slim thirty-something year old woman with dark big hair. She looked to be of Italian descent. She wore a little makeup, some red lipstick, some eyeliner, not too thick, but noticeable.

"Well aren't you handsome! I'm Lisa Canero." Lisa was smiling from ear to ear showing her pearly white teeth which were perfectly aligned. "I'll be your therapist for the next six months. After meeting your daughter, and seeing how handsome you are, I know we're going to get along fine. It's going to be hard work, but we're going to have a lot of fun along the way."

Ted's reaction was "*Great, they sent me a cheerleader. I'm trying to figure out a way to get my life back on track, and I get sent a freaking cheerleader.*"

"Did you just wake up? You look a little sleepy."

"I was taking a nap. You know first time out of the hospital, a bit draining."

"Well, no more sleeping during the day when I'm here handsome. We're here to work and have fun. The first thing I want to do is look around the house. Don't worry, I'm not here to criticize, or scope out the joint." Lisa laughed as if she was trying to be a comic. "I just want to see the areas of high activity. You know, where you will eat, bathe, sleep, dress, and use the bathroom. I want to see if we have any trouble spots. I see they converted your bedroom from upstairs to down here. That's very good. You're very lucky. Some people don't have the room for a ground area bedroom."

"Yeah, I guess I am lucky. Gina can show you around the house."

"No, no, Gina has her own work to do. You're going to show me."

Ted looked at Gina who looked back with a slight shrug. "Well you can see where I sleep."

"Let's take a look in there. Do you mind?"

"Uh, no, I don't mind."

Ted and Lisa went into the bedroom. Lisa wanted to see things such as where Ted's clothes would be kept, how high Ted's bed was compared to his wheelchair, how much room there was to move around. Were there any places where Ted may get stuck? After looking around the converted bedroom, Ted and Lisa went to the kitchen, they went to the bathroom where a standing shower with a bench was installed. After going around the house, which wasn't too much of an effort since everything was close and on the same floor, Lisa stated "You certainly are lucky to have such a nice place to live. I would love to live in a place like this. Right now, I'm in a cramped one bedroom apartment".

"Thank you. I'd just rather have kept my house the way it was. If I was lucky I wouldn't have a need for a home therapist to begin with."

"While I'm here we are going to focus on the positive Ok handsome?" Ted just looked at her. "Ok?" Lisa asked again with her wide pearly white smile.

"Yeah, sure, we'll focus solely on the positive." Ted mumbled.

"That's more like it. Now, take my hands and squeeze them."

"What?"

"I would like you to take my hands and squeeze them, as hard as you can. Don't worry, they're clean and I won't break." Lisa laughed as if she had just told a really good joke.

Ted didn't understand why Lisa was asking this, maybe this was some Kumbaya moment? "Come on, take my hands and squeeze. Don't worry, I don't bite." Ted did as he was told. "Good. Very good, you're a very strong man. I like strong men. Now, I want to check your blood pressure."

"Why?"

"Am I going to have to explain everything I do? Come over here and let me take your blood pressure." Again, Ted didn't know why Lisa was asking this, but, he did as he was told. Lisa pulled out a blood pressure kit from her bag. "Hmmm, your BP is low. Do you feel tired? Any dizziness?"

"I feel fine. I was just napping, but I feel fine. What's the reading?"

"It's 90 over 80. It's not too low, but we'll have to monitor it."

"Isn't low blood pressure good? A lot of people take medication for high blood pressure."

"It is better to have low blood pressure than high. But you don't want it to be too low. Low blood pressure can lead to dizziness, fainting spells, or worse, loss of consciousness. Yours isn't too bad. I'm not too worried."

"I'm glad to hear that. I wouldn't want to worry you."

"Is that sarcasm I hear?" Ted didn't answer. "Ok, that's all for today. I got you out of bed. I've seen what I needed in the house, and we got a little exercise. Not a bad start. Monday, I'll be here at 10AM sharp. I'm bringing the heavy equipment, so you better rest up. I want you to have eaten a good breakfast before I get here because Monday starts the real fun. Ok handsome?"

Ted wanted to say – "I'm not really looking for a cheerleader to come over for the next six months." All Ted could get out of his mouth was "I'll see you Monday at ten."

Lisa gave Ted a wink, packed her bag, said goodbye to Gina, and left.

"You know dad, there's something about her I really like." Ted didn't say a word as he wheeled himself back into his converted bedroom.

The next day, Sunday, Ted had a few visitors. The Bachwel's stopped by to see if they could help in any way. People from Ted's Union stopped by, among them were Joe Wolfers and Jennifer Manley. When Joe stopped by he expressed how sorry he was to have not secured the bolt properly. He felt responsible for Ted's position. Ted assured Joe that it wasn't his fault. He told Joe he had been sloppy by not securing a safety harness, and again by using a wooden plank. When Joe felt reassured, he began talking about his exploits with his latest girlfriend. Sasha, the bartender with five kids and a boyfriend whom she didn't like turned out to have an extremely jealous boyfriend who carried a weapon. So now it was onto Nancy, the girl who worked at the tattoo parlor. "You know how I love tattoos right."

"You always have a different one on every week Joe."

"Right, well I went to the parlor on 7th street to check out what they had. I met this girl Nancy. As I'm checking out the different tats we started up a conversation. She's 22, no kids and she broke up with her boyfriend. She's not like that other girl Sasha. Man I really learned a lesson there."

"It's good to keep learning Joe."

"If you want, you can come with me when Nancy works on my tattoo. Maybe pick out one for yourself. Nancy will do it for half price. I got a real good thing going with her."

"Right now Joe I'm just concentrating on my recovery. In fact I really appreciate you stopping by, but I have to rest up for my work-out tomorrow. The home therapist is coming over at ten and she warned me about having to start exercising and how I better get my rest."

"Oh yeah, a female therapist huh, what's she like? Is she hot?"

"Joe! What the hell is it with you? Not every girl is out there to be hit on. She's Ok, but she's not coming over to ask me out on a date. She's coming over to get me out of this damn chair and walking again. From what she says it's going to take some hard work. Now get the hell out and I'll see you next week."

Joe, oblivious to anyone's insults, was happy to see Ted held no grudge against him. As Joe opened the door to let himself out, Ted said, "Hey Joe, I really do appreciate you stopping by to check on Gina." Joe, among all of his liabilities was a friend with a good heart.

"No problem Teddy. If you need anything you know you can count on me. I'll see you next week. Or maybe I can stop by during the week and check out this new home therapist you got?"

"Joe, will you get the hell out! I'll see you next week."

"Alright man, I'll see you then. You take care of yourself."

Jennifer stopped at the house a half hour after Joe left. She was happy to finally see Ted's home. "In all the years we've known each other you have never invited me over to your house. You have a very nice home Ted."

Ted never invited Jennifer over mainly because he didn't want to give off any false impressions. Ted knew Jennifer wanted to be more than just co-workers. But Ted didn't want that. Not because Jennifer wasn't attractive, or wasn't nice, it was because he still couldn't see himself in a relationship. He still thought of his wife every day.

"So how are you doing Ted? Are you feeling any better?"

"I'm getting better every day. Coming home was a big step. I'm so glad to be out of that hospital. Gina has been a big help. I don't know what I would do without her. And you've been a big help as well Jen. Thanks for all you've done with the insurance and workman's comp. You don't know how much Gina and I appreciate it."

"That's my job Ted. I'm happy to do those things for you. You concentrate on getting better."

"I'm doing the best I can. I'm hoping by spring I can get out of this chair for good."

"I know you will Ted. You have always been a hard worker." Jennifer stayed an hour longer, but noticed Ted was getting tired. Before Jennifer left she placed her right hand on Ted's left cheek, and gave him a kiss on his right cheek. "You take care, Ted. You know I think of you every day."

"Thanks Jen, I will."

"When you're up for it, you can take me out for that fun weekend you've promised."

"You got it. As soon as I'm out of this chair, the first weekend, you and me, sound good?"

"That sounds great." Jennifer let herself out of the house.

By the end of the day, Ted had felt extremely tired. It wasn't even 9PM and he could hardly keep his eyes open. He went into his room, got himself onto his bed, undressed and laid there. He thought of his wife, his daughter, himself and what he needed to do to get himself back on his feet. He felt lucky to have the good friends and neighbors that he did. He reached over, to his bureau and took his medication, then reached over the other side of the bed where he had a mini-fridge and took out a bottle of water. After swallowing his pills, he closed his eyes and was sound asleep in minutes.

Lisa knocked on the door precisely at 10AM. Ted was up, had eaten breakfast that Gina made, and answered the door. Gina had left for school a couple hours prior. "Good morning handsome. Are you ready to work?"

"Well, if it isn't my favorite cheerleader. You bet. I'm ready to go. Let's get me out of this thing."

"Cheerleader, huh? I've been called worse. Where can I put my things?" Lisa had her same bag from Saturday. She also had a walker which Ted liked to see. It meant getting out of his chair.

"You can put those things over there." Ted pointed to the table.

"First off, I'd like to get a couple things straight. Let's start with expectations. What do you expect to get out of the next six months Ted?"

"I expect to be walking naturally. I don't expect to run the mile under four minutes, but I expect to be able to walk. What are your expectations?"

"Ted, I'm going to be honest with you. I can't say for sure that by the end of the six months you'll be walking. I can't even tell you that you'll be able to walk from here to the door. And that's the point I want to get across. My expectations are to get you to a point where you don't have to depend on Gina to everything for you like cooking, cleaning, and shopping. My expectations are to get you to a point where you can live independently. I want to get you back to work. It may not be climbing up buildings as you did before, but I want to get you to a point where you will be productive. I'm not saying that you will definitely stay in a wheel chair the rest of your life. You may even be able to walk on your own, who knows. But my job isn't specifically to get you out of that chair for good. My job, in addition to helping you physically get stronger, is also to help you get independent occupationally. Do you understand?"

Suddenly the excitement Ted felt starting on the road to recovery was dealt a major blow. What was Lisa saying? *Get me to a point where I could function independently.* Ted thought he *was* at a point where he could function independently. Sure Gina did all of the cooking, cleaning, shopping, but if Ted needed to do those things, he knew he could. Maybe this was Lisa's way of setting low expectations if things didn't go so well. That had to be it. Ted was going to work his ass off. Lisa had never dealt with anyone like him. He was going to show her he was going to walk. He was going to get back to the point of *his* definition of normal, not Lisa's. "Ok Lisa, I understand."

"Really, you understand?"

"Yeah, sure, don't worry. I'm not going to sue you or anything if things don't work out."

"Ted, I'm not concerned about that. I've been doing this for over ten years. The main problem that arises in this process is the frustration that my patients have. They all expect to physically get to the point they were before their accident. But that's not always the case. In fact it hardly *ever* works out like that. I want to set expectations to try to offset the frustrations that will occur."

Again, Ted didn't like what he was hearing. But Lisa had never worked with someone like him before. "Ok Lisa. We'll do our best and whatever happens, happens."

Lisa knew Ted did not understand the point she was trying to make. How could he? How could anyone understand that the things they took for granted were most likely taken away forever? Lisa continued. "Next item, what I say goes. You do *exactly* as I say. Not only when I'm here, but anything I leave for you to do, you do. Got it?"

"Ok, you're the boss, understood."

"That goes for things I tell you *not* to do as well. I've worked with people like you before Ted."

"People like me?"

"Yes, I've read your bio. You were always athletic. You've always worked with your hands. You were never the desk jockey type. Before your accident, you probably couldn't sit through a movie. You're the type that always needs to be doing something. People like you I will never have to worry about motivating. I know you will give your all. However, I worry about people like you more because you will do things on your own that may put your health, even your life jeopardy. So I mean it. If I tell you to do something, you do it. And, more importantly, if I tell you *not* to do something, you *don't* do it. Got it?"

"Ok, you're right I don't do well at movies. But it's been 15 years since I've been to a movie. I'm sure I'm much better now." Ted said with a smile.

"I'm sure you are. Do you have any questions for me?"

"Yes, can we stop with the chit chat and get started? I see you brought a walker with you, let's get it over here and put that to use."

"I did bring the walker, yes. First grab my hands and squeeze them as tight as you can."

"What? I did this Saturday why do I need to do this again?"

"What did I say about doing as I say? Have you forgotten that already?"
Ted looked at Lisa, rolled his eyes and held out his hands for Lisa.

"And don't roll your eyes mister. When I'm here, I'm the boss, got it?"

"Yes boss." Ted held Lisa's hands and squeezed as hard as he could.

"Your strength seems to be good. Now, roll up your sleeve I want to take your blood pressure."

"What?" Before Ted could finish his sentence, Lisa gave him a look which made him stop. He rolled up his sleeve and Lisa took his blood pressure. "Your pressure is better than it was on Saturday. How do you feel?"

"I feel fine, now can we get the walker and try to walk?"

"Hold on now handsome, I brought the walker here, but not to try to walk. We are going to use the walker to work on your upper body strength. First, lock the wheels on your chair."

"They're fine. They won't move on the rug." Lisa placed her hands on her hips, and looked at Ted like a mother looking at a child in trouble. "Ok, they're locked. Don't you want to take this blood pressure thing off my arm?"

"No, I want you to hold onto the walker, bring it as close to you as possible." Ted did as he was told. "Good. Now I want you to stand for fifteen seconds. When I say go, I want you to stand, ready?"

"Yes."

"Ok, stand." While Ted stood up, Lisa counted to fifteen. "Ok, down. Nice. Now, I'm going to take your blood pressure." Ted thought this exercise was stupid. But, he wasn't about to say anything. "How do you feel?"

"I feel with my hands, how do you think I feel?"

"Wow you just set a record, you know that?"

"A record, what record is that?"

"Most of my patients take at least a few days before frustration sets in. For you it was less than two minutes."

"I just don't see the point of standing, sitting, standing, sitting. And why do you have to keep taking my blood pressure?"

"This is exactly my point. Before you can start walking, I want you to be able to stand and not have your blood pressure to the point where you faint. Because you haven't used your leg muscles in a long time and are very weak they don't have the ability to contract and get your blood pumped back to your upper body. If you stand too long all of your blood will be at your legs which will lead to dizziness. Then, if you fall, you run the risk of breaking something. And then, you're right back in the hospital. What we're doing, as simple as it seems, is building up those muscles. Now let me take you blood pressure." Ted just shook his head and held out his arm for Lisa to take.

"Maybe this frustration is doing some good. Your pressure is better. Ok, one more time stand." Ted stood while Lisa counted to fifteen. "Ok, sit down." Ted wanted to see how long he could stand. Lisa commanded again. "Ted, sit down!" Suddenly Ted was feeling lightheaded. He plopped down into his chair so hard it moved back even with the wheels locked. "Damn it Ted! Now listen. I'm not going to come here if you disobey everything I say. If that's the way it's going to be, then I'll have someone else come over. I am not going to waste my time if you are just going to go off and do as you wish. Now, are you going to listen to me or are we done here?"

Ted was surprised at how angry Lisa was. She certainly was no longer the upbeat cheerleader. He was also embarrassed at how he felt physically. Lisa was right. He was nowhere near ready to do the things he wanted. "I'm sorry. I just wanted to see how long I could go. From now on you're the boss."

"Ted, it's not that I like being a boss. I've worked with plenty of people in your condition. I know how frustrating it is."

"No, that's where you're wrong. When you're done here you get to walk out the door and get back to a normal life. I don't get to do that."

"You're right. I don't know exactly how it is for someone in your condition. But I know what we need to do to get you better. You have never gone through this type of rehabilitation before. I have. You're going to have to trust me. Tell you what, give me a month, if things aren't going well, or if you think you need a change in therapist, I'll accept that."

"That's fair. I apologize for not listening. I'll try to do better."

"Let me have your arm so I can take your blood pressure." This time Ted did as he was told. "It's down to 90 over 75. A bit low, wouldn't you say?" Lisa said with a wry smile.

Ted did feel lightheaded. He lied when he said he felt fine.

"We'll give it a few minutes and try again. Would you like some water?"

"Yes please. Thank you." Ted felt exhausted.

After several minutes waiting for Ted to recuperate they went through the same exercise of standing, sitting, taking Ted's blood pressure. They did the exercise for the better part of an hour. "That's enough physical activity for today. Let's go into the kitchen?"

"I'm not that tired. We can do other exercises, I can continue."

"I'm glad you're feeling fine Ted, like I said before I'm not here for only physical exercise. My goal is to get you to be independent. That means we have to work on occupational things which at this point are more important. You can't count on your daughter to do a lot of the things she already does. She won't be able to wait on you 24-7. She's at school now. What if you are hungry, or need to do laundry? You can't expect Gina to rush home when you need her. She's going to want a life of her own."

That last part hit Ted hard. The last thing he wanted was to be a burden on Gina. He especially did not want to be the reason Gina couldn't have a life of her own. "Ok, let's go to the kitchen."

Lisa and Ted worked on occupational exercises in the kitchen and laundry room. At 1:00, Lisa said it was time for her to go. She had another patient she needed to get to by 2:00. "Ted, you did real well today. Tomorrow we'll continue with the physical and occupational exercises. I'm going to leave the walker here but I don't want you doing anything with it, got it?"

"Ok, sure."

Lisa looked at Ted and wasn't so sure. "Remember, you do the things I tell you to do, and you *don't* do the things I tell you *not* to do. Just to be sure, I'm going to leave the walker upstairs." Lisa walked up the steps and placed the walker in the hallway.

As Ted watched Lisa, he felt a little angry, a little upset, and even a little vulnerable. All someone had to do to put something out of his reach was walk up a couple steps. "I said I wouldn't use the walker! You don't have to do that!"

"I'll sleep better knowing that it is upstairs. Besides, if you said you won't use it I don't understand why you would be upset."

Ted just shook his head. "Fine!"

"Look, we'll do more exercises tomorrow. If things go according to plan, and you listen, we'll try taking a few steps within a couple weeks. Ok?"

"Sure."

"What's wrong?"

"Nothing, I said I was fine. I'm fine."

"You know I can tell when you're mad at me."

Ted hadn't heard that statement in a long time. It was as if Linda was speaking. "I'm fine, really. I just thought things would be different that's all. I don't want to hold you up for your next patient. I'll see you tomorrow at ten."

"You got it. And I want you to have eaten a good breakfast right?"

"Yes, I'll be ready. I'll see you tomorrow."

"When does your daughter get home from school?"

"She should be home by 4:30."

"You know I've secretly trained Oreo to tell me if you do anything I tell you not to do. So don't try anything. Here, I want to give you my phone number. If you have any problems, don't hesitate to call."

"Thanks, I'll see you tomorrow."

Over the next few days Lisa and Ted worked on Ted's stamina. By the end of the following week, Lisa sensed Ted's frustration with the same routine, so she presented him with a challenge. "Tell you what; if you can stand for ten minutes and your blood pressure stays close to normal, we'll try walking. Ok?"

"Alright, now you're talking." Ted stood for ten minutes. Although most of his weight was supported by his arms, he felt relatively fine. When he sat down, Lisa took his blood pressure.

"What is it? It better be good because I feel fine."

"It's not too bad, 105 over 90."

"Well alright then, let's give this walker thing a real try."

"Hold on handsome, rest a few minutes. Can I get you some water?"

"Yes, thank you."

When Ted was ready, Lisa gave him her instructions. "I'm going to be right behind you with the chair. If you need to sit down, just let me know. When you walk I want the walker extended just a few inches, not too far. Let me show you." Lisa showed Ted exactly how she wanted him to proceed. "After you extend the walker, I want you to stabilize yourself before you take a step. Then, take a breath, and repeat the process. You got it."

"I got. I'm ready when you are."

"Ok, on my count, one, two, three stand. Move the walker out a little. Not too far, bring it back in a little. Ok, try to take a step." Ted took a step. He wasn't really lifting his leg it was rather a swing from the hip to drag his leg in front. "Ok, good. Let's try to go to the door." Ted repeated the process. "Ted you're doing great." Lisa could sense Ted was tired. "Do you want to sit?"

"No, I'm fine, not until I get to the door."

"There's no reason to push too hard. You've done really well."

"I'm fine. We're almost there." When Ted got to the door, he let go of the walker as his arms gave out. He plopped into the chair almost falling.

"Well, that was a nice landing." Lisa said sarcastically. "You did very well Ted, how do you feel?"

"I feel with my hands." Ted joked.

"It's time for your blood pressure. It's low, but not as bad as I thought. That was a nice finish to the day, don't you think?"

"Yeah, finally, now were going somewhere."

Gina walked into the house after having a half day at school. "Hi dad, you looked drained. Is Lisa working you hard?" Gina gave Lisa a smile.

"Your dad just walked across the room, that's why he's tired."

"Really dad, really? You walked across the room? That's great!"

"Don't get too excited, it was more I lifted myself across the room with my arms than walking."

"Even so, I was really proud of you. I didn't think you would make it the whole way. You really surprised me."

"Dad, I think that's great. You should be excited."

"I am sweetheart, I am. It just took a bit out of me. That's all.

"Oh, I see, with your daughter, you are human. With me, you're superman."

"I like my daughter." Ted said with a smile.

"Fine, let's take that blood pressure. It's 110 over 95. Perfect."

"You hear that Gina? I'm perfect."

"I have to see my next patient. I'll see you Monday. Take care, Gina."

"I'll see you Monday Lisa."

"You really did well today Ted. Next week, we'll mix a couple more exercises into the session."

That weekend Ted felt as good as he felt since before his accident. For the first time, there was some tangible evidence that he was improving. It wasn't much, but it was a start. The following Monday and the next couple sessions were the same. Ted and Lisa worked with the walker along with occupational tasks. By Thursday, Ted asked Lisa when she was going to mix in a few more exercises as she promised.

"I was going to wait until tomorrow but I guess we can add something now. The next thing I want to work on is your falling."

"Falling? What do you mean?"

"We have been in this safe environment, but eventually you are going to have to go outside. Someone as handsome as you shouldn't stay inside all day. We need to practice what happens if you fall out of your chair."

"That seems odd but you're the boss. What do you want me to do?"

"First, lock your wheels." Ted locked the wheels. "Now, I'm going to hold onto you while you place your arms on the legs of the chair. On my count I want to you slide out of the chair, and onto the ground."

As Lisa put her arms around Ted to help him down, Ted could smell the floral scent of Lisa's hair. He could sense the aroma of her perfume. As with all her cosmetics, she didn't apply too much, but just enough to notice. Ted felt the soft touch of Lisa's hair as it brushed against his cheek. These were senses he had not felt in a long time. For a brief instant he wanted to wrap his arms around Lisa. He wanted to bring her closer to him.

With Lisa's help, Ted slid from his chair and was now lying on the floor. "I'm going to turn your chair over, and I want you to try to set it right then try to climb back into the chair. Think you can do it?"

"I'll give it a shot." Ted slid over to the chair. He tried to lift it to an upright position but he wasn't able to support himself and lift the chair at the same time. Lisa guided him through and soon Ted was able to set the chair straight. Already he was winded and needed to rest.

"Now comes the hard part. Try to get yourself back into the chair."

Ted quickly found that getting back into his chair was harder than he expected. With limited use of his body below his waist he couldn't keep his balance. After several attempts he was exhausted and back where he started.

"Take a minute or two to catch your breath."

"I'm Ok, I just lost my balance. I'll try again." Ted made more attempts, but he couldn't get himself into the chair.

"Here is how you do it." Lisa showed Ted how to best get back into his chair. After a couple minutes to regroup, Ted tried as per Lisa's instructions. It took a few minutes, but eventually, Ted was sitting in his chair. "Wonderful!"

"You know you could have told me that from the beginning and saved me some trouble."

"I wanted to test your survival IQ."

"My survival IQ? I guess it's not too high huh?"

"I'm sure you would have figured it out eventually."

"Yeah, I'm sure I would have, eventually." Ted was beginning to have feelings he hadn't had since Linda had passed. The cheerleader that Ted didn't want was someone he now looked forward to seeing. He wanted to see more of Lisa, but he didn't want to push the relationship that was building.

"That's all for today. You know the drill. Let me get my BP kit." Ted rolled up his sleeve. "Your pressure looks good Ted."

Over the next few weeks, the exercises, the occupational therapy continued. Ted was getting stronger physically, especially in his upper body, and he was able to put more weight on his legs as he stood. Then, as they performed the walk across the floor to the door, it happened. Instead of Ted's swing from the hip, Ted's right leg lifted on its own. He was caught off guard and nearly fell. Lisa, holding on from behind, caught him, and sat Ted back onto his chair.

"Ted, what happened? Did you trip?"

"No, I think I lifted my leg. It could have been a muscle spasm, but I think I lifted my leg."

"Let's see. Stand up and try to lift your leg. Don't move the walker, just hold onto it and try to lift your leg." Ted stood up, gripped the walker, and lifted his right leg. It wasn't much, just a few inches off the ground, but he was lifting his leg when he wanted to. He couldn't keep the leg off the ground for more than a couple seconds, but it was an improvement.

"Can you do it again?" Lisa was shocked.

Ted lifted his leg once more. This time it was for a shorter period. "Ted I can't believe this! This is great! I can't believe you're doing this."

"I know, I can't explain it. It just came to me. I, I just can't..." Ted didn't know what to say. He was just happy to have gained something seemingly so small, yet to him, it was a big step forward. After resting a few minutes, Ted walked across the floor. This time instead of swinging his right leg, Ted was lifting his right leg. With his left leg, he was still swinging from the hip.

"Ted, this is so unexpected. I'm speechless. I don't know what to say."

"I know. You still think I won't be walking by the end of our sessions?"

The next few days both Lisa's and Ted's spirits were very high. There were now exercises that Lisa needed to come up with to strengthen Ted's ability to raise his right leg. The following week, which was two months into the six month stay, Ted wanted to do more physical exercises with his legs, while Lisa wanted to continue with the occupational exercises. Ted was beginning to show the frustration that Lisa knew would be coming. "Lisa, cleaning, laundry, and grabbing and replacing things I can't reach aren't going to help me walk. We only have a few months left and I think we should spend as much time working on the walking exercises as possible."

"Ted, I know we have a limited amount of time, but I wouldn't be fulfilling my responsibilities if I only focused on the leg exercises."

"Lisa, you don't have to worry. You're doing great. There's no one I can imagine being a better therapist than you. I mean that."

"I appreciate the compliment. Tell you what. I'll try to get here earlier so we can spend more time on your legs, but only if you do the other exercises as well. Is it a deal?"

"That sounds fair, deal."

"Your daughter's eighteenth birthday is coming up. Why don't we spend the occupational time making her dinner and baking a birthday cake?"

"Bake a birthday cake? I don't know how to bake a cake."

"I do. What's her favorite kind of cake?"

"I think vanilla with chocolate icing. We better get some ice cream as well. She loves ice cream."

"What's her favorite dinner?"

"I know she likes pork chops and mashed potatoes with gravy, maybe some green beans.

"Perfect. I'll make a list of things we need to shop for, then Friday, we'll go to the market."

"What do you mean 'we'? I can ask the Bachwel's to…"

"Nope, you have been in this house for two months. I think it's time you stepped outside."

Ted didn't know what to say. Lisa was right. He couldn't stay in the house forever. But, he thought of what it would be like to have people stare.

"Ted, it will be fine. I'll be with you in case anything happens. You'll see. It will be good to go out and get some fresh air."

"Ok, we'll head out Friday morning – early."

Friday morning Lisa knocked on the door at 9:30. "Ready to go, Ted?"

"I guess."

The hardest part for Ted was getting out of the car in the parking lot. He knew as soon as the chair came out of the car, everyone within eye distance would be staring at him. Once inside the market, people would go out of their way to not get in Ted's path. He knew that people would stare as he rode by. As Lisa placed the chair by his side, Ted had no choice other than to get on with it. He rushed as fast as he could to get into the market.

"Slow down there handsome. I'm not going to chase you all over the market." Lisa grabbed a cart, took out her list, and they began shopping. When all of the items were gathered, they took them to the cashier. Ted began to take out his debit card when Lisa held out her hand. "Put that away. This is my present to you and your daughter for all of the hard work you have done."

"Lisa no way, if anyone should be appreciative, it's me. You've done so much the past two months I can't begin to thank you enough."

"Ted, didn't you promise to listen to me while I'm your therapist?"

"I did but this is different."

"No it isn't. I'm still your therapist so I expect you to listen. Now, don't make me angry when I'm trying to be nice."

It was the playful arguments Ted remembered having with Linda that he never could win. "Ok, you win."

"Thank you." Lisa paid for the items and they headed home.

It was funny to Ted that once they were in the market, all of the fears he had of people staring were gone. He and Lisa shopped like any boyfriend-girlfriend or husband-wife. Lisa had been in Ted's life for only two months, but it felt as though he had known her for years. When they were home, they decided to forego the usual exercises in order to start making Gina's birthday dinner. At 1:00 Lisa told Ted she had to go to her afternoon patient. "I'll be back by 5:30 to help set the table."

"Oh, you're coming back for dinner?"

"Of course I am. You think I'm going to miss your first dinner? I am welcome aren't I?"

"Yes, I didn't think, I mean, I think it's great. I want you to be here. After all you did pay for it."

"That's right, I did, so don't mess this up. I'll see you at 5:30."

When Gina came home she could smell the dinner cooking. "Wow something smells great dad."

"Lisa and I decided to cook you a birthday dinner. We're making pork chops with mashed potatoes and gravy, green beans, and, we even baked a cake for desert."

"Thank you so much dad. Is Lisa still here?"

"No, she had to go to her afternoon patient, but she will be coming back tonight."

"Didn't I tell you there's something about her that I liked? I could tell in the beginning that you weren't too thrilled about her."

"You're right when I first saw her she appeared to be an overpaid cheerleader. But, she has turned out to be a really great therapist. She is even a better person. I really do like her."

"I can tell. You certainly look a lot better than when you first came home. And I don't mean just physically. I have some home work to do, so I'll be upstairs. Give a yell when Lisa is here."

"Ok sweetie, should be about an hour or so."

It was 5:45 when Lisa knocked on the door. "Sorry I'm late. The traffic was terrible."

"That's ok. I just set the table. I was just about to bring out the dinner."

When Lisa and Ted had the dinner ready, Ted gave Gina a yell to come down. For the first time in a very long time, Ted felt like a father and husband as the three of them ate, and talked. When the dinner was finished, Ted brought out the cake and he and Lisa sang Happy Birthday to Gina.

"Make your wish Gina and blow out the candles." Lisa said.

Gina looked at her dad, closed her eyes, and then blew out all of the candles in one breath. When they had finished eating, Gina began to clean up. "Oh no, you sit down Gina. It's your birthday. Your father will get the dishes."

"You have been so nice. This was so unexpected. The least I can do is help with the dishes."

"You and I will go into the living room so we can talk. Your father will clean up. It's part of his occupational therapy, right Ted?"

Ted smiled it was as if Linda was speaking. "Sure, you girls head into the living room."

Lisa and Gina went into the living room and talked. "How is my dad really doing? He seems a lot better than when he came home two months ago."

"Gina, your dad is doing great. I have no problem whatsoever getting your dad to work. He is so much further along than what I had planned. He keeps me on my toes to come up with new exercises because he is progressing faster than I had thought."

"He really likes you. You have been an unbelievable help for him. To be honest, he wasn't too impressed in the beginning, but…"

"You mean he initially thought of me as a glorified cheerleader?"

"Something like that, but he really likes and respects you a great deal."

"Thank you. It means a lot that I have made a difference."

"Oh, absolutely you have made a difference."

"I do worry though."

"What do you worry about?"

"Like I said, your father has been progressing better than I had expected. But, your father gets frustrated which is normal. It's to be expected. What worries me is that when I am finished with my work, there won't be anyone watching him as much when I'm not around. I'm worried that he may get so frustrated that he will try something that sets him back."

The only thing Gina heard from Lisa was *when I'm not around*. It hadn't occurred to Gina that Lisa was only going to be around for a few more months. She knew going in that the therapy sessions were paid for by insurance for six months. The past two months were going so great that she had forgotten that this arrangement was temporary. Gina knew her father was beginning to think of Lisa as something more than a therapist. When Lisa was finished with the sessions, how would that affect her father?

Lisa continued. "We still have four months to go. Let's see how things progress. I guess we can cross that bridge when we come to it."

At that moment Ted came into the room. "I hope you two aren't talking about me."

"No, just girl stuff, Gina and I haven't had a chance to get to know each other."

"I'm glad you two finally have a chance to get to chat."

Ted, Gina, and Lisa talked for another hour when Lisa said it was time for her to go. "I'll see you at 9:30 Monday morning."

"You don't want to take my blood pressure before you go?"

"Not this time. I think your fine." Lisa walked over to Gina, gave her a hug. "Happy Birthday Gina." Then, Lisa gave Ted a hug. "That was a great dinner Ted. You really outdid yourself."

"I wouldn't have been able to do it without you. Thanks for your help."

Gina could tell her father had felt something for Lisa that he hadn't felt in years. She wanted to tell him not to fall too hard. After all, Lisa was only going to be here four more months. But, the dinner was great. The night was great. Her father was in such a good mood, that Gina couldn't bring herself to say anything. And, who knows what would happen in four months.

The next day, Saturday, Ted called Jennifer to ask if she could recommend a gift for Gina's birthday. Jennifer had no problem stopping by and helping Ted pick out a gift. They decided among other items to get a necklace with a locket. Ted had asked to have an inscription written, something simple - *Love Dad.* Jennifer took the instructions and told Ted she would be back Monday or Tuesday, in time for Ted to give the gifts to Gina Tuesday night.

Monday's therapy session with Lisa went as usual. Ted, still in a good mood from Friday's dinner, didn't get frustrated, nor did he complain about the lack of exercises they were doing to actually walk. On Tuesday, Lisa and Ted were going through their exercises when Jennifer came in to show Ted the gifts she had purchased for Gina. Ted introduced the two women. "Jennifer, this is Lisa my therapist. Lisa this is Jennifer. She is our administrator at the Union Hall and a good friend."

After Lisa and Jennifer introduced themselves, Jennifer turned to Ted. "I was able to get all of the gifts for Gina. I even got the inscription on the locket like you asked." After showing Ted the items, going through the receipts, Jennifer said she didn't want to keep him from his exercises. "I'll stop back later this week. I hope Gina likes the gifts."

"I'm sure she will. Thank you for doing this."

"No problem Ted. You know I like to help out any way I can. Take care." Jennifer gave him a kiss.

After Jennifer left, Lisa asked Ted. "She is very attractive Ted. Is she your girlfriend?"

"No, Jennifer is our administrator at the Hall. She's been extremely helpful with my insurance, and such."

"I don't mean to pry. I'm just not aware of many administrators that attractive that give their co-workers kisses. It looked to me like she thinks of you more than a co-worker."

Ted now had the impression that maybe Lisa was jealous. Could it be? He didn't know what to make of Lisa's reaction. Ted decided to let it pass. He didn't want to push the relationship he already had with Lisa. They were seeing each other five times a week. There was no need to pursue it any further.

"What's the matter? Cat got your tongue?" Lisa asked.

"I'm sorry. I was thinking about tonight. I hope Gina likes her gifts."

"I'm sure she will. The necklace and locket look beautiful."

Later that evening, after Lisa had gone to her afternoon patient, after Ted and Gina finished dinner, Ted gave his daughter her presents. Lisa was right. Gina loved the birthday gifts that Ted gave her.

The start of the sixth week of therapy sessions, Ted had complained he was having some minor back pain. Because of the pain, the exercises were cut back. Midway through the day Lisa commented. "You know your observation skills leave a lot to be desired."

"Why? What do you mean?"

"You don't notice anything different about me?"

Ted looked. These were the types of questions his wife had asked. "You got a haircut?"

"Close, I didn't get it cut, but I did get it colored. It's darker than usual. You didn't notice?"

"Yes, I do now. It looks great. Sorry I didn't say anything before. You know how guys are."

"Yeah, I know. I just thought since we've been working so close you would have noticed."

"I'm sorry. I don't know what to say." Ted felt genuinely embarrassed.

Lisa laughed. "I'm only teasing. Don't take it so hard."

Ted's imagination started to take over. Why did Lisa choose now to get her hair done? Was it because of Jennifer? What did she mean by we've been so close you should have noticed? He still couldn't bring himself to asking Lisa straight up. He didn't want to risk the time he was spending with her already.

For the next couple weeks, Ted's progress had come to a halt. He was much stronger physically than when he started. He could stand for a half hour straight. He could clean, cook, and do just about anything he wanted around the house. However, what he wanted more than anything was to walk. Since gaining the ability to lift his right leg, he hadn't gained anything significant. The frustration was beginning to show again.

It was the end of the third month, half way through the home therapy sessions. Ted had to go to the rehabilitation hospital for a checkup to measure his progress. He and Lisa went together in a hospital provided van. When they got to the hospital, Ted went though some psychological tests. He answered subjective questions as well as he could. Lisa gave her perspective as well. Her main concerns were that his frustration may lead to Ted taking risks, and the other concern was that Ted hadn't really gone outside his house. She was worried that Ted may become reclusive.

Ted wasn't offended by Lisa's comments. He knew Lisa was right. All Ted could think about was regaining the ability to walk. He wasn't concerned about going outside.

Next, it was onto the physical tests. The doctors tested Ted's upper body strength which was sixty percent stronger than when he left rehabilitation three months ago. On the standing tests, he blew away the fifteen seconds he recorded three months ago. Lisa looked at him with the pride of a mother with her child. Ted was given a walker and was asked to walk around the hall. An intern would be behind him with a wheelchair. Ted was told that when he felt tired to ask for the chair and it would be brought within a second. He began walking down the hall. When he got to the end, the doctor asked if he wanted the chair. Ted declined. He began walking back, but half way through he started to turn pale. Lisa knew he was pushing too hard. "Ted, take a rest?"

"No, I'm fine."

"Mr. Stroit I agree. You have done more than enough. Why don't you take a seat?"

"I'm fine, not until I get back to the original starting point." After a few more steps, as he became even paler, Ted mumbled. "I think I need the chair." The chair was a second behind him. Ted fell to the chair and looked like he passed out. Lisa screamed. As the doctor, the intern, and Lisa helped Ted lean back in his chair to regain his blood pressure. Ted couldn't help but see how his fall affected Lisa. She had tears in her eyes. When Ted was sitting up in his chair, Lisa walked away. Ted didn't know where she went.

It took over an hour for the doctor to completely check Ted to ensure that he was Ok. In all that time Lisa had not come back. It wasn't until the doctor released Ted, when the intern wheeled him to the pickup van that he saw Lisa waiting inside the van. When he got into the van Ted tried to talk to Lisa.

"Lisa I'm sorry about that. I just wanted to…."

"Ted, don't say anything about it. I don't want to hear it."

"I know I…."

"Ted! Did you not hear me? For once, will you listen to me! I said I don't want to hear it."

Never before had Ted seen Lisa so angry. For the remainder of the ride home, nothing was said. When they got back to the house, Lisa stepped out of the van, went straight to her car and drove away. The driver of the van helped Ted out, wheeled him into his house and left. Ted was by himself. He wanted desperately to talk to Lisa. He hated the silent treatment. He knew for sure that Lisa did care for him. He wasn't just her patient. He thought about calling her cell phone, but decided against it. The worse thing was that it would be three days until he would see her again.

The next day, all Ted could think about was Lisa. Several times he had his phone in his hand, dialed her number, only to put the phone away before hitting 'Call'. At night Ted couldn't sleep. He had to do something to explain himself. He couldn't call her, so he decided to write her a letter.

Lisa,

I realize that I have hurt you. Please believe me when I say, that aside from Gina, you are the last person in the world I would ever want to hurt. Sometimes I get too frustrated. And when I do, I don't see or hear the people around me, I only see myself. I only see what I want, and what I don't have. When I am like this, I don't realize what I already do have. What I already have is a wonderful person who is trying her best to help me. I'm sorry I that I didn't listen to you. I know you are only looking out for me. You are only saying and doing these things to help me. Unfortunately when my frustration gets the best of me, I shut everyone out, even those who are helping me.

All I can ask is that you please don't give up on me. Please don't let my frustrations turn you away. In return, I will do my best to listen to the things you say. You are the best friend to have come into my life since Gina was born. It would hurt me deeply to know that I pushed you away due to my frustration over my limitations.

Sincerely,
Ted

Finally, for Ted, Monday morning arrived. At 9:30, Ted expected Lisa to knock on the door. 9:45, 10:00 came and went. Ted began to think that Lisa wouldn't show. She had been prompt at 9:30 ever since she changed her schedule. 10:15, and still no Lisa. Ted wanted to call her to see if she was coming, but decided to wait until 10:30. At 10:25 Lisa knocked on the door. Ted was relieved to see her. "I was beginning to think you weren't coming."

"Honestly Ted, I was struggling all weekend whether to come or send someone as a replacement. I don't think I am the person who can take you to the level you want. I think that I've done all I can. You are at the point where you can do everything you need to at home. But I'm not strong enough to catch you when you fall."

"Lisa you don't have to. What I did at the hospital was stupid. I tried to prove to myself that…"

"That's the point Ted. You're always going to try to prove one thing or another. It isn't about listening to me, or playing it safe. I really think I may be holding you back. I can't tell you not to try something you think you can do. I think you need a man to help you take it from here."

"No Lisa that's not true. I don't want anyone else. We've come so far in just three months. You're not holding me back. I'm too impatient, too frustrated. I wrote this letter. Please, just read it."

"Ted, I just don't know. I want to stay because we have accomplished so much. I want to see this to the end, but my fear is that maybe you would do better with a male therapist, someone who is stronger than I."

"Lisa, no one understands me as well as you do other than Gina. I can't imagine anyone getting to know me as well as you. Please, read the letter. If you still want to leave, then Ok."

As Lisa read the letter tears were swelling in her eyes. "Ok, Ted, we'll continue. But I'm not going to stay today. I want to go into the office to talk to a few other therapists and see if I can get some ideas on some exercises we can try. Since you are doing so well occupationally, we'll concentrate on the physical exercises. Hopefully I'll get some ideas on things we can try tomorrow."

"Thank you Lisa. If you want take tomorrow off as well I understand. You haven't had any days off since you've been here. No one's been able to work with me for three months straight. I've heard I can sometimes be a little difficult to deal with." Ted tried a little humor, but Lisa didn't even smile.

Lisa wiped away her tear and gave Ted a hug. "I'll be back tomorrow. I'll be here 9:30 sharp."

"I'll be ready. I'll see you then."

When Lisa left Ted felt a great deal of relief. Lisa wasn't leaving. He was going to see her for three months at least. Ted started to feel regret however. He should have told her then how he really felt. It was an emotional conversation. It was the perfect time to put all his cards on the table. But he just couldn't do it. Why couldn't he do it? Why couldn't he tell her? It was obvious she thought of him as more than a patient. She felt she wasn't helping *him* enough. Ted was comforted in the fact that she was still in his life. Soon, he had to tell her how he really felt.

Lisa showed up the next day more excited than any prior day. "Ted, I have a surprise for you."

"For me? Oh, you shouldn't have."

"This is going to make your day. What I have is an electro stimulator."

"What is that?"

"What this does is send electric shocks to your muscles to wake them up. I'm going to stick these prongs to different areas on your leg, and then as you walk, I'm going to send a shock to help stimulate the muscles."

"You're going to shock me? You're not still mad at me are you? I've been shocked before and it doesn't particularly feel too good. This isn't your way of getting back at me is it?"

"I am still mad at you but no, this won't hurt a bit. It will feel a little weird, but it won't hurt."

"I'm willing to try anything."

Lisa put some jelly on several pads. "This may feel cold at first." She applied the pads to areas on Ted's right leg. "Hold onto the walker and stand. I'm going to turn on the stimulator, ready?"

"I'm ready."

Lisa turned the dial and Ted's leg began to lift. "How's that feel?"

"Weird, it feels like a muscle spasm."

"I'm turning it down." As Lisa turned the dial back, Ted's leg went back to the ground. "Let's stand here and get used to the feeling of lifting your leg. Once we get better control, we'll use this to walk. This time when I turn on the stimulator, I want you to try to work with the muscle and lift your leg and step forward, understood?"

"Understood, let's go."

They practiced using the electro stimulator. As they worked, Ted was able to raise his leg a little higher each time. When they were finished, Ted's legs were extremely fatigued. "Try to lift your leg on your own, without the stimulator." Ted tried as best he could, but he could barely budge his leg. He looked worried. "Don't worry Ted, that's normal. Using the stimulator excites the muscles, but the side-affect is that they are going to be tired."

After resting for an hour, they tried again. "Let's see if the leg muscles are ready to work, stand up please. Let's take this as slow as possible. I want you to stand as straight as possible, work with the stimulator to lift and place your right leg forward. Then, bring your left leg up even to your right leg, place the walker a few inches in front of you, then repeat the process until we've come full circle. We're going to the door, then back, ready?"

"I'm ready when you are." The first couple strides were awkward. But, they made it to the door. The walk back was much better. Ted was getting used to working with the electro stimulator to raise his right leg.

"Ted, that was great. Your right leg lifted to a normal height and it looked like you were comfortable putting it in front of you. How did it feel?"

"It felt fine for a first time. I'm excited about this electro thing. Can we hook it up to my left leg?"

"Let's do one leg at a time. Let's rest a few minutes and try again."

The second walk was better than the first as Ted was able to control his leg with the use of the electro stimulator right from the jump. By the end of the day both Lisa and Ted were extremely happy with the entire session. "I'm going to leave these here, and we'll pick it up tomorrow. I don't want you to do anything with this until I come back tomorrow, got it?"

"I got it. I promise not to do anything you tell me not to. Today was the most progress we've made in a few weeks."

"I think this will definitely help get some more strength in your legs."

"I'll see you tomorrow."

For the next few weeks Ted and Lisa worked almost entirely on getting Ted's legs stronger. He continued to use the electro stimulator and it was successful to a degree. Ted was able to raise his right leg higher, as well as keep the leg raised for longer periods of time. Ted's left leg however was still much weaker than his right. He could stand on both legs for up to an hour. However, when he walked, he still swung his left leg from the hip as opposed to actually lifting his leg and placing it in front of him. The progress was minimal, but it was progress. What tempered any enthusiasm Ted had was the fact that he was beginning to realize that his time with Lisa as his therapist was nearing an end.

From Lisa's perspective, the last few weeks went above her expectations. She had never had a patient who made such improvements nine months after the accident. Normally, the patient would see the most improvements in the first two to four months from the date of their accident. After the fourth month working with Ted, Lisa too felt the end of their sessions coming close. Lisa was worried that Ted had still shown discomfort when asked to do anything outside the house. "We have been working in this house for over four months. And while I love your home, I think it's time we try some sessions outside. What do you think?"

"I know we have spent most of our time inside, but it's safer in here. If I fall, the phone is close, and I can also make it back onto a couch or chair. What would happen if I fell outside?"

"Aren't you the one who wanted to stand for as long as he could? Aren't you the one who wanted to walk as long as he could in the hospital? Aren't you the one pushing me to the limit? Why so careful now?"

"I was pushing myself but it was always in a controlled environment. You or a doctor, were always close by. We go outside and no one is around."

"Ted, I'll still be with you. I'll have a cell phone in case something happens. I'm surprised someone as handsome as you wouldn't want to go outside for people to see."

That was just the point Ted thought. He didn't want people to see him as he was. He certainly didn't feel handsome, he felt different. He felt like a circus freak that people would stare. He didn't want to be seen by anyone. "How about we finish up this week's sessions here, and beginning next week we do whatever you like outside?"

"Ok, fair enough."

Over the weekend, Ted kept to himself more than usual. All he could think about was Monday's session outside. "Dad, are you Ok? You haven't said anything all day. You seem preoccupied."

"Monday Lisa and I are going to start sessions outside."

"I think that's great. Where are you going? What will you be doing?"

"I'm not sure."

"You two should go down to the Missonian Path. Remember how you used to go jogging there? The creek is really nice. They put up a new restaurant right by the waterfalls."

"The Missonian Path, I hadn't thought of that. You're right. It is nice this time of year." Ted also liked the idea because most likely he wouldn't know any of the people who would be there. He didn't want to picture himself using a walker like some ninety year old man. Perhaps if he could use crutches it would look as if he was recovering from a broken leg. The more he thought about it, the more it had to be. If Lisa wanted to go outside, they had to go outside using crutches, not a walker. When Lisa stopped by for their Monday session, Ted gave the ultimatum.

"Ted, are you ready to go? I thought we would start by going out the door, down the ramp and onto the sidewalk. I'll follow behind with your chair."

"Lisa I know we said we would start having sessions outside, but I don't want to go outside using a walker."

"What do you have in mind? Do you want me to carry you?"

"I want to try with crutches instead of a walker."

"Ted, we have never tried using crutches. I can't agree to that."

"Let's try in here and see how it goes. I know I can walk with them."

"Ted, I don't have crutches with me."

"Can't you get them from the hospital?"

"Ted, I don't know about this."

"Come on, you were saying last week how I was becoming so careful. You're right. Let's take the next step. At least let's give it a shot. If I can't do it, then we go back to the walker."

"What about today? What do you want to do today?"

"Let's just keep on working with the electro stimulator."

"Ted, you really disappoint me. I was looking forward to going outside for a walk today."

"We'll go for a walk, just not today. What do you say, please?"

"Ok Ted we'll try with the crutches tomorrow. But we are going to have some sessions outside. I'm worried that you're becoming reclusive. And you're too handsome to be a recluse."

"Thanks Lisa."

The next day Lisa brought over a pair of crutches. Lisa measured Ted's height, and set the crutches accordingly. "These are going to be trickier than the walker." Lisa demonstrated how she wanted Ted to proceed using the crutches.

"I got it." When Ted started, he was a bit shaky, but after a while, he began to move around as if he had been using crutches for months.

"Ted, once again, you surprise me. You look like a natural with the crutches. I actually feel comfortable with you walking with those. You are amazing."

"Thanks Lisa. Thanks for letting me try using them. I feel pretty comfortable with them. I think I'm ready to have some sessions outside."

"Walking on a flat surface is one thing. Walking outside where you can't predict what the ground will be is another. What we need to do is go back to the hospital and walk around in there."

"Why go back to the hospital?"

"We can set up some obstacles. They have ramps where we can simulate walking up and down hills. We can make the ground curve rather than walk on a completely flat surface."

"Ok, I get it. That's a good idea."

"For now, let's keep walking here and let's get you as comfortable with those as possible."

For the remainder of the session, Ted practiced with the crutches inside. When Gina came home she saw her father and Lisa. "I thought you were going to start exercising outside?"

"That's what I thought too Gina. But your father had other ideas."

"Why change of plans, dad? You need to get outside. You can't stay a hermit all your life."

"Sweetie, believe me I've heard that before." Ted gave a smirk in Lisa's direction. "The change in plans is a good change. Today I started walking with crutches. So I can throw that walker out."

"Seriously?"

"I don't know about throwing the walker away, but yes, your father started walking with crutches. I'm very proud of him." Ted's felt embarrassed. "You should be proud of what you did Ted."

"I am, but it's not like I'm a two year old child learning to walk."

"I'm not so sure about that. Sometimes you act like a two year old."

"Dad I think that is great. To think of where you were a few months ago, I can't believe it."

"You can thank Lisa. She really has done wonders. I couldn't have done it without her."

Now it was Lisa blushing. "Ted, that's so nice of you to say."

"I mean it Lisa. I really do."

"Before I burst into tears let me get out of here. Tomorrow we'll head down to the hospital."

"Sounds good, I'll see you tomorrow."

Gina knew her father looked at Lisa as more than a therapist. She couldn't help but feel worried about her father's feelings. "She is a very good therapist dad. Isn't she?"

"She's a great therapist. She is also a wonderful woman, a God send."

Gina wanted to tell her father that Lisa was only here for two more months. Once her time as a therapist was up, she would be moving on. But Gina couldn't bear to hurt her father. And who knows, maybe, just maybe Lisa would feel the same towards her father.

The next day Lisa was at the house at her usual time. Ted was ready to go and asked for the crutches. "Ted, we'll use the crutches once we get to the hospital. To get to the car, we'll use the wheelchair." If it were up to Ted, the chair would be put away for good, though he didn't argue.

Over the next few days the sessions were spent at the hospital. Ted practiced walking up simulated hills, curved surfaces, up small steps, down small steps, etc. Lisa felt safe having Ted begin sessions outside walking with crutches. At first, the sessions were outside his house. They walked up and down the ramp. They walked out on the side walk. After two weeks, Ted and Lisa walked to the corner and back. Ted was beginning to feel normal.

There was less than a month remaining until the insurance would stop paying for the home therapist. The walks that Ted and Lisa were taking seemed like those that a husband and wife would take. Instead of talking about what exercise to do, they talked about Ted getting back to work. They talked about Gina, who decided she wanted to go to nursing school. Ted was so proud of Gina. He was grateful to know that she was going to school to become what she wanted. He was grateful the way things were turning out that he wouldn't be a burden to her.

The next three weeks, Ted didn't have any improvement. But, because in Ted's mind it looked as though he was normal, he didn't let that bother him too much. He knew as long as he and Lisa kept working, the improvements would come. Ted also knew that very soon, he would have to lay all his cards on the table and tell Lisa how he really felt about her.

The final day arrived. Lisa came to the house for the last time as Ted's therapist. "Well, this is it, our last day."

"I know. I can't believe it's been six months. So much has happened. I still remember that first day when you arrived. You were a tall, thin cheerleader coming over to perk me up. But, you've become so much more. I also remember how I was that day. I remember how miserable I was, how I couldn't even get out of my chair. I remember thinking to myself I'm trying to get my life back and they send me a cheerleader. And now, I'm so much better, not just physically, but better. And a lot of that is due to you."

"I remember that day too, how miserable you were. You didn't even want to show me around your house. But it wasn't your fault. It was only natural. I look at you now, how much you have improved. I was worried that you would become reclusive. However these last few weeks have made my work seem worthwhile. I'm really going to miss working with you Ted."

"I'm going to miss our sessions too. We can still keep in touch though. I know you have to move on to other patients, but...."

"Well, Ted, actually you are my last patient."

"Oh, you quit your job?"

"I did. I'll be getting married in two months. My fiancé just accepted a position in California. We'll be moving there in two weeks."

BAM! Ted felt as if he had been shot in the heart. He could hardly breathe, let alone speak. His heart was in his throat. "You, you're married?"

"Engaged, I'll be married in two months."

"I never realized you were engaged. I never saw you wear a ring. You never mentioned that you even had a boyfriend."

"I never wear my ring while working with patients. I have to be hands on and the last thing I need is for my ring to get caught on a patient's shirt, or something that may cause a rip, or scratch."

"I see." Ted couldn't believe it. How could Lisa not have said she was engaged or ever mention her boyfriend? "Your fiancé is certainly a lucky man."

"Thanks Ted. I'm sure the next woman you meet will feel the same about you. You are a big, strong, handsome man."

Ted was becoming angry. What the hell was all this handsome talk? He couldn't believe he fell for all of Lisa's fake feelings towards him. Why did Lisa get upset when he fell at the hospital? Why was she jealous when Jennifer gave him a kiss? How could Lisa pretend to have these feelings towards him? How dare she pretend to be something she wasn't!

Ted looked at Lisa and didn't know what to say. He wanted to tell her that he was in love with her. He had been in love with her for some time. *Lisa, if you look closely, you'll see that you are in love with me too. You have to know you're in love with me. Look at how well we worked together. Look at how much progress we made. We have gone through so much together. Remember how angry you were at me, but remember how we worked it all out. Remember the letter I wrote and how it made you cry. You know you have feelings for me. You know you love me!*

And then Ted looked at himself. He saw himself not as a man. He saw himself as someone barely out of a wheelchair. He saw himself as a person who could no longer do the things he used to do. He saw himself as a person who couldn't treat Lisa like a woman in love should be treated. Who was he to tell her to leave a man for someone like himself? It was wrong to tell her how he felt, so he said nothing.

"Are you Ok? You're not saying much."

"I'm fine. I guess I'm a little sad that I won't be seeing you any longer."

Lisa's eyes began to water. She came up to Ted, gave him a hug and a kiss. "Ted I wrote you this letter. I want you to read it after I leave. It took me a long time to write and I mean every word I wrote." Ted took the letter and said nothing. "Ted, is there something you want to say? I just get the sense you want to tell me something."

I love you! I want to spend the rest my life with you! If you look inside yourself, you will see that you love me too. Ted couldn't say what he wanted. "I don't know what to say. I wish you all the happiness in the world. You deserve that and more. I hope for the best for you and your fiancé."

"Thank you, Ted. I wish only the best for you and Gina as well."

Chapter 6
FEEL THE PAIN

Conscientia High School – Freshman Year

Pat sat in the bleachers watching his son participate in his first football practice. He watched the kids on the team, run laps, toss footballs, learn blocking techniques, etc. When practice was over Brandon walked over to him. "Hey dad I'm surprised to see you here."

"I wanted to see how your first practice went. You looked really good out there. Have the coaches told you what position you'll play?"

"Well, because of...."

"You must be Brandon's father. I'm Coach Rick Lemmor, nice to meet you. I'm glad your son decided to try out for the team."

"Hi Coach, Pat Leshing. I thought he could be a good player, that's why I asked him to try out."

"He does have good size and speed. You can't coach those things. We'll see how he does when we get the pads on. That will start Monday."

"What position do you think he'll play?"

"Right now I can't say for sure. He is big enough to play the line. But I don't want to waste his speed, so I may try him at receiver, or running back, on defense probably linebacker. If he can hit, I think we have a real talent. I wanted to introduce myself. I hope to see you around."

"It's nice to meet you to Coach." Pat turned to Brandon. "Are you ready to head home?"

"I have to get my books, I'll be right out."

Cindy was surprised to see Pat and Brandon come home together. "You picked up Brandon from school?"

"I watched some of his practice. Coach said he has talent and will make a great football player."

"Dad, he said I might be able to play. We'll know better when we put the pads on Monday."

"Brandon, are you sure this is what you want to do? Football can be pretty rough in High School. This isn't Pee Wee Football you played in Virginia. You can play soccer, or run cross country, those sports aren't so rough."

"Cindy, his coach said he has talent and Brandon is one of the biggest kids on the team. If anyone will be dishing out the pain, it will be him."

"You see Pat, that's what I mean. There is no reason why anyone should be dishing out any pain. He can play other sports if he wants."

"No mom, I want to play football. It was fun. We'll see how it goes next week when we really start playing."

"There, it's settled. What's for dinner hun, I'm starving. I bet you're hungry too hey Brandon?"

"Yeah, I am kind of hungry."

"Dinner will be ready in thirty minutes. Why don't you get washed up before we eat Brandon?"

With Brandon out of the room, Cindy turned to her husband. "Pat, I really don't approve of your manipulating our son because of your work. What if Brandon gets hurt?

"Cindy, I'm not manipulating our son. I admit, I flat out asked him to play. But he's not complaining. He had fun out there today. His coach said he looked good out there too."

"I don't understand you. You have never been like this before. You know I hated the fact that you worked fifty, sixty hours a week. You never went to any of Brandon's school functions, never went to the PTA meetings unless it was absolutely necessary. However I could put up with that because that's what you wanted to do. You set a goal for yourself, and by God, you made it. But now you're taking Brandon with you. Although I can't do anything about it now, the first sense I get that he doesn't want to play football, I'm going to be sure that doesn't play football. You got that?"

"He's playing with other freshman and sophomores. Yes, there is a possibility that he might get hurt. Cindy, you can get hurt playing any sport. He can break a leg playing soccer. You can't baby him forever."

"Patrick, I'm not babying him. I'm just saying he can make his own decisions about what he wants to do with his life. If this isn't what he wants to do, then he won't do it. And I don't want you convincing him he *needs* to play."

"Fine, all I asked was for him to give it a shot that's all."

"Well you got your wish. Dinner will be ready in a half hour."

Pat looked forward to going to work the next morning. His projects were taking off. The incentive programs he implemented were the main reason that the service reps were handling more calls per hour than at any time prior. Brandon was playing football and he couldn't wait to talk about it with his coworkers, especially his boss. "Hey Jim, Brandon just had his first practice at football yesterday. The coach says he has some real talent."

"That's great Pat. I'm glad to hear it. So he's kicking some butt already, huh? Good for him. Hopefully he can help bring Conscientia another title. They haven't done too well since my son graduated."

Larry Minkoff, Pat's co-worker walked by. "Good morning Larry."

"Morning Jim, what school does your son go to Pat? I couldn't help hear he's playing football."

"He goes to Conscientia."

"Conscientia, that's a nice school. Not much of a football program though. They're Ok, but they're certainly not big time like La Salle."

"Careful there Larry, my kids went to Conscientia as well."

"Hey Jim, I'm not saying it's a bad school. It's a great school academically. It's just not a big school, especially for a top football program. What do they have about a hundred kids in a class?"

"It's about 150. But what they lack for number, they make up in heart."

"Tell that to the 150 pound running back going up against the 220 pound lineman. My kid would eat that running back alive."

"Your son plays at La Salle?"

"Yep, he's a two way starting lineman, and one of the tri-captains on the team. Last year they won the state championship. Let me get the team picture from my desk."

"Good luck shutting Larry up now Pat." Jim said with a chuckle.

"Here you go, that's him sitting with the football in his hands, #77. Here are some newspaper clippings. He has offers from a half dozen colleges."

"Larry that's great. Has he decided where he wants to go to college?"

"You're damn right it's great. It will save my butt from having to pay an arm and a leg for college. If I had to pick, it would be Ohio State. I'd love for him to stay close to the area. But there's not a better coach in college than Urban Meyer. That guy is a winner with class."

Jim had enough of Larry's bravado for one day. "Ok, Larry, now that you got the bragging out of the way let's get back to work."

Monday was Brandon's first practice with pads. Pat wanted to be there to see his son in action. He really wanted to be sure Brandon would maintain his interest. The last thing Pat wanted was for Brandon to quit. How would he explain that to Jim and Larry?

Practice was moving along fine when Coach Lemmor called for the players to participate in 'two on two' drill. The 'two on two' drill placed one offensive lineman face to face with a defensive lineman. Behind the offensive lineman was a running back. Behind the defensive lineman was a defensive back. The objective for the running back was to use his lineman to get past the defensive lineman, then try to break the tackle of the defensive back and gain as many yards as possible. The only stipulation was that the running back had to run between two pylons that were five yards apart.

Brandon started the drill as the offensive lineman. When the whistle blew Brandon sent the defensive lineman back peddling five yards for a good block. Then, it was his turn as the defensive lineman. Because he was half a foot bigger than the offensive lineman, Brandon was able to stand up his opposition, throw him to the side, and tackle the running back for a loss.

"Nice job Leshing, nice job." Coach Lemmor yelled. Pat looked on like the proud papa he was.

Then, it was Brandon's turn as the defensive back. When the whistle blew, the offensive and defensive linemen immediately went to the ground in a stalemate. That left Brandon up against the running back. Brandon came up as fast as he could to tackle the runner, but the runner, a couple inches shorter than Brandon, and running with a full head of steam, was able to put his shoulder into Brandon's chest. Brandon was nearly lifted off the ground as he was thrown back several yards. The running back kept going as he celebrated the mock touchdown.

Brandon laid there barely able to breathe. The coaches came over to see if he was Ok. Pat, still in the stands looking on, stood up immediately hoping Brandon wasn't hurt. Brandon laid there for couple minutes as he tried to regain his breath. Finally he was able to pull himself together and said he was fine. When Pat saw Brandon up and walking he sat back down.

After sitting out of the drill for a couple turns, Brandon went back in as the running back. When Coach Lemmor blew the whistle to start, Brandon saw the two linemen locked up in battle so he went to his right to get around them. Just as he took a step up field, he was met head on by the defensive back. The defender put his helmet right under Brandon's chin, wrapped his arms around Brandon's waist, lifted him off the ground, and then planted him on his back. The impact left Brandon gasping for air again. Blood trickled down his chin.

"Perfect tackle Tony! That was beautiful! Gentleman, that's how you make a tackle." Brandon was oblivious to Coach Lemmor's remarks. All he was concentrating on was getting back up. He didn't want his coaches, his teammates gathering around him again seeing him hurt. Wincing, gasping for air, Brandon took his place as the offensive lineman. As he approached his position, Coach Lemmor blew his whistle and told everyone to gather around. Brandon was grateful for the end of the drill. Coach told the kids to jog a lap around the field, and hit the showers.

Pat noticed how slow Brandon was jogging. Most of the kids ran off the field as fast as they could. Brandon went off in a slow jog. Pat watched his son every step of the way, Brandon never once looked in his father's direction.

"Your son did a nice job today Pat." Pat, still watching Brandon walk off the field, didn't notice Coach Lemmor had come up by his side.

"I'm not so sure about that. He looked good when he played the line positions, but he got killed in the backfield."

"He took some pretty good shots. But I like the way he bounced back. A lot of kids would have sit out the entire practice after taking a shot like that. He got right back into it. He would have taken his place on the line again had I not ended the drill. He's got a lot of heart. I'll take a kid with twice the heart over a kid with twice the size any day. Brandon's got both. He could be something special."

Coach Lemmor headed off the field and Pat sat down waiting for his son. At least the coaches weren't disappointed in Brandon's play. The real question on Pat's mind was will he quit the team after taking so many hard hits.

After several minutes, Pat saw Brandon walking his way with his book bag strapped to his shoulder. As Brandon got closer, Pat could see that his chin had swollen and was black and blue."

"How do you feel champ? Coach said you did really well out there. He said he hasn't seen too many kids with as much heart as you."

"It's not my heart that's hurting dad."

"Ah, your chin doesn't look too bad."

"It's not just my chin. My back, my butt hurts. My whole body hurts."

Pat knew this was Brandon's way of letting his father down easy. He knew Brandon was leading up to the – "I don't think football is for me" - line. And after seeing him take a beating, he didn't think he would be able to convince his son to stick it out. "I'm sure as you practice you will be able to prepare yourself for those hits. Besides, Coach said next week they will be separating you guys to focus on your positions. I'm sure he'll have you playing the line where you did really well."

"I hope he doesn't play me on the line. I'd rather play running back."

"Even after taking those hits?"

"Yeah, I kind of liked it."

Pat was shocked. He wanted to ask why on earth you want to play the positions where you were knocked around. He wanted to ask, but didn't. He was happy that Brandon didn't quit. "I don't suppose your chin will heal by the time we get home huh? Your mother is going to have a fit. How does it feel?"

"It probably looks worse than it feels. It's not too bad."

Cindy heard both Pat and Brandon walking into the house. She wasn't happy about Brandon playing football from the start. But, she did like the fact that Pat was taking an interest in his activities at school. When she saw Brandon's face, she went back to not liking the idea of Brandon playing football at all. "Brandon, what happened to your face? Are you Ok?"

"I'm fine mom I just took a shot at practice that's all."

"I hope whoever did that to you, was kicked off the team!"

"Mom, they don't kick people off the team for making tackles."

"Pat, you see what I was talking about? What if he suffered a concussion or worse?"

"Cindy getting bumps and bruises are part of the game. Playing football is a contact sport. You can't avoid things like this. He'll get better. His coach said he's never seen a kid with so much heart."

"What good is having a heart when you're knocked unconscious?"

"Mom I wasn't knocked unconscious, I'm fine. Besides, it was my fault."

"How was it your fault?"

"I didn't position myself right."

"I don't want to hear about this. Go wash up for dinner." After Brandon went upstairs, Cindy turned to her husband. "Pat this is exactly what I was talking about. You talked him into this, so you talk him out of it."

"Cindy, Brandon is fine. I'm not going to talk him out of playing. If he wants to stop playing, he will. But he wants to keep playing. Remember it's up to him to decide what he wants to do."

"Oh no you don't, don't you dare throw that back at me. We both know you talked him into playing. If you hadn't said anything about football, his face wouldn't be bruised right now."

"Cindy he's fine, he said so himself. You ask him if he wants to stop playing. I won't say a word. If he says he wants to quit. I won't say a word."

"Pat you have him so brain-washed you know he won't quit. He wants to please his father for Christ's sake! This is the first time you have ever taken an interest in his activities. He isn't going to want to disappoint is father now. Of course he won't quit."

"That's not true. Maybe he wanted to please me when he signed up. He has talent Cindy. He likes playing. And he's not immersed in his books and computers all day. To tell you the truth, after practice I expected him to tell me that he wanted to quit. But he didn't, and I didn't suggest anything at all."

"Yeah, I bet. Maybe he isn't immersed in his books, but now he's walking around with two chins! I hope you're proud of yourself Patrick!"

Pat didn't say it, but he was proud. He couldn't wait to tell his coworkers how tough of a son he had. His son took one on the chin, literally, and got up, brushed himself off and went back for more.

The following week, Brandon was excited about the first football game. "Hey dad our first game is Saturday. It's a non-league game against Olney. Do you and mom think you can make it?"

"Make it? Your mom and I wouldn't miss it for the world. Of course we'll make it right hunny?"

Cindy didn't like football. She didn't understand football. And, most of all she didn't want to see her son getting hurt playing football. But she was backed into a corner and did not want to come across as a mother who did not support her son. "Of course we'll make it."

"Great! The game starts at eleven. I need to be there by ten. Can you give me a ride?"

"Sure, your mom will make a big breakfast, and then we'll get you to the game."

"Awesome! I can't wait for the game. It's been a while since I played against another team."

Pat looked over at his wife as if to say *I told you so*. Cindy pretended not to notice. She still did not like her son playing football, but she did like the idea of making a big breakfast for the family, then spending the day together outdoors. It had been a long time since the family did anything together.

On game day, Coach Lemmor had two rules. One, everyone plays no matter what the score. Two, everyone plays hard to the whistle no matter what the score. Olney was a public league school that had over forty players on their squad. When the teams were warming up on the field Cindy and Pat couldn't help but notice how big Olney's team was, both in number of players and the size of each player. While Brandon was easily the biggest player on Conscientia's team, he was the average size of an Olney player. Pat thought of the words Larry said – *"Tell that to the 150 pound running back going up against the 220 pound lineman. My kid would eat that running back alive."*

"Pat the other team looks so much bigger than Conscientia. Are you sure they're not playing the varsity team?"

"That's their Junior Varsity team."

When the game started, Conscientia was the first to go on offense. The first play was a hand off to Brandon who was to run off the right tackle. As soon as he touched the ball, there were two Olney players ready to tackle him. Brandon had no time to react as both Olney players picked him up and dropped him like a sack of potatoes for a four yard loss. Cindy winced, seeing her son get hit so hard.

Unfortunately for the Conscientia fans, that was just a pre-cursor of things to come. Every time Brandon touched the ball he was hit hard by several Olney defenders. Conscientia's defense couldn't stop the bigger Olney offense from scoring. By halftime Olney had a 28 to 0 lead.

In the second half, Olney took possession of the football and once again, marched to a touchdown. Conscientia took the ensuing kickoff and brought the ball to mid field. The first play was a Quarterback option right. Allen Landry faked a handoff to the fullback, and pitched the ball to Brandon. Olney's safety and cornerback both came up to make a tackle. As the cornerback came close, Brandon stuck out his left arm putting his hand on the defender's helmet. The cornerback fell to the ground trying to grab Brandon's legs, but he missed. That left the safety coming with a full head of steam. Brandon was able to lower his shoulder into the safety's shoulder. The sound of the impact could be heard throughout the field. Brandon lifted the safety, throwing him flat on his back. He regained his balance, and sped down the sidelines for a fifty yard touchdown.

Although the team was still far behind 35 to 7, they finally had something to cheer about. Pat jumped up from his seat, shouting. Even Cindy felt the excitement as she stood up screaming – "Go Brandon, Go!" The touchdown run seemed to give the whole team some life. Brandon scored a second touchdown making the score 35 to 14.

At the start of the fourth quarter, Coach Lemmor stuck to his rule that everybody plays. For the final quarter, Brandon stood on the sidelines cheering on his teammates. The final score was Olney 42 and Conscientia 14.

As the players were in the locker room showering and changing clothes, Pat and Cindy were getting a lot of congratulations on Brandon's performance by other parents. Pat was smiling from ear to ear, watching as his son walked towards them receiving the pats on the back he deserved for scoring two touchdowns. Even Cindy was proud of her son's play. "You played a great game Brandon. I'm really proud of you."

"Thanks mom."

"I agree with your mom son, you really turned your team around with some of those runs. You played a great game."

"Thanks dad. I just wished we had won. Olney was tough."

"They were so much bigger than your team. I don't think it was fair for them to be so big. Someone should check to see if they really are the JV team."

"Mom, I'm sure they were. I don't think they would risk being kicked out of the league by playing their varsity. Besides, it's just non-league team. It doesn't really mean anything."

"Just the same I don't think it was fair for them to be so much bigger."

"Even so, you guys didn't back down one bit. You guys could have thrown in the towel at halftime. A lot of that was thanks to you."

"Coach wasn't happy that we lost, but he was happy how we finished. Next week we start league play so the other team should be closer to our size."

When Pat went into the office the following Monday, he spoke to anyone who would listen about his son's two touchdown performance. In a company that stressed athletics, in a city that prized football above any other sport, Pat had a lot to talk about. His desk was now like most everyone else's in the office with the family pictures along with his son's football team picture.

The following week was a visit to Christian Academy for the first league game. Pat and Cindy made the trip on the Saturday morning along with about fifty other parents, friends, and class mates of football team. Much to the liking of both Pat and Cindy, Christian's team was the same size as Conscientia. That meant Brandon was not only the biggest player on his team, he was one of the biggest players on either team.

In this game Conscientia dominated. At half time Conscientia led 21 to 7 with Brandon scoring two touchdowns. He had made several tackles on defense as well. In the second half Brandon only played the third quarter because of Coach Lemmor's number one rule that everybody plays.

When Brandon came out to meet his parents after the game, he told them that he was going to ride the team bus back to school and that he would meet them at home. It was the team's first win and Brandon wanted to celebrate with his teammates.

For Pat, it was going to be another great Monday at the office. His son once again played well, scoring four touchdowns. For Cindy, it was another perfect Saturday. Her husband was watching her son play football. Brandon seemed to really enjoy playing. They were spending their weekends as a family. Although Pat had yet to attend any other school function, Cindy took what she could get. Brandon no longer had his head in his books and computers 24/7. He had friends with which he played football.

Pat and Cindy were home by 3:00, and an hour later, Cindy saw Brandon walking into the house. "I thought you were going to celebrate with your teammates after the big win."

"We did for a little while, but we all went home. Besides, I have a science project I need to work on for school."

The next three games were all against league opponents. Conscientia won all of them with relative ease. Brandon was by far the team's most outstanding player both on offense and defense. The crowds started to get bigger as a buzz at school picked up regarding the JV team, and especially Brandon Leshing. Some of the fans started introducing themselves to Pat and Cindy during games. Most of them were parents of other players. All of them were very impressed with Brandon's ability on the field.

Pat continued to talk to anyone at work regarding his son's exploits on the football field. Cindy was coming around on her view of the game. Seeing how well Brandon played, and how much he enjoyed playing, she looked forward to going to the games.

The last game of the season was against the school's rival Romitis Academy. Not only was a big deal being made because of the heated rivalry, but both teams were undefeated in league play. This game would be for the Junior Varsity league championship. Conscientia's varsity team had won only one game thus far this season. As far as football was concerned for Conscientia, the JV team was the school's only chance at any bragging rights.

When Pat and Cindy dropped Brandon off at the field, they could already tell this game was different. It was over an hour before game time and there were already more fans in the stands than at any game prior. This was going to be the largest crowd yet to see their son play.

There was a nervousness that Pat could sense as the game drew closer. This was for the league championship. When the teams came out to warm up the crowd began to yell. Cheerleaders began to jump. The school students began their chants. Parents stood to get a good view of their sons. Pat and Cindy were no different. Pat tried to peer into his son's helmet to see if he could get a sense of Brandon's nervousness. Cindy held her hands close to her mouth never taking her eyes off her son.

The game started out as a hard fought contest with no scoring from either team mid-way through the second quarter. Knowing that Brandon was Conscientia's main offensive player, all eleven Romitis defenders focused on Brandon on each play. Every time he touched the ball, Brandon was met by at least two defenders. With so many defenders focusing on Brandon, Coach

Lemmor decided it was time to design a play to offset the defender's aggressiveness.

It was first and ten at the thirty yard line. Quarterback Allen Landry pitched the ball to into Brandon's hands. As was the case in every prior play, all of the Romitis defenders were focused on Brandon. Just as he was turning to go up field, he pulled up and stopped. As Brandon was about to get tackled he cocked the football to his ear and let go a spiral pass to the wide receiver Billy Winder running alone across midfield. Brandon was laid out on the ground as Billy caught the ball and sprinted to the end zone for a touchdown.

Everyone on the Conscientia sideline was euphoric. The fans went wild, the students were picking up their chants, and the cheerleaders were being flipped in the air. Some of the parents looked over to Pat and Cindy clapping their hands and shaking their heads at what a great play their son had made.

The rest of the quarter was a stalemate. The only score was a twenty yard field goal by Romitis Academy. The halftime score was Conscientia 7, Romitis 3.

One of the other player's parents approached Pat and Cindy. "Great game so far, isn't it?"

"It has been an exciting season hasn't it Cindy?"

"I really didn't get the whole football mentality. I always thought it was just a guy thing. I can't believe all the excitement. So many people taking time to watch a football game, it's unbelievable."

"And this is the JV team. Wait until we get to the varsity games."

When the second half started, Brandon remained on the sideline, not playing at all. Pat and Cindy wondered if Brandon had gotten hurt. Brandon never came out of the game unless it was late and the team was well ahead. Pat yelled as loud as he could to get his son's attention. But it was no avail. With the fans cheering loudly Pat could not get his attention. With Brandon standing on the sideline, Romitis was able to score a touchdown taking a 10 to 7 lead.

"What's wrong with Brandon? Why isn't he playing?"

"I don't know Cindy. He doesn't look like he's hurt. I'm not sure why he isn't playing."

"Pat, go down and find out if Brandon is hurt."

"You're damn right I'm going to find out." When Pat got to the sideline, he finally was able to get his son's attention. "Brandon, why aren't you playing? Are you hurt?"

"No dad, Coach's number one rule is that everybody plays. I'm sitting out the first two series. I'll be back in after this series."

"What? Are you kidding me? This is for the championship. What the hell is he doing? Doesn't he care about winning?" Seeing that his complaints were not going to change things, Pat walked back to his seat. "I can't believe it. Why would the coach pull his players now? They were ahead and now they're losing. Why would he do that to his players?"

"Pat, there is still a lot of game left to play. I'm sure Brandon will get back in. They're not losing by a lot. They can come back."

Romitis took possession of the football, this time starting at the thirty-two yard line. When Conscientia's defense took the field, Brandon was back playing linebacker. "There you go Pat, Brandon's back in playing again."

"It's about damn time! Alright Conscientia let's go! Let's get that ball back!"

Cindy couldn't believe how Pat was acting. She had never seen him so animated. "Pat, will you calm down, people in the stands are staring at you."

"I can't calm down Cindy. The team would be winning the game if it wasn't for that idiot coach."

"So now he's an idiot?" Cindy leaned over, grabbed Pat's sleeve and whispered into his ear. "Patrick, *you* have been the one acting like an idiot."

The game remained tough, the only subsequent score was Romitis field goal to increase their lead to 13 to 7. Conscientia was still only one touchdown away from taking the lead. But there was only a little over three minutes left in the game when they started their drive needing seven points to win.

Conscientia's offense was able to take the ball to the three yard line with ten seconds remaining in the game. With the clock stopped, the Romitis Academy coach called timeout so he could inform his players on what to look for on the next play. With ten seconds remaining, Conscientia would have to attempt a quick pass into the end zone in order to have two shots at scoring. If the pass was complete, Conscientia would win the game. If the pass was incomplete, they still would have a second or two left to try again.

As the teams lined up, the crowd was silent. "Set! Hut! Hut!" Quarterback Allan Landry dropped back to pass, the Romitis defenders dropped back to cover the end zone. The defensive line was rushing to get to Allen. Brandon was in the backfield ready to help block any defender he saw. The clock was ticking down, nine, eight, seven … All of the receivers were covered. Allen dropped back two more steps. Brandon slipped out of the backfield to his left. Everyone expected Allen to throw the ball away as there was only three seconds left. But he threw the ball to Brandon who caught it at the four yard line. Three Romitis defenders were charging hard to make the tackle. By the time Brandon took the ball to the two yard line a defender hit him shoulder to shoulder. The impact was loud. Everyone stood on their feet not wanting to miss the play. As a second defender came up to help bring Brandon down, he saw the goal line just a yard away. Dragging both defenders, Brandon crossed the goal line as a third defender came to finally bring him down. It was too late, Brandon scored the tying touchdown. Everyone on Conscientia sideline went wild, ready to storm the field. All that was needed was for Sam Palazzo, the kicker, to make the extra point to win the game. The game ended in a one point Conscientia win and a Junior Varsity league championship.

Players were jumping on one another. Most of the crowd spilled onto the field trying to reach the player who scored the winning touchdown.

Brandon, his helmet still on, seemed to take it in stride. He didn't jump up and down. He didn't pile on the other players. He simply took the congratulations, and in a few minutes, looked up into the stands and caught his mother and father. After that, he led his team into the locker room.

Dozens of people in the stands wanted to congratulate Pat and Cindy on the terrific game that Brandon played. After waiting for nearly an hour for the players to come out of the locker - and Pat could have waited longer as he was in his glory - Brandon came out to meet his parents.

"That was a great game Brandon! That was a terrific win!"

"Thanks dad."

"You played a wonderful game Brandon. We're so proud of you."

"Thanks mom."

Quarterback Allen Landry came running up. "Hey Brandon a bunch of us are heading to the Peanut Gallery to celebrate the championship. Natalie is going to be there. She told me to tell you that. Are you coming?"

"I got some work to do back home. I'll catch up to you on Monday."

"Are you sure? Natalie specifically told me to tell you she would be there. Natalie man! Natalie, you know just the hottest girl in school?"

"I know who you mean, but I have some work I gotta do back home."

"You don't mind if I eh, you know celebrate with her?"

"You go ahead. I'll catch up with you on Monday."

Allen just shook his head. "Alright man, it's your loss."

"Honey, why don't you go with your friends? I'm sure work can wait."

"Your mom's right Brandon. The work can wait. Trust me when you get to be my age, you'll look for any excuse to get away from work."

"I have some stuff I need to do for school. You ready to go home?"

"Sure, if you say so."

Later that night Cindy knocked on Brandon's bedroom door.

"Hi mom what's up?"

When Cindy opened the door she saw Brandon with a couple books open and his laptop on. "Hi, I just wanted to see if everything was Ok."

"I'm a little sore from the game, but I don't mind that, why?"

"I don't know. I was wondering why you didn't go out to celebrate with the other players."

"I told you, I had some work I needed to do. What's the big deal?"

"It's no big deal. I wanted to make sure you were Ok, that's all. I'm a mother looking after her son. What kind of work are you doing?"

"It's a biology project. Everyone has to write up a study on some part of the body. I chose the neurological system."

"Can I get you something to eat to help keep up your energy level?"

"No thanks mom, I'm good."

"If you need anything, give me a yell ok?"

"Ok."

Cindy left the room seeing that Brandon was Ok, at least physically. She thought how advanced the work was for a high school freshman. When she was a freshman, she was dissecting frogs. Now kids were studying the neurological system of the human body?

After football season, Brandon was hardly going out after school or on the weekends. He was consumed in his studies. Pat went back to his 60+ hour work weeks. Maybe it was a trait in the Leshing family that caused them to be workaholics. Cindy couldn't really complain. Brandon was getting straight A's and he wasn't getting into any trouble. But Cindy couldn't help but feel as though something wasn't right with her son.

"Pat, I received a letter from Brandon's school. Next Wednesday, is their PTA meeting. You're going aren't you?"

"Cindy, those things are a big bore. You don't need me there. Brandon is getting all A's isn't he?"

"Yes, but I think it would be nice if you took an interest in his school. Don't you think it's odd that he never goes out after school or on weekends?"

"He's a hard worker. Besides, he was going out playing football."

"Pat playing football is different than going out after school with his friends. He never seems to have any fun with any friends. He's always studying. It's not normal. We both need to go to the PTA meeting to see if Brandon is having any issues we're not aware of. What if he's being bullied and not saying anything about it? There has to be a reason why he doesn't socialize."

"Well isn't this a role reversal. Weren't you the one who said he was fine the way he was? Weren't you the one who said there were worse things he could get into besides his school work?"

"Yes, I did say that and I'm not complaining. This is his first year at a new school. There has to be a reason why he doesn't go out with anyone. Doesn't that bother you? Wouldn't you want to know if there was something wrong at school?"

"Cindy, if there was anything wrong at school Brandon would have said something by now. I'm sure after his football season the other kids love him. If there was anything serious going on at school I'm sure one of the teachers would have called."

"I guess, but just this once can't you take off from work? I haven't asked for much. You certainly were able to watch Brandon play football. Can't you once take off for his school work?"

"Ugh! What time is the PTA meeting?"

"It starts at 10AM and goes until 3:00."

"Ok, how about we go at 1:00? I'll put in for a half day Ok?"

"Yes, thank you."

On Wednesday at 12:30 Pat beeped the horn on his car as he waited for Cindy to come out of the house. Cindy finally stepped into the car ten minutes

96

later. Pat was irritated by the wait. "We're going to a PTA meeting. We aren't going anywhere to impress anyone."

"I want to look presentable. This is Brandon's school and I don't want his teachers thinking he comes from a dysfunctional home."

When they arrived at school Pat and Cindy went to the greeting desk. "Hello I'm Cindy Leshing. Our son Brandon is a freshman."

"Oh yes, I have his curriculum here. These are his classes, the class room number and the teacher's name. You can step into any class you like. On the first floor down the hall on your right are class rooms 100 through 120. Down the hall on the left are class rooms 130 through 150. You can take the steps over there or at the end of each hall to the second floor where you will see classrooms 200 through 220 and 230 through 250. If you are hungry or thirsty down the steps and to the right you will find our cafeteria."

"Thank you. Brandon's English and Math classes are close. We'll go there first."

"Fine with me, let's get this over with."

Pat and Cindy talked to Brandon's English, Math, and French teachers. All of them had the same thing to say, that Brandon was an excellent student that got along well with other students.

"Cindy this is a complete waste of time. I told you he was fine."

"Yes Pat but it's nice to hear that from his teachers don't you agree?"

The next stop was Brandon's Biology teacher. When they stepped into the classroom they took a seat and listened as Mr. Riling spoke of the lab projects, and his grading system. When Mr. Riling was finished he answered each parent's questions. On their way out Cindy introduced herself and Pat.

"I must say, kids are learning more at such an earlier age than when I went to high school. I didn't think neurology was studied in high school. I thought that was a college or medical subject."

"Oh, you mean the Biology project I gave the students at the end of last semester. Brandon chose that subject on his own. My project was for each student to evaluate a part of the human body. Most kids chose parts like the foot, or the hand. Brandon was adamant on evaluating the neurological system. I tried to talk him out of it as it is such a difficult subject. For some reason he stuck to it. I have to be honest, his paper taught me some things I wasn't aware. I'm a biology teacher and we do discuss anatomy as well, but I'm certainly not a neurologist. His paper would make a first year medical student proud. Have you ever thought of putting him in Advance Placement classes?"

"No we haven't. He has always done well in school. But we didn't want to push him too hard. It's his first year here as we recently moved from Virginia. He seems to study enough as it is. In fact we both would like him to be a little more social. We were afraid that by placing him in those types of classes that he would just become more engrossed in studies."

"He does seem to enjoy the science classes. He's by far my best student. He also seems to get the grades very easily. He isn't bored in my class, but he does strive for the extra work. I would consider putting him in some AP classes. I think they would be more of a challenge to him."

"We'll discuss that possibility with him. How do the other students treat Brandon? Does he have any issues with other students that you can see?"

"From what I can tell, the other students like him, especially the girls. From their point of view he's very easy on the eyes. Most other students run as fast as they can to be his partner in lab projects."

"Thank you Mr. Riley. We'll give the AP classes some thought. It was nice meeting you."

"There, you see honey, no issues at all. The teachers love him, the other students love him. Everything is fine. You worry too much."

"Maybe Pat. I guess."

As they walked down the hall on their way out of school, Pat and Cindy could hear a grizzly voice. "Mr. Leshing, Mr. Leshing." Pat and Cindy turned to see a heavy set man with a graying beard walking quickly their way. The man was bald on the top of his head with graying hair on the side. "Mr. Leshing, I'm glad I got a chance to meet you. I'm Ed Buzerow, the head football coach."

Pat's eyes lit up. "Coach Buzerow, it's nice to meet you. Call me Pat. This is my wife Cindy."

"The pleasure is mine, Pat. It's nice to meet you Cindy. I wanted to commend you on your son's fine football season this year. Spring practice begins next week and it would be great to see your son at the orientation."

"I didn't know you started so soon."

"Spring practice is when students and coaches develop a summer program. We have the players do some running and weight lifting exercises. We try to keep them in shape for the upcoming season. As coaches, we like to get an early look at the players."

"Brandon never mentioned that. I'll ask him if he plans on attending. He had a great time this past fall. I'm sure he is planning on playing next year."

"Fantastic. With the incoming talent from that championship JV team, we have a good chance to do the same at the varsity level. I'm looking forward to working with some of the players from that team, especially Brandon."

"I'll let him know. I'm sure you'll be seeing him next week."

"Terrific! It was nice meeting the both of you."

"It was nice meeting you too Coach Buzerow."

When Pat and Cindy walked into the house, Pat yelled for Brandon. "Brandon, come on down. Your mom and I just got back from your school and we want to talk to you."

"Ok dad, I'll be right down."

When Brandon came down the steps, Pat started. "Brandon we just got back from PTA meeting at your school."

"Is everything Ok?"

"As far as school everything went great. Every teacher we talked to said you're doing well."

"Yes Brandon, your father is right. Every teacher we spoke to said you were a model student. In fact one of your teachers, Mr. Riley..."

"He's my Biology teacher."

"Yes, Mr. Riley suggested that we consider placing you in Advanced Placement classes. We told him we would discuss that with you first. He suggested maybe taking AP classes in science and math. What would you think about that? The classes are more challenging. But when it comes time for college if you do well, it would make it easier to get into more schools. It's up to you though. We don't want to force you into anything."

"I think that would be cool, especially science."

"We'll discuss it with your teachers. It wouldn't start until next year since you are half way through this semester. And, if after next semester if the class is too advanced, then you can always go back to the regular classes."

"That sounds great. Anything else you want to talk about?"

"We did run into Coach Buzerow on our way out. He introduced himself to us, didn't he Cindy?"

"He did. He seems like a nice man."

"Nice indeed, he asked if you were going to the spring workouts next week. I told him I assumed that you were after the year you had, but I wanted to check with you first."

"Now Pat, I told you Brandon will play only if he wants to."

"Yes, exactly, I didn't say for sure, 100 percent he was playing. But he came up to us to ask if you were playing. I doubt he goes up to every student's parents to ask if they'll play. It's entirely up to you if you want to play or not. But he was really hoping that he would see you next week."

"Patrick!"

"What? Am I lying? You saw how anxious he was when he said that he hoped to see Brandon at the spring practices."

"Yes but you're putting too much pressure on your son. It doesn't matter who wants Brandon to play. If he wants to play then he will play. If he doesn't want to play, then he won't play. Brandon it is totally up to you."

"I knew spring practice was starting next week. And I'm going to play. I just hadn't said anything because I didn't think it was such a big deal."

"Well you made quite an impression on Coach Buzerow. To him it is a big deal. Coach said he thinks with the players coming up from that championship JV team that he thinks the varsity team can be good next year."

"The varsity team hasn't been too good for a few years. Last year they only won two games and this year they won only one."

"With you and your teammates coming up, I'm sure the team will be a lot better next year."

"Brandon, are you sure you want to play? You don't have to play just because your father or Coach Buzerow wants you to play."

"I want to play mom."

"There, now can we put an end to the prodding and nagging your son asking if he wants to play? He had a heck of a year this year and he wants to play next year, Ok?"

"Fine Pat, I won't ask any more. I guess I was wrong. However, I'm going to say this one more time. Brandon if you ever decide you want to do something else, you do that. You don't have to play just because someone else wants you to. Do you understand?"

"Yeah mom I understand. I wouldn't play if I didn't want to. I enjoy playing. I kinda like it."

"All right so we're all settled." Pat stated.

When spring football practice started Coach Buzerow introduced himself along with his coaching staff. When he was finished with the introductions Tim Boseman and Eddie Palindro, who were soon to be seniors, introduced themselves as the team captains. Tim was slated to be the starting quarterback while Eddie was penciled in as the starting middle linebacker. Though both Tim Boseman and Eddie Palindro were the team captains, most players were more interested in what soon to be sophomore, Brandon Leshing had to say. Tim didn't seem to mind the attention being given to Brandon. Eddie didn't like the fact that someone who hadn't played one down of varsity football was looked upon as the team's best player.

Over the summer Brandon kept up with the weight lifting he had begun in the spring. He didn't lift weights necessarily because he wanted to be a better football player. He liked the way the burning of his muscles felt after a hard workout. The harder Brandon worked out, the more sore he felt the next day. The sorer he felt, the more he liked the workout.

Captain's practice for the upcoming football season began on August 1st each year. The practices ran for the entire month and as a league rule, no coaches were allowed to participate. However Coach Buzerow usually met with the captains off the field to go over drills he wanted the players to perform. The practices were more or less a continuation of what the players did in the spring, running drills and studying the playbook. Coach Buzerow expected everyone to know the playbook by heart by the time full pad practice started on September 1st. On the last Saturday of Captain's practice, the team had a party that included the hazing of the incoming new players.

Brandon knew he would have to go to the hazing party, even though he hated the idea. The party was at Jimmy Stringer's house. Jimmy wasn't on the team but he was friends with just about everyone in school. Mainly because he could get anything any high school kid wanted – beer, pot, concert tickets, etc. Jimmy's parents also had money. His house was huge and had a swimming pool and a hot tub. This weekend Jimmy's parents were away on vacation, so he had the house to himself.

Everyone from school was there. Brandon arrived with Allen Landry, the quarterback from the JV team. It wasn't too long before Natalie, the hottest girl in the sophomore class, came up to talk to Brandon. "It's about time you came out to have some fun Brandon. You know this house has a hot tub. You want to try it out?"

"Hey Natalie, I don't think so. It would be a bit awkward being in a hot tub with other people around. I'm only here because the football team has to be here."

"Suit yourself. I think it would be kind of sexy to be together in the hot tub don't you think? Or maybe you don't find me attractive enough?"

"Are you kidding? Every guy thinks you're the hottest girl in school."

"That's every guy, but what does Brandon Leshing think?"

"I think you're hot too."

"Then how come you haven't asked me out on a date?"

"I don't go out much. It's not that I don't like you, honest. I think you're real cool. One of the coolest girls I've ever known. It's just that I have some things I need to get done."

When the 11PM hour came, Tim and Eddie rounded up the football players. "All football players meet me on the front lawn. Let's go!"

"Well Natalie, I guess I have to go. I'll see you around."

"Ok, be careful."

"I will."

Eddie explained this year's hazing. "Ok rookies, this year you get blindfolded. This year we learn to trust our upper classmen. After your blindfolds are secure, we'll place you in a car. We'll drive to an undisclosed place and then we will see if you can find your way home."

The upper classmen drove the blindfolded players, including Brandon, around the neighborhood so they didn't know where they were. They eventually drove to Misty Lake then parked the cars on top of a slope. The rookie players all got out of the cars, led by the upper classmen, still blindfolded. The upper classmen led the blindfolded players to the top of the slope facing the lake.

Eddie continued explaining the rules. "Ok, ladies this is your drop off point. Now, we will be heading back to Jimmy's house. After we leave, you can then take the blindfolds off and see if you can make it back within the hour. Are you ready? Ok, on the count of three we will be heading back. One, two, three." The upper classmen pushed the blindfolded players down the hill. Each player tumbled down into the lake. Brandon couldn't help but be reminded of the blind fall that Louie took.

When he got out of the water Brandon was pissed. "What the hell is your problem Eddie! You could have killed him!"

"Killed who asshole? No one got hurt. What the hell are you crying for? You're Mommy never lets you out, then when she does let you out one time you cry."

"Fuck you Eddie. You're an asshole. You know that?"

"What are you gonna do about it freshman sensation? Freshman year is over. You're playing with the big boys now."

"Yeah right, the big boys. You could have seriously hurt someone. You don't blindfold someone and push them down a hill."

"Seriously man, what is your problem? It was a prank. We do this every year. You don't like it get the hell off my team."

Tim came between Brandon and Eddie. "Brandon, calm down man. It was just a prank."

"Let him go Tim let's see what he can do? You really want a piece of me? You really think you can take me? I see you've been beefing up but you're out of your freaking mind if you think you can take me."

"It ain't about you and me Eddie. You have no fucking clue. You could have seriously hurt someone, believe me."

"Yeah, well do something or go home. I hear your Mommy calling anyway. You're out way past your bed time."

"Come on Brandon let it go man. No one got hurt. It's over. Let's go back to the party."

"Ah, fuck you too Tim. You were in it just the same."

"Hey man, I'm trying to calm things down. Why are you fighting me?" Brandon looked at the two captains, turned, and walked home.

When full practice began Coach Buzerow ran his version of the 'two on two' drill. Every time Brandon lined up to play running back Eddie was sure to line up as the defensive back. Even the coaches took notice of Eddie's positioning. "No cutting in front Eddie, this is an equal opportunity drill. You line up and play the guy you get."

"Sorry coach, I just want to play against the best."

Eddie matched up against Brandon as much as he could. On one play when Brandon took the ball, the defensive lineman was able to push the offensive lineman aside and hit Brandon square on his thigh stopping him in his tracks. Eddie, seeing Brandon couldn't move, came up and put a lick on him knocking Brandon flat on his back.

"Take it easy Eddie we don't want our players hurt before the season starts." Eddie stood over Brandon watching him as he winced. Eddie knew he hit him good. "This ain't JV football anymore kid. You're with the big boys now." Brandon got up and slowly jogged back into line. Eddie went back to his place in line high fiving any player who would raise his hand.

The next day at practice Coach Buzerow ran his 'two on two' drill. Again, Eddie tried to line up so he could play against Brandon. When the whistle blew, Brandon took the handoff, both offensive and defensive linemen were on the ground in a standstill leaving Brandon one on one against Eddie. When Brandon went right to go around the linemen, Eddie expected Brandon to try and run around him. But Brandon cut right back into Eddie catching him by surprise. Before Eddie could react Brandon had his helmet in Eddie's chest, Brandon's left arm in Eddie's gut. With Brandon's force and Eddie off balance, Brandon planted Eddie on his back then placed his left cleat right on Eddie's stomach, leaving his cleat mark on Eddie's jersey. When the whistle blew stopping the play, Brandon walked up to Eddie who was still on his back. "Liquid Tide will get my cleat mark off your chest." Brandon ran back to his place in line. Eddie slowly got up and limped back to his place in line. Though no other player openly showed it, everyone who saw the drill had a new respect for Brandon's game. Even the coaches were impressed. For the rest of the day Eddie didn't run the drill against Brandon.

When the season opening game started Pat was as anxious as any player and couldn't wait for the opening kickoff. Brandon was now on the varsity team where the crowds were bigger and the games were captured by the local press. When Conscientia's defense took the field against Lincoln, Brandon remained on the sideline. Pat didn't realize that Brandon wouldn't be playing both sides of the ball. Maybe it was best since the players were bigger, the stakes were higher and Brandon needed to save all of his energy for the running back position.

The defense was able to hold Lincoln to one first down. As the Conscientia offense came onto the field, Brandon remained on the sideline watching. It had never occurred to Pat that Brandon wouldn't be starting. He envisioned another great year of football. He envisioned going into work on Mondays bragging how his son scored the winning touchdown. He envisioned telling his co-workers how Brandon took the team on his back and won the game.

At the end of the game, Conscientia was on the losing end of the score 27 to 7. Brandon had played a total of two plays, both coming on kickoffs. On the ride home Pat had hoped there was some explanation as to why Brandon wasn't playing. "I don't understand. Coach Buzerow came up to us last spring practically begging you to try out for the team. Didn't he Cindy?"

"Pat, he didn't beg. He asked if he was going to try out for the team."

"It's not like he goes up to every parent and asks that, right? I can't see him doing that."

"Dad, there are two senior backs that are ahead of me. Coach likes to play the guys that have been in the system. Next year after Joe and Ty graduate, I'll get more playing time I guess."

"So you're saying the coach doesn't play his best players just because they haven't played before? That's stupid. No wonder the team stinks."

"Pat there's no reason to start berating the coach just because Brandon isn't playing."

"Cindy what he's doing is a disservice to the team. The coach's responsibility is to play the best players that give the team the best shot to win. You don't sit players because it's their first year. You saw the game today. The team stunk. The game plan stunk and the players they had running the ball stunk. Someone should say something to Buzerow. He's there to win. This isn't the JV team where it's all fun and games. Varsity, you play to *win* the game."

"Pat that's enough and you are not going to say anything to the coach. Brandon will play when the coach thinks he is ready to play. I'm sure he wants to win as much as anyone."

"I don't know Cindy. I'm not going every Saturday to watch Brandon sit on the bench when I know he's better than the people playing in front of him. I'm certainly not taking off from work when they start playing on Fridays."

Cindy said nothing, but looked at Pat incredulously. Brandon sat in the back seat not saying a word. He did feel that he could have done just as good, or a better job running the ball. But he didn't, and wasn't going to complain. Brandon didn't play for the glory. What he missed most of all were the hits he would have taken had he played.

The next three non-league games were all losses. Worse, was that none of the games were close. Pat and Cindy still showed up to watch. Cindy liked the family weekend outing, but Pat complained that if he was going to give up his Saturdays it should be better spent than watching his son stand on the sideline. The team had zero wins and four losses going into the first league game to be played the coming Friday against Ashton.

The game against Ashton started at 7:00 Friday night. Pat didn't get home from work until 6:30 and he and Cindy made it to the game minutes after it started. When Pat and Cindy took their seats they tried to find their son. "There he is Pat. He is standing down to the right."

"Ok, I see him. He's standing on the sideline as usual."

"Yes but look, Conscientia is winning seven to nothing."

"Ashton must have fumbled the ball. I doubt the offense scored."

"Pat will you knock it off. The team is doing well. If you're going to be like this for every game then maybe you shouldn't come down to watch."

In the beginning of the fourth quarter Conscientia was up 21 to 7. The offense had the ball again at their own 22 yard line when Joe Williams took a handoff and was met by two Ashton defenders. As the tackle was made a player's high pitched shout could be heard throughout the field. The players got up after the whistle had blown, but Joe remained on the ground clutching his ankle. The medical staff ran onto the field to give aid to the running back. After several minutes, Joe got onto his feet and was helped off the field. When the team huddled up, Brandon ran onto the field to take Joe's place.

"Oh Pat, Brandon's going into the game."

"Finally! Now the coach will see what he can do. All right Brandon!"

The first play with Brandon on the field was a running play to the left where Ty Walker, took the ball to the 36 yard line behind the blocking Brandon provided. The next play was another run by Ty. On third down quarterback Tim Boseman threw an incomplete pass and Conscientia punted the football.

The defense held Ashton again and the Conscientia offense took the football at the 35 yard line with a little over four minutes left in the game. On the first two plays Ty ran the ball for a total of three yards. It was obvious that Coach Buzerow was not going to put the football into the hands of a rookie player. On third down, Tim Bozeman again handed the ball off to Ty. He was met almost at once by Ashton's defenders. When he was hit, he fumbled the ball. Brandon saw the ball right away and was able to pick it up and run twelve yards for a first down. Finally Pat had something to cheer about.

Coach Buzerow called Ty over to the sideline and chewed him out for dropping the ball. On the next play, Tim handed the ball off to Brandon who cut to his right, stiff-armed a Ashton defender, continued up field, cut back to his left where he was met by a Ashton linebacker. Brandon put his shoulder down and ran over the defender, then cut to the sideline where he turned up field and outran the Ashton safety all the way to his first touchdown of the year.

The fans stood and cheered, Pat of course was the loudest. "Way to go Brandon! Now we know what you can do! All right here we go now!" People turned to Pat and Cindy to congratulate them on the great run their son had made. It was like old times. It took a while but now things were turning out the way Pat had expected. He had something to brag about on Monday. Conscientia went onto win the game 28 to 7.

Conscientia's second league game was the following Friday at Orion Prep's field. Even though it was on the road, Pat and Cindy were able to make it to the game on time. Pat actually left work early so he wouldn't miss a minute of his son's playing time.

On their first possession of the ball, Orion was able to march the length of the field for a touchdown. When Conscientia's offense took the field, the usual senior running back tandem of Joe Williams and Ty Walker were in the backfield. It was as if all the air was taken out of Pat's lungs. All of the excitement Pat had coming to the game was gone. "What's going on here Cindy? What the hell is Coach Buzerow doing?"

"Pat calm down. Obviously Joe is fine now. Maybe if someone gets hurt, God forbid, Brandon will get back into the game."

"What the hell is that supposed to mean? You saw how Brandon played last week. What does he have to do to get this idiot coach to notice?"

"Patrick! Now I'm telling you to calm down or we're leaving."

Brandon continued to watch from the sideline as the senior running backs continued to play. With 3:48 left in the game, Conscientia was behind 28 to 24. The offense had the football at Orion's 32 yard line. Brandon had yet to get into the game on offense. On second down, quarterback Tim Boseman pitched the ball to Ty Walker who took off to the right and cut up field trying to make the first down. When Ty was hit by two Orion defenders, he fumbled the ball which was recovered by a Orion player. Everyone in Conscientia's stands fell silent. They knew the game was over. Pat wasn't so quiet. He began to shout to the coaches on sideline. Cindy tried to calm him down, grabbing Pat by his jacket to sit him down.

When the game was over, Pat jumped out of his seat. "Coach! Coach Buzerow! Do you know what the hell you're doing out there! Why the hell aren't you playing Brandon at running back? You saw how he played last week. When are you going to try to *win* a game? Isn't that kid who lost the game the same kid who fumbled last week?"

Coach Buzerow had heard parents complain before. Last couple years his teams hadn't been too good. He normally could let the comments go. When he heard Pat berating one of his players, he had enough. He walked up to Pat and stood nose to nose. "You listen here Mr. Leshing! As long as I am coaching this team I'll play the players I think gives me the best chance to win the game. You can yell, scream, or holler at me all you want. I can take it. But don't you ever talk about one of my players. If I ever hear you yelling about one of my players I'll have you removed from the game. That kid feels bad enough that he lost the ball. He sure as hell doesn't need some jackass berating him from the stands. Do you understand me?"

"Yeah, I understand. What I don't understand is why you don't play your best players. Aren't you coaching to win?"

"I'm going to say this one more time and then this discussion is over. I decide which players give this team the best chance to win the game. Your son will play when I think he is ready to play. That's it, end of discussion." Coach Buzerow ran back to the locker room where his team was waiting.

Pat walked back to Cindy who was embarrassed. "Patrick what the hell has gotten into you? You never acted like this before. I don't understand what you're trying to accomplish. It's a football game. It's a *kid's* football game. This isn't life and death. They play the game to have fun."

"Are they having fun Cindy? Do you think those kids in there are laughing and having a good time? Is that what you think? It's only fun when you win. It's only fun when you can actually play the game, not stand on a sideline."

"I don't hear Brandon complaining, do you?"

"Brandon's not going to complain because he isn't going to rock the boat. He's going to do whatever the coaches tell him to do."

"Maybe you should start acting like your son. Maybe you shouldn't be rocking the boat for him. Or is it more for you? Are you yelling for Brandon to play for his sake? Or are you yelling so you can walk into your office and tell everyone how great Brandon played? Your bitching isn't going to get Brandon more playing time. Hell Pat, the coach may play him less just to spite you. Did you ever think about that?"

"Cindy let's get out of here. I'm sure Brandon is riding back to school with the team bus."

"I'm sure he'd rather ride home on the team bus. I wouldn't want to ride home with a maniac."

The next two weeks Pat sat silently watching Brandon stand on the sidelines as Conscientia lost both games. Heading into the final week of the season, Conscientia was to play their rival, Romitis Academy at home. The team had a record of one win and seven losses overall. Romitis had a record of four wins and four losses overall. This game would not be for a championship, it would be played for rival bragging rights alone.

The game started poorly for Conscientia. Within the first five minutes into the game, Romitis had a 14 to 0 lead. Before the end of the first quarter, the Conscientia fans were numb. They had nothing to cheer for and some, including Pat, were beginning to boo. When Conscientia's offense took the field for their third possession of the game, Joe Williams took the ball, cut to the right, broke a tackle, and then cut back up the middle. As he cut back, he didn't see the Romitis linebacker coming to make a hit. The linebacker put his helmet on the hand that held the football and immediately the ball popped out. A Romitis defender scooped up the ball and ran back 50 yards for another Romitis score. Conscientia was down 21 to 0 and they weren't even out of the first quarter.

Suddenly there was more than a trickle of boos in the stands. Whether the fans were booing or not, they certainly heard Coach Buzerow chewing out his team for their lack luster performance. When the first quarter came to an end, the two captains, Eddie Palindro and Tim Boseman, gathered the team to try to put the first quarter out of their mind. They urged their teammates to treat the second quarter on, as if it was a new game. They didn't want to go out without a fight. Conscientia played the second quarter better, but gave up another touchdown. The first half came to an end with the score Romitis 28, Conscientia 0.

Pat wanted nothing more than to go down to the sideline as the teams walked off the field. He wanted so desperately to urge Coach Buzerow to put Brandon into the game. But Cindy was able to keep Pat in his seat. However, Pat wasn't the only person in the stands who wanted to see Brandon get into the game. Some of the fans remembered how well Brandon played last year. Those fans also wanted to see a change. Obviously what the team was doing certainly wasn't good enough.

After 15 minutes of half time, the teams came back onto the field with Romitis set to receive the kickoff. After three plays and gaining seven yards Romitis punted the ball to Conscientia. When the offense took the field the fans noticed immediately that Brandon had taken over as running back for Joe Williams. Pat stood up and was now cheering wildly as Brandon took the field.

Whether it was the half time speech, the change in running back, or the players digging deep down to play harder, Conscientia began to pick up some momentum. The offense was able to take the ball down to the RA 32 yard line. On the first down play, Tim Boseman took the snap and handed the ball off to Ty on a power sweep to the right. Ty followed the pulling guard and Brandon around the right end. The pulling guard blocked the defensive end, Brandon led Ty right off the guard's shoulder and knocked the Romitis linebacker right on his ass with an overpowering block. Ty cut up the right sideline with only the safety to beat, but the safety was able to reach out and grab Ty's jersey. As the safety tried to wrap Ty up with his other arm, Brandon hustled over and smacked the safety square on his chest. The safety couldn't hold onto Ty and he ran the remaining 18 yards for a touchdown. When Brandon got back to the sideline every player made their way to him to let him know how much they appreciated his hustle. Even Eddie came up to tell him how good of a play he made. "Way to hustle out there freshman sensation. Welcome to the big time."

The score was 28 to 7. No one from Conscientia expected a win, but at least they hadn't quit, and they had gained some momentum. That was until the Romitis returner took the kickoff all the way back to Conscientia's 15 yard line. Eddie gathered his defensive unit together before heading out to the field. "Come on now, the offense is coming back. No matter what, we don't let them in our end zone!" Romitis was only able to drive the ball down to the ten yard line where they kicked a field goal to take a 31 to 7 lead with 5:17 remaining in the third quarter.

The Conscientia offense took the field and on first down, Tim Boseman took the snap and pitched the ball to Brandon who was able to break two tackles on his way to picking up 13 yards. Three plays later, Tim faked a hand-off to Ty, dropped back three steps and threw a swing pass to Brandon on the right flat. Brandon had plenty of room but there was one Romitis defender who followed him out to the flat. Instead of trying to juke the defender, Brandon placed the ball in his right hand, lowered his shoulder and literally ran over the defender. He sprinted the remaining 55 yards for the touchdown. The Conscientia crowd went into frenzy with Pat hollering louder than anyone. The score was now Romitis 31, Conscientia 14 with two minutes remaining in the third quarter.

The defense again held Romitis in check and three plays later, Romitis punted the ball. With the start of the fourth quarter Conscientia drove the ball to the Romitis 22 yard line. It was third down and one yard to go for a first down. Everyone knew what was coming - a handoff to either Ty or Brandon. Tim Boseman took the snap, turned to hand the ball off to Ty, but then pulled the football back. Tim swung to pitch the ball to Brandon. Brandon caught the ball, saw two Romitis defenders coming and immediately threw the ball down the middle of the field to a wide open Timmy Smith. Timmy caught the ball and sprinted to the end zone for a touchdown. With over nine minutes remaining, the score was Romitis 31, Conscientia 21.

As flawless of a game Romitis Academy had played in the first half, Conscientia reversed that thus far in the second half. On their next possession Romitis was able to make a couple first downs, but again, the defense kept them from scoring. Romitis punted the ball to Conscientia who took possession at the three yard line, 97 yards away from the end zone. Conscientia was down two scores and the clock was their biggest opponent with 5:33 remaining in the game.

Up ten points with little time remaining, Romitis decided to play a prevent defense letting Conscientia gain yards but keeping them from hitting a big score. That prevent defensive scheme backfired when Tim Boseman took the snap, faked a handoff to Ty, and kept running to his right. After Tim ran past the Romitis defender, he turned up field where the linebacker was waiting to make a tackle. As the linebacker came up to make the hit on Tim, he flipped the ball to Brandon who was running behind Tim in stride. When Brandon caught the football on the sprint option play, a safety was tracking him down. This time Brandon showed his speed as he took off down the right sideline. The safety never even touched Brandon as he sprinted down the sideline scoring his second touchdown of the game drawing Conscientia to within three points. The problem however was there were only 3:18 left in the game.

When Conscientia lined up for the kickoff, they lined up for an on-sides kick. As the ball trickled down five yards, the ball point hit the ground causing it to bounce high into the air. Two of the three Conscientia players that lined up on the left side didn't even look at the ball. They ran down to knock out as many of the Romitis players as they could. When the ball came down onto the ground, the third Conscientia player was able to fall on the ball giving Conscientia their last chance to try to win the game. Romitis Academy still had the lead but was now just hoping it would hold. Conscientia had 3:10 to change the outcome.

The offense was able to drive down to the 18 yard line where it was fourth down and four yards a first down. There were only 16 seconds left on the clock and Coach Buzerow called his last time out. Down by three points, he elected to try and kick a 35 yard field goal. Everyone agreed it was the right call. Chuck Hayes was a senior kicker who had made every extra point thus far in the season. He was six for eight in field goal attempts with his longest successful kick at 42 yards.

Conscientia was playing at home. They had all of the momentum. All they needed was to put the game into overtime. The players took the field to line up for the kick. The holder yelled out "HUT", the ball was snapped, the holder caught the ball, and he lined it up for the kick. Chuck took three steps, and swung his right leg as hard as he could. The ball began to ascend into the air turning point over point heading straight for the goal post. Everyone stood to watch. Every fan jumped and took one last gasp of air as the ball ascended. Then, an arm was seen sticking straight into the football's path. With a sudden *thump* the ball bounced back. The long hard fight to get back into the game ended in a heartbeat. Conscientia's season was over. The Romitis Academy players jumped for joy. The Conscientia players fell to their knees.

When the players met in the middle of the field Romitis players and coaches caught up to Brandon to congratulate him on such a fine game. The *Player of the Game* honors almost always went to a player on the winning team. For this game, the *Player of the Game* Honors went to Jim Frickle from Romitis Academy and Brandon Leshing from Conscientia. When the Conscientia players walked off the field most were in tears, but not Brandon. He walked off the field as if it was just another game.

The Conscientia players' parents tried to console their sons on the loss. When Pat and Cindy reached Brandon, Pat was overjoyed at how well his son played. He congratulated him on his *Player of the Game* honors. "I can't wait to show this off to the people at work."

"Thanks dad. I'm going to get a shower and change. I'll be out in a bit."

"Brandon, you played a great game. So sorry it was in a loss."

"That's Ok mom. No big deal. I'll be out as soon as I can." Brandon trotted to the locker room.

"Pat isn't it odd that Brandon didn't seem upset about the loss? Look at the other kids. Most of them are in tears. Look at poor Eddie with his parents. He can hardly control himself."

"If it wasn't for that stupid Coach Buzerow sitting Brandon all the time, they would have won this game and a lot of the others. Hopefully he learned this year how good of a player Brandon is so we won't have to go through another losing season. Brandon has two more seasons. Eddie's high school career is done. It's a shame he had to go out with a loss."

"Maybe, I just think it's odd that Brandon is taking the loss so well."

"Brandon knows if it wasn't for him the game wouldn't have been close. He's got nothing to be ashamed of and he knows it. Look hun, I got a nice picture of Brandon and the Romitis player holding the *Player of the Game* trophy. I can't wait to show this on Monday."

Cindy rolled her eyes. "That's wonderful Pat. I feel bad for those kids."

"Ah, Cindy, don't worry. They're high school kids. They'll get over it."

On Monday, not only did Pat have the picture of his son holding the *Player of the Game* trophy, he carried in newspaper clippings. He told anyone who would listen that Brandon almost singlehandedly brought Conscientia back from a 28 to 0 deficit.

Later that fall Pat had even better news for his co-workers. Brandon was picked to be a co-captain of the football team next season. Team captains were usually held by senior classmen, but his teammates elected Brandon to be captain during his junior year. Even Eddie Palindro picked Brandon to be a captain. For the remainder of the fall and early spring Pat went back to 60+ hour work week. Brandon went back to spending all of his time with books and on his laptop.

Brandon completed his sophomore year receiving straight A's again. He began his summer weightlifting program and continued to get bigger and stronger. August 1st was the beginning of captain's practices. This year Brandon was slated to be the starting running back and as such, he was involved in most of the offensive drills. None of the practices involved any contact. The players dressed in t-shirts and shorts. As the summer heat beat down upon the players everyone noticed how well defined Brandon had become. Some of the school girls stopped by to watch the practices just to get a glimpse of Brandon. Coach Buzerow who watched the practices from the school bell tower was pleasantly surprised at how much Brandon had grown. He was a powerful runner as a sophomore. With the added muscle built onto his frame he was going to be unstoppable as a junior.

When the summer captain's practices came to an end, Co-captain Sammy Turgin approached Brandon as to what prank they should pull for rookie hazing night. "I don't think we should do any hazing Sammy. If you want to, go ahead, just don't include me."

"It's tradition Brandon. We gotta do something."

"Is it also a tradition that we have a losing record every year? Maybe we need to change some things if you want to go out your senior year as a winner."

Sammy had gone through two football seasons where the team's combined record was two wins, and sixteen losses. He didn't want to break with tradition, but maybe Brandon was right. He *was* right in knowing that Sammy wanted to go out a winner. He remembered the painful losses felt last year, especially to Romitis Academy. "Maybe you're right Brandon. Ok, let's forget about hazing night. But you're going to the end of summer party though right? This is the last time we'll be together as a team this summer. As a co-captain you have to go to show team spirit."

Brandon didn't want to go, but as co-captain, he felt obligated. "Where is it this year?"

"It'll be at Stringer's house." His parents are away on vacation again.

"Ok, I'll be there."

"Great! Man it's going to be a blast."

"I'm sure it will be."

The party started at 8PM. Brandon didn't show up until ten. Allen Landry saw Brandon arrive. "Hey finally, the captain's here."

"Hey Allen, Mikey what's going on?"

"Brandon you missed it. A couple of the guys were messing around by the pool and four girls were pushed in. That started a wet T-shirt contest and guess who won?"

"I have no idea."

"Well it's about time you showed up captain Leshing."

"Hey Natalie, that's an odd get up you have on."

"That's because you're looking at the wet T-shirt contest winner. It looked like some of the girls were having some fun so I thought I'd join." Natalie could be the girlfriend of any guy in the entire school. Yet the guy she wanted was Brandon.

"Well, be careful Nat."

"Be careful? Be careful! That's all you can say? Be careful! What's with you Brandon? I can't be any more obvious and you treat me like I'm your little sister. Don't you like me? Don't you find me the least bit attractive?"

"Natalie I do. You're pretty, you're smart, and you're nice. You're all of that. I just, it's just that."

"What? It's just what? What are you gay or something?"

"Oh man, no way, she didn't just use the 'G' word." Mikey couldn't help but chime in.

"Mikey, Allen, can you give us some privacy?"

"Yeah, sure captain. We'll leave you two uh, brother and sister alone."

As Mikey and Allen headed to get a beer, Brandon turned to Natalie. "Natalie, I mean it. I really do think you are sexy, smart and all of that. And I'm not gay. It's just that I don't want to disappoint you in the end. What I want isn't here in high school. I can't explain it, but I need to spend my time on other things. I can't spend my time partying, dating, and socializing."

"What the hell is that supposed to mean? We're in high school. What else is there but partying and dating and socializing? There's school work, but that's not what life is about. We're young we should enjoy the time we have because sooner or later we won't have time to party and socialize."

"Now you're starting to sound like my mother."

"Your mother! It was bad enough being your little sister, but your mother!"

"I didn't say you were like my mother. You're saying the same things she told me about enjoying my time now because there will be plenty of time to work later."

"She's right. So what do you say? Want to spend some time with me?"

"Natalie I can't. I can't be the person you want me to be. It has nothing to do with you. It's me. It really is."

"Oh I've heard that before. *'It's me. It isn't you'* bullshit. But I've always been the one telling that to other guys because of you. You know what? Maybe this once it really is because of you. Maybe I'm the one who's been wasting my time. Maybe I'm the one who needs to find someone who wants to have fun in high school instead of playing football and being cooped up inside all the time."

Brandon didn't stay at the party much longer. He stayed long enough for the team to sing out their fight song. He stayed long enough to watch Natalie get drunk and make out with Allen. A part of him wanted to tell Natalie that she was right. They should start having fun together. But that was only a small part. He couldn't date Natalie because that would take time away from keeping his promise.

Conscientia's first game of Brandon's junior year was on the road against a team from New Jersey. Cindy waited for Pat who went into work early to finish up some customer service call center programs he was leading. By the time Pat made it home there were only thirty minutes until kickoff. Pat drove like a mad man with Cindy in the passenger seat. Cindy hollered at Pat to slow down several times. Pat simply said "We'll be fine dear. I don't want to miss too much of the game."

By the time Pat and Cindy arrived the game had less than four minutes left in the first half. Conscientia was up 35 to 7. They immediately saw Allen Landry's father. "Pat! Cindy! What kept you? You missed your son scoring four touchdowns. Allen threw a touchdown to Mikey for the last score."

"Are you serious Allen? Damn it Cindy. If you hadn't been nagging me the whole ride over here we may have made it to see Brandon score."

"Pat, if I hadn't nagged you we may have never made it here at all. Besides, it's not my fault you choose to spend your Saturdays in the office."

"Why can't they play on Sundays anyway? Who works just five days a week? Am I right Allen?"

"I can relate Pat. I've been working overtime too. There's still over three minutes left in the half and then you'll get to see the second half."

Pat and Cindy took their seats and watched as Conscientia's offense, with Brandon at running back, was on the field. Just before the half ended, Brandon took a pitch from Allen and took off around the end, straight up field and scored another touchdown, his fifth of the day. "Well Cindy, at least we got to see that one. Way to go Conscientia! Way to go Brandon!"

When the players took the field in the second half with the score 42 to 7, Brandon remained on the bench. Pat and Cindy knew Brandon wasn't hurt. Pat knew Coach Buzerow intentionally sat Brandon because he and Cindy had just shown up for the game. "Well, Pat I guess you and Cindy rushed to see one score. That's too bad because the boys played phenomenally today."

"Yeah Allen last year Buzerow wouldn't let any underclassmen play unless someone got hurt. Now he can't wait to sit his starters."

"Pat it's not the coach's fault we couldn't make it here on time. From what Allen said we should be really proud of the boys today."

The game ended with Conscientia winning 49 to 14. After the game the players had their choice to ride home on the team bus, or ride home with their parents. Brandon left with Pat and Cindy. "It's a shame we couldn't make it on time Brandon. We got here as soon as we could."

"Yeah Brandon we're real sorry about that. We did see you score your last touchdown at the end of the first half. I heard you scored five today. I wonder if that's some kind of record for most touchdowns in a half."

"I don't know dad. It's no big deal mom. The game wasn't too good anyway."

"What do you mean it wasn't too good? Your team won."

"I know but it was too easy. Those guys really didn't hit too hard."

"If you ask me, I think that's good. I don't want any team hitting you too hard. I want you to have fun out there."

"It's more fun when the other team is more physical."

"What do you mean by that?"

"What he means Cindy is today wasn't competitive. Yeah they won but it was too easy, like it wasn't worth the effort, right Brandon?"

"Yeah dad, something it's like that."

114

Cindy turned to watch the road ahead. Pat was driving normal now so she could relax. It was odd how Brandon felt after winning the game. Maybe it was another guy thing that women didn't understand. Pat was relaxed too. All he could think about were the newspaper clippings he was going to show the people at work. "Hey how about we pick up some nice steaks for dinner? What do you say?"

"That sounds good dad."

"That does sound good Pat." A nice dinner with her two favorite men sounded very nice.

Conscientia won their next two games handedly. In the three games played thus far, Brandon had scored ten touchdowns. He was the highest scoring player in the state. He was gaining notoriety from colleges who started sending letters describing their football and academic programs.

The final game before league play was against a team from Hershey Pennsylvania. Not just any team, they were the top ranked team in the state. It was an hour and a half drive to the game and this time Pat did not go into work on a Saturday. He was not going to miss his chance to see his son play against the best team in the state. When Pat and Cindy arrived at the stadium, yes a stadium built for a high school team, they hadn't seen anything like it. None of the Conscientia players or parents had seen anything like it. It was as if the boys were playing against a college team. There were programs, ticket sales, turnstiles, and the works.

When the Hershey team took the field, Cindy was shocked to see what the Conscientia team was up against. "My goodness Pat, look at that team. There must be 80 players. Are you sure this isn't a college prep team?"

"Cindy, Hershey is a high school team, the number one rated high school team in the state. I can see why. Here they take their football seriously."

"God Pat I just hope no one gets hurt."

The game started with Hershey taking their first possession for a touchdown. When Conscientia took their first possession they ran three plays with Brandon running on two of them, and punted. It was obvious from the start that this game would be a rout. By halftime Conscientia was down 24 to 7. Brandon had carried the ball 14 times gaining 52 yards. Forty of those yards came on one run where he broke three tackles and scored the lone touchdown.

The final score was Hershey 45, Conscientia 14. Brandon ran the ball 25 times for 98 yards, caught three passes for 21 yards, and scored both touchdowns.

"Tough game hey kid?" Pat asked, stating the obvious.

"That was a good game dad. That Hershey team really came to play."

Cindy was shocked. "That was a good one? What do you mean? I don't understand. When you win you say the game wasn't good. When you lose, you say it was a good game. How can you say this was a good game? At least five of your teammates got hurt. I saw the one player with a cast on his leg. Look at you. My God Brandon you have bruises up and down your body. Are you Ok?"

"I'm fine mom." Brandon poked at the bruises on his arm. He could still feel the pain of the many hits he took. "Today was a good day."

"Don't hang your head son. You did everything you could out there. If the team had 22 players like you, you would have won."

"Thanks dad but that Hershey team was really good."

"I was telling your mom they are the number one team in the state. I guess we can see why. Next week starts league play and I think playing a team like this may actually help you guys in the long run. A loss like this brings you back down to earth."

Conscientia ran the table winning every league game on its way to its first championship in six years. The team ended its season with a 31 to 10 win over rival Romitis Academy. Brandon again won the *Player of the Game* award after scoring three touchdowns. When the All-League team was announced, Brandon was a unanimous first team choice. He also won the league's Most Valuable Player award as a junior.

Pat was gushing at work. He brought in newspaper clippings, and college letters Brandon was receiving to work. Everyone at work was happy to hear of Brandon's success. Well, everyone except Larry Minkoff. Maybe it was because Larry's son was no longer the star high school player in the company. Larry still brought up the fact that Conscientia was a small time school. "If Brandon had played at La Salle he would be just another good player. My son's playing at Ohio State. Urban Meyer himself came to my house. Let's see if Urban drops by next year when recruiting starts."

Pat's boss, Jim Lawry, was right when he told Pat how much of a sports town, a sports company Universal was. He was especially right when he said football was the number one sport in the city. Pat couldn't be happier. He was working for one of the biggest cable companies in the U.S. His call center incentive program was a big success. His department was handling more calls than ever. Pat was gaining recognition throughout the entire company.

At the company's Holiday dinner nearly everyone wanted to introduce themselves to Pat, Cindy and especially Brandon. Several of the company CEO's walked up to introduce themselves. All of this and Brandon was just a junior. Pat could hardly contain himself thinking of his future at Universal when Brandon returned for his senior season. By then he was sure he would be offered some type of promotion, maybe even a seat on the board.

At the end of spring Conscientia held its junior prom. A couple girls had asked Brandon to go to the Prom, but not Natalie. A couple senior girls also asked Brandon to the Senior Prom. But Brandon always declined gracefully. Some of the kids at school were thinking maybe Brandon was gay, but there were no indications that he was gay or not. Because of his stature as a

116

football player, no one really pushed it. Most of the guys at school thought Brandon was cool, and most of the girls at the school thought he was out of their league when it came to dating. Some thought Brandon was dating a college woman since no one really ever saw Brandon outside of school. There were other rumors but Brandon didn't really pay much attention.

Cindy knocked on Brandon's bedroom door. As always, Brandon had his head in his studies. "Brandon, Allen's mom told me that the Junior Prom was coming up. Have you asked anyone yet?"

"I don't think I'm going to the prom mom."

"Why aren't you going? I bet any girl would be happy to go with such a football star. You're the captain of the football team, you get good grades. You'd be a great catch for any girl."

"It's not that mom I just don't want to go."

"You only get one junior prom. If you don't go you'll always look back and regret not going. I remember my Junior Prom. Two boys had asked me to go, but I had my eyes on your father. He hadn't asked me yet but I knew he wanted to. He was just too shy. So I had one of my friends tell one of his friends this sob story of how I was left all alone and really wanted to go and no one had asked me and sure enough he finally got up the courage to ask. We had a great time."

"That's great for you mom but I'm not really interested in taking anyone to the prom."

"What are you interested in Brandon? I'm sorry, I don't mean to pry. You're the best son a mother can ask. But I worry about you."

"Why is that? I'm fine."

"I worry because you never seem to do anything fun."

"I play football."

"I know but outside of football you never go out. When I was your age I couldn't wait for the weekend to come. I loved going out with friends, going to movies, or to the mall. You spend so much time with school work and on your computer I worry that you're going to realize how much fun you missed. Like your father said, when you get to a certain age you will be expected to work. There won't be as much time to hang out with your friends."

"Mom that was great for you. I'm just not into all that. I know what I want. And if I don't do it I don't want to look back and think of all the time I wasted going out to the mall and dating and such."

"What is it that you want?"

"I made a promise. I made a promise and I just need to see it through."

"Who did you make a promise to? What kind of promise? Does it have to do with Louie?"

"Yeah, to Louie."

"Brandon, I'm sure Louie wouldn't want you to throw away your high school years on a promise. He would want you to have fun. Whatever promise you made there will be time enough to keep it."

"That's easy to say mom but I'm not sure. No one knows for sure how much time they have. I would hate myself if one day it's too late and I look back and see that I didn't give it my all. I don't think I can make you understand but it's what I have to do. Believe me I'll be fine. I need to do it my way. Ok."

"Ok Brandon. I told your father not to force you into anything you didn't want to do, and I'd be hypocritical if I forced you into going to your Junior Prom. Just think about what I said. You're not going to solve every problem as a junior in high school. There will be plenty of time to work on whatever you need to do."

"Ok mom I'll think about it."

Cindy left Brandon's room knowing he wasn't going to his Jr. Prom.

Brandon's senior football season started with high expectations as co-captain for the second straight year. Expectations were high for the team as well being the defending league champions. No one was more excited to start the season more than Pat. When Pat saw the upcoming season schedule, the first game he noticed was that Conscientia would be playing La Salle. "Larry looks like Conscientia will be playing your son's alma mater this year."

"Well, now we'll get to see just how good of a team they have. I guess we'll also get to see how good of a player Brandon really is. Of course this isn't one of La Salle's best teams. After my son graduated they haven't been back to the City championship."

"So you're coming up with excuses already huh?"

"No, no, even in a down year for La Salle they should mop the field with a team that small. Listen, I've got nothing against you or your son. I'm sure he's a heck of a player. I'm just stating the obvious. Conscientia is not as big of a school as La Salle. Let's be honest."

"We'll see if it's the size of the dog in the fight, or the size of the fight in the dog that matters."

Larry laughed. "Ok Pat, I guess we will see. Good luck to you and your kid. I mean that. I hope he does well this year." Even Larry's sarcastic gestures couldn't bring Pat's euphoria down. Not only would this be Brandon's best year playing football, but this was the year that he would choose which college to attend. Pat had been asked by people at work many times where Brandon was leaning when choosing a school. Pat's boss, Jim had suggested Boston College, Jim's alma-mater. One of the Board of Directors, who didn't know Pat existed until Brandon's junior season ended, suggested Michigan.

The season started out as Pat had envisioned. Conscientia breezed through their first three games winning by an average of 28 points. In those first three games, Brandon had scored 11 touchdowns and had over 650 yards running the ball. He would have had much more if Coach Buzerow hadn't sat Brandon in the fourth quarter of each game. Even without playing every quarter he led the city in touchdowns and rushing yards.

Next was the final non-league game of the season, a home against La Salle. Pat invited Larry to watch. Larry obliged and sat with Pat and Cindy in the stands. "Hunny this is Larry Minkoff. He works with me down at the office. Larry, this is my wife Cindy."

"Hello Larry."

"Hello Cindy. I've heard a lot about your son I had to come down and see for myself. My son played for La Salle a couple years ago. He has graduated and is now playing for Ohio State."

"I must apologize for my husband's rants at work. I'm sure he bends anyone's ear that is in hearing distance."

"Don't apologize at all. That's the way we are at Universal, very competitive. Every parent brags one way or another at the office. I must admit your son has been getting a lot of attention."

"Thank you Larry. I'm glad he found something he enjoys outside of school work."

"Looks like Conscientia will be kicking off. " Pat was anxious to get the game started.

"Yep, does Brandon play defense Pat?"

"No, Coach Buzerow has him playing running back."

With La Salle's first possession, they drove to mid-field and punted. On Conscientia's second play from scrimmage Brandon took a pitch to his right and ran 74 yards for a touchdown. Cindy cheered and clapped for her son. Pat stood and smiled. He was waiting for Larry to say something.

"Nice run. La Salle's safety slipped trying to cover the flat. Brandon does have nice speed."

"Thanks Larry." Pat couldn't contain himself and let out a yell. "Way to go Conscientia!"

Cindy could sense something was going on between her husband and Larry. The smugness on her husband's face was a dead giveaway.

The game was close and at the end of the first half Conscientia led 17 to 14. Brandon had two touchdowns and had rushed for over 100 yards. The second half the game remained close. With less than three and a half minutes remaining in the game, La Salle led 28 to 24. In the second half Brandon was held in check. He hadn't scored and was held to 30 yards rushing. With time running down, Conscientia had the ball on their 27 yard line. Eight plays later, seven of which had Brandon receiving or rushing the football, Brandon ran straight up the middle breaking three tackles, for a 22 yard touchdown. Conscientia held on and won the game 31 to 28 to remain undefeated.

"Well Larry, the size of the fight in the dog beat out the bigger dog."

"Congratulations Pat. Conscientia has a real fine team. They probably would have given my son's senior team quite a battle." Larry just couldn't give in totally to Pat.

When Brandon made his way to his parents after the game Pat introduced his son to his co-worker. "Hell of a game Brandon, great win! I want to introduce you to Larry Minkoff. He works with me at Universal."

"Hello Mr. Minkoff."

"Hello Brandon I think we met at last year's at the Christmas party. Nice game you had today. Have you decided on a college yet?"

"No sir I'll probably wait until the end of the season to decide."

"Ohio State has a real good team this year. I hear they'll be even better next year. You would make a nice addition."

For the first time Pat saw that Larry was being sincere. It looked as though the final critic had been converted.

"I'm sure Ohio State is a nice school sir. I'll give it some thought."

On Monday Pat brought in the news clippings to read to his co-workers. They described how his son scored three touchdowns and ran for over 160 yards as Conscientia remained undefeated and risen to the 9th ranked team in the state. Brandon remained the top football star in the area.

Pat usually worked late on Mondays but this Monday he was home in time for dinner. "Brandon you're having a heck of a year so far. I know you are only half way through the season and league play starts up next week. But have you given any thought to where you want to go to college? With your grades, the sky's the limit. We have letters from Rutgers, Purdue, Florida State, Michigan, and there must be two dozen more. Have you thought about it?"

"I've thought a little bit about it dad."

"Come December you're going to have a lot of coaches calling. Maybe you should give it some serious thought."

"Pat, don't rush him. He has another semester to decide where he wants to go to college."

"That's not true Cindy. Football signing day usually starts mid-February. I'm not saying he has to decide now. However he should start to give it some serious thought. He can visit five schools so maybe by the end of next month he should try to narrow it down. When the season is over it is going to be crazy. I'm sure the colleges can't wait to come visit us. There's a limit to the number of schools Brandon can visit but there is no limit to the number of schools that can visit us."

"For now let's just enjoy his senior season. He can wait until after football to start thinking about college, right Brandon?"

"Yeah mom I'm sure I'll decide by then."

Brandon *had* already decided on which school he wanted to attend. The problem was that none of the letters he received so far had been from that school. Maybe by the end of the season he would hear from the school's coach.

In league play Conscientia, riding on Brandon's back, ran through everyone. They went undefeated on their way to their second straight championship. Brandon became the first player ever to win *Player of the Game* award three times after beating rival Romitis Academy. He was again named league's *Most Valuable Player*. He had set state records for most touchdowns scored, and most rushing yards gained.

In early December, Brandon received a certified letter. It was from the Philadelphia Athletic Club.

Dear Mr. Leshing,

It is with great pleasure to inform you that you have been selected as this year's **High School Football Player of the Year**. *We invite you, your family and your coach, to the Waying's House at the Rittinghouse Square for a dinner banquet to present you with your award. The dinner will take place Saturday, December 22nd, at 6:30 PM. The dinner will require formal attire. Hors d'oeuvres will be served starting at 6:00 PM.*

Honorary chairman will be former Philadelphia Eagles quarterback Ron Jaworski. Guest speakers will include:

> *Former Philadelphia Phillies pitcher Steve Carlton*
> *Former Philadelphia 76er Julius "the Doctor" Erving*
> *Former Philadelphia Flyers goalie Bernie Parent*

Brandon casually gave the letter to his mother. "Brandon you have been named the *High School Football Player of the Year*. This is tremendous!"

"I'm really surprised I won."

"That's it? No jumping up and down?"

"I'm happy to receive the award. I really am. I guess I'm not the jumping up and down type."

"I know someone who will jump up and down. Do you want to call him? Or should I? Why don't you tell him?"

"You tell him mom. I'm sure we'll talk when he gets home from work."

"Are you sure? If that's what you want I'll call. I think he may enjoy it more hearing it from you."

"You can call him mom. I'll talk to dad when he gets home."

"Ok, if that's what you want."

Brandon headed to his room. Cindy called her husband to tell him the great news.

"He what? Cindy that's great! Wait until I tell the people here. Wait until I tell Larry. This is awesome! With this he can write his ticket to any college he wants. Do you know the people who won this award in the past? Jim Kelley, Dan Marino, Joe Namath for Christ sake! Every high school player to win this award went on to play in the pros. Where's Brandon? Does he know?"

"Yes Pat. He's the one who opened the letter."

"Oh damn I would have liked to have told him. No matter, I can't believe this!"

"Pat, now that you mentioned Brandon I have to say that when he found out he didn't seem all that excited."

"What do you mean?"

"He was happy to win the award but you're more excited than he is."

"Maybe that's because Brandon doesn't know how prestigious this award is. I'm sure when he gets to meet Ron Jaworski he'll get excited."

"I don't know. I guess. It' just strange that's all."

122

"Cindy, we'll talk when I get home. I have to head to a meeting now. In fact I don't want to be late since I can start out with this great news."

"Ok Pat I'll see you when you get home."

"I'll see you when I get home love."

The week leading up to the award ceremony Coach Buzerow called Brandon into his office. "Brandon a reporter from the *Daily News* is coming for an interview. She will be here Friday at noon. I tried to schedule it around your lunch time."

"Ok coach I'll be here."

"Hey Brandon!"

"Yeah Coach?"

"You really deserve this award. I want you to know that. You're the best high school player I have ever seen. Not just here but *any* high school. I want you to know I'm real proud of you."

"Thanks Coach."

"Hey, one more thing, have you decided on a college yet?"

"No, not yet Coach."

"Well you have time. Any school would love to have you on their team, *any* school. I'm sure you're getting lots of letters too. Pretty soon coaches will be contacting you for a visit. Then coaches will start showing up at your door. The longer you put it off, the more calls you're going to get. My advice is if you have it narrowed down to a couple schools and you're sure about them, let them know and we can set up some visits. If you need any help, any help at all in contacting any coach from any school let me know."

"Thanks Coach. I may take you up on that."

Friday at noon Brandon was in Coach Buzerow's office waiting for the *Daily News* reporter. When Diane Latner walked in she immediately shook Coach Buzerow's hand, then focused her eyes on Brandon. "You must be Brandon Leshing. I'm Diane Latner. I've heard a lot about you."

Brandon extended his hand. "Hello, nice to meet you Ms. Latner."

"Please, call me Diane. This won't be too bad. After all this is to celebrate your *High School Football Player of the Year* award. I'm just going to ask you some questions. I'll have the recorder on so if you could talk into the microphone that would be great. Are you ready to start?"

"Sure."

"I'll let you two alone. I'll be just outside here." Coach Buzerow closed the door behind him.

Diane pushed the record button. "It must be an honor to receive such a prestigious award."

"Yes it is. The players who have previously won the award are unbelievable. I'm very honored."

"When did you start playing football?"

123

"I started playing organized football when I came to Conscientia, my freshman year."

"What made you decide to start playing football?"

"My dad suggested it. He thought I'd be good at it."

"You have had a tremendous year. What drives you to play so well?"

Brandon thought of the real reason but he knew he couldn't tell a reporter. He couldn't tell her that it wasn't necessarily football that he loved. It was the pain he felt when playing. "The competition drives me. I love when the game is tough, the tougher the game the more I like playing."

"So you enjoy a close fought game over a game your team easily wins?"

How could he explain it to her? It wasn't the score that mattered. It was how hard the opponent hit him. It was how much pain he could endure. She wouldn't understand. No one would. "Yes, it's the close games where the team finds its character."

Diane went on for another 45 minutes with her questions. Finally she came to her last question. "Have you decided on a college yet? I'm sure they will be knocking down the door to have you on their team."

Brandon thought about it. He couldn't give the answer he wanted because the college he wanted hadn't even sent a letter. "I haven't decided on a school yet."

"Thank you for your time. I look forward to taking your picture at tomorrow night's ceremony."

"Thank you Diane for taking the time to come down to interview me."

The ceremony went better than Pat had envisioned. The fine crystal was laid out. Brandon sat on stage at the honorary table. Pat and Cindy sat with Coach Buzerow and his wife. Many people came up to shake Pat's hand to congratulate him on his son's achievements. Ron Jaworski walked up to Pat to introduce himself. The crowning jewel came when Diane Latner asked to take a picture of the family with Brandon holding his award. The picture would make the sports page in Monday's paper.

Coach Buzerow was right. Calls from college coaches were coming in non-stop. West Virginia, Rutgers, Minnesota, Florida, Florida State, Michigan, Michigan State all called or visited. Then schools from the West Coast started calling USC, California, Stanford made their pitch to recruit Brandon.

At first Pat was happy as a lark. He was important. People wanted to talk to him. As the weeks went by the calls became a nuisance. "Brandon, have you made any kind of decision yet? Surely you have narrowed your choices down. You see all of these calls we are getting. At first it was fun listening to all of the coaches making their recruiting pitch. But now it's time to make a decision. They aren't going to stop until you do."

Cindy agreed with Pat. "Brandon your father's right. At some point you need to decide what school you want to go to. It isn't right to keep all of these coaches and assistants in the dark."

"I'm waiting to hear from one school. I know where I want to go, but I haven't heard from them yet."

"What school is that? I'm sure any school would be ecstatic to know you want to go there."

"I don't want to beg to go to the school."

"Believe me Brandon you don't have to beg anyone. You can go to whatever school you want."

"Let's give it another couple weeks. If I don't hear from them, I'll narrow my choices to five schools and we'll decide from there ok?"

"That's fair."

The calls kept coming non-stop. However there was one call that Pat wanted to receive. He was sure it was the school Brandon wanted to receive as well. Then, on January 18th, Pat got the call he had been waiting for. "Hello Mr. Leshing, this is Nick Saban, head football coach at Alabama."

Pat thought it was funny that Nick Saban thought he had to specify what school he coached. "Hello Coach Saban, how are you?"

"After winning our 15th National Championship we are very well. The reason I haven't called earlier is due to our run at this year's Championship. Now we're looking forward to winning another one next year. I wanted to call you to see if you wouldn't mind me stopping by to talk to you and your son."

"Do I mind? Of course not, we would be honored to have you at the house. Anytime you are available we'll make ourselves available, anytime at all."

"How about this Saturday, say around noon?"

"Saturday at noon is fine. I'll make sure my wife and Brandon, are available. We'll see you then."

As soon as Pat hung up the phone he called for his wife. "Cindy, Brandon, come quick!"

"What? What is it Pat?"

Brandon came running down the stairs. "What's wrong dad?"

"Wrong? I'll tell you what's wrong. That was Nick Saban on the phone. *The* Nick Saban! He's coming this Saturday at noon to talk to you Brandon. He wants you to come to Alabama. Finally the call we've been waiting for. I can't believe it. Normally Coach Saban sends an assistant to a recruit's house. But he's coming down *in person* to see you. Can you believe it?"

"That's great Pat. I guess this Nick Saban is a big time college coach?"

"A big time college coach? Hunny this is the *biggest* big time college coach. Alabama just won the National Championship. Alabama only recruits the very best of the best. Can you believe this? Nick Saban, here in our house!"

"Should I make something to eat? What should we wear?"

"Cindy why don't you make the best lunch your culinary class can think of. Since Coach Saban is from the south, something Southern. As far as what we should wear, I'm not sure. It's not like we're going to a formal occasion. But this is Nick freaking Saban! Brandon, now I know this is a big deal but try not to look too anxious. Try not to look too nervous."

"Pat, why don't *you* try not to look too anxious or nervous?"

"I'll be fine dad."

Finally Pat had an answer to everyone who kept asking where Brandon was going to college. He couldn't wait to tell them, that Nick Saban was coming over to his house.

On Thursday Pat heard the knock he had been waiting for. It was Alabama Coach Nick Saban standing at his doorstep. "Cindy, open the door."

"Hello. You must be Mr. Saban. It's nice of you to come all this way to visit us. Please, come in."

"Thank you Mrs. Leshing."

"Please, call me Cindy."

"Thank you Cindy. You must be Pat." Nick extended his hand.

"Hello Coach Saban, yes I'm Pat and this is Brandon."

"Brandon it's nice to meet you. I've been keeping track of your football accomplishments. You have had an extraordinary year. Congratulations on winning the *Philadelphia Athletic Club Award*. I know how prestigious that award is. Joe Namath who played quarterback at Alabama won the award."

"Thank you Mr. Saban, thank you very much."

"I hope you'll call me Coach when you decide on the school you like."

Coach Saban made his recruiting pitch. Cindy and Brandon listened and were very polite to the coach. Pat was star struck the whole time. In the end, Pat asked if Coach Saban would mind if he could take a picture. "Of course I don't mind."

"Great! Cindy, take a picture of me and Coach Saban. I can't wait to show the people at work."

After the picture taken, Coach Saban asked if Brandon would like to have his picture taken. Pat thought that would be terrific. "Yes, would your assistant mind taking a picture of you and my family?"

"I'm sure he wouldn't mind. Hey Jerry, take a picture of me and the Leshing family."

When Coach Saban left the house, all that was left was for Brandon to make the official announcement.

Chapter 7
TO BE WHOLE AGAIN

Ted sat in his wheelchair, holding the letter Lisa had written. He sat there for what seemed like hours. Perhaps, hopefully, maybe, Lisa would walk back inside. Finally, the door opened. Ted looked up at his daughter. Gina immediately noticed the tears streaming down her father's cheeks. She knew Lisa was gone.

"Dad, are you Ok?"

Ted quickly wiped away the tears. "I'm Ok Gina. I was just saying goodbye to Lisa."

"I know she cared for you a great deal. I know you really liked her too. Think of how much you have improved since she started. It's amazing how much better you look."

"That's what makes it hard I guess. I know I owe a great deal to her. She did a tremendous job." Ted didn't like Gina seeing him depressed. He tried his best to shake it off. "Now it's just you and me kid! So what do you want for dinner?"

Later that night, while lying in bed, Ted opened Lisa's letter.

Dear Ted,

I have never worked with anyone quite like you. You have made me so proud to be your therapist. You don't know how fulfilling it was to help you improve as much as you did in the time we had together. I know you are going to turn out great in anything you do. As much as I may have helped you, you have helped me. You made my work worthwhile. It is because of people like you that I decided to make physical therapy my profession.

I have never been more challenged with any patient as much as you have challenged me. I hope with all my heart that I had risen up to those challenges and you are happy with my effort. I will miss the talks we had especially those last few weeks where we were able to take walks outside.

I know how self-conscious you are about how other people see you. Ted, you have to realize that it's not how you look on the outside that matters. It's what's on the inside. Once you start letting people see you, you will find that they will like what they see.

If I ever come back to the Philadelphia area I hope we can get together. If you ever find yourself in the San Diego area, I hope you will look me up.

Take Care,
Lisa

Though it wasn't the letter, or the words that Ted was hoping for, he decided right there that he would do whatever it took to become whole again. He was finally able to connect with a woman in a way that he never was able to since his wife had passed away. For the first time in a long time he now wanted to be in a relationship with someone. But he had to get to a point where he was comfortable with himself. Lisa was right. He was self-conscious of how people saw him. He was going to change that. Ted was willing to work as hard as he could to get stronger. Instead of having a therapist come to his house to help, Ted was on his own. But he knew he could do it. He knew he could make it.

Gina wasn't Ted's little girl any longer. She was a soon to be senior in high school. In a few years she would become a registered nurse. Ted knew that it was because of his condition that Gina chose the nursing profession. She had always wanted to become a veterinarian ever since she found her kitten Oreo. However her goals changed once she saw her father come home from the rehabilitation hospital. He was proud that Gina had chosen such a giving profession, but part of him didn't like that it was because of him that Gina chose the profession.

For several months, Ted had worked as hard as he could. But he saw little progress in his ability to walk. He had not improved much at all since Lisa had left. Without Lisa to talk to, Ted stopped going outside. He was too self-conscious and being outside alone was close to unbearable. Gina tried her best to get her father out of the house. The only time Ted did go out, was when he and Gina visited his wife's grave. Ted was thinking of Linda more and more since Lisa had left.

Ted's friends were stopping by less often. When Ted first arrived home from the hospital, people were stopping by every week. Joe Wolfers who used to stop by every Saturday was now visiting once a month. Jennifer who had been stopping by a couple times per week had also cut back the number of visits. Ted wasn't angry at them. It was human nature. Everyone has their own life to live. Ted didn't expect others to plan their lives around him.

On the first Saturday in October, Joe Wolfers did stop by. He brought a flyer for the company *Night at the Races* event which was being held the first Saturday in November. The *Night at the Races* was an annual event that the Iron Workers held at their Union Hall. The event was a chance for the workers to help their fallen brothers in the coming holidays. Proceeds from the event benefited the families who lost loved ones or had trouble making ends meet. The money raised helped pay for rent, mortgages, children's school tuition, or help make the holiday more bearable by buying children Christmas gifts. "Hey, Teddy boy you're going to the *Night at the Races* right? Everyone from work is going. A lot of people had been asking me if you would be there. I told them of course you would. You wouldn't miss this right?"

Gina chimed in. "Dad the *Night at the Races* sounds like fun. You always had gone before. I think you should go. You haven't been out of the house in a while. It will give you a chance to meet some of your friends and co-workers. You haven't seen some of them in over a year."

Ted looked at the flyer. "I'll think about it, we'll see."

"Oh come on Ted. Jen Jen will be there. You know how much she likes you. Everyone's been asking about you. I'm getting tired of telling them about you. You would be doing me a favor if you could tell them yourself."

"Dad you should go."

"I said I'll think about it, ok?"

The following week Joe stopped by again. With his and Gina's prodding, and a phone call from Jennifer, Ted relented and said he would go to the *Night at the Races* which would be held the Saturday night November 7th.

Joe picked Ted up at 7:30. Ted wasn't sure if he should try to make it through the night using his crutches, or if he should attend in his wheelchair. He hadn't seen a lot of his co-workers since his accident. Ted knew that no matter how he walked into the room, everyone would stop and stare. He thought it would be a much easier entrance if he walked in with the crutches. Not only would Ted feel less self-conscious, he would give the impression that he was well on his way towards a complete recovery. Gina was against her father's decision. She was afraid that he may slip and fall, especially with the amount of alcohol that people would consume. She wasn't worried about her father getting intoxicated. She was worried that someone else, while intoxicated would bump into her father accidentally and knock him to the ground. Ted said it was either that or he wouldn't go. When Joe told Gina that he would watch out for her father, she felt a little more comfortable, but not much. Gina could already smell the beer on Joe's breath.

When Ted and Joe left, Gina took the opportunity to clean her father's room. She wanted to wash the clothes that were dirty and replace the bed sheets. When she went to the head of the bed to strip the bed of its sheets she couldn't help but notice the medications on the side table. She noticed the full bottle of Baclofen, the full bottle of Paxil, but the bottle of Vicodin was nearly empty. Ted wasn't taking any more than what was being prescribed, so Gina wasn't too concerned. She continued with the wash wanting to have everything done by the time her father returned from his night out.

When Ted and Joe walked into the hall Joe yelled out at the top of his lungs "Ladies and gentleman may I have your attention please."

Ted looked incredulously at Joe. "What the hell are you doing?"

"Ladies and gentlemen for the first time this year may I introduce you to a man you all know and love, Mr. Ted Stroit." All Ted could get out was – "Joe you fucking idiot!" - before a dozen people made their way to him. Many extended their hand to shake Ted's but Ted was still not 100% stable on crutches. So after extending their hand and not getting Ted's in return, most just went to patting Ted on the back. Ted's weakening legs left him more and more unstable with every pat on the back. Ted wanted desperately to get to a chair. Finally he had to just come out and say – "What's a person gotta do to get a chair around here?"

"Alright everyone let the man through." Joe cleared a path to a table. "There you go Teddy boy, all settled in. Can I get you a drink?"

"A coke is fine Joe."

"Coke, you got it. I'll be right back."

Once Ted was seated, more people came up to him asking how he was and when he would be back. Now that Ted was more secure, he was happy to talk and shake everyone's hand. He actually felt better than he thought he would. He wasn't as self-conscious as he imagined he would be. After greeting a dozen people, Ted wondered where his drink was. Then, he saw Joe at the bar with a beer in his hand. He was talking to the female bartender who seemed to be trying her best to look as busy as possible. Ted shouted – "Hey Joe, how about that drink?"

"Oh shit man I'm sorry." Joe grabbed his beer and Ted's soda. He gave the bartender a wink and walked back to the table. The bartender caught Ted's eyes and she gave him a look - "Thank You!"

In a few minutes the first race of the night went off. Ted gave Joe $5.00 to put the number four horse. If the horse won Ted would get back $20.00. The number four horse ended up in seventh place, but that didn't matter to Ted. The money was for a good cause and he was having a good time talking to friends he hadn't seen in a while. Ted lost another $5.00 on the second race. "Hey Joe, Jennifer did say she was coming tonight, right?"

"That's what she told me. Hey speak of the devil."

Jennifer Manley walked into the hall. She was by herself and was wearing tight jeans with a white jacket that had a fur lined hood. She had curled her hair and put in some blonde highlights. She stood at the door looking around the room. Many of the guys stopped what they were doing just to get a glance at her. Some of the men's wives saw this and immediately took a dislike to Jennifer, though she didn't notice, nor would she care. Finally when Jennifer saw Ted she began walking towards his table. As she walked some of the men stopped her to say hello. Some asked if they could get her a drink to which she politely said – "Not right now, thank you". She finally made it to Ted's table.

Ted, feeling as well as he had in a long time started the conversation. "Well hello there stranger. It's nice to see that you made it. I was beginning to think you wouldn't show up."

"Ted, you know me. I have to show up fashionably late."

Joe came up from behind Jennifer and put his arm around her. "There's my little Jen Jen."

"Hello Mr. Wolfers I actually got lost on the way over here but then I rolled my window down and followed the scent of your cologne and WA LA! Here I am."

Joe gave Jennifer a squeeze. "You can smell a lot more of me tonight if you like."

"How about we just start with a drink? Get me one of those hard lemonades, Joe, please?"

"You got it Jen Jen. Ted, you want another coke, or a beer?"

"Another coke is fine Joe, thanks."

"You got it."

As Joe walked away, Jennifer sat down next to Ted. "Oh God I hate it when he calls me Jen Jen. My name is Jennifer, ok, just Jennifer!"

"Oh come on my little Jen Jen you know that's his way of letting you know he likes you. You think I like it when he calls me Teddy boy?"

"Don't *you* start with that Jen Jen shit!" Jennifer leaned back to get a good look at Ted. "How have you been Ted? You look nice. It looks like you've put on a couple pounds. I like it. You were getting way too skinny."

"I've been ok. I'm able to walk a bit with the crutches now."

"I see that. That's great!"

"I can't walk too far with them. I think by spring I should be more comfortable with them. My goal is to use only one crutch, then none at all."

"I think that's great. You do look a lot better than you did a couple months ago. I'm really proud of you."

The words, *I'm really proud of you*, hit Ted off guard. He couldn't help but think of Lisa. Was she married now? Was she happy? Would he ever see her again?

"Here we go, a coke for Teddy boy, and hard lemonade for my Jen Jen. You guys want anything for the next race? I'll put it in while I'm up."

"What do you say Jen Jen? You have a lucky number?"

Jennifer gave Ted a slap on the thigh. "What did I tell you about that? My lucky number is two."

"Joe here's ten bucks put it all on the two horse."

When the race ended, the number two horse came out on top. Ted turned his $10.00 bet into a $50.00 win. "Well alright, that's more like it!"

"Hey Mr., that was my pick that won you fifty bucks. Where's my cut?"

"I say we let it ride baby! Let's break this bank!" Ted, Joe, Jennifer and a couple others at their table were laughing. Ted was having a good time. It had been so long he couldn't remember the last time he was out enjoying himself.

As the night went on, the laughs kept coming. Joe was circulating around the room trying to hit on any girl that he came in contact. Jennifer was having a good time as well. She had put down a couple more of the hard lemonades and was a little buzzed. She and Ted laughed every time they sent Joe for a drink. They played a game of what is the bartender thinking each time she took an order from Joe.

On the last race of the night, Ted was up $35.00. Once again he asked Jennifer what number they should play. "I told you my lucky number is two. Don't you ever listen?" Jennifer tilted her head a bit and folded her arms. Again,

Ted had a flashback to Lisa telling Ted to listen to her. But it was brief. Ted's attention went back to Jennifer. He was happy to be in a flirtatious conversation with her. "Ok dear we'll let it ride on the number two horse."

When the horses came down the stretch it wasn't visibly clear which horse had won. When the announcer shouted out – "The winner is the number two horse by a nose" - Jennifer wrapped her arms around Ted. He could feel Jennifer's well-endowed breasts press up against his chest. He wrapped his arms around her. Ted wanted this feeling to last, but Joe was there to once again bring Ted back down to reality.

"That's what I like to see. It's about time you two hooked up. Now if I could just find a little something, something for Joe Joe we can all be happy."

"Calm down. No one is hooking up. We're just having a good time."

"I can see that."

"Here, cash this ticket in for us, will you?"

Joe returned with $140.00. At the end of the night Ted donated his winnings back to the charity. He gave Jennifer a kiss goodbye. "After all that money I won for you all I get is a kiss on the cheek?"

Ted was a bit surprised. All night they had been flirting but it had all been playful, innocent fun. Could they take it up a notch? With one arm holding him up with a crutch, Ted wrapped his other arm around Jennifer as best he could and gave her a kiss on the lips. Ted asked. "You know if you like we could go back to my place. Gina is most likely in bed by now."

"Ted normally you know I would love to, but I can't. I need to get back home to the kids. Maybe some other time ok? I had a nice time tonight. It's great to see you up and about. You really look great."

"That's fine Jen, definitely, some other time. I had a great time myself. Alright let me find Mr. Wolfers. I'll talk to you later."

Jennifer gave Ted another kiss, this time on his cheek. "I'll give you a call Ok Ted?"

"Sure Jen, anytime." Jennifer put on her coat and left the room.

Ted shook the hands of the many co-workers still at the hall then he and Joe left for home. When Ted and Joe walked into the house Gina was watching TV with Oreo on her lap. She wanted to stay up to make sure her father got home Ok and most of all to see if he had a good time.

"Hi Daddy, you're home late. I was going to call the cops to check up on you."

"We had a good time tonight sweetie, a really good time."

"That's great dad! I told you going out would be good for you. So you enjoyed yourself tonight?"

"I'll say he did. He got more action than I did tonight. Tell her about Jen Jen, Teddy boy." The Jen Jen and Teddy boy routine was starting to annoy Ted. But, he was feeling too good to say anything.

"You mean Jennifer from work?" Gina asked.

"Yep, Jennifer from work, tell her Ted."

"We had a good time that's all. We had a good time and the night is over, end of story."

"She was all over your dad. I told you that she was into you Teddy."

"Alright, that's enough. Maybe you're right, but let's take it slow ok?"

"Take it slow! Damn Teddy how long are you gonna wait. Just ask her out already."

"We'll see. We'll talk about it later. Right now I'm just looking to hit the sheets. I'll call you tomorrow Joe. Thanks for picking me up and dropping me off tonight I really appreciate it."

"Don't mention it. I'll talk to you tomorrow. Take it easy Gina."

"You too Mr. Wolfers, I mean, Joe. And thanks for helping to get him out of the house." Gina gave her dad a wink to which Ted just rolled his eyes. To Gina it looked like her father had a good night out. She was happy. Joe walked out and shut the door behind him.

"Dad I hope you don't mind, I did your wash and cleaned the sheets."

"No, I don't mind at all. It was nice of you to do that. Come give your dad a kiss good night."

"Good night dad."

"Good night sweetie."

After a week of not hearing from Jennifer Ted thought of calling her, but his self-consciousness came back. After two more weeks, and still no improvement, Ted was becoming frustrated. If Lisa were still here, he knew he would be getting better. Ted called the hospital to see if he could purchase the electro stimulator that Lisa had used on his legs. The hospital said only a licensed health care provider could apply. He went into his bedroom, opened up the Vicodin and swallowed a couple pills. He didn't need it for the physical pain, but he wanted it to feel better. He found himself taking more and more recently. With no improvement, no one to help, seemingly no options, and with the increase in his self-medication, Ted was becoming lost. He was too self-conscious to go outside, yet being alone was mentally painful. The only way he could make it through some days was through the medication.

As Thanksgiving approached, Gina noticed that her father was becoming more and more distant. She knew her father was depressed but she didn't know what to do about it. Her father's high spirits that he had just three weeks ago had quickly disappeared. She didn't know if he was still exercising while she was at school. He certainly wasn't exercising while she was home.

When Thanksgiving arrived it was quiet. Joe Wolfers had called to wish Ted and Gina well. Jennifer had called to wish Ted a Happy Thanksgiving as well. She apologized for not keeping in touch, but she had been busy at work, her one child was doing poorly in school, and she was having issues with her ex-husband. After eating very little turkey dinner, Ted went back into his room and downed a couple more pain pills. When he got into bed he grabbed the picture of his wife. He missed her so much. He wanted to be with her.

The next day, at Gina's request and unknown to her father, Joe came over the house to visit. "Hey Teddy boy you know the Christmas dinner is coming up. Its fifty bucks a plate. I hear they'll be putting out a nice spread. It's open bar all night too. You're going right?"

"I don't know Joe, we'll see."

"Oh come on man. You know Jen Jen still talks about the *Night at the Races*. She'll be disappointed if you don't show."

"Joe, it's not Jen Jen, it's Jennifer. I doubt very much if she'll be disappointed if I don't show."

"Have you called her? How do you know?"

"I spoke to her yesterday. She didn't mention it one way or the other."

"Then how do you know? What are you waiting for? You want her to ask you?"

Ted thought about it. Maybe Joe was right. Ted shouldn't expect Jennifer to ask him out. He was the man, he should ask her. But he didn't, he couldn't. He should have said something when she called yesterday. But his self-consciousness got in the way again. Now he hoped he would see her at the Christmas dinner. "Maybe you're right Joe. Maybe you're right."

"Of course I'm right."

Over the next few weeks Ted went back to his exercises. If he could improve just a little, just enough for him to see there was hope, he could gain some confidence. Although there was still no improvement, Ted wasn't losing any ground either. As the Christmas party drew closer, Gina received a phone call. "Dad, Jennifer is on the phone."

"Ok I'll take it, thanks. Hey Jen what's up?"

"You know you can be such a jerk sometimes Mr. Stroit!"

"Why what did I do?"

"What did you do? Nothing, that's why you're such a jerk, did you expect me to go to the Christmas party by myself?"

"I wasn't sure what your plans were to be honest. If you like I can get Mr. Wolfers on the phone I believe he hasn't picked out his date yet."

"Maybe I should take Mr. Wolfers up on his offer. At least he doesn't completely ignore me like some men I know."

"That is true. Joe does have some qualities that are very appealing. You certainly know where you stand with Joe Joe. I'll see if he has a date yet. You want me to call you back and let you know."

"Alright stop it! You know you are taking me to the dinner. So you decide what time I should pick you up. No is not an option."

"Well in that case, I guess you can pick me up around 6:30."

"6:30 it is, I'll see you then."

Ted hung up the phone. So maybe Joe *was* right after all. Joe Wolfers in all his obnoxious, arrogant, and seemingly oblivious to anyone around him was actually right. Ted *should* have called Jennifer. After all Jennifer knew Ted before his accident. She knew the real Ted, not like Lisa. Jennifer had always liked Ted, always wanted to get closer to him. However Ted could never let anyone get close to him. Linda had always been in the way, and now his self-consciousness was in the way, but not any longer. Ted was going to take a chance with Jennifer. He owed that to himself, but more important, he owed that to Gina. Soon, very soon, Gina would want to live on her own. No way could Ted expect Gina to stay and take care of him. It wouldn't be fair to his daughter.

"I couldn't help but over hear dad. Are you and Jennifer are going to the Christmas dinner?"

"You heard it right sweetie. Jennifer is coming at 6:30 to pick me up."

"Great. I really like Jennifer. She helped a lot when you were in the hospital. She is very nice."

"Yes, she is nice isn't she?"

On the night of the Christmas dinner, Gina let Jennifer in the house at 6:15. "Dad is still getting ready. Why don't you have a seat? Can I get you something to drink?"

Jennifer took off her long, ankle length black coat. When she did Gina couldn't help but notice how attractive Jennifer really was. Prior to today Gina only saw Jennifer in business or casual attire. Now Jennifer was wearing a black mini-dress that accentuated her full figure. The dress was strapless and with Jen's full size breasts there was no worry about the dress slipping. The makeup on her face was certainly noticeable but not plastered. She wore a light red, almost pinkish lipstick. Her eyes were accentuated with black eye-lash thickener which was applied perfectly. She wore a little rouge on her cheeks that was barely noticeable. Jennifer had such a naturally pretty face and the makeup didn't cover any of that, it made her more attractive.

When Ted walked out with the aid of his crutches, wearing his suit and tie, he had to pause for a few seconds before he caught himself staring.

"Are you ready to go mister?"

"Uh, yeah, sure I'm all set." Ted hoped that Jennifer didn't realize him staring at her figure. "Gina I'll see you when we get back."

"Ok dad you two have a great time."

"I'm sure we will. I'll see you when I get home."

When Jennifer and Ted arrived at the dinner, there was no announcement at the door. This time no announcement was needed. Almost everyone who was there stopped to look at the two of them standing at the door. Ted noticed and was anxious. Jennifer noticed and smiled as she was in her element. She still had it, she thought. She still could make an entrance.

"Hey, it's Teddy boy and Jen Jen! There's the happy couple. Come over here, our table is this way." Joe was already three sheets to the wind.

"Well Jen Jen looks like our table is ready."

"What did I tell you about that? I'm still mad at you for not asking me to this thing Teddy boy!"

The dinner went well, but the fun certainly seemed a lot less than at the *Night at the Races*. Jennifer wasn't drinking as many of the hard lemonades as she had before. Whenever Ted tried to get close by holding Jennifer's hand, or giving her a hug she seemed a bit stand-offish. Jennifer wasn't being rude, nor was she saying or doing anything to stop Ted from trying to get close. They were both amused at Joe and his date.

Joe certainly had no trouble getting close to his date of at least twenty years his elder. While Jennifer knew exactly what she was doing when she applied her makeup, Joe's date looked as if she used a putty knife. Her red lipstick, heavily applied when she arrived at the dinner was now all over her face. Every time Joe brought his date back a beer, he asked for and received a kiss for payment of services. The first and second beers were pecks on the lips. The third through fifth beers were open mouth tongue twisters. By the eighth beer Joe had more lipstick on his face than his date had on hers.

Maybe that was the reason Jennifer wasn't so much fun. Maybe she saw what might become of her if she let herself go. Ted had to admit watching Joe and his date was like watching an alien movie. You kept watching waiting for Joe's date to turn into some sort of gargoyle. By the end of the dinner Joe and his date wanted to keep the party going. "Why don't we head to The Tavern? It's still early and it's the holidays. Come on Teddy boy what do you say?"

Joe's date chimed in. "How 'bout it Jen Jen we gotta keep our men on a leash. As soon as we let them out of our sight some bitch will come sniffing their ass."

"It's Jennifer."

"I'm sorry?" Joe's date asked, slurring her words.

"My name is Jennifer, not Jen Jen. Joe likes to call me that because he thinks it's cute."

"Oh God, and all this time I thought your name was really Jen Jen, how about that?" Joe's date started a laugh that quickly turned into a hacking cough.

Ted, sensing that Jennifer was somehow not really in the mood to continue on for the night excused the both of them. They said their goodbye's to those still at the Christmas dinner and left for home. Jennifer dropped Ted off at his house. "The night is still young would you like to sit out on the porch for a bit before you go home?"

Jennifer said "sure", though it didn't sound too enthusiastic. Nonetheless, she sat on the porch swing next to Ted. They talked small talk. "Do you have any plans for New Year's Eve?"

"I'm not sure Ted. I usually don't go out for New Year's."

"I haven't done anything on New Year's for the last decade. Why don't we do something? The Tavern does put out a nice spread. Open bar from ten to midnight. What do you say?"

"I don't know Ted. I'm just not a New Year's party type of person."

"Come on. Don't shoot me down. I'm not doing anything, you're not doing anything."

"Well, I didn't say I wasn't doing anything. I just didn't plan on going out New Year's Eve."

"What do you have planned?"

"Nothing special Ted, I…"

"Don't make me beg. Gina will be out with her friends, which means I'll be home alone. You'll be home alone. So why don't we go? If you don't like it we can leave early."

Jennifer didn't want to disappoint Ted. She genuinely liked him. The thought of him all alone was enough for her to accept. She would go to The Tavern with Ted for New Year's Eve celebration.

"Great, is 9:00 Ok? I'm afraid you will have to drive. My daughter won't give me the car until I'm old enough to drive."

"Sure Ted, 9:00 is fine. I'll see you then." Jennifer gave Ted a kiss on the lips, squeezed Ted's hand gently, then got up and left.

When Ted walked into the house Gina was sitting on the couch with Oreo in her lap just as she had done when Ted came home from the *Night at the Races.* "You know kid you don't have to wait up for me every time I go out."

"I wasn't waiting up for you. Oreo wasn't feeling well. Weren't you Oreo? I wanted to take care of him. How did your date go?"

"It wasn't technically a date. We went to dinner but it was more a work party than a date."

"Yes but next week will be a date though right?"

"What do you know about next week? Were you listening to us?"

"Dad I couldn't help but hear. I'm sorry. Jennifer did agree to go out next week right?"

"Yes, she agreed to go out next week. She's stopping by around nine. How about you? Do you have plans for New Year's Eve?"

"Of course I do. I'm not a total geek. Some friends from school and I are heading to center city."

"That's good. Well, I'm done for the night. I'll see you in the morning."

"Good night dad. Say good night Oreo."

That week Ted kept up his exercises. He worked as hard as he could but still no improvement. It had been several months of no improvement at all. At night he began to think of the possibility that this was as well as he was going to get. What would happen as he got older? Would he have to depend on Gina for the rest of his life? He stared at the picture of his wife. He thought back to the times when it was just him and Linda without a care in the world. He thought of the times they would go on walks, or lay in the park talking about the things they wanted in life. At that time whatever they dreamed of they could have. All Ted wanted now was to be able to support himself. He knew that very soon Gina would be like any other young adult. She was going to want a life of her own. Though she never even hinted at the idea, Ted knew it was only a matter of time.

Ted lay back on his bed and thought maybe Jennifer was the one. She had always wanted to get closer to Ted, even Joe saw that. Jennifer was attractive. Her and Ted had a lot in common. The last couple times out together Ted had a good time. He thought it was time to put away all that self-consciousness and try to make a go of it with Jennifer. At the New Year's Eve party he was finally going to try to have a relationship with someone.

The day before the New Year's Eve party Ted received a call from Jennifer. "Ted would you mind if I met you at The Tavern rather than pick you up at your house?"

"Is everything Ok? We don't have to leave at nine if you need more time."

"It's just that my kids are going out to a New Year's Eve party and I don't know the people they are going with. I want to stay here until I meet them. You understand right? I'm being paranoid I know, but I worry and at least if I meet them I'll hopefully feel better."

"Sure I understand. It's normal for a mother to worry. Like I said we don't have to leave at nine, if you pick me up at ten I wouldn't care."

"I don't know Ted. It would be a lot easier if I could meet you there. I hate to do this but Joe and his date are going and I was hoping that they could pick you up. Would that be Ok? Would you mind?"

"No, I wouldn't mind. If that's easier for you then I'll meet you there. What time do you expect to be there?"

"I can't say for sure. It depends on my kids' friends and what time they get here. But I *will* be there so don't go picking up any other women you got it? You know how jealous I can get right?"

"Don't worry there's no one I'd rather celebrate with than you. I'll see you when you get there. Try to hurry though ok?"

"I will Ted. Thanks for understanding. I'll be there as soon as I can."

New Year's Eve night had arrived. Joe and his lovely date from the Christmas dinner stopped by to pick up Ted. "You ready Teddy boy?"

"I guess I'm as ready as I'll ever be."

"Then let's get this party started." Joe as usual had started his celebration a few hours before.

When Ted got into the back seat of Joe's van he could smell the alcohol. "Jesus Joe what did you do spill a case Windsor in here?"

"I got the Windsor right here hunny." Joe's girlfriend had the bottle open. "Would you like a pop? It will get you in the New Year's Eve mood."

"No thanks. I'll wait until we get to the Tavern."

"Soot yourself Teddy boy." Joe's girlfriend took the bottle to her lips and downed a mouthful. Red lipstick remained on the lip of the bottle. Ted just shook his head.

"Baby, get me a beer will ya?" Joe's date reached into the cooler sitting at her feet. "So Ted this is twice this week you and Jen Jen are hooking up. Are you two making this a permanent thing or what?"

Joe's date handed him a can of Budweiser and gave her opinion. "I gotta tell you Teddy boy I really like that girl. And she's so pretty. If I was a guy I'd do her. She's a bit shy though. Give her a couple belts and I'm sure she'd be outgoing like me."

"That's what I like about you baby. I love your personality. Don't you love my baby's personality Teddy boy?" Joe reached over to grab his date, losing sight of the road. "Come here give Joe Joe a little somethin', somethin'." Ted couldn't wait to get to The Tavern, hopefully in one piece.

When they finally got to The Tavern Joe made his way to an empty table. He pulled the chair out for his date. "Oh quite the gentleman you are tonight. Someone's working his way to pleasureville."

"You're damn right I am. Not many men act like a gentleman these days. So consider yourself lucky. I treat all my women with respect. That is until they don't respect me. Am I right Teddy boy?"

"All of your women? How many women does the gentleman have?"

"Now hush, we've been through this before. When I'm with you there *are* no other women?"

"Sure, whatever you say."

"Hey! Let's not get into that tonight. I'm here to have a good time. It's New Year's Eve and I'm here to celebrate. What can I get everyone to drink?"

"Get me a beer and a seven and seven. And make sure they put some whiskey in the drink."

"Ted? You want a coke?"

"No Joe, why don't you get me a Bud?" Ted didn't know how long he was going to have to put up with the scintillating conversation of the two drunken lovers before Jennifer showed.

"A bottle of Bud it is."

Ted looked at his watch. It was 10:30. He thought of calling Jennifer but didn't want to seem too pushy. Finally at close to 11:00 Jennifer walked into the bar. She was dressed to the hilt. She wore a long black dress and when Ted first saw her he immediately thought of the Hollies song, *Long Cool Woman in a Black Dress*. Jennifer looked around the room, showed a slight smile that Ted knew only he picked up. It took a few seconds before Jennifer saw Ted. Before walking to the table she turned and gave a quick glance to the man who had walked in behind her then she made her way to the table. The man, whom Ted hadn't ever seen before, made his way to the bar.

"Sorry I'm late. One of these days I'm going to kill those damn kids."

"That's Ok. Joe and his date were regaling me in proper relationship etiquette."

"Hey Jen Jen it's about time you showed up. Teddy boy was starting to get a little worried."

"I said I might be late, but I also said I would be here and I never break a promise. I'm here now so let the celebration begin." Jenifer leaned down to give Ted a quick kiss on the cheek.

"That's the spirit. What can I get ya? Drinks are on me."

"Isn't it open bar?" Jennifer asked.

"That's why drinks are on me. Ha! Ha! Ha!"

"I'll have one of those hard lemonades. Thanks Joe."

"Ted, you want another Bud?"

"Yeah thanks Joe."

"And for you my Sugar Baby?"

"You know what I want my little stud muffin!"

"Oh I know what you want, but how about a drink first? Later we'll get to what you want." Joe let out a loud laugh as if he had just told the world's all-time greatest joke. He looked around to see if everyone else was as hysterical.

Joe's date pulled out her lipstick. Apparently ten coats weren't enough. "You know it stud muffin." She applied so much that the lipstick made her look almost like the joker in the Batman movie.

Ted leaned over to Jennifer. "Thank God you showed up."

"I'm sorry I couldn't get here sooner." Jennifer gave Ted another kiss on his cheek.

Ted sensed that Jennifer had already started the New Year's celebration. She seemed like her old self anyway so he wasn't going to question it. For the next hour the drinks were flowing, Jennifer was constantly close to or touching Ted. Ted was a happy man. Then the midnight hour came. The countdown began ten, nine, eight … one, Happy New Year!

Joe and his date were embraced, Jennifer leaned over to Ted, wrapped her arms around him. Once again Ted felt invigorated as her body was pressed against his. She whispered into Ted's ear – "Happy New Year Ted" - and then gave him a long kiss on the lips. Ted felt enormous pleasure that he hadn't felt in a long time. Why had he waited so long to get involved with Jennifer? He had wasted so many years being miserable, alone, remorseful after his wife had passed. He had missed the touch of a woman. He had nearly forgotten how his body felt when a woman had become sensuous to him. For one brief instance all of his physical, emotional pain had disappeared. No amount of Vicodin could make him feel this good.

The music, the drinks, the party went on for another hour. "Hey Teddy boy, me and my woman are going to take off. She's starting to pass out and I got to get me some before that happens you know what mean? I see you are in good hands so I'm sure you'll make it home fine."

"Sure Joe, you take good care of your woman. Jennifer went to the ladies' room but I'm sure she can drive me home. I got to hit the head myself." Ted was flying high he didn't know if it was the few beers he had, or not, but he felt it was most likely the connection he was making with Jennifer. Because of his slight intoxication, it took him nearly fifteen minutes before he came out of the men's room. Just as someone opened the door for him on the way out, as soon as he took a couple steps, Ted's world was crushed.

Ted couldn't believe what he was seeing. Jennifer had her arm around a man's neck embraced in a kiss. Neither Jennifer, nor the man could see Ted looking at the two of them. When they finally stopped kissing, Ted could see that it was the man who had walked into the Tavern behind Jennifer. Jennifer had her hand on the man's ear then began stroking his thick black hair. She whispered something to him that Ted couldn't make out, but when the man came close for another kiss she gently pushed him away. The man walked away oblivious to the fact that Ted had seen everything.

Ted was heart-broken. He felt angry, disillusioned, used. He didn't know whether he wanted to smack Jennifer, or break down and cry asking her why. *Why*? He looked down at his legs and he knew why. Ted didn't even like himself, how could he expect anyone else to like him, let alone love him?

When Ted got back to the table Jennifer was all smiles. "I thought maybe you had left with Joe and his date. Are you having a good time Ted?"

He wanted to put his fist right into her mouth. At the same time he wanted to cry like a baby. "I'm having a great time. How about having another drink, another toast to the New Year?"

"Ok, Ted, sure."

Ted yelled over to one of his co-workers. "Hey Henry, can you get me and this lovely lady a Bud, two shots of Tequila and hard lemonade?"

"Sure Ted, no problem."

"Tequila? Since when did you start drinking Tequila?"

"It's a new year Jen Jen. Come here." Ted grabbed her, brought her in and gave her a kiss. He was hoping the man sitting at the bar was looking on.

"Ted, are you Ok?"

"I told you I'm having a great time."

Henry came over with the drinks. "Here you go Ted."

"Thanks Hank. Here you go Jen Jen. Let's make a toast. To the New Year, I hope everyone gets what they want in the end." Ted then slammed down his Tequila. "You didn't drink your shot."

"I don't like Tequila Ted."

"Then I'll finish it off for you Jen Jen." Ted slammed down her shot.

"Ted what the hell is wrong with you? You know I hate that Jen Jen shit."

"I'm sorry come here." Once again Ted brought Jennifer in close and gave her a kiss. Was the man at the bar getting jealous? Ted had hoped so. Then Ted thought what does that man has to be jealous of.

141

"Ted you're acting weird. What is wrong with you?" Although Jennifer already knew. "I'm ready to go. It's getting late are you ready? I'm driving you home."

"One more round Jen Jen. Hey Hank one more round."

"Ok Ted whatever you say." Henry obliged.

"Ted I don't think you should have any more. Can you walk like this?"

Ted just looked at her and smiled. "Who the fuck cares?"

"I do Ted, I care."

"Do you? Do you really?"

"Yes Ted you know I care about you."

So many emotions were going through Ted's mind. He didn't know what to say. When the drinks came he looked at the shot sitting in front of him. He didn't pick up his shot, he just stared at it.

"Ted, let's go home. Ted, did you hear me? I want to take you home."

Ted slowly raised his head and looked at Jennifer. "Home, where Gina is, where Gina will always be, because of me."

"Ted you're really scaring me now. Can you make it? Can you stand?"

"Yeah, let's go." Ted took the shot, brought it to his lips and slammed it down. "Let's go."

Ted leaned on the table with all his might to stand. As soon as he got to his feet, he fell back into his chair. Ted hadn't had a drink in a long time. He was now drunk. He needed the help of Hank and another person to get him into Jennifer's car.

On the ride home, after 15 minutes in the car Jennifer finally spoke. "Ted you know I care about you. I honestly do." Ted said nothing. He blankly stared at the street ahead. "Ted did you hear me? Did you hear what I said?"

Ted mumbled. "Yes, I heard you. Thank you."

"Ted I don't know what to say. You're mad at me and I didn't do anything wrong. I don't want you to be mad at me."

"I'm not mad at you. You don't have to apologize." Ted still stared blankly at the street ahead.

When they got to Ted's house, Jennifer noticed that the lights in the house were on. "Ted do you think Gina is home? It looks like she's home."

"I'm sure she is home. She'll be in that home as long as I live."

"Ted what the hell does that mean? You're really starting to scare me. Give me your keys."

"Why?"

"In case Gina isn't home so I can get your wheel chair."

"I don't need no fucking wheelchair. I'm fine."

"Ted you're not fine, now give me your keys."

"I said I'm fine." Ted reached into the back seat, grabbed his crutches and opened the door. As he tried to get out he fell immediately to the ground.

"Ted! Ted, are you alright?" Jennifer ran over to help.

Hearing the noise outside, Gina came out of the house and ran to her father. "Dad, are you Ok? What happened?" Gina saw that her father was incoherent. "Dad have you been drinking?"

"Its New Year's Eve sweetie, of course I've been drinking."

"Gina, get his chair and we'll lift him into it."

"Ok Jen, I'll be right back."

"Ted, are you Ok? Why are you doing this? I hate to see you like this."

"I'm fine. Just give me a minute."

Gina came back with the wheelchair. "What's the best way to help get you in your chair?"

"Gina put your arm under his shoulder. I'll do the same. Hold on let me lock in the wheels first."

Ted began to laugh. "What the hell is so funny Ted?"

"Nothing, I was just thinking of someone."

"Ok, are you ready Jen?"

"Yes, I'm ready." The two were able to get Ted into his chair.

"Do you need help getting him inside Gina?"

"No, I can handle it. Thank you."

"Ted, call me tomorrow, do you understand?"

"Yeah, sure." Ted mumbled. "Happy New Year, to you and yours."

Jennifer hesitated for just a second knowing exactly what Ted was inferring. She debated telling him her side of the story. She didn't believe she did anything wrong. She decided to let it go. She got into her car and drove off. Jennifer was late for her date.

After wheeling her father into the house, Gina was surprised, upset, and angry that her father was this intoxicated. "Dad what happened tonight? Why are you so drunk?"

"Its New Year's sweetie, I'm celebrating."

"Dad I don't *ever* remember you being this intoxicated. Why did you drink so much?"

"Who are you my mother, my wife?" Ted's voice was getting louder.

"Dad I'm just worried that's…"

"Stop worrying about me. Why don't you start worrying about yourself! It's time you started living your own life. What are you going to do, become an old maid and stay here with me your whole life?" Ted was now screaming.

"Dad why are you like this? I'm just trying to take care of…"

"I don't need to be taken care of! I'm your father! I'm supposed to take care of you!"

Gina's eyes were beginning to tear. "I know you're my father. What do you want me to do?"

"Just go upstairs Gina. Leave me alone. Go upstairs. I'm going to bed."

Gina had never seen her father like this before, never. "Ok Daddy, I'll see you in the morning."

Ted wheeled himself into his bedroom. Still drunk, it took a while before he finally got himself into his bed. When he did, he leaned over to the side table and grabbed the picture of his wife. Like a flood that couldn't be stopped all of Ted's emotions came pouring out. He longed for the times when he and his wife were together.

Ted was angry at Jennifer for acting like she wanted to go out with him. He was angry at Lisa for acting like she cared for him. Ted was angry at himself for believing that he could have a meaningful relationship with a woman. Most of all he hated himself. He hated to be a burden to his daughter for the rest of his life. He couldn't bear with that. Ted wasn't a true believer in God. He didn't believe in an all-powerful being that watched over everyone. But he did believe in an after-life. There just had to be something when this life was over. There was only one way he could ever be with Linda and not be a burden to Gina. First, Ted needed to explain to Gina what he was about to do. He opened the drawer on the side of the bed and took out a pen and notebook.

My Dearest Gina,

Next to your mother there is no one I have ever loved more than you. The only time in my life I was truly happy was the time spent with your mother, especially after you were born. The day you were born my life became complete. It didn't matter how much money we had, or where we lived, as long as I was with you and your mother I was truly happy. Please don't feel sorry, or worse, angry with me for what I am about to do. Gina I don't want to be a burden to you for the rest of my life. More than anything I need to be with my wife, your mother. I need to feel her warmth next to me. I need her to tell me that everything will be Ok.

I've seen you grow up into such a beautiful, intelligent and caring woman. I know I am in no position to ask any favors but I want you to promise me something. I want you to promise me that one day you will find someone to love. Falling in love and being in love doesn't happen automatically. I know you just can't pick someone and decide to be in love. But if you ever meet someone you truly care for. If you meet someone that you would give up all your possessions in order to make him happy. If you find that this person truly cares for you, and would give up all of his possessions in return. Promise me that you won't be afraid to give love a chance. No amount of money, no amount of fame, no amount of possessions will ever truly make you happy. It's only when you find someone that you can share those things with that you will be truly happy. Life is too hard to go through alone. Promise me that given the chance to go through life with someone you truly love, that you will take that chance. Remember that I have, and always will, love you.

Ted opened the Vicodin and Baclofen. He leaned over to the mini-fridge and took out a bottle of water and swallowed the pills. Ted lay back on his bed, reached over, and grabbed the picture of his wife and the note he had written to Gina. He placed them on his chest, and closed his eyes. A single tear trickled from the corner of his eye. Ted drifted off thinking of Linda.

When Gina came down the steps the next morning she was hoping the previous night would be forgotten. She walked by her father's room with the door open and saw him lying there with his clothes still on. Then she saw the picture of her mother on his chest along with a piece of paper. She began to get nervous when she saw the open bottles of his prescription medications. "Daddy?" Gina hesitantly asked. "Daddy?" Gina walked closer to her father. Seeing how still he was, she knew what had happened. She knew but didn't want to believe it. She couldn't bring herself to speak, or worse, touch her father. With her hands trembling, she took the note atop his chest and read it. All she could bring herself to say was – "Oh Daddy, no".

Chapter 8
IT'S MY LIFE

Althaia University – Freshman Year

"Larry, it's official."

"What's official Pat?"

"My son will be heading to Alabama. Nick Saban himself came to our house to recruit Brandon. Here's a picture of me and the coach."

"Congratulations. Did Brandon officially sign?"

"No not yet. But this is the school he wanted to go to all along. He's been an Alabama fan since he was seven. He should be signing soon."

Brandon laid in bed that night thinking about all of the schools that had sent him letters, all of the people who called, all of the coaches, who had visited. The very best coaches in college had recruited him. However there was one coach that Brandon still had not heard from. It was time he took matters into his own hands. The next day he made a phone call.

"Hello, I was hoping to speak to Coach Ringle."

"Who may I ask is calling?"

"Brandon Leshing, I'm a senior at Conscientia. I was hoping to speak to Coach Ringle to see if I could play for his football team next season."

"Hold on please, I'll see if Coach Ringle is available."

Coach Buddy Ringle, the head football coach at Althaia University, had been a football coach for one team or another for over 50 years. In 1982 he won a NCAA Championship. He even spent four years as a coach in the National Football League as an assistant for the Chicago Bears. However Coach Ringle's best years were well behind him. He took the head football coaching position at Althaia for a couple reasons. One, he still enjoyed the game. Two, he took the job as a favor to his longtime friend Athletic Director Mark Beheran. Most important, he took the job because no one else had made an offer after he was fired at Northwestern. Although Althaia was a division one football program, it was a long way down from the heights of Alabama. Althaia didn't put too much money into the sport the way other schools did. The expectations were never high for the football team. The Althaia job was a nice way for Coach Ringle to wind down his career. The job wasn't too stressful and it kept Buddy involved in the game.

"Coach Ringle you have a call on line two, Mr. Brandon Leshing. He is a senior at Conscientia. He's calling to see if he can try out for the team."

"Brandon Leshing, are you sure?"

"Yes, Coach I am. Would you like me to pass him through?"

"Brandon Leshing, huh, I bet it's one of my old assistants pulling a fast one. Sure, put Mr. Leshing through. I'll play along."

"Yes Coach Ringle, go ahead Mr. Leshing."

"Hello Coach Ringle, this is Brandon Leshing. I was calling to see if I could try to gain a football scholarship to Althaia. I don't know if you have heard of me but…"

"Heard of you?" Coach Ringle let out a laugh. "Of course I've heard of you, I've read all about you son. You're the top football player in the state. How could I not have heard of you?"

"Well, I've received letters from other schools. I was wondering why I hadn't heard from you."

"Why? It's simple Brandon. You're not the type of player that goes to a school like Althaia. Don't get me wrong, we have a top notch academic program. We're the top school in the nation, probably the world, in science and medicine. But players like you generally aren't interested in becoming a doctor. Players like you are more interested in becoming a professional football player. I'm sure you have had many coaches from top football programs contact you."

"Sir I hope you don't take offense, but you don't seem to be doing a very good job in recruiting."

"Recruiting? If I thought I had any chance in hell in recruiting you I'd put on a sales pitch the likes you've never seen. Seriously would you even consider choosing Althaia over an Ohio State, Michigan, or USC? I'm sure they have approached you to go to their school."

"Yes sir they have. But if you give me the chance I'd like to play at Althaia. I would have to attend on a scholarship though. It wouldn't be right to ask my parents to pay for college when I can go for free."

"You would be interested in coming to Althaia, even when you have full rides to any other top ranked school in the nation?"

"Yes sir I would."

"Ok, you got it, a full four year scholarship to Althaia. All you got to do is come down and sign. When you get here I'll be sitting with all of the documents, sound good?"

"Yes sir that would be great. When would you like me to come down? I'm still in school but I can come down Saturday if you would be willing?"

"This Saturday is perfect. How does 1:00 sound?"

"1:00 Saturday would be great. I'll see you then."

"Ok kid I'll see you then." Coach Ringle hung up the phone with a chuckle. The number one player in the state, one of the top five players in the nation asked to play for Althaia, the team that finished last season with one win and nine losses. The team that had all of four wins in the last five seasons. For the rest of the day Coach Ringle waited for the prankster to call and come clean. However, that phone call never came.

"Mom I've decided where I want to go to college next year."

"Brandon that's fantastic, hold on let me get your father you can share it with the both of us."

"Wait mom. I want to tell you first because I think dad might be angry when I tell him."

"Why would your father be angry?"

"He wants me to go to a school like Alabama or Ohio State. The school I want to go to isn't good in football. Don't worry though the coach said he would give me a scholarship. You and dad won't have to pay. He told me to come down Saturday and he would have all of the paperwork for me to sign."

"That's great Brandon. You know a lot of schools are willing to give you a full scholarship. But your father and I would gladly pay for school if need be. You don't have to worry about us. We both want you to be happy wherever you go to school. What school did you decide to attend?"

"I, I want to go to Althaia University."

"Why Althaia University?"

"Mom they have the best medical programs in the world. When I graduate I want to become a neurosurgeon. It's what I want to do and going to Althaia will give me the best chance to be a good neurosurgeon."

"I know you have put a lot of thought into this. I couldn't be more proud or happier with your choice. I think it's wonderful."

"You do mom? Do you think dad will think it's wonderful too?"

"Brandon I'm sure your father will be proud."

"He wants me to go to a school that has a better football program."

"Brandon it doesn't matter what school your father wants you to go to. All that matters is the school that you want to go to. Believe me he will be just as proud if you attend Althaia or some other big football school. Now let's go downstairs and tell your father the great news."

Cindy walked to the living room where Pat was watching TV. Brandon was right behind her.

"Pat, turn off the TV. Your son has something he wants to tell you."

Pat looked at his wife who looked as if she was about to burst. Brandon stood behind her looking down at his feet. "What is it Brandon?"

"Dad I've made my decision on what school I want to go to."

"Don't tell me, I already know. It's Alabama right? You were waiting for Coach Saban to come and recruit you and sure enough he was ready to sign you when he came. I can't blame you. They run a top program at Alabama. Coach Saban is one of the top coaches in the nation. Alabama is pretty far from here but your mother and I..."

"Dad I don't want to go to Alabama."

"No? Where do you want to go?"

"Dad, I want to go to Althaia."

"You want to go to Althaia, Althaia University? Brandon, why Althaia? That school hasn't won anything. I don't even think they are a real division one football school."

"They are dad, I checked. I even talked to Coach Ringle. He's the head coach at Althaia. He said if I want to go there he would give me a full scholarship. You and mom wouldn't have to pay at all for me to go to college."

"I bet he'd give you a full scholarship. Brandon what do you think those other coaches were offering you, every single one of them, including Coach Saban? They are all willing to give you a full scholarship. Why would you want to play for a school that isn't any good when you could go to a school that will compete for a national championship all four years you are there?"

Brandon gave a look to his mom as if to say, *see, I told you he wouldn't like it.* "Go ahead Brandon. Tell your father what you told me."

"Dad I want to go to Althaia because they have the best medical science program in the nation. I want to be a neurosurgeon."

"You want to be a neurosurgeon? Brandon you have the talent to be a professional football player. Do you know how much money those guys make?"

"Patrick that's enough, Brandon has made up his mind. If he wants to go to Althaia, then he is going to go to Althaia whether it's on a scholarship or not. He is going to go to the school that he thinks is best for *his* future. If he wants to be a neurosurgeon instead of a pro football player then that is what he will be. Now tell him how proud you are that he has decided on a fine school."

"Proud? Proud has nothing to do with it. Of course I'm proud of you Brandon. The guys at work are sick of me telling them how proud I am of you. It's just that you can play football for any school in the nation, any school at all. They all have fine programs academically I'm sure. Think of what it would be like to go to the Championship game, or maybe walk up on stage in New York if you get drafted by the NFL. Think of how famous you would be."

"Patrick I can't believe you! Why don't you take a page from your son and think about how fine of a surgeon he could be? What if he did go to a big football school? What if he did and got hurt in his first year, then what?"

"Cindy, will you stop with getting hurt? I'm asking Brandon to give it some thought that's all."

"He has given it some thought Patrick, and he has decided where he wants to go. Now you can mope around all you want about this and that, or you can be an adult and support your son's decision."

Pat was still in shock. Of all of the schools that came begging for Brandon to play football, he chose Althaia. Pat realized that the decision was final. "Brandon, whatever decision you make is fine with me. If Althaia is the school you choose, then Althaia it is. I don't remember anyone from Althaia calling. When did you talk to the Althaia coach? Is he coming here?"

"I talked to him yesterday. I told him I would go to his office Saturday at 1:00."

"You are going to his office? What the hell kind of recruiting job is that? Not only does he run one of the worst teams in college, he can't take the time to come to you?"

"Dad the way he explained it he didn't think someone like me would say yes to a school like his."

"You see Cindy even the Althaia coach doesn't think Brandon would go to Althaia."

"Well Patrick Brandon *is* going to Althaia."

"Brandon, all I ask is that you give it some serious thought between now and Saturday. Once you sign that's it. You can't turn around and say you didn't mean it. Once you sign if you want to go somewhere else you'll have to sit out a year. Just give it some serious thought Ok?"

"Ok dad I will."

"Fine, and if you still want to go to Althaia, then Althaia it is."

At night as Pat and Cindy lie in bed, Pat still was in shock at his son's choice of school. "I don't get it Cindy. Brandon could go to any school in the nation. You've seen all of the letters, all of the phone calls, all of the coach's visits, and he chooses Althaia. I just don't get it."

"Pat, what is wrong with Althaia? He's getting a full scholarship to play football. What difference does it make?"

"What difference does it make? Cindy the difference between Althaia and a school like Alabama is like comparing a TV dinner to a meal prepared by chef Emeril. In case I lost you in the comparison, Althaia is the TV dinner."

"Pat he's going to a school that has one of the best science programs in the nation for free. What I don't understand is why you're not happy for our son who, by the way, is going to save you a lot of money in college tuition."

"Cindy, believe me I am grateful and thankful that his education is paid for. But you have to understand, he has a real chance of making it to the pros. He has that much talent. I hate to see him waste that talent going to a school like Althaia. Yes, he's going for free. He'll probably start playing is freshman year." Pat hesitated before continuing. "Maybe that's it. Maybe he thinks he isn't good enough to go to a big time school like Alabama. He was the best player on his high school team but Conscientia is a small school. Maybe he thinks he isn't ready to go big time. I should have a talk with him…."

"You'll do nothing of the kind! You asked him to think it over until Saturday. If he changes his mind he will do it on his own. You will not steer him into thinking one way or another, understand?"

"Cindy, I just…"

"Do you know why he told me first about his decision?"

"No, I hadn't thought about that but come to think of it…"

"It's because he knew you would be upset with his choice. He really thought you would be disappointed. Can you believe that? A son is about to tell his father the biggest decision in his life and he was afraid you would not approve. So you promise me that you will not say anything to try and change his mind. You promise me right now."

"Ok, I promise. I won't say anything or suggest anything about his decision. And it's not that I disapprove, or I'm upset about his decision. It's just that he really has a talent Cindy. I believe he has what it takes to be a pro football player. I'm not saying that as his father. I really believe in him. And going to Althaia will make it that much harder."

"Pat it's great that you think he has talent to be a pro football player. But in the end it's his life. Whether he wants to be a pro football player or anything else, is up to him. He told me he wants to be a neurosurgeon. And if he wants to be a neurosurgeon then I believe he will be a great one."

"You don't get your picture on the cover of Sports Illustrated being a neurosurgeon. And you certainly don't sign a contract for millions of dollars coming out of college to become a neurosurgeon."

"Well, you promise me you won't say anything to sway his decision."

"I did promise. I won't say anything to sway his decision."

"Ok then, turn the light out. I'm tired, goodnight."

As Pat drove into work all he could think about was what he was going to tell his co-workers. In Pat's mind his co-workers genuinely cared about Brandon's college choice. Even his boss, Jim asked about Brandon's decision and suggested Boston College as a great choice. Yes, in Pat's mind all anyone at work really cared about was Brandon's college decision. Pat had no idea how to break the news to everyone that Brandon had chosen to go to Althaia. He knew everyone would be shocked. Some would be disappointed.

All morning Pat sat in his office trying to come up with a spin to ensure that Brandon's choice was the right choice. Then it occurred to him. Pat looked back on Brandon's high school years remembering how bad the football team had been before Brandon started playing. Brandon carried the team to two league championships. Pat saw a new spin on how to break the news to his co-workers. He couldn't wait for the staff meetings to start.

At a 12:45 Pat walked into the conference room for Jim's staff meeting. He was the second to arrive. Larry Minkoff was sitting in the back row working on his laptop. "Larry, I have some big news."

"What's that Pat?"

"Brandon has made his decision where he'll attend college to play ball."

"Yes, Alabama right?"

"I'll make the announcement when everyone's here. That way I'll only have to say it once and I can answer any questions people may have."

"Ok." Larry focused back onto his laptop.

As the minutes passed other managers walked in and took a seat. At precisely 1:00 Jim Lawry arrived and took his seat in the front facing the people he managed. "Jim, I have some big news and I would like to take five minutes at the start of the meeting to make an announcement if that's Ok."

"Sure Pat, what's the big news?"

"Brandon has made his decision where he is going to play football."

"Oh, I heard its Alabama right?"

"I'd rather tell everyone at the same time if you don't mind. This way I can answer any questions."

"That's fine, Pat." Jim began his meeting. "Before we start the meeting Pat would like to make an announcement to the team. Pat, it's all yours."

"Thanks Jim. As everyone knows my son has had to make the biggest decision of his life. He has had just about every college football coach contacting him to go to their school. Needless to say with so many great schools it has been a trying time for him. This week, Brandon has decided." Pat paused for dramatic affect. "Brandon has decided to attend Althaia University." Pat's co-workers clapped politely. Pat stood there soaking it all in. He tried to continue. "Now I know…."

Jim interrupted. "Pat that's great news, we are all happy for Brandon. If you'll take your seat we can get started on the coming spring projects."

Pat looked at Jim with astonishment. Didn't Jim realize he was there to answer everyone's questions about why Brandon chose Althaia? He spent the night and the first half of the day thinking of the reasons why Althaia was the perfect choice. What was Jim's problem? Was he upset that Brandon didn't choose Boston College?

Later in the afternoon, Pat held his own staff meeting. This time, Pat took up the sixty minute meeting discussing every reason why he thought Althaia was the perfect choice. He discussed the proximity of the school. He told his staff how Brandon wanted to turn a perennial loser into a champion. He rationalized how Brandon wanted the chance to turn not just a school, but the city of Philadelphia into winners. Pat's staff couldn't help but stare in astonishment at the idiocy of their boss. At the end of the meeting Pat felt great pride shaking everyone's hand as each congratulated him on a job well done. After the last person left, Pat pumped out his chest, tucked in his shirt. He felt great joy as he heard laughter outside the room.

Saturday, as Pat drove Brandon to Althaia University to meet Coach Ringle, he couldn't help but admire his son. "Brandon I'll be honest with you. At first I didn't like your choice of school."

"I know dad. I thought you would be disappointed."

"I wasn't exactly disappointed, but I was surprised. But you know, the more I thought about it, the more I like the choice."

"You do? Why the turnaround?"

"Like I told the folks at work, who by the way are happy you finally made a decision, I told them at Althaia you won't have to wait for playing time. You'll be the feature back right away. Even at a school like Althaia, the pro scouts have to be impressed with that. You'll turn that team from losers into winners just like you did in high school. The more I think about it, the more I like your choice."

"I don't know about being the feature back right away and I don't know if I will turn the team around. In high school it wasn't just me who won the league championship. We had some pretty good players. The main reason I like Althaia is because of their school of science. It's the best in the nation."

"Yeah, that too, their academics are impressive.

Sarah Brandt, the coach's secretary and a student at Althaia, picked up the phone. "Coach Ringle, Mr. Leshing and his son are here to see you."

Coach Ringle was sitting in his office, going over his roster for the upcoming season. The #1 high school football recruit in the state was waiting to see him. Buddy would finally meet his pranksters. "Ok Sarah let them in."

When Pat and Brandon walked in, Buddy was in shock. This wasn't a hoax. There were no pranksters. Coach Ringle had seen many photographs of Brandon Leshing by now that there was no mistaking. The top football player in the state was here to sign on to play at Althaia.

"Thank you for allowing me to attend Althaia Coach Ringle. I appreciate the opportunity."

"Well, Brandon, I would really like to thank you. I don't understand though. Why Althaia? Don't get me wrong, we love to have you here. But with your credentials, you could have chosen any school."

"That's what I told him coach. But my son would like to attend Althaia. Let me tell you, before he went to Conscientia, the football team stunk. They were just like your team. He turned them around by his junior year and he can do the same for your program."

Buddy gave Pat a wry smile. "Yes, I am aware of your son's talent. So what it is it son?"

"What is what sir?"

"Call me Coach. Why do you want to play football here at Althaia?"

"Coach the reason I want to play at Althaia is I want to become a neurosurgeon. I believe Althaia gives me the best chance of doing that."

"You want to be a neurosurgeon? Son with your football talent you should be thinking pros."

"That's what *I* told him Coach."

Again, Coach Ringle gave Pat a wry smile. "Yes. It is nice to have something to fall back on. Even the best of the pros stop playing at some point. Usually they become reporters, motivational speakers, or broadcasters. You don't see too many football players falling back on neurosurgery."

"That's what I want. In fact, before I sign I would like to ask two favors if you don't mind."

At that instant thoughts of prima-donna went through Buddy's mind. Here sits one of the best recruits waiting to sign on to play at Althaia, but he already has demands. He didn't seem to be a prima-donna. His father seemed aloof, but the kid seemed to have his head on straight. "Ok, kid, what would you like from me?"

"As I've said, my goal is to become a neurosurgeon. Therefore, school work comes first. I'm not saying I will miss any games, and I will try not to miss practices. But if there is a conflict between school work and football, school work takes precedence."

"The school is pretty good about working around an athlete's schedule. There shouldn't be any issue there. What's the second favor?"

"I don't like talking to reporters. I would appreciate it if I didn't have to do interviews or talk to reporters, even the school paper."

"That's it? You don't like to talk to reporters huh? Well you won't have to worry about that at Althaia. Our football program takes a back seat to our academics. Most reporters, if any, usually come to talk to our school professors. We don't get too many reporters hanging around the football locker. Ok, kid I can live with your requests. Anything else I need to know?"

"No Coach, that's it. I'm looking forward to attending Althaia."

"Brandon, Pat, we at Althaia are looking forward to having you. Now let's sign some papers and we can make this official."

Brandon graduated from Conscientia High School a couple months later, ready to start his college career.

In August, when Brandon walked onto the Althaia football field for the first time he couldn't help but notice every other player staring at him. Here walked the new big man on campus. Here walked the savior of the Althaia football team. Brandon didn't care about how he was perceived. He didn't feel any pressure of being "the man" even though he hadn't played one down of college football. All he wanted to do was put in the work, to play the game, and feel the pain.

Althaia's first game of Brandon's freshman season was against Villanova, a lower tier division II football program. Because Villanova was a division II team, it was one of the few games that Althaia actually had a shot to win. However Althaia had lost to Villanova the three previous seasons.

This was the first time Pat and Cindy had seen a live college football game. Pat had seen a few on TV and his expectations for Althaia's home opening game were overly exaggerated at best. He envisioned 100,000 screaming fans, the student body section all decked out in school colors cheering for their home team. He envisioned the coaches followed by the players running out of the smoke filled tunnel to the cheers of the crowd. When he got to his seat (from which he could choose just about any seat in the stadium) he realized that Althaia football wasn't like what he saw on TV. There were many more empty seats then filled seats.

Cindy, who had never seen a college football game live or on TV, was ecstatic. "Pat, take a look at the football program. They have a bio of all the players. Here's a picture of Brandon. Can you believe this? I'm so excited, our son playing his first big time college football game!"

"Well, I don't know about *big time,* but it is exciting."

Within a few minutes, the teams were lined up on the field. Villanova kicked off to Althaia to start the game. Cindy stood to cheer as Brandon took the field as Althaia's starting tailback. On the first play Brandon carried the ball to the right side of the field for eighteen yards. For Pat it was like Brandon's senior year of high school again. Ten plays later, Brandon carried the ball again and ran eight yards for a touchdown. The Althaia fans, all 5,000 or so, cheered with Pat and Cindy leading the way. That first offensive possession was a sign of good things to come as Althaia won the first game of the season 24 to 14. In his first college game, Coach Ringle awarded Brandon the game ball.

Althaia's second game was against a division I school, Akron. Like Althaia, Akron wasn't a highly touted school. But Akron was a step up from Villanova. The game was in Ohio, and Pat and Cindy were unable to attend. The Akron fans were treated to an outstanding individual performance, albeit by the opponent. Brandon had broken the NCAA freshman single game record by running for 396 yards. His 53 carries also set an NCAA single game record for a freshman. He also scored four touchdowns in the game. For the first time in over 20 years, Althaia football made headlines across the nation. Brandon's NCAA freshman record setting performance was noted on ESPN.

Pat was on cloud nine. His predictions that Brandon would be a feature running back as a freshman in college came true. His prediction that Brandon would turn the perennial losing Althaia team into winners was coming true as well. Brandon was receiving nation-wide attention and Pat made sure everyone at work was made aware of his son's stardom.

Week three would be Althaia's biggest test thus far, a home game vs. Penn State. Althaia had played Penn State 38 times since 1931. Althaia won the first two games in 1931 and 1932. Since then, Penn State had a record of 38 wins, one loss and one tie. The last three years, Pen State outscored Althaia 124 to 17. The meeting was nothing more than a tune-up game for Penn State.

This year, because of Althaia's two wins coming into the game and the national attention Brandon received during the week, the game had more hype than in previous years. Ticket sales had doubled for Althaia from those sold for their previous home game. Even though the ticket sales had doubled, the stadium was still half empty with the Penn State fans out-numbering the Althaia fans by more than two to one.

The game started with Althaia kicking off to Penn State. The first play from scrimmage the Penn State running back carried the ball up the middle of the field for 33 yards. Two plays later, a Penn State receiver caught a pass for a touchdown. In three plays, Althaia was down 7 to 0.

When Althaia took possession the first three plays called was a run by Brandon for no gain, an incomplete pass for no gain, and a swing pass caught by Brandon who carried the ball for three yards before he was gang tackled by four Penn State defenders. Althaia punted the ball back to Penn State who scored another touchdown, this time in six plays, making the score 14 to 0. The rest of the first half was more of the same. Penn State scored every time they had the ball. Althaia could only get the ball across mid-field one time. The half time score was Penn State 35, Althaia 0.

The stadium that was half empty at the beginning of the game was now only one quarter filled. Pat and Cindy remained, wanting to see their son play in the second half. Unfortunately for Althaia, the second half wasn't much better than the first half. By the end of the third quarter, Althaia did manage to score a touchdown, but they gave up two, for a 49 to 7 deficit. The only person from Althaia who enjoyed the game thus far was Brandon. All during the game, every time he touched the football he was hit hard, by bigger players than he had been hit in his life. After every hit, he wanted the ball more. It felt right.

By the start of the fourth quarter, Penn State began playing their second and third string units. When Althaia offense took the field Coach Ringle yelled to Brandon who was trotting out onto the field. "Leshing!"

"Yeah coach?"

"Take a seat I'm putting in the second unit."

"Why coach? Are you quitting?"

Everyone within earshot stopped still in their tracks. Brandon's backup who was ready to go out onto the field stopped to hear Coach Ringle's response. Noticeably infuriated, Coach Ringle shot back. "No son, it's just that you didn't look so well that last series."

"I feel fine coach."

"Ok son let's see how fine you are."

Brandon ran back onto the field, his replacement went back to the sideline. Coach Ringle immediately spoke to his offensive coordinator who was up in the coach's box and hadn't heard the exchange between Buddy and Brandon. "I don't care what plays you call, I want Leshing to get the ball every single damn play from here on out you understand?"

"Why is that Buddy? I thought we were putting in the second unit."

"Just do it!" Coach Ringle mumbled. "Let's see just how tough he is."

"What was that Buddy I didn't get that last bit?"

"Every play from here on out, I want the ball in Leshing's hands!"

"Ok Buddy, every play."

"Every Play!"

The next two plays were handoffs to Brandon who once again was met by at least three Penn State defenders who planted him hard onto the turf. On the third play, Brandon caught a screen pass where once again, there were three Penn State defenders waiting to bring him down hard. Brandon was able to stiff arm the first defender, he then put his shoulder into the second defender's chest and ran him over. As the third defender began to make a hit, Brandon spun around which left the Nittany Lion grasping at air. Brandon headed down the left side line running right past Coach Ringle to the screams of his teammates as he sprinted 61 yards for a touchdown. The offensive coordinator yelled through the ear phones to Buddy. "Nice call giving the ball to Leshing. It never hurts to get the ball into the best player's hands."

Coach Ringle said nothing. He stood perfectly still as Brandon's teammates congratulated him on the great run. Pat and Cindy along with the remaining Althaia fans finally had something to cheer about. The final score of the game was Penn State 56, Althaia 21.

After the game, as the players showered, an assistant came up to Brandon and told him once he was dressed to see Coach Ringle in his office. When Brandon walked into the office, Buddy immediately told his assistants to leave. Once they left, he told Brandon to shut the door.

"You wanted to see me Coach?"

"Sit down." Buddy pointed to the mettle chair right in front of his desk. "I understand the talent you bring to this football team. And I appreciate that you chose to play here for whatever reason you may have. My biggest worry was that you would be some prima-donna who would be more trouble than you were worth. Up until now you have been a model teammate, and a model student. But don't ever question my decisions when it comes to playing time. That comment about me quitting in front of every player and coach will never, and I mean never come out of your mouth again. Do I make myself clear?"

"Yes Coach. I apologize for the comment. It's just that I hate to give up when there is still time left in the game. No matter what the score, I don't want to come out."

"I admire your commitment. I really do. But son you were getting pummeled out there today. You have to look at the big picture. There was no way in hell we were competitive in that game. The last thing I need is for you to get hurt in a game we have no chance in winning. I need you for the entire season. I need you for the three or four years you're at this school. Do you understand what I'm saying?"

"I do coach. I just hate to give up. And I wasn't getting hit that hard. It was rough but I can take the hits. They don't bother me."

"No one is questioning your toughness. However in times like this, in games like this, you can't look at it as quitting on your team. It's a long season and sometimes you have to regroup the troops in order to fight another day. I don't want you to have a good game against Penn State. I want you to have a great career at Althaia. Do you understand?"

"Yes coach, I do. It won't happen again."

Coach Ringle looked carefully at his prize recruit. Even today, he still could not understand how a kid with this much talent had landed on his lap to play football at Althaia. If the worst thing about this kid was that he hated to come out of a game no matter what the score, then he was grateful to have him on his team. "Ok Brandon head on home. If it means anything to you, even though we got our asses handed to us, you played a hell of a game. Christ son is there any part of your body that isn't bruised?"

"There is Coach but if I show you I might get locked up for indecent exposure."

"If you need anything for the pain, go see the trainer for some meds."

"Thanks coach, but I don't mind the pain."

The momentum the Althaia team built after the first two wins of the season were gone. Althaia didn't make another ESPN highlight for the remainder of the season. The team that started out undefeated after two games was back to being the Althaia everyone had known for years finishing the season with two wins and nine losses. For the fifth season in a row, they finished in last place in the league. The lone bright spot for the team was that Brandon made honorable mention on the NCAA all-freshman team. In the forty years that an NCAA All-Freshman team had been named, no player from Althaia had ever made the team or made honorable mention.

A week after the final game of the season, Coach Ringle was called into the Athletic Director's office. "Come in Buddy, have a seat."

When Buddy sat down, Mark Beheran, Althaia's A.D. picked up a piece of paper and stared at it. "What's this about Mark? Is my time here up? Just give it to me straight. I'm a grown man, I've been fired before."

"No Buddy, you're not being fired."

"You keep staring at that paper. The results back, are you pregnant?"

Mark didn't appear to hear the joke. "Buddy, you knew when you were hired that Althaia didn't put too much of a priority on the football program."

"I realize that Mark. The weight room alone should have been upgraded twenty years ago."

"That may be true, but along those lines your job has always been secure no matter what the team's record. The only reason we have a division one program is because the school gets a share of revenue from the league. What I have here is something that puts us in an awkward position."

"What's on the paper Mark, out with it already?"

"It's from the commissioner. The league has decided on criteria that each school must maintain membership in the league. Naturally I was opposed to such criteria since we can't meet any of them, but I was out-numbered."

"What's the list of criteria?"

"There are many, but the ones that concern you are that the team must be competitive. Also a home attendance level must be met. That means we need this football team to start winning, and winning now or we will be kicked out."

"Do you really care if we stay in this league? Maybe getting kicked out is a blessing. We would be free to negotiate a deal with another league, one that is more on the level of our program."

158

"I've looked into that possibility. Truth is there aren't many other leagues that would take us in with our attendance revenue. Going to another league would mean a bigger travel expense. I've spoken to the Board of Trustees and they gave us two options. One is to remain in the current league, or two, disband the entire football program."

"So you're saying that the team needs to be competitive or the entire program will be dropped."

"That's correct. Look, if it was up to the school we would be perfectly happy running things as is. But now that the league has put in place the competitive criteria, we have no choice. Either become more competitive, or drop the program entirely."

"When do the league's criteria come into effect?"

"I'm afraid as early as next season."

"So what's the bottom line? Obviously we aren't going to become league champions overnight."

"From what I've been told if we don't finish with a .500 record in the league, and we average below 20,000 fans in league home games, we stand a good chance of being kicked out by the end of next season."

"Mark, I can't guarantee fan support. They'll either show up or they won't. What if we finish with a .500 record but fall short on the attendance?"

"Then we can make a case that we are improving. And as the team improves, our attendance will improve. In that scenario we may buy ourselves another year, maybe two."

"So somehow I have to get this team to win some league games. This team that has won a total of three league games in the last five years and hasn't won a single league game in the last two years."

"That's the gist of it. Do you think you can somehow get it done?"

"Why not just fire me and bring in some young hot shot to breathe new life into the program?"

"We can't hire a coach without disclosing the fact that this might be the last year the school has a football program. There aren't too many coaches who would be willing to move their family here just to coach one year, especially at the salary we pay. So, it's up to you Buddy."

"We do have a kid to build around. And, it looks like we have no choice but to do it. I'll get my assistants together and discuss the situation. In light of the circumstances what are the chances of raising the recruiting money? I've never asked before but if we could get some real recruitment money, I can send some assistants out on the road, we would stand a better chance of getting some quality players."

"I'll see what I can do. Buddy, while I understand you need to discuss this with your coaches, keep this situation solely to them."

"Sure, but you know the media will pick up on this sooner or later."

"That's true but nothing has been finalized as of yet. When the time comes, we'll have a press conference to discuss it."

When Buddy got back to his office he sat at his desk pondering the situation. For the first time in his tenure at Althaia he was under the gun to produce a competitive team. When he took the job several years ago, he took it because he loved the game. He loved mentoring young men. Now, if he failed to turn the team around in one year, the Althaia football program, as well as his coaching days, would come to an end. Buddy was going to do whatever it took to prevent those things from happening.

Mark Beheran was able to help by adding money to the recruitment budget. With the additional funding, Coach Ringle and his assistants were able to land four mid-grade high school seniors to commit to Althaia. The recruits weren't mentioned in any national publication of the top players in the country, but they were a step above the players that had been recruited in previous years.

On August 15th, the official announcement came from the league office. A new competitive standard policy was going to be enforced.

Brandon's second season started out like the previous year. The team beat Villanova on the road and Akron at home. In his first two games Brandon had over 600 yards rushing. He scored seven touchdowns which led the NCAA. People again had begun to take notice of the Althaia football team and in particular, Brandon Leshing. The biggest test on how much the team had improved was the next game against Penn State at Beaver Stadium.

While Althaia had trouble getting 20,000 fans at their home games, Penn State easily sold out every home game with over 100,000 people in attendance. Pat and Cindy were able to secure two seats for the game. Though they were high up in the crowd, they had a good view of the field. Both brought binoculars to help focus their sights on their son. However neither had brought ear plugs to drown out the sounds of the home crowd. "My goodness Pat, look at all of these people. I've never seen such a sight. I can hardly hear myself think with all of the noise."

"Cindy, this is what a real college football school is like. They have more student body in the stands than Althaia has in their entire stadium."

"And the way they sing all together like that. We are! Penn State! That is amazing. I wonder how they learned to do that."

"I just hope our guys can give Penn State a better game than last year."

As the players lined up for the initial kickoff, the fans began to hush. As the Penn State kicker approached the football, the crowd noise built up to a crescendo as the kicker pounded the football out of the end zone. Unlike last year, when Althaia could not move the ball, they were able to drive their opening possession to the Penn State 24 yard line where it was fourth down and six yards to go for the first. Brandon led the way with five carries for 22 yards. Coach Ringle sent out the field goal unit to try for a 41 yard kick. However, the kick went wide right and Penn State took possession of the ball.

Penn State drove the ball down to Althaia's 17 yard line when the Lions' kicker trotted out to the field and nailed a 34 yard field goal to give Penn State a 3 to 0 lead mid-way through the first quarter.

The game continued to be much more competitive than the previous year. With a little over three minutes remaining in the first half, Penn State held a 6 to 0 lead when the Penn State quarterback threw an interception. The newly recruited Althaia safety returned the ball to the Penn State 19 yard line. Six plays later, Brandon took a handoff and carried two Penn State defenders into the end zone to give Althaia a 7 to 6 lead. The Penn State crowd which had expected another usual blowout had quieted down significantly.

With the opening possession in the second half, Penn State took nine plays to score a touchdown for a 13 to 7 lead. Althaia's offense continued to struggle, but their defense held tight and the third quarter ended with no additional points put on the scoreboard.

Midway through the fourth quarter, down 16 to 7, Althaia took possession of the football at their forty yard line. Althaia had done virtually nothing on offense all day except turning a Penn State interception into a touchdown. Brandon had carried the ball 27 times for 81 yards as the Penn State defense had been keying on him throughout the game. It was obvious that if the play calling had continued, Althaia would be hard pressed to score again.

Desperate for any spark to ignite the offense, Althaia's offensive coordinator suggested to Brandon that since every Penn State defender had been keying on him, that it might be time for a little trickery. "Brandon what do you think of a halfback option pass? Do you think you can set up and hit Williams down field on a hitch and go route?"

"I'm all for it coach. We did the same thing in high school and it worked pretty well."

"All right, first play from scrimmage I want the half back swing right option hitch and go."

When the ball was snapped, Brandon took the pitch from the quarterback. Ernie Williams, the speedy new recruit from Miami sprinted down field. Penn State's defensive back had his focus on Brandon and came up to try to make a tackle. That was when Ernie sped past him down field and was wide open. Ernie caught Brandon's pass and sprinted the remaining 35 yards into the end zone. With the extra point kick, Althaia now trailed by only two points. The Nittany Lion crowd again became anxious with the score so close with over six minutes left in the game.

"Cindy, Brandon is playing so great today! It's a shame that kicker missed that first field goal or we would be winning right now. Wait until I tell the guys at work about that pass Brandon threw for a touchdown. He's carrying that team out there. They really have a chance to win this game."

"Pat the whole team is playing well. The defense is doing great. I really hope they win but no matter what I'm so proud of them. They are doing a lot better than last year."

As well as Althaia had played, they couldn't muster up enough offense to score any more points. The final score was Penn State 16, Althaia 14. Even though they had lost the game, Coach Ringle felt real good about his team. They had played well and if they continued to play this well throughout the season, they were certain to be competitive in league play.

Althaia started league play at home against West Virginia. The Las Vegas odds had the Mountaineers as a three point favorite to win the game. However, the smart money was on Althaia as they pounded the Mountaineers with a crushing running game, winning 24 to 10. Althaia had their first league win in almost three years.

Althaia went on to have a record of six wins and five losses. In league play, they had a losing record with three wins and four losses with one game remaining. Althaia was receiving a little national attention through Brandon, who was ranked in the top five nationally in most rushing and scoring categories.

Athletic Director Mark Beheran called Coach Ringle into his office. "Buddy, have a seat. I want to discuss the team's standing within the league."

"With a win next week we'll meet the league mandate of fielding a competitive team. Our record will be seven and five overall and four and four in the league. We've done the best we could this year Mark. Hell we may even get a Bowl game out of it."

"Buddy, you, your staff, the entire team has done a hell of a job. No one doubts the competitiveness of the team."

"Well what's the problem? I realize next week is a must win."

"It is a must win. However that may not be enough. The league mandates us to have an average of 20,000 fans. We're lucky if we can get 15,000. I don't think winning next week will be enough."

"I can't sell the tickets. I can only coach the team. Talk to the Marketing department. Oh, that's right we don't have a marketing department."

"Buddy, you know how the budget is at this school. You knew it coming in, and you know it now. Most of the students, faculty, and alumni couldn't care less if we had a football team."

"That's not my problem Mark. I'm getting mixed signals here. At the beginning of the year you were practically crying to me that the program is on the outs. Now I get the feeling you're one of the faculty that couldn't care less."

"I'll be honest with you Buddy. Sometimes this team is more of a headache to me than it's worth. I get calls all the time asking why we have a team. People ask why isn't the money, the little money we do spend on the program, spent on better lab facilities, or building up the school library, or used to sponsor more students. When I came to you at the beginning of the year no one thought the team would be doing this well."

"So what do you want me to do now? Throw the game Saturday so you don't have to fight for the program?"

"The league will hold its annual meeting next month. My true feelings about the program are that I would like it to stay. But I'm in the minority on that, both within the league and even here among the faculty and alumni. I've seen how hard you, your staff and the players worked this season."

"It's nice to know you don't want me to throw the game."

"On the contrary, I want you to kick ass Saturday. I *need* you to kick ass. I need you to win big and I need Leshing to have a big part in the win."

"We're certainly going to try, but I can't guarantee a big win like that. South Florida isn't coming up here just to lie down."

"No, but hear me out. Even if you're up 20 with a minute to go, I need you to keep your foot on the pedal. You can't take Leshing out of the game."

"What do you mean?"

"Look, the record is what it is if you win. You certainly put a competitive team out on the field. But we would need over 100,000 people to show up to get our average attendance up to meet the guideline that's been set. We both know that isn't happening."

"Like I said, I don't sell the tickets."

"I know, but you do control the team's play. The one selling point I can make to the league is the Leshing kid. He's one of the top five backs in the entire NCAA. If he has a major game where he can run for a couple hundred yards and score a few touchdowns, that might put him in the top three. I can sell him to the league. In fact I may be able to get some support to market him next year. At the very least market him on a local level, and then build him up throughout the league. Hell, with is stats, I can make a case for him to be a Heisman candidate."

"Ok, I see your point. But I can't promise anything. South Florida isn't coming here just to watch the kid run. They're going to key on him the whole game. And their defense isn't too shabby."

"Well, here it is. You get your team to win, get the Leshing kid to score big, and I'll sell him as best as I can to the league. If they see things our way it will be almost impossible for them not to give us another year or two."

Leading up to the final regular season game Buddy felt anxious as he had ever felt since his days at Georgia. When game time finally arrived, the pre-game speech Buddy had written was thrown away. This one was from the heart. He knew, the coaches knew, the players knew, losing this game meant a probable end to Althaia football. When the speech was over, the team jumped up ready to head out to the field. As the players passed, Buddy pulled Brandon aside. "How are you feeling today son?"

"I feel great Coach. I'm ready to give it my all."

"That's good. I've never asked this of any player in all of my years of coaching. But today I'm gonna ask it. Brandon I need you to be special out there today. I don't mean just play to win. I mean I need you to play big. I need a big game out of you. Do you understand?"

"Sure Coach, I understand."

The game was played before a crowd of a little more than 26,000 people. The attendance was above the average set by the league, but for the season it wasn't enough to qualify. Pat and Cindy were in their usual fifty yard line seats ready to watch their son play what may be, his final game for Althaia.

"Cindy, if the team can pull this one off, they qualify for a Bowl game."

"What's a Bowl game?"

"It's a prize for having a good season. The team will get invited to play one more game. The school gets money for having played the game, and the students get some gift packages."

"That sounds so nice. They deserve it. They played so hard this year."

"The best part is that the Bowl game will be televised nationally. That means NFL coaches will see Brandon play. And, if he plays well, which he always does, it could be the start of his NFL career."

"Start of an NFL career? Brandon has two more years of college."

"Don't be so sure Cindy. A lot of players leave of school early. Then, while getting paid to play football, they come back to graduate."

"Patrick, don't start with this pro football stuff. Let our son enjoy college while he's here."

"I'm not starting anything. I'm just talking, just thinking of his future."

"Yes Pat *his* future, not yours, not ours, *his* future."

The game with South Florida didn't start off too well for Althaia. With their first possession South Florida took the ball and drove down for a field goal for an early 3 to 0 lead. To make matters worse, Althaia's quarterback fumbled the ball to give South Florida possession right back. Once again, the Althaia defense held South Florida to another field goal making the score 6 to 0.

Althaia quickly gained momentum when Brandon took a swing pass to the left side and ran 68 yards for a touchdown. The crowd was back in the game with Pat and Cindy leading the cheers. On South Florida's next possession, Althaia's safety intercepted a pass. Six plays later, Brandon scored his second touchdown. Althaia took a 14 to 6 lead heading into halftime.

As the players and coaches made their way to the locker room, Coach Ringle was met by Mark Beheran. "Nice comeback out there. I was beginning to think I wouldn't have a chance keeping the team in the league. I knew Leshing wouldn't let us down, and our defense has really stepped up their game. Now, we need to finish strong. You know what we discussed in my office. This win has to be impressive and we need Leshing to lead the way."

"Mark, their defense is focusing on him. I can only call the plays. I can't do the blocking myself."

"Think of something. The future of Althaia football is at stake. Your coaching career is at stake."

"Hey! Let's get one thing straight. I'm not doing this for my sake. I'll be just fine. But I damn well don't want to see an end to this program. Not now. Not while we are coming around."

"Then, let's get this thing done!"

In their first possession to start the second half, Althaia took the ball and drove to the South Florida 42 yard line. It was fourth down and two yards to go. Normally, with the lead, and the defense playing well, any coach would punt the ball and let the defense take over. But Buddy kept thinking about what

Mark had said. He needed Althaia to not just win, but win big. Coach Ringle called a timeout.

Buddy told the team that they needed to go for the first down. He needed the team to take any hope of winning that South Florida had, out of the game out. He asked his offensive coordinator, Jim Rotterdam, to come up with the best way to get the two yards needed. "Coach, I really think we should punt here. We're taking a big risk going for it, if we don't make it…"

"I don't want to hear us not making it! Come up with something that will get us those yards!"

With no choice but to design a play, Jim knew the South Florida team would have at least two, maybe three defenders keying solely on Leshing. He decided to run a fake right to Brandon, and have the quarterback sprint left for an option pass. Buddy's gamble paid off. Althaia was able to gain the two yards for the first down and eight plays later, Brandon scored his third touchdown of the game giving Althaia a 21 to 6 lead. Just as Buddy predicted, South Florida lost their will to compete.

With just over a minute left in the game, Althaia was leading 35 to 6. Brandon had scored all five touchdowns and had over 200 yards rushing. When Althaia got the ball back one last time, everyone expected Coach Ringle to take the starters, including Brandon, out of the game. But Buddy was reminded of the words Mark Beheran had said. *Even if you up big with a minute left to play, keep your foot on the pedal.* Coach Ringle kept Brandon and the rest of the starters in the game. This was surprising to everyone, especially the South Florida coaches who had taken his first unit out of the game.

Even Offensive Coordinator, Jim Rotterdam was surprised by Buddy's decision. In all of the years he had known Buddy, he was never a man to run up the score. Once the game was in hand, Buddy had always taken the foot off the gas in respect to the opposing coach. Not that there were many times this had happened at Althaia, but at other schools, this was Buddy's way. He never embarrassed the opposing team. "Buddy, why not take the first unit out, especially Leshing? I'm sure he's had enough."

"Not now Jim. And I need you to keep feeding him the ball."

"Buddy, why?"

"Just do it! I'll explain later."

"Ok, but those South Florida coaches aren't going to forget this."

"I can't worry about them right now. Just do as I say."

The next several plays were all designed for Brandon. With South Florida's second and third string units going up against Althaia's starting unit, Althaia drove down to the South Florida 13 yard line. There were less than ten seconds left in the game when Buddy called a time out. Everyone was stunned, the South Florida coaches were livid. Buddy called a play to give the ball to Leshing one last time. Sure enough, he scored his sixth touchdown, the most touchdowns he had scored in any game in his life.

People were stunned at how disrespectful Coach Ringle was to rub it in on the South Florida team. Pat though, was ecstatic, *six touchdowns!* People at work would be amazed at his son's performance. Pat's prediction that Brandon would turn Althaia into winners was coming true.

When the coaches came out onto the field to shake hands, the South Florida coach refused to shake Buddy's hand. All he said was – "I'll remember this" - and ran off the field. Buddy wanted a chance to explain his actions to the South Florida coaches. But he couldn't and he felt bad about it.

Heading into the locker room, Buddy was met by Mark Beheran. "Great job Buddy! A great win! A great day for Leshing! This really gives me something to defend our right to stay in the league."

"Yeah, well, I know one school that won't support your petition."

"Don't worry about that, I'll handle the South Florida AD."

In the locker room Coach Ringle told his players how much he appreciated their effort throughout the season. He told them how proud he was for turning the team from perennial losers into winners. Buddy pulled Brandon aside and expressed his appreciation. He knew that without Brandon, the football program would be done for good.

After today's effort, Brandon finished the season third in the NCAA in scoring, and fourth in rushing. Never before had an Althaia running back finished in the top twenty.

Two weeks later, Mark Beheran called Coach Ringle into his office. "Buddy, I wanted to tell you first of the great news I just received."

"What is it Mark, are we staying in the league?"

"It took some persuading, but yes we are! Going into the league meeting I was certain that we had earned the right to stay. Initially, the league had actually decided to drop us. You were right, the South Florida AD pretty much headed up a sub-committee to cut us off. They argued that one year with a .500 record in the league after so many years of futility wasn't enough to guarantee our stay. The attendance was well under the league minimum as well."

"So how did you convince the league to keep us?"

"Leshing. I convinced the league that we had a legitimate Heisman candidate to market. He's only a sophomore and he's third in the NCAA in scoring, and fourth in rushing. With one more game to play, he has a chance of leading the NCAA. No one has ever done that as a sophomore."

"Ok, he had a great year. How does that help us to stay in the league?"

"Don't you get it? This kid is a marketing giant! I promised the league that we would do everything in our power to market him as a legitimate Heisman Trophy candidate. I promised that we would spend money to create a marketing team specifically for Leshing. With the marketing exposure as the local kid from the small school going for a Heisman Trophy, he will draw enough people to the games that our 20,000 attendance criteria will seem tiny in comparison to the number of fans who show up. The league has never had a

Heisman trophy winner. Leshing's Heisman campaign means exposure for the entire league."

"I don't know Mark. The kid is a hell of a player. But he isn't one for publicity. In fact, one of the promises I made to him was that he wouldn't have to do interviews. Now you want to explicitly market him nationally? He won't go for it, and you and I can't make him do it."

"Buddy, this is a once in a lifetime opportunity. If we get the national exposure that I think we can get, that means better players for you. It makes your job easier. It keeps Althaia football on the map. And it will be good for the kid when the NFL draft comes. If we market this right, and the kid plays well enough, he may be a top five pick after his junior year."

"I just don't know Mark."

"What don't you know Buddy? This is an opportunity for all of us. What's not to like?"

"The kid isn't going to like it. It's not in his DNA to market himself. He's a quiet kid who likes to play football that's all."

"Buddy, I'm not asking him to go on tour. All I'm asking is that the kid take some photos, and do some interviews. If it gets in the way of his practice, we'll pull back the reigns. Talk to him. You get along with him. Explain how this is bigger than himself. This is the Althaia football program he's saving."

"I'll talk to him but I'm not guaranteeing anything."

"You talk to the kid. I'll talk to his parents. If you can't make him see the light, maybe his parents can."

"I'll see what I can do." As Buddy was about to leave he realized something. "Hey, you mentioned that he has one more game left."

"I almost forgot. That's the other great news. We've been asked to go to the Alamo Bowl in Texas on January 1st. We made it to a New Year's Day Bowl game! We'll be on national television."

"*That's* something I can tell Leshing and the team. Who do we play?"

"It isn't official, but we will probably be playing Nebraska."

Buddy called his players into the team's conference room. Though Althaia's acceptance wasn't official, most, if not all of the players already knew what Coach Ringle's announcement would be. When the team was told that they would be heading to Texas to New Year's Day Bowl game, everyone yelled with joy. After the meeting Buddy spoke to Brandon privately. "Brandon, can I have a minute?"

"Sure Coach, what's up?"

"First, I wanted to tell you how proud I am of the season you've had."

"Thanks Coach, but as you said, football is a team game."

"It is. It is. I wanted to talk to you about next season."

"Already?"

"Never in the history of Althaia football, has any player had as much success as you have had this season. But, that success brings exposure, the kind

Althaia has never seen before. As well as you have played this year you may be looked upon as a possible Heisman Trophy candidate next season."

"If that happens, great Coach, but I'm not concerned with that stuff."

"I know personal glory isn't why you play. As well of a player that you are, it's hard to fathom the fact that you aren't interested in that stuff. Unfortunately, like it or not, next year will bring a lot of attention to yourself."

"What do you mean?"

"Even with our record this year, and getting a Bowl game, the league had intentions of dropping us next year. But, the Athletic Director was able to convince the league that we were worth keeping."

"I knew there was a chance that we would be dropped, but I thought since we had a good year that wouldn't be an issue."

"There were other factors in determining which teams would remain in the league, but that's not important. What is important is that we have been given a reprieve to stay for at least two more years. The reason we were given that reprieve is mainly due to you."

"How do you mean?"

"With your talent the school has told the league that we would build a marketing campaign around you to drum up fan interest."

"What kind of marketing campaign?"

"The school would probably have some photo shoots to place in papers and magazines. Along with those photos your statistics, and a bio of yourself. Now I know you are a private person."

"Yeah Coach, can't they just take photos here and send them out?"

"I'm afraid not. The worst part is that you will probably be expected to do some interviews to talk about yourself."

"Coach, you promised I would never have to do interviews."

"I know I promised, and that's why I'm talking to you now before anyone else approached you. I feel awful about this. But I don't think I can control it. When you signed to play here, the program wasn't on anyone's priority list. A lot of people wouldn't have minded to see the football program fold. However things have changed. Some restrictions have been applied. And now, the team, the program needs your help to keep afloat."

The last thing Brandon wanted was to be a public figure. He thought of the last interview and the questions about his childhood. He remembered how hard it was to avoid the one subject that made him who he was today. But he felt he had no choice. He finally concluded that he had to perform the interviews he had dreaded. "Ok Coach. How many interviews do I have to do? How often do I have to do them?"

"Brandon, honestly, I'm not sure. I will promise this, and this I will keep. Anytime anyone asks to do an interview, they will have to go through me. Even if the A. D. himself asks you to do some type of publicity stunt, he will have to clear it with me. This way you and I can discuss when and where it will take place. If you are dead set against an interview, I promise to do my best to get you out of it. I won't be able to get you out of all of them, but I'll try my best to work with you."

"Ok Coach, that's fair. One thing though, school work still comes first. That still holds true."

"That's fair enough."

When Coach Ringle met with Mark Beheran, Buddy set the terms. "Mark, the kid agreed to go along with the marketing campaign, but to a point. For starters, no publicity stunt interferes with his school work, or the team."

"Ok, we can work around his schedule as best we can."

"No, not as best you can, you *will* work around his schedule. Second, any interview he is asked to give comes through me. No one goes directly to him, including you."

"I can work with that, but I can't control the media. I, or you can't be his shield twenty-four seven. There will be times when someone I'm not aware of asks for an interview."

"For those times his response is to have the person clear it with me."

When Pat heard about the team's acceptance to the Alamo Bowl, he immediately called his son. "Brandon, I just heard the great news, Texas! That's fantastic! This is so exciting, and to play on New Year's Day in front of a national audience. You must be bursting! I knew you could turn that team into winners. I thought it would take until your senior year, but in two years! Brandon I'm so proud of you. You're all everyone talks about at work. I have senior directors coming to me to ask about you."

"Thanks dad I meant to tell you as soon as I had heard, but I had some things I needed to work on before I called. How about if I stop by for dinner sometime this week? Is Friday good?"

"Brandon, any time you want to stop by is fine with us. Friday is even better. It will give me a chance to clear up some things at work and head out early. I'll ask your mom to whip up something special to celebrate. Or better yet, why don't we head out for dinner? This is, after all, a special occasion. Plus, we don't get to see you as much with you in college."

"I'd rather just stay at home if that's Ok. Plus I have some other news to tell you as well."

"It doesn't have to do with some pro scouts asking about you is it?"

"No dad nothing like that, but you'll be happy to hear it. I'll tell you about it on Friday."

"Brandon, I'm already looking forward to it. I'll see you on Friday."

When Brandon hung up the phone, he wasn't lying when he said his dad would be happy to hear the news. He was going to tell his parents about the promotional campaign that the school had planned for next year. Brandon was already dreading the year to come.

170

Pat and Cindy were given four tickets to the New Year's Day Bowl game, plus airfare, and two hotel rooms courtesy of Althaia. Naturally Pat and Cindy would take up two of the packages. The question was who would take up the other two? They did have a few friends and relatives that Pat could give the tickets. But Pat thought that this would be a great way to make him ingratiated with the senior directors at Universal Cable. "Jim, I have two extra packages for the Alamo Bowl. It includes two tickets to the game, airfare, hotel room, and meals. How would you like to go with me to watch Brandon's game?"

"Pat, that sounds great. I appreciate the offer. Unfortunately, neither I nor anyone here can accept those tickets. It's a company policy. Any gifts must be within a total of $50.00 in value, any gift more than that must be approved by the board."

"I can't give anyone in the office a package to the Bowl game?"

"Not without approval from the board."

"How do I get approval?"

"I'll send you the forms to fill out."

Pat filled out the forms and sent them to the compliance department. Within two days he received his answer. As a middle manager, he could not give the package to anyone that he managed. He also could not give the package to anyone who was within his managerial hierarchy. If he did, it could compromise any opinions or year-end ratings that he would perform, or receive. However, he could set up a lottery that anyone may enter to win the package.

The news was disappointing at first, but after thinking about it, Pat relished the opportunity to advertise that his son had turned Althaia into a Bowl eligible team. He sent out e-mails to everyone within the company that he was going to have a raffle to give away a package to go to Texas with him and his wife to watch his son play in the Alamo Bowl. There were thousands of people who worked at Universal Cable. He couldn't wait to hear the responses. Plus, Brandon was coming home for dinner to tell him some more great news. It was a banner day for Pat Leshing.

When Brandon walked into the house, carrying two bags of laundry, his mother ran up to greet him. "Well, well, look who it is. It's nice to finally see you Brandon. Here, let me take those. I take it those aren't big presents for your dear old mom."

"Hi mom, it's nice to see you too. No, I'm afraid those are the clothes that I haven't had a chance to wash. I was hoping that since I'm home, maybe I could get some laundry done."

"And by 'I' you mean 'me' I guess?"

"Well, I was hoping…."

Cindy laughed. "Brandon, I'm never too old to do my son's laundry. I'll take these down stairs."

"I'll take them down mom. Is dad home yet?"

"No, but he did call. He should be home in about an hour. It will give us a chance to catch up. I don't hear from you as much as I would like."

"I know mom, with football and school being really hard this year, I don't have much free time. This year has been science, math and computer classes. There just aren't enough hours in the day it seems."

"I hope there are some hours where you can socialize. I'm still waiting for you to bring home a special girl for me to meet." Cindy could tell her son was embarrassed so she switched topics. "Your father and I are really proud of you. Your father constantly talks to anyone who will listen about your football."

"I know he does."

Cindy noticed some discomfort in her son. "Your father tells me you have some great news."

"I do. At least dad will think it is great news."

"You want to talk about it before your father gets home?"

"Well, I really had a good year with football."

"I know. It isn't just your father talking. A lot of people have noticed how well you've played."

"Yes, well, the Athletic Director, he kind of made some promises to the league we're in. Because the team hasn't done so well in the past, and because we don't get a lot of fans to the game, the league was considering dropping us."

"What would happen to the team?"

"Althaia would have dropped football altogether. But that's not going to happen. The league is keeping us for another two years."

"That's great. Was that the news you wanted to tell us?"

"No, not exactly, the reason the league is keeping us is because the Athletic Director told them that he will create a marketing campaign to try and sell me as a Heisman candidate. That would give the team and the league a lot of exposure"

"And you're not exactly happy with this marketing campaign I take it."

"No, not really, I'm just not comfortable with that kind of stuff."

"Did you tell this to the Athletic Director?"

"I didn't tell him anything. I talked to Coach about it. He's the one who told me."

"What did you tell your coach?"

"What could I tell him? The Athletic Director already promised the league he would do the campaign. If he didn't it might mean the end of Althaia football. I would feel bad if football was dropped knowing that I could have done something about it."

"If you don't want to do it you could have said no. At the very least this Athletic Director should have asked you before making such a promise."

"There's nothing I can do about it now. I just hope it doesn't get too crazy."

"Brandon even if you *think* it's getting crazy you need to speak up. You didn't choose to go to Althaia to save their football team. You chose to go there for the education. It's not your job to save the football program. I know you try to do everything for everybody but sometimes you have to say no."

"I know mom but if I say no, I'll be letting a lot of people down. Anyway, that's the news. I'm officially a Heisman Trophy candidate."

"I hope you won't get mad at me for asking, but, what's a Heisman Trophy candidate?"

Brandon smiled knowing that no matter how people viewed him, his mother would always see him as her son. That was comforting to know since most people saw him as a successful college football player on his way to making it to the pros. "The Heisman Trophy is an award given to the best player in college football."

"I knew you had played well, but the best in college football? Whether you like it or not, that sounds very prestigious. Congratulations."

"Thanks mom but I haven't actually won it. The school just wants to run a campaign showcasing me so I have a better chance to win it."

"I can see why you think your father will think this is great news. He is going to flip over this."

When Pat had walked in Cindy was setting the dinner table. "Is Brandon home yet?"

"He's upstairs. I'm putting the dinner out now. You made perfect timing. Why don't you call Brandon down to eat?"

Pat still worked late hours a lot and Brandon was seldom home from school so this was a rare treat for Cindy to have her men home for supper. Pat was happy to have a rare face to face conversation with his son. "Brandon you know the school gave us four tickets to the Alamo Bowl. It includes air fare, hotel stay and all. I'm so excited to watch you play in your first Bowl game on national television! You must be really excited?"

"I am. The team played great this year. This is the first Bowl game in a long time for Althaia."

"I knew you would turn that school into winners. When people at work asked why Althaia, that's what I told them. They didn't believe me but now look. Heck, I wasn't even on board at first, but boy was I wrong. I'm so proud of you son."

"Thanks dad."

"I didn't even tell you the best part about the tickets. I wanted to give two of them to one of my bosses. You know, try and grease the wheel. But they have some rules at work and I couldn't give them to anyone. Universal did allow me to set up a raffle. This will give everyone a chance to win them. I was disappointed at first. I wanted to give them to someone who could, you know, do me a favor in return, but..."

"Maybe that's why they don't allow things like that Pat."

"Yes dear, of course. This raffle is a mixed blessing. For the raffle I sent an e-mail to all of our employees. Now anyone who thought – "I wonder if that Pat Leshing guy is related to Brandon Leshing" - will know for sure. There's not a person in the company who doesn't know who you are. Of course with my luck the winner will be the person who scrubs the toilets."

"Patrick! Sometimes you can be so insensitive. What if it is the person who cleans the bathrooms? I for one will be happy to have him or her on the trip. It would be better than one of those high nosed suits you're always trying to impress. At least I know that person would appreciate it."

"Oh Cindy you know I'm just joking."

"It didn't sound as if you were joking."

"Anyway, I sent the e-mail out today. I bet I'll have over 500 responses by Monday morning. Say, you said you had some great news to tell us. Well? Let's hear it."

Brandon gave a quick glance to his mom before responding. "Well dad there was a chance that the football team would have been dropped from the league because of some new league rules."

"I had heard about that. But the league won't drop you now, right?"

"No the Athletic Director was able to change their minds. He promised to come up with a way to help draw fans to the game."

"What's that?"

"The school is going to create a marketing campaign to help me become a Heisman candidate next year."

Pat dropped his fork, his mouth wide open and full of food. He was stunned and had to let the news sink in. "Are you kidding me? Can this day *get* any better? Cindy did you hear? My son is going to be a Heisman candidate!"

"Yes Pat, I heard. *Our* son is going to be a Heisman Candidate."

"My son is a Heisman Trophy candidate! And in his junior year to boot! This is the greatest day of my life! First we get to go to the Alamo Bowl on New Year's Day to watch you play on national television. Then we get two extra tickets to raffle off at work which means *everyone* at work will know me. Now you tell me the school is going to set up a marketing campaign to help you win the Heisman Trophy. I, I don't know what to say son, except congratulations! What kind of campaign are they setting up?"

"They haven't told me anything yet. I imagine they'll have me doing interviews with newspapers and magazines, maybe television. They promised it wouldn't interfere with school work."

"Do you think they would want to have your mom and I do some interviews? Can you see that Cindy? Me and you interviewed in some newspaper? Or even better, an interview on TV?"

"Pat, they aren't marketing us, it's for Brandon. As he said his schoolwork comes first."

Cindy was speaking but Pat was far away. "Maybe we'll be on ESPN."

Pat couldn't wait until Monday to see all of the responses to his raffle e-mail. So he went into work on Saturday to see if anyone had responded. To his disappointment only two people had replied that they would like to enter. Pat had no idea who either person was. Lying in bed that night Pat couldn't believe only two people had wanted to participate. "Pat its Saturday. The weather is beautiful so I bet no one has had a chance to read the e-mail yet."

Monday morning Larry Minkoff walked up to Judy Reinhardt, Pat's secretary. "Did you see the e-mail about the raffle Pat's going to have?"

"Of course, everyone's seen it. He sent it to the entire company."

"And it isn't, *win free tickets to Texas to watch the Alamo Bowl*. Its *win free tickets to see my son*. Don't get me wrong. I've seen the kid play and he is one hell of a player. I still don't know why he chose Althaia. Can you imagine spending three days with that guy? Who wants to win that?"

"Not me, and lucky for me I'm a girl. I can say football isn't my thing. That way I don't hurt his feelings by not entering."

"I'm not entering either. I'll tell him my wife and I go away for the New Year's holiday."

"Honestly, Larry. I don't think too many people are going to enter the raffle. Everyone I've talked to are just like you. They get enough of the son's football talk at work. They don't want to listen to it over a three day holiday."

Pat was in his office constantly checking his e-mail. When he came out of meetings the first thing he did was rush back to his computer to check how many people had responded to his raffle. By the end of the day only 14 people had responded that they wanted to enter. The only person Pat knew was the security guard that he barely talked to on his way out of the office. At lunchtime he called his wife. "Cindy, I just don't get it. We have thousands of employees. I get 14 people who want to enter?"

"Are you sure you said the package was free?"

"Yes, it's in the e-mail. I even asked a couple people if the e-mail was clear enough. It states, two free tickets, airfare, hotel, the works. It seems everyone I've asked told me they were either going away, not interested in football, or had some party they couldn't get out of."

"Pat, it was only one day. I'm sure by the end of the week you'll have a lot more people enter."

"I guess."

By the end of the week there were a total of 22 people who entered the raffle. Of the 22 people, Pat still only knew the security guard. The e-mail stated that the raffle would go off the following Monday. When Pat thought of the idea he imagined a big conference room full of people. He imagined streamers coming down as he announced the winner on a stage. But on the day of the raffle Pat had his secretary Judy write down the 22 names and put them in a box. As she carried them into Pat's office she tried her best to contain her laughter. On one hand she felt bad for her boss who had thoughts of grandeur.

After all, Pat was a nice guy at heart. But the thought of him waiting for a small shoebox of names to pick the winner was hard to contain. "You'll have to stay with me to make this official Judy."

At this moment she couldn't help but let out a burst of laughter.

"Is something funny Judy?"

"No Pat, I had a sausage burrito and it's now coming back to bite me."

"Alright, let's get this over with. I'll hold the box, you pick the name."

Trying not to laugh, Judy reached in and picked Greg Brottum."

Pat had never heard of that name in his life. He later found out that Greg was a driver of the campus bus. With three buildings on campus, Greg had the position of driving a minivan which made stops at each building every thirty minutes transporting employees. "Please inform Mr. Brottum that he has won and set up a day and time when he can pick up his package."

"I'll do that Pat."

At home Cindy couldn't help notice that her husband seemed down. "What's wrong Pat."

"Huh? Oh, nothing, I'm just thinking of something at work."

"Pat, last week you were like a kid in a candy store alone with the doors locked. Now you look like someone stole all of your candy. What's wrong?"

"It's just that I thought there would be more people who wanted to enter the raffle. I thought it was such a great idea. But only 22 people entered. I'm wondering if people think of me as some kind of jerk or something."

"Pat, I doubt anyone thinks of you as some kind of jerk. If your bosses did, they would have fired you long ago. If one of the people you manage did they would have complained or would have asked to move to a different department. I'm sure there is a reasonable explanation why you didn't get the number of responses you expected."

"Why do you think I got so few responses?"

"For one it is on New Year's Day. Most people have already made plans. Two, I'm sure your bosses would feel that maybe there would be some reciprocation that may be expected. You said it yourself you would have liked to have given the package to someone who may help you get promoted later. I wouldn't worry about it Pat."

"You wouldn't huh?"

"No, I wouldn't worry about it. Work is work. This is going to be a fun getaway. You get to watch your son play in a Bowl game on national TV. His school work has been excellent with him getting straight A's. You have too much going on to be worried about who entered some raffle."

Pat thought about it. There *was* too much going on that was too exciting for him to worry about some stupid raffle. "You're right hun."

"I always am Pat." Cindy said with a wink.

"This time you really are. If they don't want to go to Texas on an all-expenses paid trip to see a Heisman Trophy candidate, then it's there loss. Thanks, I *am* feeling better."

Pat was back to his happy self, talking up the big game to anyone who would listen. Poor Greg Brottum, who had never met Pat before, had to listen to him throughout the plane ride to Texas. When they had landed, Pat suggested that they check in, unpack and meet for dinner. Greg politely declined saying he and his wife were going to meet a relative that they hadn't seen in years. Pat was fine with that and suggested they meet in the morning for brunch before heading off to the game. Greg and his wife agreed and then they set off to check in, unpack, and visit the relative who didn't exist.

The team had checked in earlier in the morning. Mark Beheran had already set up three interviews for Brandon. Since all interviews had to go through Coach Ringle, he was the one who told Brandon when they would take place. Brandon felt the world was beginning to close in on him. It was a matter of time before everyone knew his secrets. "Coach, why do I have to do three interviews? Can't they just all come in at the same time and I can answer them all in one shot?"

"It doesn't work like that Brandon. Although I hate this stuff as well, I do think the national television interview is important. The station from Philly is important too because it's our home. If you don't want to do the third one, I'll make something up for you."

"Ok Coach, I'll do the first two but if you can get me out of the third one, I'd prefer not to do it."

"Sure son, I'll let them know."

The first interview with the TV station went well. The questions only lasted about 20 minutes and all were focused on this year's team, the big turn-around from the prior year, and the Alamo Bowl game. The second interview wasn't as smooth and lasted over an hour. The Philadelphia reporter asked about the Althaia turnaround, Brandon's health, and the upcoming game. The reporter also remembered Brandon from high school. She knew he had won the *Philadelphia Athletic Award*, and began asking questions about Brandon's life prior to Althaia. What was his childhood like? Why had he chosen Althaia when he could have chosen a high profile school? Brandon didn't tell the reporter his real reasons. He answered that he chose Althaia for its academics and he believed in Coach Ringle. Before she could dig any deeper, Brandon politely told her that he had a team meeting and had to end the interview.

Before the Alamo Bowl game, Mark Beheran met Coach Ringle. "Buddy listen, this is the start of the campaign for Leshing's Heisman. You have to do whatever it takes for him to have a big game. I don't care if you need to feed him the ball a hundred times. He has to get noticed and this is a nationally televised game."

"Mark, I appreciate all you did to keep us in the league. Leshing will get his touches. You don't have to worry about that. But I'm playing to win. I owe it to the entire team to do what I can to get them a win. They worked too damn hard for me to throw it away for one person."

"All I'm saying, is if you have a choice, Leshing has to be the go to guy. I'm not asking you to throw the game. I'm just saying if we're close to the goal line, let Leshing take it across."

The Alamo Bowl game was a tightly fought contest through three quarters as Nebraska held a 20 to 17 lead. But after Althaia's quarterback threw an interception which was returned for a touchdown, add to it another field goal by Nebraska, Althaia fell behind early in the fourth quarter 30 to 17. Althaia was able to hold Nebraska scoreless for the remainder of the game but Althaia could only muster one more touchdown, a 37 yard run by Brandon. Althaia had lost its first Bowl game appearance in over a decade by a score of 30 to 24.

After the game Coach Ringle applauded his players for their effort. He told the players they had nothing to be ashamed of after the loss. This was the team that turned the Althaia football program around.

Most of the players dressed and went out to various clubs and parties later that night. Brandon had dinner with his parents and was introduced to Mr. and Mrs. Brottum who were lucky enough, according to Pat, to watch Brandon play. The next day Brandon went with some of his teammates to visit some of the Texas sights. Pat and Cindy planned to see some sights with the Brottum's. But Greg Brottum once again made plans to visit their imaginary relative. Cindy saw right through the lie but understood why Greg had made it up.

Brandon's sophomore football season had come to an end. He had trepidations about what was to come. What would be expected of him to help the school maintain its status in the league? How much personnel information would he have to reveal of himself? He wished he could just play football and go to school. At least for a couple months, he could drop out completely from the world around him and envelop himself in his studies.

Coach Ringle had looked back on the season with great pleasure. On the plane ride home he began to think of next year's team. With as much improvement as the team had this year, and with most of the players coming back next year, Buddy felt that with two or three blue chip recruits, next year's team could be something special. He also knew that he only had a few precious years left to coach before he would leave the game for good. He wanted to make them count.

Pat could hardly wait for the start of Brandon's junior season. Althaia would be marketing his son as the best football player in the entire nation. Pat wouldn't have to tell everyone at work about his son. Anyone who watched television, read a newspaper, or followed college sports online would know about Brandon. Perhaps someone would be interested in his thoughts about how to run the campaign. After all, it was his son they were marketing.

The next two months went by quickly for Brandon. Before he knew it, spring football practice began. Along with the practices, Mark Beheran set up a series of photo shoots, interviews, and a web site campaign.

Brandon Leshing – Althaia's Heisman Trophy candidate.

Initially, Brandon tried to get out of as many interviews as he could. But, he couldn't get out of all of them. They started with the Althaia newspaper, Althaia's web site dedicated to his Heisman candidacy. There were local newspapers, magazines and television interviews. With each passing interview Brandon became more adept at handling the questions. He became proficient at steering the questions away from himself and steering them towards the team.

Buddy worked hard recruiting talented high school players. Buddy's biggest selling point was anyone who came to Althaia would have a chance to play right away. He was able to sell the fact that the team played in a major Bowl game. Most of all, he was able to sell the fact that anyone who played at Althaia would be playing with the Heisman hopeful Brandon Leshing. The hard work and extra recruiting money paid off as Buddy had his best recruiting class ever at Althaia.

Althaia University – Junior Year

The fall of Brandon's junior season had a lot of anticipation for the Althaia football team. The team's 24th ranking in the pre-season poll was their first pre-season ranking in the school's history. Pat bought every magazine he could find that had any mention of his son. One local magazine, *Philadelphia Family Today*, conducted an interview with the entire Leshing family. The centerfold page was a picture of the Leshings with the caption – *Philadelphia's Leshing Family*. Pat bought twenty copies of the magazine. While his co-workers had family photographs on their desk, Pat had the magazine centerfold picture cut out and framed on his desk. He had another copy blown up and hung on the living room wall. Cindy thought it was very tacky to have the picture blown up and hung in the house, but she did like the aura of having the perfect family.

In all of the interviews, photo shoots, TV appearances, not one mentioned Brandon's secret. Not one went back and dug up what Brandon did to Louie. It was as if the Leshing's didn't exist prior to moving to Philadelphia. All that was mentioned was the Leshing family had moved from Virginia when Brandon was 13 years old.

Althaia's football season in Brandon's junior year started off with two easy wins against Villanova and Akron. In the two games, Brandon scored seven touchdowns and had rushed for over 500 yards. Everyone at Althaia, the fans, the players, the A.D. - Mark Beheran and especially Pat, was pleased with how the season had begun. Coach Ringle knew the season's first real test would come in the home game in week three against the team that Althaia seldom had beaten – Penn State.

Over 60,000 were on hand to watch Althaia take on the visiting Nittany Lions. Mark Beheran's vision had come to fruition thus far this season. The team had started out strong, the fan base was strong. Brandon Leshing was ranked near the top in every rushing statistic in the NCAA. At this rate Althaia wouldn't have to worry about being dropped by the league anytime soon.

Coach Ringle's vision was going to be tested. He had a returning class that had played Penn State close the previous year. He had a strong recruiting class that added strength and speed to his team. He felt that this was the year Althaia could come out on top against the Nittany Lions.

While Pat and Cindy were ecstatic over the attention that had come their way, and the fact that Brandon and the team were doing so well, they had yearned for the days when they could buy a ticket and sit in the seat of their choice. Now, they could hardly hear themselves speak. Althaia was now a big time football school.

The game started out close. Penn State had taken a lead at the end of the first quarter 10 to 7. The Penn State defenders had done a good job of containing Brandon as he had only 22 yards and one touchdown. Coach Ringle began to think the psychological advantage that Penn State had in never losing to Althaia may be a factor.

In the second quarter Althaia started to gain some momentum and the half ended tied at 17. Midway through the third quarter Althaia began to take over. With 5:45 remaining in the third quarter, and the score still tied at 17, Althaia took control of the ball at their own 13 yard line. Thirteen plays later Brandon scored on a three yard run to give Althaia their first lead in the game. The longer the game went, the stronger Brandon got, and the more tired the Penn State defense had become. Althaia, behind Brandon's powerful running, dominated the fourth quarter. They went on to win the game 31 to 20.

Althaia started the season with three wins and zero losses for the first time in over two decades. Mark Beheran brought the latest rankings to Coach Ringle. "Buddy, can you believe it? We are ranked 20th in the nation."

"The season is young Mark. We haven't played one league game yet."

"I know Buddy, but come on. You have to be impressed with the way the team is playing. And Leshing is living up to all of the Heisman expectations. Tell me, how do you feel about this team?"

"Mark, I honestly feel that this could be a special year. The kids are playing tough, smart football. Most important is that after beating Penn State, they really believe they can beat anyone. That's a feeling that's never been around here. But league play is different. I've seen a lot of teams start off great only to crash hard in league play."

"Keep the faith Buddy. I just wanted to stop by with the great news. And congratulate you on the win. The fans are showing up, we're getting national exposure, and Leshing has been really impressive. I've spoken to a few Heisman voters and they are impressed as well. Keep up the good work!"

Althaia started league play on the road against Rutgers. The Scarlet Knight squad had played in three consecutive Bowl games coming into this year. They were two and one on the year and had a twelve game winning streak at home over the last three years. The league opener was going to be a good test for the Althaia team. At least that was the way it looked coming into the game. The Vegas odds had the game as even. But Althaia took it to the Scarlet Knights right from the opening possession winning 35 to 10. Brandon Leshing rushed over 200 yards and scored three touchdowns.

The next game was at home against Syracuse. Althaia was a 17 point favorite according to the Las Vegas odds makers. Althaia had never been more than a four point favorite in any game in over seven years. Althaia's national ranking had jumped to 18th in the polls and more people had taken notice of the team. When the game began there were close to 45,000 fans in the stands. Leading the fans cheers were Pat and Cindy. Just as in high school, fans were beginning to recognize the Leshings and many stopped to congratulate them on their son's play. Some wanted to converse with them asking about how Brandon was raised to such a wonderful player and person. Many asked if Pat had played football when he was younger. Pat and Cindy greeted anyone who stopped to say hello. Pat loved the spotlight.

As for the game, Althaia could not cover the 17 point spread. But, they did win 24 to 13. With five wins and zero losses Althaia was ranked 17th in the nation. Brandon Leshing was the nation's second leading rusher and leading scorer. His Heisman Trophy campaign was coming together nicely. He was growing accustom to the interviews that Mark had set up. Brandon still didn't like talking about himself, but he always found a way to steer the interview towards the team.

The next three games for Althaia had them on the road against Cincinnati, on the road against Connecticut, followed by a home game against Louisville. Althaia had won each game with relative ease and their record improved to eight wins and zero losses. In the history of Althaia football, Althaia had never started out with eight wins and zero losses. Their national ranking jumped to 11th. There were only eight teams in all of college football who were undefeated and Althaia was one of them.

Game nine was a home game against Pittsburgh. The Panthers were ranked 19th in the nation. With two top 20 teams playing, ESPN chose this game as their *Game of the Week*. Althaia would be playing on Saturday night in front of the entire nation. Of all of the players and coaches, only Coach Ringle had ever participated in a game of this magnitude. As such, Buddy wasn't sure how the players and coaches would react to nationally televised game.

Mark Beheran was sure to not let this national exposure slip away without everyone getting to know Althaia's Heisman hopeful Brandon Leshing. Mark had made a deal with ESPN for an exclusive 15 minute interview. Brandon was billed as the player who turned the Althaia football program around. ESPN wanted the nation to get to know Brandon Leshing – off the field and personal.

Leading up to the game Brandon had become more and more nervous. Not about the game, but once he had learned of the ESPN deal, he knew this interview would be harder to steer towards the team. All he could think about was how he would tell the story of why he played football. Could he tell the nation that he only played the game because he loved the hitting, he loved the pain, he deserved the pain. Could he tell the nation why he deserved the pain? Would the nation understand?

Pat was on top of the world. He took a day off from work with the excuse that ESPN needed to do an interview with him and he needed time to prepare. When some people heard this they at first thought he was joking. Was ESPN really interested in him? Did he really need a day to prepare for answers to questions that he didn't know would be asked?

Cindy had her reasons to be nervous. Her home was going to be open to the world. It was as if she had sent out an open house invitation to the entire world to come see. Should she buy new furniture? Are the rugs Ok? What about her appearance? Should she get her hair cut? What was the latest style? Cindy had always been the quiet one. She was the listener who gave her opinion only when asked. Now, she would be front and center stage on national television.

The ESPN crew set up their equipment in the Leshing home the day before the game. The interview with the Leshing family started at 6PM. Erica Anderson, the ESPN reporter, could sense the nervousness of the family. Being a veteran reporter, Erica was able to set the family at ease. By the time the cameras were rolling, Pat, and Cindy were more relaxed. It was as if they had known Erica for years. Brandon remained nervous about what was to come.

When the cameras started rolling Erica asked if they expected such a whirlwind of attention coming into the season. Brandon and Cindy said they had no idea. Pat, on the other hand said he knew Brandon was special right from the beginning of his playing days as a kid. Brandon immediately became nervous at the mention of his childhood.

Erica picked up on Brandon's childhood and asked Brandon directly. "Did you play football at an early age? Did you have any other interests when you were younger?" Brandon didn't want to talk about his days as a child. He steered the conversation towards his time in high school. When he mentioned that his father asked him to play as a freshman.

Pat took the bait and took over the conversation. "Yes, I did start Brandon off in football. Cindy was afraid he might get hurt, but I knew he would be special. After Pat's ten minute solo act, the conversation went to Cindy to get her perspective on Brandon's football start.

As his mother spoke, Brandon again felt calm. He had successfully steered the conversation away from his childhood. Unfortunately, Erica decided to go back to his childhood and asked about other activities or sports he played as a child. *Why was this reporter so infatuated with my childhood? Did she know what I had done? She had to know what I had done. She was a reporter. I'm sure she researched my past. She knew! She knew! Now she wants me to admit what I had done in front of everyone. Why? Why is she doing this to me? I can't, I won't tell her.*

"Brandon?" Erica repeated her question.

"I played baseball. But football was my favorite sport growing up. I had a poster of Bear Bryant on my wall and I was a Redskins fan. My dad loved sports so I guess I just picked it up from him. Wouldn't you say so dad?"

183

"I've always loved sports, especially football." Pat again went on a solo act for the cameras.

After an hour of questions and answers which would be edited to meet the TV time, the interview session wrapped up. Erica thanked the Leshing family for their time and said goodbye. The camera crew took 30 minutes to clean up and leave. Brandon could finally relax. His secret was safe.

When the game started there were over 60,000 fans in attendance. No more would Mark or anyone else at Althaia, worry about maintaining an average of 20,000 fans per game. No longer would anyone have to worry about Althaia being competitive. They were participating in ESPN *Game of the Week* and had a Heisman hopeful in Brandon Leshing.

The Althaia squad showed its lack of comfort to the national spotlight. Lucky for Althaia, Pittsburgh also played nervous. The first quarter was filled with penalties, turnovers and missed opportunities by both teams. The quarter ended with the score tied at 3. In the second quarter, Althaia, again behind the power running of Brandon began to assert itself. Their first drive of the second quarter began with Brandon sweeping to the right and into the end zone for a touchdown. They took a half time lead 10 to 6 into the locker room.

Coach Ringle's halftime speech was sensational. On Althaia's first possession of the second half, they scored a touchdown. After that, Althaia never looked back taking complete control of the game and winning 27 to 13. The next poll saw Althaia rising to 8th in the nation.

Althaia's next game was against a lowly Buffalo team on the road. By the start of the fourth quarter Coach Ringle was able to play his 2nd and 3rd string players as Althaia dominated Buffalo through the first three quarters. Althaia was 10-0 on the season.

Three of the top seven teams had lost during the weekend. This meant that if Althaia could win their final game against South Florida, they would be one of only three undefeated teams in the nation since two of those teams would square off against each other in a league championship game. By winning their final game, Althaia had a legitimate case for playing in the National Championship game. Althaia rose to 5th in the rankings.

All of the South Florida Bulls coaching staff was on the field the previous year when Coach Ringle ran up the score on them. The Bulls' coaches wanted nothing more than to kill Althaia's chances of going to a National Championship game. Over half of the Bulls' players were on the field the previous year when they saw Brandon Leshing run up the score against them. They wanted nothing more than to knock him out of the game. Unknown to the Bulls' coaches, the players put together a bounty on who would be the one to take Leshing out of the game.

A new attendance record was set with over 75,000 fans coming to see Althaia's final home game of the season. In the game, the first play from scrimmage would be a prelude of things to come. Brandon took a handoff to his right and was hit hard by two Bulls defenders. But that wasn't enough. After the whistle, a third Bulls defender ran full steam and lowered his helmet into Brandon's side. It was a blatant late hit. The referees threw their flags. Players from both teams began fighting as Brandon remained on the ground trying to catch his breath. When the melee stopped, the referee had given South Florida a personal foul adding 15 yards to Brandon's modest three yard gain. Althaia trainers rushed out to see if Brandon was alright. As they came out Brandon could hear the taunting of the Bulls' players telling him to get out of the game or he would get more of the same.

Brandon had played for the pain. In his mind the punishment he took was justified. But he had never had pain like this. Just taking a breath caused him to wince. When the trainer asked if he was Ok, he said he wasn't hurt. He told the trainer that he just lost his breath and could continue playing. The trainer looked at Brandon and knew he was lying. Brandon had to come out of the game for one play. Coach Ringle asked Brandon if he was Ok to go back in and he said yes. There was nothing the trainer could do.

The game continued to be a physical battle. By half time Althaia held a slight 10 to 7 lead. In the locker room Brandon slunk to a corner with a bottle of water. He felt like he was going to either pass out from the pain, or throw up from his nauseating stomach. When the trainer came over to check on him, Brandon told her he was fine. Knowing Brandon was in pain, she asked if he wanted a pain killer. Brandon declined.

The second half was as physical as the first. Seven personal fouls were called by the time it was midway through the fourth quarter. With seven minutes to go in the game, Althaia continued to hold a slight lead 17 to 13. The hits by both teams were brutal. Every time Brandon touched the ball, and at times when he didn't, he took a hard shot to the ribs. Everyone on the South Florida team wanted to collect the bounty and knock Leshing out of the game. But every time he got hit, every time he got knocked down, Brandon got back up. After being hit by three Bulls' defenders on a play, Brandon came back to the huddle spitting blood. His teammates told him to get off the field and see the trainer. Brandon declined.

On the next play, Brandon took a handoff up the middle of the field, shook off two Bulls' defenders and ran 31 yards for a touchdown to give Althaia a lead of 24 to 13. On the Bulls' following possession, the Althaia defense was able to hold off the Bulls' drive. With 3:10 remaining in the game, Althaia took possession of the ball. All Althaia would need, is one first down to seal the victory. With a careful eye on Brandon the entire game, knowing he was hurt, the trainer suggested that Brandon come out of the game as Althaia held a big lead with little time left. Coach Ringle, not knowing just how hurt Brandon was, didn't want to leave anything to chance. If Leshing said he could play, he was going to play.

Althaia held on to the win the game. When the final whistle blew, Buddy sprinted to meet the South Florida head coach. But the Bulls' coach didn't want any part of Coach Ringle, and sprinted to his locker without as much as a handshake. Buddy did meet with a Bulls' assistant coach and begged to have the head coach contact him to explain his actions the previous year.

When Brandon heard the final whistle, he tried to get off the field as fast as he could without having to talk to anyone. However he couldn't get too far without the South Florida players stopping him to congratulate him on his play. They admired his courage.

In the locker room Coach Ringle congratulated the team on their first undefeated season in school history. They were league champions and all that awaited them was where they were going for their Bowl game. The team had done all they could to get an invitation to the National Championship game, but now that was out of their hands.

All Brandon wanted was to get a shower and head home. The good news was that he would have several weeks until the team's final game. When Coach Ringle's speech was over, Brandon tried to get his pads off. He was in so much pain that getting undressed wasn't easy.

"Leshing, let's go. I want to take a look at your ribs. I'm not taking no for an answer. Brandon didn't notice the Althaia trainer standing next to him. This time, she was in charge. This time, whatever she said goes. Brandon walked gingerly behind her heading to the trainer's table. Every player was whooping and hollering on the chance they were going to play for a National Championship. To a man, when Brandon limped in front of him heading to the table, each player quickly became quiet. Every player in that locker room knew the physical sacrifice that Brandon had made.

Being undefeated did not guarantee Althaia a spot in the National Championship game. That would be determined in a week by various computer rankings, a coach's poll, and the Associated Press poll. While many analysts, sports radio personalities, believed Althaia deserved a title shot, Althaia's chances remained slim. After winning their last game they only jumped to 4th in the rankings. The following Monday, it was official. Althaia finished third in the poll balloting and would play in the Orange Bowl against Big Ten Champion, Ohio State. Though it wasn't the BCS Championship game he wanted, Coach Ringle was ecstatic to be playing in a major BCS Bowl game. Althaia did get some good news after being rejected to play in the Championship game. Brandon was named as one of the five finalists for the Heisman Trophy.

Pat was in his glory. His son had turned a losing Althaia team into a Championship contender. His son was asked to go to New York as a finalist for the most prestigious award in college football. And Brandon had accomplished all of this as a junior. With not much more to accomplish in college football, Pat thought it may be a good time for his son to consider forgoing his senior year and declaring for the upcoming NFL draft. Pat wasn't the only one who thought it would be best that Brandon declare for the NFL. Brandon would be a first round pick which meant millions of dollars in guaranteed money. If he came back to Althaia to play his senior year and got hurt, the NFL draft pick and the guaranteed millions of dollars would all go away.

Brandon had a dilemma to think about. By declaring for the NFL now, he stood a good chance of making millions of dollars. He could contribute a great deal of money towards neurological research and thus, help keep his promise to Louie. But that also meant giving up his work. He would have to count on the work of others to come through with a cure. All of his life Brandon had sacrificed to keep his promise to Louie. All of his life he had been the one doing the work. Could he put his work aside by playing in the NFL?

Pat and Cindy had several talks with Brandon. Pat tried to persuade him to forego his senior season. Every time Pat tried to persuade him, Cindy was there to ensure that the decision was Brandon's and Brandon's alone. He decided that he would announce his decision at the Heisman ceremony. This way, he would state his intentions once for the entire nation to hear.

The five finalists for the Heisman Trophy were Brandon Leshing the only junior, and four other players who all were seniors. The Heisman ceremony was televised by ESPN. Erica Anderson who had interviewed the Leshing's in the fall prior to the Pittsburgh game, interviewed Pat and Cindy to see if they would tell her what their son's decision would be regarding entering the NFL in the spring.

Pat was more than happy to state his opinion. "Erica, Brandon hasn't told us anything officially, but he has weighed the rewards and the risks. From what we have been told, from NFL scouts, is that Brandon would most certainly be a top ten pick. I hate to say it but at this stage, it is a business now, and the rewards may be too great to pass up."

Erica went to Buddy for his opinion. "Coach Ringle, has Brandon told you anything that might be construed as making a decision?"

"Erica, he hasn't told me one way or the other. I'm just happy to be here representing Brandon on such an outstanding year and representing our Althaia football program."

The Heisman show on ESPN took a half hour to air. The decision as to who would win the trophy took less than one minute. Chris Fowler walked up to the podium and announced – "With 1,044 votes, the winner of this year's Heisman Trophy goes to…. Alabama Quarterback, Ricky Kraft."

It was revealed later that Brandon had finished second in the Heisman voting. Once the trophy was presented, Erica interviewed each Heisman finalist. When it came to Brandon, she wanted more than his reaction to the winner. "Brandon, we've just been told that you finished second in the Heisman voting.

Does this give you any incentive to want to come back to play your senior year at Althaia? Or, will you declare your eligibility for the NFL draft?"

"Erica, I wanted to wait until this moment to state my intentions for next year. I want to state it now so I won't have to answer questions about it in the upcoming months. After weighing all of my options, I have decided to come back to Althaia for my senior year."

Coach Ringle could be seen smiling from ear to ear. Cindy could be seen looking admirably at her son. Pat could be seen with a look of astonishment. Pat couldn't believe it. It was one thing to give up a chance to go to a high profile college. But it was another to give up millions of dollars to remain in school for his senior season. What did he have to prove?

Cindy, as usual, didn't see Brandon's decision from her husband's point of view. "Pat, how can you be angry with Brandon? It's his life. He doesn't owe a thing to anyone including you and me."

"Cindy, I'm not angry with Brandon. It's just that he has a real chance to make something of himself. He has a chance to be adored by millions of people. He has a chance to make millions of dollars and he is risking everything by coming back for his senior year."

"Pat, Brandon is different. You know that. He isn't looking to be adored. He isn't interested in making millions of dollars. Whatever he does, he will be fine. He's getting a top notch education for free. He is an excellent student who happens to be very good at football."

"Cindy, he can finish his degree after football. He will be in a position after a few years in the NFL to come back without any regard to his finances. If he gets hurt next year, it could all be over."

"If he continues to play as well as he has, he could win that Heisman award. Instead of being a top ten pick, he could be the number one pick."

"That's true but it's a huge risk to take when there are millions of dollars guaranteed to be picked up. There is a way we can lessen the risk."

"How is that?"

"We could take out an insurance policy."

"What do you mean?"

"We could take out a million dollar policy on Brandon, maybe more."

"You mean treat your son like a car or a house? Pat, he's your son, not some piece of property."

"Cindy listen, I'm not treating him like some piece of property. I'm looking out for his future. Let's say, God forbid, that Brandon gets hurt next year and can't play football anymore. We would then cash in and he would have money to start out after school. If he stays healthy and makes it to the NFL next year he could pay us back the premium, and all is well."

"How much would this cost us?"

"It depends on the amount we take out. It would be somewhere around forty to fifty thousand."

"Forty to fifty thousand! Pat that's not something we can just pull out of our pockets."

"We could refinance the house, or I could borrow against my 401K. Either way we get the money back in a year."

"Pat, what if Brandon doesn't want to play professional football?"

"Cindy, I can see somewhat that he would give up millions to come back for his senior year. But he isn't stupid. What choice will he have? If he stays healthy, and does become the number one pick we're talking ten million or more. No one gives up that amount of money. No doctor in the world makes that much right out of college."

"I don't know Pat. I don't want to put that much pressure on him knowing we took out a loan or refinanced our home for an insurance policy."

"Cindy, think of it this way. If Brandon hadn't received a full scholarship to school we would have had to take out some kind of loan to pay for his college tuition. We would be taking out a loan to help secure his future by sending him to college. Now we're just taking out a loan to help secure his future after he graduates."

"What you're saying does make sense. It just feels strange taking out an insurance policy on your son's health. How do you think Brandon will react knowing we bought an insurance policy on him?"

"We'll talk to him about it tomorrow. I'm sure he'll understand."

When Pat and Cindy discussed their intentions of taking out the insurance policy, Brandon suggested that they keep their money. "Dad I don't want you spending that kind of money on an insurance policy. I'll be fine. I've never been seriously hurt before and I don't plan on getting hurt next year."

"Brandon, no one plans on getting hurt. And I'm not saying you will get hurt. I just want to be sure that you are taken care of after school. I've talked to some people about this and they all agree that it is the sensible thing to do."

Brandon could see that there was no way he was going to talk his father out of buying the insurance policy. A couple weeks later, Pat had taken out a two million dollar policy.

When Pat received his complimentary four tickets to the Orange Bowl, Pat didn't offer them through a raffle within work. Instead he let Cindy choose her sister and husband to go along. Although Althaia was the talk of college football, the Cinderella Story, Althaia was a relative unknown to BCS Bowl games. Ohio State was an old guard established school that had gone to a BCS Bowl game in four of the past six years. It was also known that Althaia's star player – Brandon Leshing had suffered broken ribs and was going to play the game with special padding to help absorb the hits he would take. The day prior to the game, Las Vegas had the undefeated Althaia team as a seven point underdog against the eleven and one Ohio State Buckeyes.

The game started out as a defensive struggle. The half time score was Ohio State 13, Althaia 7. The Buckeye squad was bigger than the Althaia team and although the score was close, it appeared as if Ohio State was dominating the game. Ohio State had scored on three of the seven possessions they had in the first half. Two drives were halted by turnovers, another halted by penalties. The Althaia defense had really stopped the Buckeye offense only once.

In the second half the Ohio State offense continued their domination of the line of scrimmage, but the Buckeyes couldn't get the ball across for a touchdown. Twice the Buckeyes had to settle for field goals. The Althaia offense started to pick up steam. Rather it was more that Brandon began to get stronger as the Buckeye defense seemed to get worn down. While Ohio State kept kicking field goals, Althaia's offense was able to score two touchdowns to take a lead, 21 to 19.

Brandon's ribs were extremely sore, but he wouldn't show any sign of pain. Every time he was hit and hit hard, he got right back up. It seemed the more he got hit, the more focused, more determined he came back on the following play. The Althaia trainer was astounded at how much punishment he took as the game wore on knowing that he didn't take a single pain killing pill or injection. With less than three minutes to go in the game Althaia still held a 21 to 19 lead. But on their final possession, Ohio State was able to drive to Althaia's 32 yard line. With three seconds remaining in the game, the Ohio State kicker knocked in a 49 yard field goal to give Ohio State the 22 to 21 win.

Brandon had 26 carries for 137 yards scoring two touchdowns. Coach Ringle told his players that even though they had lost the game, they had turned the Althaia football program into champions and every player should hold their head high. The senior players had tears in their eyes knowing it was the last game they would ever play.

Coach Ringle thought how special this year's team was as they had become an undefeated league championship team for the first time in school history. He thought how special Brandon Leshing was and that he was coming back for his senior year was a gift that Buddy would never have again. He was going to lose seven starters from this year's team, but he knew he was going to have a very good sell to many highly touted high school seniors to keep the level of play at its current height. Buddy also reflected upon the fact that he too wouldn't be coaching forever. He knew next season would be his last shot at a National Championship.

Althaia Athletic Director, Mark Beheran, no longer had to sell the football program to the league. He too knew that having Leshing back for his senior year was a gift that he planned on taking full advantage. If the school was willing to create a marketing campaign for a Heisman hopeful, Mark should have no problem convincing the school to put in double the money for a Heisman front runner. After all, the money that the Althaia received from the BCS Bowl game alone was enough for the school to upgrade their science labs and library. The increase in funding also meant an increase in salary for Mark.

The one drawback from being a championship contending team was that the season was a lot longer. Normally Althaia's season was over by mid-November, thus giving the team four months until spring practice. Because they had played in the Orange Bowl, the time between seasons was only a little more than two months. Coach Ringle and his assistants had to work hard and fast to bring in high school recruits. The recruiting was easier though as Buddy now could sell the team as champions. He could sell the new training facilities. Most of all he could sell a high school senior that he would be playing along with the best player in the nation – Brandon Leshing. Buddy was able to bring in a nationally ranked top ten high school offensive lineman. He had recruited four of the top 100 nationally ranked players in the country. This had never been done before at Althaia.

In the spring of each season, Althaia played an inter-squad game called *Cherry vs. White*. It was nothing more than an exhibition pitting the Althaia offense vs. the Althaia defense. Normally only a few hundred people came to see the exhibition even though tickets were free. This year, the marketing campaign was well under way. Mark had sent out mailers, and placed ads in newspapers. He bought space on Maxim, Sports Illustrated and other magazines and web sites. He placed ads on CBS, ESPN and other networks. After a year as a Heisman finalist, Mark was going to ensure that Leshing was not forgotten by every fan, every voter in the country before his senior season even began.

However, problems began to appear. Brandon fulfilled his end when asked to save the Althaia football program. Brandon never wanted to be a marketing piece. He never wanted to be a ticket draw. He never asked to be paraded throughout the nation in interviews and media shows. All Brandon wanted was to get the education he needed to continue to fulfill his promise. When asked to do interviews, Brandon relented. He relented because he feared that the more he avoided them, the more people would want to know why.

As good of a football player that Brandon was, he was an even better student. He was ahead of the normal four year graduation rate. If he kept up the pace he was on, he would be able to graduate at the end of the summer. Being such an excellent student and that he was well ahead of the four year college term, he was presented with a rare opportunity to serve an internship at the renowned Spinal Cord research hospital – Roosevelt/Reiger Institute. The problem was that the internship would be for six weeks over the spring semester. If he accepted, it would mean that Brandon would not be able to participate in Althaia's spring football practices, including the *Cherry vs. White* game. It meant that many of the fans wanting to get their first glimpse of the Heisman front-runner would not get their chance to do so.

Mark Beheran wanted no part of Leshing missing his first chance to impress the local fans, and media. Mark has spent a lot of money advertising that this would be a great way for fans to come and see the Heisman candidate for free. Coach Ringle was also none too happy to hear of Brandon's internship opportunity. Buddy knew this would be his last chance to seriously contend for a National Championship and he wanted to do everything possible to get his team ready for fall's opener.

Brandon sat in Coach Ringle's newly built office discussing his opportunity to participate in the internship. "Coach all I asked was two stipulations. One that I not do interviews, and the second that my school work always comes before football."

"I remember. You also said you wouldn't do anything to hurt the team."

"Coach I said I wouldn't do anything to miss any games. I also said that I would try to work around the practices. Doing this internship isn't going to make me miss any games. As for the practices, I'm sorry. I can't do anything about it. Believe me I'm not doing this to get out of spring practice. And you can tell Mr. Beheran that I'm not doing this to get out of any Heisman marketing campaign."

Buddy stared into the convincing eyes of his star player. He didn't know what to say. On the one hand this was one last chance to win an NCAA Championship. Leshing was the most important piece of the team. There were a limited number of days between now and the start of the season. Buddy wanted to get the team as ready as possible. On the other hand, Buddy was sitting in a newly built office. He had his team training in a new building complete with a film room, weight room, cafeteria, and offices for each of his assistants. None of this would have been built if Leshing had not chosen Althaia. "Why is this internship so important? When you graduate you're going to be a top five pick in the NFL Draft, maybe the number one draft pick overall. You're going to make millions before even taking one snap in the NFL."

"It's important because of a promise I made a long time ago."

"You made a promise to take an internship at a research institute?"

"It's more than that Coach. It's the reason I came back for my senior year. I can't get into what the promise was or why I made it. But to me, the reasons are far more important than football. Besides, spring practice is more for the new players anyway. It's a time for you and the coaches to evaluate the team. I think you and the coaches know what kind of player I am. Do I really need the spring practice?"

On this point there was no debate. Coach Ringle and his staff knew what they had in Brandon Leshing. Buddy didn't need to have him in the backfield going through the plays he had already run hundreds of times. Besides, Buddy needed Brandon for the fall. If he got hurt while participating in the *Cherry vs. White* game or any spring practice, Buddy would never forgive himself. "Ok Brandon, you can participate in the internship. I'll keep my promise to not let football interfere with your school work. However I need a promise from you in return."

"What's that coach?"

"During this internship you keep up with your training. Come fall you are 100 percent committed to the team. We have something very special this year, something that only a few of teams truly have. It would be a shame if the one player that everyone is counting on left the team to pursue personal goals."

"That's fair coach. I promise when I come back I'll be dedicated as always to the team. I won't let you or my teammates down."

Buddy and Brandon shook hands. "What about Mr. Beheran? I'm sure he will be disappointed."

"Don't worry about him Brandon. I'll handle Mark."

"Thanks Coach."

When Buddy discussed the decision with Mark, he was not too pleased. "What do you mean you let Leshing off the team for an internship?"

"When he signed on to play here I promised that his school work would always come first."

"I made promises too. I promised thousands of fans that they would get their first free look at the next Heisman Trophy winner. I took out ads. The school spent a lot of money on this campaign."

"Did Leshing tell you to spend money on the ads? Did he tell you to come up with this Heisman campaign? Seems to me that every promise you made, you made on your own without asking the guy you're parading around."

"Hey, don't make it sound like I'm doing this all for myself. If it were up to me, things would go on as they have since you arrived. I'm doing this for the school. I'm doing this for you, to keep this football program going."

"I noticed your salary was helped as well since this campaign started."

"As well as yours Buddy."

"When this campaign started I was on board. I, like you, thought it would benefit the school by making a case to the league to keep them from dropping us. Now we don't have to worry about being dropped. The sole reason for that is Leshing. You know it and I know it. So now the kid needs to do an internship during the spring. After all he's done for the school it's the least we can do for him. Besides, I doubt I would even play him in the *Cherry vs. White* game. If I did at most it would be for two series of plays. Mark, there's nothing more to be said. I'm letting him do the internship."

Mark stood there staring right through Buddy. There was nothing he could say, nothing he could do. His campaign would have to be put on hold until the fall. The advertisements Mark paid for, stating that people would be able to get their first look at Brandon Leshing, would have to stop. He would have to explain why what was advertised was no longer true. "Ok Buddy. But we need to come out with a public statement as to why Leshing won't be playing in the *Cherry vs. White* game. If we don't say anything there's going to be a lot of angry fans. That's not the way we want to start the season."

"I can't help you with that Mark. This is where you earn your money."

A few days later, Mark came up with the perfect spin for the Heisman market campaign. "Buddy, can I meet with you and Leshing in your office tomorrow?"

"What's this about?"

"I'll fill you in when we meet. Call me back to let me know what time."

Buddy called Mark back to be in his office at 2PM. The next day, Buddy, Mark and Brandon met in the coach's office. "Ok Mark we're all here. What's this all about?"

"Brandon, Coach Ringle tells me you have accepted an internship at Roosevelt/Reiger Institute."

"That's correct. It is a great offer which I readily accepted."

"There's no way to talk you into declining the offer to get a jump on your last year of football?"

"Sir my mind is made up. This is an offer that I'll never have again in my life. I have to take it."

"Mark, we've been through this. The kid's mind is made up, he's going to take the offer and I'm willing to let him off the team to go."

"I know Buddy, but I thought I'd ask one last time. Brandon you know we've been marketing you as the face of this football program. We want you to win that Heisman trophy next year."

"I know sir. While I'm not playing to win awards, I appreciate the school backing me."

"Winning the award is good for the school too. Before you arrived, Althaia football was just an afterthought. Since you have arrived a lot of people have realized just how important a good football program can be to a school. Our enrollment numbers have gone up significantly the past couple years. It's no coincidence you've played a factor in that."

"Mark is this going anywhere? The kid's mind is made up."

"My point is, is that we have put a lot of time and money into campaigning for you to better your chance at winning the Heisman. We've put out a lot of advertising telling people that they would get their first real look at the next Heisman front runner for free at the *Cherry vs. White* game. A lot of people are going to be very disappointed."

"Mark, we've been over this. Get to the point!" Buddy didn't like the tone of Mark's voice insinuating his star player owed something to the school.

"The point is, is that we're happy to have you further your education as best as you can. What we would like to do is video some of your time that will be spent at Roosevelt/Reiger Institute. We can market you not only as a football player, but someone who really cares about his education. You're a rare breed Brandon. Most Heisman candidates are strictly football jocks. They live and breathe football. College to them is just a stepping stone to the NFL. But not you, you proved that this past winter when you decided to come back for your senior year. You're proving it once again by asking to bypass spring football in order to perform your internship. You put your education ahead of football. You are everything that NCAA Athletic Scholarships are all about. You are the true example of what it means to be a scholar athlete. We want to show the nation the complete picture of Brandon Leshing, not just the football player. We want every mother and father to think that they would want their son to grow up to be just like Brandon Leshing. And if the football season goes like we hope, you'll win the Heisman unanimously. What do you think?"

Brandon listened to everything Mark was saying. But all he really heard was that Mark wanted the nation to get to know the complete Brandon Leshing. He didn't want his teammates knowing the complete Brandon Leshing, let alone the entire nation. Brandon looked to his coach who simply looked back with his hands up. "Brandon the decision is yours. I know you don't like interviews and such. So this is completely up to you."

"Would I have to talk through the video? Would Roosevelt/Reiger Institute even allow a bunch of cameramen to follow me around?"

"No, no Brandon you wouldn't have to say anything if you don't want to. You would just go about doing whatever the people at Roosevelt/Reiger Institute asked you to do. And we would only have one camera person following you around. As for permission to do so, I will work that out with Roosevelt/Reiger. I know I'm sounding like I'm pressuring you."

"Sounding like?" Buddy reiterated.

Mark continued to focus completely on Brandon as if Buddy was just an irritating bug. "I know it sounds as if I am pressuring you but this would be good for you as well. It would be good for the school. Hell it would be good for the NCAA."

"Hell Mark, why not just throw in that it would be good for world peace?" Buddy stated.

Mark continued without even a nod towards Buddy. "There's been so much bad publicity surrounding college football. You have the issues at Ohio State, the issues at Penn State. All you hear is how college football has changed for the worse. Here's our chance to show the nation that there are good programs out there. There are colleges doing things the right way. There are people like you showing everyone that scholar athlete means just that."

Brandon let what Mark was saying, sink in. He didn't want anyone knowing Brandon Leshing. He just wanted to play football, get his education and move on. He didn't care about winning the Heisman Trophy. What did it matter anyway? He couldn't help but see that he was caught in something bigger than himself. Maybe Roosevelt/Reiger wouldn't allow a camera person to follow him around. If Roosevelt/Reiger Institute didn't allow the cameramen, he wouldn't have to be the bad guy. "If the people at the Institute say it's Ok to have someone follow me around I guess it's Ok. But I wouldn't have to do any interviews or anything like that right?"

"You have my word, no interviews. All that will happen is we video your day to day activities at the Institute."

Brandon came home from school to tell his parents the news. His father didn't like what he was hearing. "What do you mean you won't be playing spring football? What about the *Cherry vs. White* game? So many people are coming to see you play."

"It's just for the spring dad. Coach said he wouldn't have played me much in the game anyway."

"Patrick! How many times am I going to have to remind you that it's Brandon's life, not yours? If the coach is Ok with this, than there isn't any reason why you shouldn't be."

"Cindy you don't understand. This is his final year. This is the year where he has a chance to do something special. This is when he starts building up his draft status."

Brandon didn't feel like listening to NFL talk. He didn't even want to tell his parents the news because he knew how his dad would take it. But Brandon thought of a way to get his dad on board. "Dad it's just the spring practices. I'll be ready to go come fall. Besides, the Athletic Director thinks this is good for my Heisman chances."

"He does? Why does he think that?"

"He's going to have someone follow me around with a camera. He thinks this will be a great way for people to see the complete me, not just the football player. He thinks that once people see that I'm not just at school to play football, that I'm there to actually get the best education possible, they will be impressed. As long as the team keeps winning like we've done last year, this would give voters another reason to vote for me."

"So they want to do a documentary on you huh?"

"It isn't a documentary, more like a day as a college intern, instead of life on the football field."

"Yeah, Ok. I get it. There are a lot of great players in college. But throw in your exceptional grades, not to mention the types of classes that you take. Yeah, I see. Maybe he's right."

"Plus while interning, there's no chance of me getting hurt."

"Maybe this is a good thing. When does the documentary come out?"

"Dad it's not a documentary. I'm not sure what it is. I have no idea when this will come out."

It was no use. Pat was in his world where he was telling his coworkers that Althaia was making a documentary of his son. Brandon looked at his mom, who in turn just smiled back with a wink, as if to say don't mind your father.

Roosevelt/Reiger allowed Mark to have one camera person follow Brandon around but only for two days. This wasn't what Mark had hoped for but at least he would be able to showcase his Heisman hopeful in a way no other college player would. This was a big relief to Brandon who was able to put up with the camera person for two days in his six week stay. It meant that for over five weeks he had nothing to do but put his mind towards his work. He could soak up all of the knowledge he could in spinal cord research.

While interning, Brandon learned about cellular structures within the spine. He performed in-depth research of the capabilities of different substances that could be used to stimulate nerve growth. When he completed his internship, spring practice was over. During the summer, Brandon kept up his studies and continued researching what he had learned from his internship.

Mark kept up the campaign showcasing Brandon as the complete college scholar athlete. He put up a montage of football clips, highlights, and included the film conducted at Roosevelt/Reiger Institute on Althaia's web site. He sent clips of the montage to sport affiliates ESPN, CBS, as well as sport magazines and web sites dedicated towards college athletics.

Pat collected all of the film, magazine articles, newspaper clippings he could find regarding his son. He couldn't wait for fall to begin. This would be the year to remember, the year that Pat would be the envy of every coworker at Universal Cable. His son will be a Heisman Trophy winner, and an NFL first round top pick. Maybe he could be Brandon's agent. How hard could it be to negotiate an NFL contract? He knew how much previously drafted players received. Yes, this would be a great year indeed.

When the fall football season arrived Brandon was in the best shape of his life, and that was saying something. Althaia went through their non-league schedule beating Villanova, Akron and Penn State by an average of 22 points per game. Brandon racked up over 1,000 yards and scored ten touchdowns.

Althaia's league schedule was more of the same. Their home games averaged over 60,000 fans culminating in their home-coming game against Pittsburgh where the fan support was over 80,000. They ran right through the league winning every game by an average of 16 points. By season's end, Brandon Leshing led the NCAA in number of carries, yards rushed, all-purpose yards, and touchdowns scored. Althaia had come a long way since Brandon arrived. Althaia was now a national powerhouse.

When the season ended, Althaia was undefeated for the second straight year, and were ranked 2nd in the nation. But that did not guarantee an invitation to play in their first ever BCS Championship game. However all doubts were relieved when it was officially announced that they would be playing Alabama in the championship game.

After Brandon's stellar season he again was one of five finalists asked to go to New York for the unveiling of the Heisman Trophy award. This year there was little doubt that Brandon would win the award. His statistics were undeniably the best for any running back in the nation. He was one of only two finalists playing for an undefeated team. And, best of all, Mark Beheran was right about showcasing Brandon as the complete scholar athlete. Every sports media outlet in the nation talked about how every college player should emulate Brandon Leshing. Brandon was what college athletics were all about.

Everyone Brandon had come in contact with wished him good luck in the Heisman race. People whom Brandon had never met walked up to him to say 'hi' and 'good luck'. Teachers, professors, secretaries, stopped whatever they were doing to congratulate him on the wonderful year he and the team had. While everyone was happily looking forward to the Heisman presentation, Brandon was not. He always accepted anyone and everyone's well wishes. He never talked about the award himself. He never really had any close friends. Not friends he could fully confide in. He never talked about the upcoming presentation to any of his teammates, coaches, or his parents. No one really questioned Brandon's lack of talk about the award. Most knew him as an extremely private person, one who seldom if ever talked about himself. Lately he was even more withdrawn.

Pat's dream year was going just as he had imagined. Now that his son's final year of college had one game left on the season, it looked as though the money spent on his son's insurance policy would all be for naught. But Pat didn't care. It meant that his son would be a top pick by an NFL team. It meant that instead of cashing in on a two million dollar policy, his son would be receiving five times that amount in salary and endorsements. Knowing Brandon's soon to be wealth, Pat's work began to slip. The highest priority in the past had always been his work and his ability to move up the corporate ladder. That didn't seem to matter to Pat so much now.

The national Championship game wouldn't be played for several weeks. The football practices had very little hitting, they were geared towards keeping players in shape physically and mentally. The practices made sure each player knew his assignment on every play called on offense, defense and special teams. On the Friday before the Heisman presentation, the players and coaching staff threw Brandon a party. The theme was "good luck". Everyone brought in some kind of good luck charm, whether it was a bracelet, a coin, a four leaf clover. One teammate gave Brandon his lucky shirt. It was lucky for him because he was wearing the shirt the first time he had 'gotten lucky' with a girl. Brandon thanked him as another teammate shouted – "Good thing it wasn't his underwear!" This drew laughter from everyone. Brandon simply smiled.

When the party was over, and everyone had left, Coach Ringle asked Brandon. "Are you Ok son? You seem to have something on your mind. It isn't just today I've noticed. You seemed to have been in deep thought for weeks now. You're not nervous about winning the award tomorrow night are you?"

"No Coach, I'm not nervous about winning the award."

"That's good because from what I've heard you're well ahead in the voting."

"It would be nice to win the award, but if I don't it won't be the end of the world would it?"

"No I guess not. But son, let me tell you, if you don't win the award I'll personally file a protest and ask for a recount of the votes."

Brandon thanked Coach Ringle for his support on and off the football field. Brandon still had a look that something was heavily on his mind. He turned to the one person he always could turn to whenever he wanted to talk about anything personal.

Brandon arrived home just in time for dinner. After dinner, when Pat had gone into the living room to watch TV, Brandon asked his mother. "Mom, can I talk to you for a minute?"

"Brandon you can always talk to me. What do you want to talk about?"

"Now that college is almost over, I have to think about what I'm going to do next."

"We assumed, well your father assumed, that you would go onto play professional football. Your father has said, it's a pretty lucrative career."

"Yes, I know. If I play in the NFL I could make a lot of money."

"But you don't want to play in the NFL, do you?"

Brandon knew how much money his parents had spent taking out the insurance policy. "I want to continue my career in the medical field. I learned a lot while I interned. I'm considering announcing at the presentation tomorrow that I am electing to bypass the NFL altogether. The only thing is that I know dad would be really disappointed, especially with the insurance policy."

"Brandon I don't want you to ever worry about your father and me when deciding what you want to do in your life. It's your life to live. I'd rather you decide to do something that makes you happy rather than do something you will hate just to make us happy. The insurance policy was your father's decision. Besides, you've saved us a more than that by going to school for free."

"I guess. I know he will be greatly disappointed. Plus, many other people are counting on me playing in the NFL."

"Who is counting on you playing in the NFL?"

"There's the coaches, everyone I meet expects me to play. It's going to look pretty dumb for me to give up all that money don't you think?"

"Brandon it doesn't matter what anyone else thinks. You are the one who is going to have to look in the mirror and ask 'am I happy'? No one else is going to live your life but you."

"So you wouldn't be upset if I gave up millions of dollars to continue school? You wouldn't think that I'm crazy or stupid?"

"As for the millions of dollars, no, I wouldn't be upset. As for thinking you are stupid or crazy, no, I know you have your reasons. Do you want to go tell your father your decision?"

"Not right now. I think if I told him now he wouldn't be able to enjoy tomorrow's presentation. Besides, I haven't totally decided yet."

"You're still very young. You have a long life ahead of you. There are many things you can do with your life. It's up to you to decide what makes you happy."

"Thanks mom. I feel a lot better now."

"I'm glad Brandon. You can talk to me any time."

The next morning, Pat, Cindy, Brandon, Coach Ringle, and Mark Beheran rode together by way of limo from Philadelphia to New York. At noon, Brandon would have to do some press interviews. They wouldn't be anything tough, just his opinion of the other finalists, a look back at his season and career at Althaia. Pat and Cindy also had interviews, which Pat was more than happy to give. Coach Ringle had his interviews discussing his star player and the remarkable turnaround at Althaia.

The ride to New York was pleasant, filled with small talk. "Coach Ringle, congratulations on winning the *Coach of the Year Award*. It certainly was well deserved." Pat started off.

"Thank you, Pat. I would never have won it without the team's hard work, especially your son. He's certainly something special."

Brandon lifted his head briefly to acknowledge Coach's mention of him. However he hadn't said a word thus far the entire ride down. "Are you Ok son? You look a little nervous. You've been through this before. And this year, I think you are a shoe-in to win."

Before Brandon could answer, his father jumped in. "You think so Coach? Have you heard from anyone about the voting?"

Mark answered. "The votes are sealed. No one is supposed to know who has voted for whom. Of course people do talk and from what we've heard Brandon should win in a landslide. People really connected with Brandon as the true scholar athlete once they saw the film on his internship." Mark couldn't help but self-promote his campaign strategy being a major factor in the voting.

"Who actually does vote?" Pat asked.

"It's a combination of previous Heisman Trophy winners and about 145 writers in six regions across the nation that vote. There is also one vote that is made up of a fan poll."

As Mark and Pat continued their small talk, Buddy realized that Brandon wasn't right. He never did get an answer from him but he didn't want to ask again. Cindy also noticed how quiet Brandon was, and she was the only one besides her son who knew why. She turned to give Buddy a quick glance and a smile. Coach smiled in return.

When they arrived in New York's Downtown Athletic Club they were given their itinerary for the day. First, the groups, along with the other Heisman finalists were treated to a luncheon. Afterward they were given instructions on where and when they would be conducting their interviews for ESPN. They were shown a 'green room' where they could watch TV, listen to music, or whatever they needed to relax. They could also meet previous Heisman winners, all of whom would be on stage as this year's recipient received his award. At 8:00, the ceremony would start. Clips of each finalist's football exploits would be shown as Chris Berman described what each player meant to his team. The actual unveiling of the award would be announced at precisely 8:50.

As the final moment came closer, Brandon became more and more nervous. Cindy began to worry as her son seemed to turn pale and sweating more than usual. Pat shrugged it off to nerves, but Cindy knew better. Finally, at 8:50, ESPN's Chris Fowler made the announcement: "This year's Heisman Trophy winner is: Brandon Leshing, running back from Althaia University."

Though it came as no great shock, Coach Ringle, Mark Beheran, Cindy and Pat were all relived to hear Brandon's name. They all stood and clapped as Brandon walked upon the stage to accept his award. Cindy had tears in her eyes which were perfectly captured by the ESPN camera crew. Brandon walked

201

across the stage shaking hands of the previous Heisman winners. He shook Chris Fowler's hand and took hold of his award. "Brandon Leshing, congratulations on winning the Heisman Trophy. Would you like to say a few words to the audience here at the Downtown Athletic Club and the millions of college football fans watching on ESPN?"

"Thank you, Mr. Fowler." Brandon took several seconds before speaking.

"I'd like to thank first and foremost my family, my teammates, and my coaches. Without whom I would not be standing here today. I would like to thank the Downtown Athletic Club for their gracious hospitality and to those who have voted for me. I also would like to thank the Althaia fans as well as the fans across the nation."

Brandon then stood still. Chris Fowler thought Brandon was done speaking but as Chris took a step towards him, Brandon grasped the microphone. Chris stepped back to let Brandon finish his speech. Brandon looked to his mom who nodded slightly as if to say - go ahead son.

Brandon continued. "I enjoyed playing football. The game is so beautiful to play. It takes skill, speed, strength, intelligence, and team work to be successful. There are only two places I truly feel at peace, and that is when I'm involved in my studies, and when I'm on the playing field. I would like to take this time to announce", Brandon paused. "I would like to take this time to announce that I will not be entering the NFL draft this upcoming April. I will be continuing my studies in neurology."

A collective gasp for air was heard from everyone in the room. ESPN camera shots went from Brandon to his mother (who had her clasped hands at her mouth), to Pat (who looked like his eyes were about to pop out of his head), to Coach Ringle (who looked on with open mouth in amazement), back to Brandon (who for the first time all night finally looked at peace).

"The reason I am making the announcement here is that I wish to make this announcement once. I'm sure a lot, if not all of you are asking why I am giving up a career in the National Football League. First, let me say that playing in the NFL would be an honor and a privilege. However I have a personal reason why I am choosing a different path, one that I have never told anyone." Brandon paused again to collect himself.

"When I was eight years old I made a promise to my best friend." The peacefulness that Brandon had shown had disappeared. It was obvious he was trying to hold back tears. "His name was Louie Buccelli. He was the smallest kid in class, but man could he run. He was the fastest kid in the block. He was fun to be around and would always make me laugh. I remember like it was yesterday how we used to play in the neighborhood. He was like a little brother to me. He always looked up to me. Whenever anyone picked on Louie I was always there to protect him." Brandon paused. You could hear a pin drop among the crowd.

"We used to play a game called Prison Break. And when we were picking teams, I didn't pick Louie. I don't know why, but I didn't. For some reason, on that day I wasn't looking out for him." A single tear dropped from Brandon's right eye. "When it was decided that my team would run and hide and Louie's team would have to catch us, I decided to build a trap for them to fall into. When they came looking for us, Louie ran ahead of everyone. I know he wanted to prove that it didn't matter how small he was, he was going to be the one to catch us." Brandon paused again. He found it difficult to continue.

"When he came up to find us he fell right into the trap I built." Tears were streaming down Brandon's cheeks. "And when he fell, he fell right on top of a water pipe, and, and…" Brandon gulped hard. He found it difficult to breath. "And he broke his back paralyzing him." Tears were flowing from people in the crowd. Cindy especially couldn't control the streams of tears.

"At just seven years old Louie's life was over." The next words from Brandon were barely audible. "And it was my fault." Brandon gathered himself as best he could. "He spent months in the hospital until he came home right before Christmas. When I went to his house to see him he was so tiny, I couldn't believe it. Like always Louie was so positive. When I should have been the one consoling him, he was trying to make me feel better. I told him I would fix it. I told him I would help him like always, like I should have that day. I promised I would make it all better." Brandon gulped hard trying to breathe.

"But I didn't, and shortly after, Louie passed away." Now you could hear many people in the room sniffling as there was hardly a dry eye in the room. "Louie never had a chance to finish school. He never had a chance to play sports. He never had a girlfriend or drove a car or go to college. He never got to play football like I did and it's because of me." Brandon once again had to stop for several seconds.

"So tonight, I'd like to dedicate this award to Louie Buccelli. I'd also like to state that the next game I play on January 8th in the BCS Championship will be my last. I hope that people will not ask me to explain, or ask questions about the matter. I'm trying to move on with my life. Thank you."

Brandon walked off the stage straight to his mom who was waiting with open arms. Coach Ringle and Mark Beheran put their hands on Brandon's shoulder to console him. Pat realized that he was going to have to work at Universal Cable until he retired. The big company that he originally had hoped to move up the corporate ladder hadn't worked out as planned. He was still in the same boring position he had when he first took the job eight years ago. Now he realized that his son had to make his own decisions in life. If bypassing the NFL and the millions of dollars was what his son needed to do, then Pat wouldn't say anything to change it. He wrapped his arms around his wife and his son.

Leading up to the BCS Championship game all the media could talk about was the speech Brandon had given at the Heisman presentation. Some understood Brandon's reasons for not wanting to go to the NFL. Some thought he needed psychiatric help bypassing a lucrative NFL career.

When the Championship game arrived, and when reporters had come up to interview Brandon, all were adhering to his request to not ask about Louie. Most questions solely centered on the game itself. Though reporters are told to be unbiased in their rooting teams to win, everyone wished Brandon good luck and meant it.

The game was the most watched college football game in history. None of those who watched were disappointed. After a hard fought first half, Althaia went into the locker room trailing Nick Saban's Alabama team, 17 to 14. By the end of the third quarter, the deficit had grown to 27 to 21. Midway through the fourth quarter Althaia was down 34 to 21. With less than six minutes left in the game Althaia cut the deficit to six points as Brandon took a pitch left, broke two tackles and ran 22 yards for the touchdown.

On the ensuing kickoff, Althaia ran an on-side kick and recovered the ball. Althaia drove 52 yards to the two yard line. On the next play, with two seconds remaining, Brandon took a handoff and ran off the right tackle for the game tying score. The extra point kick gave Althaia a 35 to 34 win for their first National Championship in school history. Brandon Leshing was named the game's *Most Valuable Player* after rushing for 186 yards, scoring four touchdowns. It was a perfect ending to Althaia's perfect undefeated season. It was the end of Brandon Leshing's football career.

A week after that championship game, Brandon received a letter in the mail. The return address was not familiar to him. When he opened the letter he couldn't believe what he was reading. The letter was from Claire Buccelli. She wrote that she had seen him on TV giving his Heisman acceptance speech. She was asking forgiveness for how she had treated him before he had moved from Virginia. She was angry that she had lost her son, and she channeled all of that anger towards Brandon. But in her heart she had always known what had happened was an accident. She also wrote that she and her husband Dominic had moved from Virginia as well. She included a picture of their five year old daughter Louise. Claire had hoped that one day maybe they could meet and talk.

Brandon was happy to hear that Claire and Dominic had moved on with their lives. It was time that he moved onto his next phase in his life as well.

Chapter 9
CARRY ON

The autopsy report stated that Ted Stroit died as a result of a drug overdose. The official ruling was death by suicide. Months after her father's death, Gina battled the insurance company to collect the life insurance policy her father had taken out when she was born. Jennifer Manley helped Gina in any way that she could and provided her a lawyer paid for by Ted's Union. Gina assumed that Jennifer had always liked her father and that was her reason for her assistance. Unknown to Gina, the reasons were more from a feeling of guilt.

Jennifer had never intended to hurt Ted that New Year's Eve night. She started dating Roy Renstad, the man Ted saw Jennifer kissing on New Year's Eve, a few days after the November *Night at the Races* event. Jennifer had asked Ted to take her to the company Christmas dinner because she didn't want Ted to be alone during the Christmas holiday. When Ted asked Jennifer to be with him for New Year's Eve, she didn't want to go because she had already made plans with Roy. But again, Jennifer didn't want Ted to be alone. She explained the situation to Roy who said that he understood. Jennifer planned to have dinner, a couple drinks and some laughs with Ted, then after Ted was taken home, spend the rest of the night with Roy. Ted must have seen them kissing and this is what Jennifer believed drove him to his fate. With the amount of guilt that Jennifer felt, she did whatever she could to help Gina.

Gina was eventually able to collect the full amount of the insurance claim. Although there was a suicide clause in the life insurance policy, the clause was deemed void if the policy was in force for more than ten years. Ted also had insurance on the home mortgage, thus, the house was paid in full. All Gina needed to pay was the taxes and utility bills. Between the insurance policies Ted had taken out, and Ted's savings, Gina did not have any immediate financial worries and continuing her education in nursing.

The uncertainty and fear of surviving financially prior to collecting on the insurance was nothing compared to the sorrow and the emptiness Gina felt. She was now without both her mother and her father. It took her over a month before she could even step forward into her father's bedroom. She constantly kept the letter he had written just prior to his death with her.

As was the case whenever tragedy struck, Gina's neighbor, the Bachwel's were there when Gina needed anything. Julie felt more like a sister to Gina than a friend and neighbor. The only family Gina had left was her eleven year old cat, Oreo. As the summer passed, Gina knew that she had to carry on with her life. A lot of times she thought back to her father's days while he was home trying to rehabilitate. She remembered that while he was home he felt his best while Lisa had been working with him. She decided that what she wanted to do with her life was become a therapist as Lisa had been. Not so much to help people physically, though this was definitely part of her plan, but to help anyone in need emotionally as well.

In the fall she enrolled in school with the hope of becoming a nurse/therapist as well as obtaining a degree in psychology. Within two years, Gina had received her degree in nursing. After graduating she passed the National Council Licensure Examination for Registered Nurses. Shortly after passing her nursing exam, Gina took a nursing position at St. Helena's hospital. The same hospital where her father had fallen on the job. Since this was her first job in the field, she worked odd hours, sometimes ten to twelve hours per shift.

Gina didn't mind the long shifts since this was her first full-time job. She didn't have an extensive social calendar to keep. Gina always had Julie to go out with, and she had several other friends, but she didn't have a steady boyfriend. Between her work hours at St. Helena's and her studies in psychology, Gina didn't have much time for socializing. In the spring at 22 years old, Gina received her bachelor's degree in psychology.

While on the night shift at St. Helena's, there was an emergency call from an ambulance indicating that they had three patients coming in after a horrific car accident. A middle aged driver of an SUV was driving while under the influence and ran a red light, crashing into a small car that was driven by a man approximately thirty years old carrying his ten year old daughter in the passenger seat. The father of the ten year old never saw the SUV coming as the SUV blind-sided the car smashing right into the driver's side door. The man driving the SUV, and the ten year old girl were treated for minor injuries. However, the driver of the small car was unconscious and bleeding badly. Gina was one of the nurses who assisted the doctor who operated on the driver.

After three hours in the operating room, Gina and the surgeon came out of the room and were met by the driver's wife. The doctor had told her that her husband was seriously hurt. He had broken his left forearm, his left leg was broken in two places, and he suffered from a fractured hip. He also had lost a lot of blood but was brought to the hospital in time to save his life. Though her husband was listed in critical condition, he most likely would recover.

After the woman thanked the surgeon, Gina took her to her daughter's hospital room to give her the good news. Gina felt exhausted after assisting in the operating room. Seeing the ten year old girl reminded Gina of the time she got the call that her father had been injured on the job. Gina wanted to be there to ensure the little girl not to worry and answer any question she could.

This was the reason she went into the nursing profession, to help people. She had never felt as proud as she had that night. But when she left the hospital to go home, she knew that in a short time, the man would be released from the hospital. She knew that as soon as the patient was able, he would be transferred to a rehabilitation center and that would be the last Gina would hear from the patient, his wife, and their ten year old daughter. The hospital's job was to make people better physically. Gina wanted to help people get better physically and mentally. A few months later, Gina gave her notice at St. Helena's hospital so she could take a full-time position as a physical therapist at Macgregor Rehabilitation Hospital.

Macgregor Rehabilitation Hospital specialized in Spinal Cord injury. They had one of the top successful rehabilitation rates in the world. While the pay for a first year therapist was less than she was making as a full-time nurse, she felt that the position was perfect for her. Before she put in her last day at St. Helena's, her coworkers set up a going away party.

The Ultimate Getaway club was a couple blocks away from St. Helena's Hospital. Gina and her co-workers met for drinks at 8PM. By the time Gina arrived, there were over twenty people already at the club for Gina's party. Gina was well liked by everyone at St. Helena's, as witnessed by the big turnout. Gina was especially close to Jill Woodley.

Jill was an African American who was a couple years older than Gina. What brought them together was that like Gina, Jill had a tough childhood growing up. Her father had passed away at the early age of 48 from a heart-attack. Jill had four brothers and two sisters that her mother had to raise practically by herself. She was the youngest of the children and was seven years old when her father had passed away. Because she was the youngest, her siblings made sure she was raised properly.

"Oh my God Jill, I can't believe how many people turned out. Are they glad to see me go or do they just want an excuse to have a couple drinks?"

"Believe me girl no one is happy to see you leave. But it doesn't hurt to have an excuse to go out for drinks. I can't believe you're leaving St. Helena's for a therapist's job. You're such a great nurse. In a few years you could have a cushy administrative job. Everyone likes you, you know that."

"And I love everyone at St. Helena's. But I don't want an administrative position. I love working with people. It's not about the money."

"You're crazy girl. Sooner or later don't all of the patients' problems get to you? It gets depressing. I know for myself I was just like you when I started. I felt really good knowing I was helping people. However, after a few years, sometimes it just gets to me. As soon as someone gets better, they ship them out and a new person replaces them and you start all over."

"That's one of the reasons why I'm leaving. Here all we get to see is that they come in injured, and most of the time they leave to go to a rehabilitation hospital. We never get to see them get to the point where they can take care of themselves. I want to work with people and get them to a point where they are self-sufficient. I want to help a patient more than just physically. Physically there's only so much we can do. It's the mental part that is the toughest. When patients leave here we have no idea how well they will be. Sometimes it feels like we ship them in, give medications, make sure they rest, and then when the insurance company deems them physically fit, we ship them out. We don't heal the mental side of their injury. I want to go someplace where I can work one on one with someone to help get them feeling whole again."

"I think you're crazy. How are you going to meet a doctor to marry?"

"I didn't get into this field to find a doctor to marry. Besides they have doctors at Macgregor."

"Yeah but they don't have the high paying surgeons like they have here, am I right?"

"Oh Jill you're always thinking about the money."

"Darn right girl! I've *been* married for love. Look where that got me. Three kids from what turned out to be drunken bum and now I'm busting my ass just to make ends meet. Take it from me girl, the first marriage, marry for money, then have the kids, get a divorce, get a big settlement, then you marry for love."

"Yeah, yeah, you need a refill? I'm heading up to the bar to get one."

"I'm good, but bring me back that bartender though will you? He's what I've been waiting for, for a long time."

"I'll see what I can do."

When Gina got to the bar to get her drink she noticed that both bartenders were looking intently at the television. She looked at the people at the bar and everyone was glued to the television as well. She turned to the guy on her right who looked to be about forty years old. His hairline was receding. He was dressed in blue jeans and a nice, but inexpensive shirt. Gina could tell he worked in some kind of construction because although his hands looked clean, under his finger nails were still dirty. One thumb nail was black and blue. He had calluses on both hands as well. He had a half bottle of Budweiser and a shot of whiskey in front of him. "What's all the excitement on TV?"

The man turned to Gina slowly. "Huh?" He looked Gina up and down and smiled. He liked what he saw. "Well hello there beautiful. I'm Gene, who might you be?"

Gina could smell the alcohol on his breath very easily. Right away she regretted sparking any conversation with him. "Hi, the name is Gina. Why is everyone glued to the TV?"

"Gina, everyone is watching an idiot give away millions of dollars right before our eyes."

"What do you mean?"

"You see that guy talking on the podium? He just won the Heisman Trophy award. Do you know what that is?"

"No I don't sorry. Is that some sports award?"

"Some sports award? It's the greatest sports award a college kid can get. It means you are the best college football player in the country. And do you know what that means?"

"Sorry, I'm going to have to give you another no on that."

"It means beautiful, that come April, some NFL football team is going to offer him millions of dollars to play. Not only that, he would have made millions more in sponsorship deals."

"If he's going to get all that money why are you saying everyone is watching him give away millions of dollars?"

"Because he's just announced that he doesn't want to play football. He's giving some sad story from his childhood and now he wants to pay him back by not playing football. He wants to become a doctor. Can you believe that? He's throwing away millions of dollars to become a doctor. I bet his girlfriend breaks up with him when he gets home tonight after hearing her big pay day has been thrown away. What girl would stay with an idiot like that?"

"I don't know. I think it's refreshing that someone isn't planning their life goals by dollar amounts. I bet his girlfriend sticks with him."

"Oh yeah, tell me then, if he was the first pick in the draft and he said, no, you keep your millions, I'm going to be a doctor. And I was the second pick in the draft and I took the millions, who would you pick as a boyfriend?"

"If I had to choose between you and him?"

"Would you pick the guy going to medical school or me walking around with millions of dollars?"

"I don't think you want to know the answer."

"Yeah right, that's easy to say now, but I guarantee any woman would pick me in that situation. Millions of dollars buys a lot of love and happiness."

"You're probably right. In fact I know a girl sitting at my table that would pick you."

"Well then, why don't you introduce me to her?"

"You have to show me your millions first."

"That's what I figured. A man's got to have a lot of money to have a chance with a girl. No one wants a working stiff like me."

"Don't be so hard on yourself. My father was a construction worker."

Gene then raised his shot of whiskey. "Here's to your father." He slammed back the shot and followed that with a slug of his beer.

Gina finally got a hold of the bartender and ordered. As the bartender went to make her drink, she looked closely at the television. She knew that she didn't know the person speaking at the podium personally, or that she had ever met him, but she felt as if she had known the man. He seemed to be a big football star, and the caption on the screen said he had played for Althaia University. Althaia wasn't too far from where Gina lived so she thought that maybe she had seen his picture in the newspaper. When the bartender came back with Gina's drink, she gave the bartender a twenty dollar bill. As she waited for her change she continued to stare at the television screen. She didn't know why, but for some reason she felt some sort of connection with the guy who was speaking. It wasn't infatuation, and it wasn't a celebrity crush. It was an odd sensation that she felt. She could see the sorrow in his eyes as he continued on with his speech. Maybe the connection Gina sensed was a reminder of how she felt when her father passed away. She immediately thought of the letter her father wrote to her. It was the letter she carried with her at all times. When the show went to commercial, Gina asked Gene the name of the person speaking.

"That's Brandon Leshing. He played football at Althaia. He was going to be a local legend. Now he's going to be a local idiot."

The bartender came back with her change. "Get this gentleman a drink on me and keep the rest for yourself."

Gene raised his Budweiser. "Thank you beautiful. Say, if you are the type that doesn't go for money, maybe you and I could head out of here and get to know each other a little better."

Gina smiled. "Maybe some other time Gene, right now I have to get back to my friends." Gina walked back to her table. As she walked back Gene yelled out - "You can't blame a guy for trying."

When Gina got back to her table, Jill asked. "Well, did you get the bartender's number for me?"

"Sorry Jill I didn't. But there's a half drunk middle-aged man desperately looking for someone sitting right over there. His name is Gene. Would you like me to introduce you two? He would be more than happy to meet you." Jill saw the man Gina was referring.

"No thanks. I've already had that type. I'm looking for a boy-toy I can play with for a while."

Gina's first days at Macgregor Rehabilitation Hospital were spent being shown around by Kevin Stenlar. Kevin was in his mid-twenties. He had blonde curly hair, blue eyes, light skin. He looked to be athletic and was soft spoken. Maybe he played basketball Gina thought. He was tall and his gait was long but very coordinated. Gina had to take two steps to his one just to keep up his pace. When Gina shook his hand she noticed how meticulous his nails were and how soft his hands were. As Kevin showed Gina around the various areas in the hospital, she noticed how everyone stopped what they were doing to say hello. Kevin not only introduced Gina to the staff, but he also introduced her to the patients. Gina was amazed at how Kevin knew every patient's name. In all there must have been over thirty patients they had met. Some were there after hip replacement surgery, some were amputees, some suffered a stroke, and there were a couple who had suffered a spinal cord injury. The patients varied in age. Some were as young as eighteen years old, while others were as old as eighty in the case of Harriet Goldsmith who had just received a knee replacement. Gina would get to know Harriet very well as Harriet would be one of the first patients that Gina would care for in her start at Macgregor.

Most of Gina's patients were those who had knee or hip replacements. At Macgregor, these were relatively the easiest patients to care. The injury itself was not life threatening, and the patient's lives were generally much better when they left Macgregor than prior to surgery. Mentally, these patients were what they had been before their surgery. There were some patients like Harriet who took getting a knee replacement in stride. She couldn't wait to get out of the hospital so she could get back to her bridge club. Others looked at their replacement as a sign that they were getting old. For these people Gina did her best to ensure the patient that their replacement meant that they were now stronger and would have less pain than before. No matter what type of patient Gina cared for, the patient always liked Gina. She always had a smile and genuinely cared.

Almost immediately Gina fit in with the staff at Macgregor. However just like the work at St. Helena's, most of her patients spent just a week or two at Macgregor. Then, the patient would go on with their lives and in most cases Gina would never see or hear from the patient again. As successful as Gina was at working with her patients, she wanted more challenging work.

A form of therapy for Gina's patients was walking around the hospital so they could get used to their new knee or hip. For these exercises Gina would make it a habit to go to Kevin's area. Kevin worked with more difficult cases, those recovering from strokes, or spinal cord injuries. These patients could spend three to sometimes six months at Macgregor, depending upon the patient's insurance. These were the types of cases that Gina wanted. But that wasn't the only reason to see what was going on in Kevin's ward. "Hi Kevin, Peggy and I were going through our daily walk and we thought we would come see how the upper half lives. Peggy, this is Kevin. Kevin, this is Peggy Lichter."

"Hello Peggy. How is your new knee holding up?"

"It's been quite sore but this one doesn't care." Peggy rolled her eyes towards Gina. "She's got me walking around this hospital more than I've walked in twenty years."

Gina turned red. She didn't want Kevin to think that she was pushing her patients more than they needed. Gina began to say something to Peggy but Kevin spoke just before she could get a word out. "Well that's good to hear. You're saying that Gina has you feeling better than you did twenty years ago." Kevin looked at Gina and smiled. Gina gazed back at Kevin. She looked as if she let out a sigh of relief that Kevin understood.

Peggy looked at both of them who seemed for a second to forget that she was there. "That's not what I meant!" Peggy said sternly. "I can't wait to get out of here so I can get back to my apartment and live in peace!"

"And that's why we are working as hard as we are." Gina said. "You know that the doctors won't let you go home until they are satisfied that you are able to get around without injuring yourself."

"My apartment is thirty feet long, why do I need to walk ten miles?"

"Alright, if you're tired we can go back to your room. After that I'll let you relax for the rest of the day, but only if you cheer up a little. Is it a deal?"

Peggy looked to Kevin. "It was so nice meeting you Kevin." Then Peggy turned to Gina and gave her a sarcastic smile.

"That's much better! See, it isn't so hard to be pleasant. Come on Peg, we'll leave Kevin alone so he can get back to work. I'll talk to you later Kevin."

"I'll see you later Gina. Goodbye Peggy."

Peggy had already turned and started towards the door when Gina looked back at Kevin and gave a wave of her hand. Then she turned and noticed that her patient was already ten feet ahead of her. "Wait for me young lady, there's no need to race back to your room!"

As Peggy and Gina got into the elevator, Peggy asked. "How long have you two been together?"

"Excuse me? You mean Kevin and me?"

"No I mean the ninety year old man in the wheel chair and you. Of course I meant you and Kevin. It's written all over your faces."

"First of all if we were seeing each other it wouldn't be any of your business. Kevin and I aren't seeing each other outside of work. He was the one who showed me around the hospital when I started. He's a nice guy, and a great therapist. He's taught me a lot but we only have a working relationship."

"What a waste, what a shame."

"Now Peggy don't read anymore into what you think our relationship is or should be. I like Kevin but we work together. If we were more involved it might put a strain on our work relationship."

The elevator door to their floor opened. "Is that what you think or what he thinks?"

"Is what, what I think or he thinks?"

"That getting involved would put a strain on your work relationship."

"I think you're prying a little too much, but to answer your question, it's what I think."

"What a shame."

"And what is that supposed to mean?"

"Well dear let me tell you what I know."

Peggy's voice became softer. It was the first time Peggy had called Gina, 'dear'. "I've been around the block a time or two. I know to look at me now I seem to be a crusty old lady. But back in the day I could make a few men's heads turn. I too was in love with a man I worked with. I was a waitress at a restaurant down town. It isn't there any longer but when it was, it always had a great crowd, especially on weekends. The restaurant had a bar and Friday and Saturday nights we had a piano player who would take requests. That man could play any song anyone asked. When he started playing at the club I thought he was so handsome. He was a sharp dresser and always seemed to be in control. He seemed to be so confident, he was never rattled. The more he played, the more talented I knew he was. It got to the point where I realized that I was in love with him. But I was just a waitress at the restaurant. He was a hot shot piano player that the women loved. *What would he see in a waitress?* I used

212

to think. We worked together and he never saw me outside of the club. At first I didn't say anything or let on how I felt because I didn't want to rock the boat. It went on like this for months. Finally I thought to myself, *why not?* Why not just tell him how I feel? What was the worst that could happen? He could say he didn't feel the same way. He could say he was married, I didn't know. Even if it came to the point where I had to leave the place, what would be the big deal? I was a waitress, and there were plenty of other waitressing jobs out there."

"So one Saturday night I finally said to myself, *Margaret, don't be afraid to give love a chance.*" As Peggy said those words, Gina immediately thought of her father's letter. "I walked up to Al, and I said Albert, I've been listening and watching you play for months. I've been afraid to say this but now I need to say it. I think you are a wonderful, talented, handsome man. I would love it if we could get to know each other more. And you know what he said?"

"He said he would love to." Gina assumed.

"No. He said *go away, you're bothering me!*" Peggy paused to see the look on Gina's face. "I'm kidding, he said he had wanted to tell me the same thing but he was afraid to because he didn't want to make the workplace uncomfortable. To make a long story short, Albert and I married a year later and had four wonderful children. Who, by the way don't come to see their mother enough!"

"That's a wonderful story Peggy. Does Albert still play the piano?"

"Well dear, unfortunately he passed away a few years ago."

"Peggy I'm so sorry."

"Don't be dear. I'll tell you, not a day goes by that I don't think of that man. Every day we were together was the best day of my life." Peggy's voice began to trail off. She looked up at Gina and spoke up. "Now you take it from me. I see the way you look at that man, and I see the way he looks at you. Life is too short not to take a chance on love. Tell him how you feel. I know people think it isn't proper for a lady to be so forward with a man, but if women waited for the man to take the initiative, the human race would be lost for good!"

"Ok, I'll think about it."

"Don't think too long dear."

"It was nice talking to you today Peg. I have to get to my other patients. I'll see you tomorrow."

As Gina left Peggy's room to see her next patient, she thought about what Peggy had said. She had basically said what her father had asked Gina to promise. Gina did like Kevin, and she sensed that Kevin felt the same about her. Gina decided that she would tell Kevin how she felt, or, maybe just ask if he wanted to meet for lunch or dinner. She knew that Kevin always left the office at 6:00 sharp. Today, she kept herself busy until the same time so she could meet him on the way out. "Hey Kevin!"

"Hi Gina, how is Peggy doing? You're working her hard huh?"

"Some patients think no matter how hard, or how little you work it's always too hard."

213

"I know. Believe me I've had plenty of patients who just wanted to eat and sleep the day away. But she looks terrific. From what everyone has been saying you are doing a great job."

"Thanks Kevin, that's nice to hear."

"Do you like working in there? Have you ever thought of moving to more challenging patients?"

"Actually that's what I wanted to talk to you about. I love working with my patients, but it's not really the type of work I wanted when I came here. I know I just started and I can't start out working with the more challenging cases, but I was hoping I could make my way up the ladder so to speak."

"I know what you mean. The patients you work with are important, but not challenging or rewarding enough."

Gina and Kevin kept walking and talking until they came to Kevin's car. "Well, this is my car. How about we talk about this tomorrow?"

"I would love to but work is so busy. Maybe we could meet some time outside of work. Maybe we could do lunch or something."

"Miss Stroit, are you asking me out on a date?"

Gina became embarrassed. "No, oh no, it doesn't have to be a date. I was just thinking. You know how things are at work. We both have so many patients to work with. Someone is always asking for our attention, and..."

"Gina, Gina, I'm kidding. I would love to do lunch. Why not have dinner? Are you free this Saturday? I have a couple coupons where if you buy one Big Mac you get the second one for free?"

Gina was relieved to hear Kevin say he would love to have dinner. Did he say McDonald's? Not wanting to offend Kevin, she told him that she was free to go out Saturday for dinner and McDonald's would be fine.

"Great I'll see you tomorrow and we can decide on a time."

"Sounds great Kevin, I'll see you tomorrow."

When Gina worked with Peggy the next day she told her the good news. "I took your advice and decided to see if Kevin wanted to meet outside of work. This Saturday, we're going out for dinner."

"Good for you dear! See I told you. I knew you two would hit it off."

"Yeah, but now I'm kind of having second thoughts."

"Why is that?"

"Well, when he said he wanted to go out to dinner he said he had a coupon to go to McDonald's. Don't get me wrong, I wasn't expecting him to take me to a five star restaurant. If this is his idea of a first date dinner then maybe there's a reason he is still single."

"McDonald's huh? Well you like the person, not the meal. Just go with it and make up your mind after spending some time with him. If he is the right man for you it won't matter where you are as long as you're together."

Gina and Julie had discussed the date and Julie thought Kevin was a cheapskate to go to McDonald's. Especially if he thought he could get away with Gina having a Big Mac just because he had a buy one get one free coupon. "Gina when you go, order something else. Tell him you're allergic to Big Mac's. Then buy the most expensive meal on the menu."

"Julie, I don't want to make him mad on the first date. I'm sure there is a perfectly good reason why he is saving his money. Besides the most expensive meal on the menu is only a couple dollars."

When Kevin knocked on the door to Gina's house, Julie was waiting along with her. Gina wanted to get Julie's opinion of Kevin, and Julie couldn't wait to see the cheapskate. Knowing that they weren't going to a fancy restaurant, Gina had dressed in jeans, black boots, and a blue long-sleeved cotton pull-over shirt. Kevin wore tan slacks with a nice pair of brown shoes and a buttoned down dress shirt. He looked very nice, especially for McDonald's. After introducing Julie to Kevin and a few minutes of small-talk, they were on their way to dinner. Before they walked out the door, Julie handed Kevin her own coupon for a buy one get one free order of fries. Gina didn't know Julie had the coupon so when Julie gave it to Kevin she looked at Julie as if to say - *what the hell are you doing?*

"Oh this is great! Thanks Julie. This will save us a couple bucks! Your friend is really nice Gina." Julie held in her laugh as long as she could. When the door closed she busted out laughing.

Kevin opened the passenger door to his Chevy Volt for Gina. As they drove they neared the McDonald's restaurant. Gina expected Kevin to turn into the lot, but he passed on by. "I thought we were going to McDonald's?"

Kevin laughed. "You really thought I would take you to McDonald's on our first date?" He could hardly contain himself. "I did like the coupons Julie gave me. I almost lost it right there."

"Well how was I to know? You said that was where we were going." Gina saw Kevin still laughing. "Besides, I think a cheap person is a better date than a liar. Do you always do this to women on the first date?"

Kevin finally stopped laughing. "No, you're the first. I'm sorry for laughing. It's a beautiful night. I know a Mexican place where they make the best margaritas. They also serve a great Chicken Quesadillas with Roasted Peppers and they also have an awesome Steak Fajitas. If you aren't into Mexican food, they also serve burgers and salads."

"I like Mexican food. I don't drink too much though so I couldn't tell the difference between a good margarita and a bad one."

"The best part is that the tables are outside. The scenery is beautiful and there is a mariachi band that plays."

"That sounds nice. Is this where you take all of your dates?"

"Only the special ones."

The rest of the night couldn't have gone any better. Gina and Kevin talked about why they got into their professions. Gina enjoyed the margaritas, the scenery, and the band that played. They talked about their interests, their goals in life. As the night went on, Gina fell more and more for Kevin. Kevin enjoyed being with Gina as well.

When they approached Kevin's car for the ride home, he unlocked the passenger door for Gina and let her in. As Kevin walked around to his side of the car, Gina reached over to unlock the driver door for Kevin. When they got back to Gina's house, Kevin walked Gina to the front door. "Kevin I really had a wonderful time tonight."

"I had a great time as well. You know I had wanted to ask you out before, but I didn't want to jeopardize our relationship at work."

"Kevin I thought the same thing! Peggy was the one who said I should take a chance."

"You mean the patient I met a couple days ago?"

Gina didn't hear Kevin's question. "Gina? Gina, are you Ok?"

"Yes, yes, I'm sorry, I was thinking of something my father had asked."

"I hope I didn't bring up any bad memories."

"No, Kevin you didn't. You were asking about Peggy, yes the patient you met a couple days ago."

"I didn't think she liked me too much."

"She can be irritable on the outside, but she is a very sweet lady."

"I see. I hope we can do this again soon. I had a great time and besides, you passed the tests."

"I passed the tests?"

"Yes, the first was the McDonald's dinner. You really thought I would take you to McDonald's because I had a coupon for a free Big Mac. Yet, you didn't complain. The second test came when we got into the car when we left the restaurant."

"What do you mean?"

"My father always said, if you open the car door for a lady and she unlocks your door before you get to the driver's side, it means she is thinking of you. If she doesn't unlock the door she is only thinking of herself."

"I didn't know that. It was just by instinct that's all."

"Yes, but nonetheless you did unlock the door for me."

Kevin raised his right hand to graze Gina's cheek and gently brush back her hair. He leaned over and kissed her on her lips. Gina placed her hand upon his cheek and drew him close. With both of their eyes closed they kissed for what seemed as if timed had stopped. Yet the kiss was over in an instant. They looked into each other's eyes, each knowing the other wanted more. Gina blinked, she stepped back. "Kevin, I really do like you but this is our first date. I hope you don't mind."

"It's Ok. I'm hoping this is the first of many dates. I'll call you ok?"

"Please do Kevin. I would really like you to call me." Gina watched Kevin get into his car and drive away. When she walked into her house Julie was there to discuss all of the details.

216

As time went on, Gina graduated to more challenging work. Though Kevin put in a good word for her to help with her promotion, it was Gina's hard work, her care for her patients that got her the promotion. She began working with people who were recovering from strokes, people who were dealing with multiple sclerosis, and more closer to her heart, those who had suffered paralysis. These were the types of patients Gina wanted to help. These were the patients who required several months of rehabilitation. These were the patients she could build relationships. She knew first-hand how difficult the lives of these people were.

Gina found it very rewarding when she could help just one more patient regain their will to live. Every patient she was able to help was one less person feeling the way her father had felt. However there were patients that Gina just could not reach. No matter what she tried, there were some who just couldn't, or wouldn't try to regain their self-esteem. Every time a patient like this left the hospital, she felt as if she had failed. It wasn't just the patient she felt she failed. She thought back to thinking that she somehow failed her father.

It was at times like these that Kevin was a big to help Gina. Their relationship had grown to where Kevin would sometimes spend the night at Gina's and Gina would sometimes stay at Kevin's. Gina loved the fact that Kevin wasn't in the profession for the money. He genuinely cared for his patients' well-being as much as she did. Both were idealistic. They celebrated their successes and helped each other through their hardships.

Kevin was more pragmatic when it came to dealing with the hardships at work. He realized that his work not only depended upon himself working up to his capabilities, but that the patient must also work up to their potential. If a patient didn't want to, or wasn't going to put in the effort needed to get better, then that wasn't Kevin's fault. To Gina that was the crux of her work. She believed that her work began with getting the patient to be willing to accept his or her responsibility of the effort that was required. She felt that it was her responsibility to get the patient to see that it was worth the effort to try to become independent. In Gina's view, the physical nature of their work as a therapist was secondary to the work they needed to do emotionally. Because of this, Gina sometimes became emotionally attached to patients to a fault. One patient in particular personified the differences between Gina's emotional attachment and Kevin's pragmatic approach.

Ronald Jenkins arrived from Trinity Hospital on May 7th. He was involved in an automobile accident which left him paralyzed from the waist down. He was an eighteen year old African American kid who had been the starting point guard for his high school basketball team. He had just graduated and was headed to St. John's University on a basketball scholarship.

When Ronald arrived at Macgregor Rehabilitation he was assigned to Kevin since it was thought that because both had played basketball, they would be able to get comfortable with each other quickly. Prior to meeting Ronald, Kevin was given notes on his new patient. The notes included Ronald's prognosis (Ronald was given a less than five percent chance for a complete recovery) and his psychological profile (deeply depressed, not receptive to treatment, bordering on giving up).

Kevin was ready for the challenge. He spent the first week, trying to get to know Ronald. Physically there wasn't much Kevin could work on. Because Ronald had been kept in a bed, unable to move for over a month, he was unable to even sit up for more than a couple minutes. When he did, his blood pressure dropped almost immediately to a point where Ronald was close to passing out. For the first week, all that Kevin could examine, and work on was Ronald's psychological profile and the building of the trust that would be needed between the two. Kevin immediately found out that the psychological profile was worse than reported. Every question Kevin asked was seemingly ignored or answered with a quiet 'yes' or 'no'. Creating a conversation was impossible. It wasn't until Kevin began telling Ronald of his own basketball exploits that Ronald finally spoke. It wasn't just an answer to a question, it was an eruption heard throughout the third floor of the building.

"I remember when I played JV basketball my junior year. It was our second game and I went up for a rebound and landed on my opponent's foot. I came down so awkwardly that my ankle almost broke. I remember taking off my sneakers and watching my ankle blow up like a balloon. I knew then that my season was over so I know how you feel Ronald."

Ronald looked up at Kevin. He couldn't believe what this blonde, geeky, do-gooder, know-it-all had said. "You know how I feel? You sprain your ankle and that gives you the right to know how I feel?"

"I know spraining my ankle isn't the same…"

"You're damn right it isn't the same!" At this point everyone in the entire room, patients, hospital staff, especially Gina had stopped what they were doing and looked over at Kevin and his patient. "You're trying to put yourself in my shoes? You lost a season on the JV team! Your life would go on just fine with your Mommy and Daddy sending you off to college where you could fuck around for four years and come out with a white collar job. You lost nothing when you sprained your ankle! You know what I lost? I lost my fucking life! The only chance I had coming out of high school was playing basketball. That was the only way I'm making it out of the hood! I got no chance now! Not a fucking chance in hell! Mommy and Daddy aren't sending me to college are they! What the fuck am I going to do now white boy! Tell me, what the fuck am I going to do now! You think you know how I feel? Give me a fucking break!"

"Ronald I didn't mean to belittle you I …"

"You what! You want to get to know me? You want to be my boy? You want to be best buds?"

"Ronald I…"

"Its Ron mother fucker, Ron, not Ronald! Just let me be. I'm tired."

Kevin looked at Ron who had turned his head to avoid eye contact. Everyone in the room waited to see what Kevin would do next. Gina wanted to rush over to Kevin's aide, but she knew she couldn't. "Ok Ron, I'll get you back to your room." Kevin said quietly.

Ten minutes later Kevin was back in the therapy room. As he walked in everyone had turned to see him. Kevin looked as if he were coming into the room for the first time. He went to his desk, picked up his itinerary, looked up and smiled at Patricia Smythe. "Hello Patty. Are you ready for your exercises?" It was as if the previous twenty minutes had never happened.

Gina knew that this would be a night that Kevin would spend at Gina's. He would need some comforting and she wanted to be there for him. Later that night, as expected, Kevin stayed at Gina's. They discussed what had happened with Ron. "I just tried to set some common ground between us. I didn't mean to belittle him. Did it sound like I was trying to belittle him?"

"No Kevin, not at all. Everyone knew that you were just trying to talk to him. You knew coming in that he had been difficult to talk to. I know you were just trying to get to know him."

"That's all I was trying to do. Now I don't know what to do. I can't ignore him. Monday we'll be right back where we left off. It's not like I can take back what I said. What do you think I should do?"

"You can start off by telling Ron that you didn't mean to say that what you had experienced is what he is experiencing now. I'm sure he'll understand that you didn't think that what had happened to you is the same thing that happened to him. Tell him what you were trying to do. Tell him that all you wanted was to try to get to know him. He has to realize that he is going to be working with you for the next several months whether he likes it or not. All you wanted to do is make the best of it."

"What if he doesn't listen? What if he spouts off like he did today? I thought we could get along. What if he just shuts me out completely?"

"Kevin, it's going to take time. You can't judge what will happen based on one day. I'm sure more than anything he's scared about his future. I wouldn't take anything he said personally. I'm sure if you continue to let him know that you are here to help him that sooner or later he will come around."

On Monday Kevin again tried to get through to Ron, but Ron continued to shut Kevin out. There wasn't any hollering. Ron wouldn't answer any of Kevin's questions or attempts at conversation. This continued throughout the week and by the end of the week, Gina knew that Kevin was extremely frustrated at the lack of progress that had been made. Though Kevin was extremely frustrated, he never once raised his voice towards Ron. He kept his composure throughout the week. When Gina asked Kevin if he wanted to come over her house Friday night, Kevin said no. He told her that he needed to figure things out on his own. This was the first time since they had picked up their relationship that Kevin would think things out on his own. Since they had been dating whenever one person had a problem with a patient, the other would be there for support. Gina had not heard from Kevin all weekend even though she left two messages asking him to call her.

The following Monday morning Gina was at her desk putting together her schedule when she saw Kevin walk in. He still had not returned any of her calls so she didn't get up and walk over to him to say hello. If he wanted some space, she was going to give it to him. She continued to work on her list of patients when Kevin came over to her. "I'm sorry I didn't return your calls. I went away to clear my head and try to figure out how to handle Ron."

"That's Ok Kevin. I'm not your guardian. It's not like you need to report to me. You could have called to let me know what was going on. But I understand that you needed some space."

"Thanks for understanding. I should have returned your calls though."

"No big deal. Did you think of anything new?"

"Gina, I tried to work with things we might have in common. That didn't work. I tried being nice. That didn't work. I hate to say it but I have to come down hard on him. He has to know that if he doesn't try, he won't get better. If he doesn't like me that's one thing, but he has to know that we're here to work. I'm here to help him. I'm not here to waste my time baby-sitting him."

"Don't come down on him too hard. It's going to take some time before Ron gets over the shock of what has happened to him. Some people take longer than others. You know that."

"Gina it's been nearly two months since his accident. You know I hate playing the bully. But the time has come for him to realize that sulking all day isn't going to do any good."

When Ron was wheeled into the room by one of the assistants Kevin walked over to him. "Are you ready to work today Ron?" Ron stared straight ahead not saying a word. "Ron, look at me." Ron kept looking straight ahead. "Ron you are only going to be here for a limited amount of time. The amount of time you are here depends upon you. Each week I have to fill out paperwork on your progress to your insurance company. If you continue to make progress they will continue to pay for your stay here. But if you make zero progress over a period of time, they will ask why they should keep paying your bills if nothing is getting done. Then, they will no longer cover you and you will be sent home. I don't want to send you home in the condition that you're in. But you have to work with me." Ron kept staring straight ahead, not saying a word. "Ron! Did you hear what I said?"

For the first time Gina had seen Kevin raise his voice towards a patient. Ron continued to stare straight ahead, he softly replied. "You got to do what you got to do. It doesn't matter to me."

"Damn it Ron! Now you listen! You have been here over a week and you are still lying back in your wheelchair. By now you should be able to sit up and begin some upper body exercises. I can't work with you if you won't let me.

So here's the deal. I am not going to waste my time with you. If you want to give up that's fine. I'll work with patients who want to get better. When you are ready to go to work you let me know."

Kevin left Ron in his wheelchair in the corner of the room. Kevin began working with other patients. A couple hours later Ron was still in the same corner of the room. Gina constantly looked over to see if Kevin would make any attempt at communicating again. Kevin continued to work with other patients completely ignoring Ron as if he wasn't in the room at all.

By lunch time one of the assistants came into the therapy room to gather the patients for their lunch. Ron was wheeled back into his room where he ate his lunch alone. When the room was empty of patients, Gina walked up to Kevin. "Hey want to grab a bite downstairs?"

"Sure I'm hungry."

When Gina and Kevin sat down at the cafeteria table, Gina started up the conversation. "So now that playing the tough guy hasn't worked what will you do now?"

"Gina there's nothing I can do now. It's up to Ron to tell me when he wants to work. I meant what I said. I can't waste my time with someone who doesn't want to get better. I have other patients who do want to get better and I'll focus my attention on them. I'll keep writing that no progress has been made and at some point the insurance will stop payments and he'll be sent home."

"So you're going to give up, just like that?"

"I'm not the one who's giving up. He is."

"Kevin, before you can work with him physically, you have to work with him mentally. Obviously he is still shock over what has happened to him."

"Gina we're not psychologists, we're physical therapists. Maybe he should be sent to a psychiatric ward. I can't coddle him."

"All I'm saying is that you can't give up on him after a week."

"And all I'm saying is that he is the one who has given up, not me. When he is ready, he will let me know. Until then, I have other people who want to work on getting better."

After lunch, Gina and Kevin were back in the therapy room getting ready for their afternoon patients. At 2:00 an assistant wheeled Ron into the room. Kevin immediately walked over to Ron. "Are you ready to get to work Ron?" Once again Ron stared straight ahead not saying a word. "Well, I still have other patients who do want to work. When you're ready give me a yell." Kevin walked away leaving Ron alone in the corner of the room once again.

Gina listened to the conversation as she worked with her patient. Another hour had passed. Kevin continued to work with other patients. Ron continued to sit quietly. An assistant came into the room to take one of Gina's patients back to her room. Gina asked where Mr. McGuinty was as he was to begin his 3:30 session. The assistant told Gina that Charles (Mr. McGuinty) wasn't feeling too well and that he would not be showing up for his session. Gina looked over at Ron and could not bear to see him alone. Since Gina's next hour would be relatively free, she decided to try to talk to the lonely kid in the corner of the room.

"Hi I'm Gina. I hear your name is Ron." Ron gave Gina a quick glance but turned his attention straight ahead. "I hear that you played basketball. Were you any good?" Ron paid no attention, but Gina continued. "I'm not too big on sports. I don't see what the big deal is to take a ball and put it through a hoop. I've noticed on TV that thousands of people go crazy just because some guy jumped in the air and shoved the ball through the hoop. I know you don't like to talk much, and I won't stay if you don't want me to. But can you explain why some people go so crazy watching a guy shove a ball through a hoop?"

Ron looked at the girl standing next to him. He knew she was here to get him to talk. Was she really this dim-witted? It's one thing to not like basketball, or any sports for that matter. Was she serious when she described the game he loved in this manner? "There's more to the game than just shoving a ball through a hoop."

"Isn't the object of the game to put more balls through the hoop than the other team? Don't you get a point every time you do that? Then the team with the most points wins?"

Ron looked at Gina wondering if this was a trick to get him to talk. No one was this naïve were they? "The game of basketball is a lot more complicated that. It's more than just one guy putting a ball through a hoop. Basketball is a team game. On one hand the team with the ball has the objective of scoring, or as you say, putting the ball through the hoop. The other team has the objective of stopping the team from putting the ball through the hoop."

Kevin noticed that Gina had actually begun a conversation with Ron. As he watched, he didn't know how to feel or what to say. On the one hand he was angry at Gina for going over to his patient without asking. He also felt a bit of jealousy that Gina was able to talk to Ron. He kept quiet seeing how far the conversation would go.

"Why doesn't the team with the ball just give it to the biggest player on the team, let him run up to the hoop, jump up, and shove the ball through? It seems so simple."

Ron smiled for the first time in months. Maybe this girl really was this stupid when it came to basketball. Ron's smile did not go unnoticed by Kevin. "There are rules in the game of basketball. First you can't run with the ball. You have to dribble, or bounce the ball as you run. If you take more than two steps without bouncing the ball you have to give the ball back to the other team."

"Is that hard?"

"Dribbling? For me it isn't." Ron thought of his predicament. "I mean, for me it wasn't."

"But for other people it is hard huh?" Gina tried to get Ron's mind back on basketball.

"For most big men it is hard to dribble the ball and move around easily. It takes a lot of coordination to do that."

"So you were the one on your team who dribbled the ball?"

"You could say that. I was the guy to dribble the ball. I was the guy who set up our offense."

"What do you mean you set up your offense?"

Ron's mind was back on the court. For a few minutes his focus was on the game he loved, not on his physical condition. "You have five guys on the court for your team. The opponent has five guys as well. The offense has 35 seconds to shoot the basketball. You set up plays to give yourself the best chance to score. You want to set up your teammates to be in positions that they like when they shoot the ball. To make it simple, most big men like to score close to the basket. Some players like to shoot the ball from around ten feet from the basket. It depends on the defense too. Some teams have good big defenders. Some teams have good perimeter defenders. You need to set up your plays accordingly. I was the guy who set up the other players."

"Sounds like you need to be mentally prepared to play basketball too."

"Yeah, you do. You just don't show up and start running plays. You have to be in top physical shape, but you have to be mentally focused as well."

"You said you have 35 seconds to shoot the ball. What happens if you don't?"

"That was my specialty. If the plays we set up aren't working. If every other player on my team is covered and can't shoot the ball, the coach would tell me go one on one against my opponent. That's where it becomes a battle of wills. It's me against him. He's trying to do whatever he can to stop me from succeeding. I'm going to do whatever it takes to make myself and my team successful. And more times than not, I came out on top."

"I see what you mean when you said that basketball is more than just putting a ball through a hoop. You can probably say that in some ways basketball is a game that mimics life."

"What do you mean?"

"You stated that in some situations it's a battle of wills. I can think of instances in my own life where I thought some setbacks were more or less a battle of will. It's kind of like what you are going through now."

"The difference is that in this game I already lost. I got nothing to play for anymore. Everything I had is gone."

"So you're going to quit without even trying? I would never be able to put myself in your shoes. So I'm not going to tell you something I have no knowledge. But I have had setbacks of my own. Everyone does."

"Yeah but you were always able to walk away from your setback and start over. That ain't happening with me."

"That's not true. I've lost both of my parents, my mother when I was four, and my father just a few years ago. In fact my father was in the same predicament you are in right now. He is what made me choose this profession. There were many times I wished I could go back and start over with my parents. But I never will. There is absolutely zero chance of that happening.

223

With you, there may be a chance. It may be small, but there is a chance. But that chance *is* absolutely zero if you quit. After losing my father I was afraid of what would become of me. I was too old to be raised by other parents. There were times when I felt completely alone. I read a quote while in school that has stuck with me whenever I seem to be losing it. The quote is that *winners are not those who never fail, but those who never quit.* Everything you have told me about basketball and yourself tells me that you were a winner. I can't tell you what to do. I can't tell you that everything will work out. No one is going to fix your problems. There are no teammates. It's just you, one on one against yourself. The question is - are you going to quit?"

Ron couldn't look at Gina. He sat silently. He knew if he spoke it would come with a burst of tears. He couldn't bear to let anyone see him cry. Ron knew he was had. This dim-witted girl who knew nothing about the game of basketball just took him to school. He didn't know what to say. He knew she was right. He also knew that this wasn't a game. There would be no do-over. There would be no next game to make amends.

After several seconds Gina knew Ron wouldn't reply. "It was nice talking to you Ron. Whatever you choose to do I hope it works out for you." Gina got up and left Ron. Kevin stared at Gina as she walked back to her desk to wait for her next patient. As Gina sat down she sensed Kevin's eyes upon her. The same assistant who wheeled Gina's next patient into the room walked over to Ron to take him back to his room.

Kevin didn't say a word to Gina throughout the remainder of the day until it was time to go home. "Mind if I walk out with you Gina?"

"Sure Kevin."

When they got out to the parking lot Kevin grabbed Gina's arm to turn her to face him. "You should have asked me if you wanted to talk to Ron today. We can't coddle him through this. He is going to have to face facts that he will have to work if he wants to get on with his life. He isn't going to have people coming up to him all day asking what he wants. He is going to have to start making decisions on his own. Now he knows if he sits and stews long enough someone will come up to coddle him."

"Coddle him? Is that what you think I was doing? Kevin you are great with your patients. You, more than anyone else always gets the most from their patients."

"That's because I don't cave in to them when they feel sorry for themselves. I make them realize that no one owes them anything. If my patients want to get better, then it's up to them. No one can do it for them. That includes Ron. Sooner or later he will have to realize that for himself. I just hope your little talk didn't set him back."

"Kevin I can't believe you. You think I might have set him back? For your information I told him exactly what you are saying. I told him he has zero chance of getting better if he does quit. But I didn't yell at him like you did. I don't get it. Why are you so mad that I talked to him? It was obvious that you weren't going to say anything to him. It's not like you to be so angry."

"Maybe I'm mad because I've never had anyone question my authority. Maybe it's because no one has ever questioned my methods. You said it yourself I always get the most out of my patients. You may not like my methods but I always get results."

Gina looked into Kevin's eyes. He had never been angry with her. It was true that Kevin was a great therapist. No matter how hard he worked his patients, he always had their best interest at heart. Maybe she was wrong talking to Ron without asking Kevin. Maybe Kevin's way was the right way. Maybe if Ron had sat there alone for another day or so he would have realized that it was up to him and him alone to get to work. "I'm sorry for not asking you before talking to Ron. It's just that he looked so alone. He looked scared. He looked like he needed someone."

"And that was precisely the reason for my letting him sit by himself. I'm sure he did feel alone, and scared. I also know that those feelings would make him reach out to me to try to help him get better. I know you tried to help. I just wish you would have come to me first so I could explain."

"So you're mad at me now, right?"

Kevin looked into Gina's big, soulful, brown eyes. She looked at Kevin like a child who had her hands caught in a cookie jar. "No my love, I'm not mad at you. I could never be mad at you." Kevin then kissed Gina gently on her lips. He reached down to hold her hand.

"I'm glad you're not mad at me. I'll try to be more considerate in the future."

"And you will never, never question my methods, right?" Kevin playfully scolded Gina.

"No sir, I will never question your methods. Why don't you come over and I'll cook you dinner?"

"That sounds great."

At work, a note was sitting on both Gina's and Kevin's desk asking that they meet with the administrator, Eleanor Randolph. Before looking over their day's itinerary both Gina and Kevin walked to Eleanor's office. Kevin knocked on the office door. "Come in, please." Eleanor shouted. When Kevin and Gina walked in, Eleanor was on the phone. She put her hand on the talking end and quietly asked Kevin to shut the door behind them and have a seat.

Eleanor was an African American woman in her mid-forties. She was tall, standing over six feet, and big boned, but hardly any fat. You could tell that in her youth she had played, and excelled in sports. When she was off the phone she spoke to Gina and Kevin. "It has come to my attention that we have a patient who isn't quite happy with their assigned therapist." Gina and Kevin knew exactly who the patient was of course.

Kevin immediately spoke. "Eleanor, Ron is a difficult patient. All of his life he has been very gifted athletically. So much so that when that was taken away from him, he believes he now has nothing. Naturally he is very depressed. So much so that he doesn't want to try or do anything to help himself. I've tried communicating with him. I've tried being nice with him. Nothing has worked to get him to realize that he has to put in a great deal of effort in order to get some functionality back in his life. So I took a hard stance with him. I can't coddle him or spend time with him that would jeopardize time I need to spend with other patients. I know it looks cruel. I know it looks callous, but believe me I've dealt with patients like this before and this is the only way to get through to them."

Eleanor turned her attention to Gina. "And what is your opinion?"

"Eleanor, let me start off by saying it was wrong of me to interfere with Kevin's patient without first consulting him. I won't do that again and I've apologized. But I didn't say anything to Ron that Kevin hasn't pointed out. I basically told him that it was up to him to give himself a chance at recovery. I told him that if he did quit, he would have absolutely no chance at all. I don't think that I set him back." Gina gave Kevin a quick glance. "I realize that what I did was wrong and I'm sorry."

Eleanor glanced back and forth between Gina and Kevin. The longer Eleanor went without speaking, the more nervous Gina and Kevin became. "Gina, what you did was wrong. There are many reasons why it was wrong. First, the relationship between a patient of this type and his therapist is essential to the patient's chances of recovery. This type of patient will be spending the next several months, five days a week in the therapist's care. Therefore the patient must be able to trust his therapist. Second, even though you work close to the other therapists and their patients, you don't know what plans, goals, or decisions that are made by the therapist for his or her patient. You may, unintentionally foil some of the work that had been done, or is planned to be done. Third, we have a busy schedule. Therefore, we have to assign patients to the therapist we see that fits the patient and the staffing needs best. We can't have every patient that comes through the door choosing their own therapist." Eleanor paused, looked at Kevin, then back at Gina. "Unfortunately, we now have such a case where Ron specifically asked to be assigned to you."

Kevin's eyes widened. Gina looked at Kevin, and then back at Eleanor. "You told him that isn't the way things work here right Eleanor?" Kevin asked. "You just said we can't have patients choosing their therapists."

"Normally I would agree with you Kevin. However, in this case, because Ron seems to be more responsive towards Gina, I'm going to have to make the change. Gina, since you have only worked with Sue Millicker for a few weeks, I'm going to switch her with Ron. Kevin you will pick up Sue starting today." After several seconds of quiet, Eleanor finished. "That's all I have to say, any questions?" Neither Gina nor Kevin said anything. Both were stunned.

After closing the door behind them on the way out of the office, Gina turned to Kevin. "Kevin I had no idea this would happen. I don't know what to say, I'm so sorry…"

"Gina, it's Ok. You don't have to apologize." Kevin was stoic in his response. He was angry, and upset. Had the other therapist been anyone but Gina, he would have exploded. But he cared for Gina and he knew Gina cared about him. He knew she would never intentionally go behind his back, but still, this is the first time this had ever happened to him.

The change had been good for Ron. For the first time be began putting in an effort to get better. After a few weeks, Gina had Ron in an upright position for short periods of time, though he was being held by a machine. After working a few more weeks, the progress had been slow. What Gina had Ron working on was his stamina. Kevin, who hadn't said one word to Ron since the switch, kept a close eye on his progress. Whenever Gina discussed Ron's progress, or lack thereof with Kevin, he would listen, but seldom spoke. The romance between Gina and Kevin still went well. Any subject other than Ron was fine. Gina noticed Kevin's reluctance to talk about Ron, so she seldom brought him up when she and Kevin were together.

Each week Gina filled out paperwork to Ron's insurance company. For most of the first couple months, she was able to state the progress that Ron was able to achieve. There were a couple weeks where progress had slowed, but she never had to stretch the truth about the benefits of Ron's stay at Macgregor. As long as she was able to state the benefits and reasons why Ron should continue with his rehab, the insurance company was willing to keep paying the bills. After four months of rehabilitation, Ron's progress was beginning to be negligible. In recent weeks, Ron was able to stand while holding onto parallel bars. He was able to get himself in and out of bed, or transfer from one seating area to another. He was able to undress/dress himself, shower by himself, and use basic toiletries. But the past couple weeks saw no improvement. The insurance company, seeing that Ron was able to function on his own for basic necessities, and seeing that the benefits of staying in the hospital was minimal at best, wanted to transfer him to out-patient, or in-home therapy.

Knowing that the insurance would soon run out, unless some significant progress could be reported, Gina began to "fudge" the reports. She submitted the improvement in his walk, even though the walking Ron did was little more than him holding onto the parallel bars and lifting himself a few inches with his arms.

Eleanor came down to see Ron progress. She knew Gina wanted to keep working with Ron, but she also knew that Macgregor was liable to provide the insurance company the truth regarding all patient progress. Eleanor asked Gina to show her some of Ron's latest improvements. When Gina got Ron settled into the parallel bars, Ron stood up with no problems. Gina was visibly pleased at how well Ron was able to stand. Now came the time where Ron had to show Eleanor how well he was able to walk. Gina urged him on. "Go ahead Ron, just like we have been working." Ron grasped each bar firmly and tried to put his right foot forward. Unable to lift his leg, Ron lifted himself with his arms and slid forward a few inches. Then, he tried to lift his left leg forward. Much to his and Gina's surprise, for the first time since they had been working together, Ron was able to bring his left leg forward a couple inches on his own. Gina's surprise showed as her hands went to her mouth. Ron looked down at his left leg, immediately looked at Gina. "Well that is a new improvement, I must say. Ok Ron, now let's get that right leg in tune with your left."

As hard as Ron had tried, he again had to lift himself up with his arms. "That's Ok. The right leg must still be asleep. Let's do that again with the left." For the second time Ron lifted his left leg and brought it forward. He did the same until he got to the end of the parallel bars. "You can see he is still improving a great deal." Lisa stated to Eleanor.

Eleanor looked to Ron. "Well done. Gina speaks of you as if you were her star pupil. I can see why. It looks like you two are working well together. Keep up the good work." Eleanor said hello to a few other patients, and then left for her office.

After Eleanor left Gina ran up to Ron and placed her hands on his face. "I can't believe what you just did! When did this start happening?"

Ron, obviously excited, "I don't know. I just tried to imagine my brain telling my leg to lift like you have been saying. You know try to envision the move, and it worked. That felt great! I was beginning to think I was done, but now I know I'm still getting better."

At the end of the week Eleanor asked Gina to stop in her office before she left for the day. When everything was in order, Gina put on her coat. "Are we still on for dinner Gina?" Kevin asked.

"Sure, I have to stop by Eleanor's office though. I'll stop over your apartment when I'm done."

"I thought we could try the new sushi bar that opened last month."

"Sushi, really? I've never had that before but I guess I can give it a shot. I'm in a really good mood so I'm up for anything tonight." Gina walked up to Kevin, and gave him a quick kiss on the lips. "I'll see you in a few."

When Gina opened the door to Eleanor's office, Eleanor asked her to have a seat. Eleanor did not look happy, and Gina quickly noticed. "Hi Eleanor, is something wrong?"

"Gina, it's about Ron. I'm afraid the insurance is up for his stay here. They want him to either go to out-patient care at a facility near his home, or receive in-home care."

"Why, I just filled out my report for the week. You saw the progress he made. For the first time he is able to put his leg forward. If he has a couple more break-through, we could really be onto something. Wait until they read my report. They can't give up on him now."

"Gina, it's not for us to decide. If it were up to me, I would let you two keep working together. They believe that Ron is able to perform basic life functions. Therefore they believe the next step is to end his stay here."

"When is his last day?"

"In two weeks."

"Two weeks? But we just made so much progress. Isn't there anything we can do to let him stay longer? He is going to be crushed. You know out-patient, and in-home care isn't the same. He is going to regress. After all that work we put in. Isn't there anything that can be done?"

"Gina I'm afraid there isn't. It isn't up to us to decide."

"I was so happy for him. You should have seen the look on his face after you left. He was so excited. Now he is going to be so disappointed."

"If it will make it easier for you, I can break the news to him."

"No, it would be better coming from me. I don't know how I'm going to tell him. This is one of the hardest things I've ever had to tell a patient."

"Think it over during the weekend. If you want me to be with you when you tell him I will. I realize how difficult this will be for you."

"Thanks. I guess I'll see you Monday."

When Kevin opened the door to let Gina into his apartment, he knew immediately that something was wrong. "Are you Ok? You look like you just lost your best friend."

"In a way I did. Eleanor told me that the insurance will be stopping payments for Ron. He only has two weeks left."

"Gina, I'm so sorry. I know I've been a jerk when it came to handling the switch. You really did a great job in getting him to where he is right now. I know it doesn't help but think of how far you two have come. I couldn't even get him to sit up, let alone work as hard as he did with you."

"That's what is so hard. We really did come so far together and now that damn insurance company, who doesn't give a shit about the person, wants us to stop. If they could only see him, but all they see is the dollar amount. He's nothing more than a ledger item on their spreadsheet. They don't care about the person. If they did, they would send someone to take a look at him. See the person who is making progress. But they won't."

"Gina, I know sometimes you think I'm a hard ass with some of my patients. You're the opposite. We love our jobs because we make a big difference in people's lives. Most of the time, when a person leaves us, they are much better than when they first met us. Ron is certainly no exception. With you, you get so attached to the patient. It's not only Ron, every person you treat you want to make perfect. But that's not within our power. You have to learn to let your patient go."

Kevin didn't know if Gina was listening or not. She seemed deep in thought. Finally she looked at Kevin. "If I could get someone from the insurance company to see Ron, and how hard he works, they would change their minds. I wonder if Eleanor could arrange that. Kevin do you think Eleanor could arrange that?"

"Gina, you know that won't happen. It doesn't work like that. You can't work with someone forever. You do the best you can with the limited time you have and you move on."

"Move on? I'm supposed to just move on after all of the time and hard work we put in? How am I supposed to move on knowing that if I could work with him a little longer, we might actually make a miracle happen?"

"Baby, I know how you feel. I was like you when I first started. It seemed as if *just* when I was making real progress with a patient, they had to leave. I know how hard it is, but believe me, as time goes by, you begin to accept how things are."

"Kevin I don't think I can ever accept how things are. It isn't fair. Ron is going to be crushed when he hears this. I know how he is going to feel. I've seen it before. Should I tell Ron to move on?"

Instead of going out to dinner, Gina and Kevin stayed at his apartment. They drank a couple bottles of wine, and after many hours of Gina saying how unfair the system is, and Kevin trying to console her, Gina fell asleep on Kevin's couch. In the morning, before Kevin awoke, Gina left for home where she spent the rest of the weekend wondering how to break the news to Ron.

When Gina arrived at work, she found a message asking her to see Eleanor before she speaks to Ron. Maybe Eleanor had some good news. Maybe Eleanor had found a way to allow Ron to stay. After dropping her coat and bag, Gina rushed to Eleanor's office. After Gina knocked, she opened the office door before Eleanor had a chance to say come in. "You wanted to see me?"

"Yes, I have some good news. It isn't the news you wanted, but it's better than nothing."

"What is it?"

"I've asked Ron's primary doctor to write a note that Ron has had a fever and may not be ready for transport in two weeks. I've asked that he recommend Ron stay and additional two weeks. It isn't much, but now at least you will have a whole month to work with Ron.

"That is good news. I wonder if I should tell Ron his time is almost up. Maybe in another two weeks Ron may get another fever. Who knows?"

"Gina, you can't push this. I've asked the doctor as a favor to me. I would take what you have and make the best of it. As for telling Ron, my advice would be the sooner the better. Maybe that will give some extra incentive to work that much harder. But don't push too hard. The last thing we want to do is something that sets him back."

"You're right. I'll tell him this morning. Thanks Eleanor for what you have done. I appreciate it."

"You're welcome Gina. Now go work your magic."

When Ron came into the therapy room he was raring to go. The progress made last week had been the incentive he needed to believe again. "I'm ready when you are Gina."

"Ok, Ron, I'll be right there." Gina walked slowly over to Ron. He could sense something was not right. "Ron, as you know, I always fill out a weekly progress report to your insurance company".

"Your last report must have been easy."

"Yes, it was. In fact you are getting around so well the insurance company thinks that you're ready for out-patient or in-home care."

"What does that mean? We'll still work together right? I can still come in here right?"

"Ron as much as I would love to keep working with you, I'm afraid it means that our time together will come to an end. I don't handle out-patients, and where you live, you wouldn't be treated at this facility. You would be treated at a facility closer to your home."

"We were making such great progress. How can they do that?"

"I know Ron and I'm sorry. The good news is that Eleanor has convinced the insurance company to give us a month. I know we can do some great things in that time. Are you ready to give it your all for the next month?"

"I guess. What happens if things stay the same?"

"Let's not think like that. We'll see what happens and plan from there."

The next four weeks Ron and Gina worked as hard as they could. However the progress was minimal. The final day was rough for both Ron and Gina. Gina wrote Ron a letter telling him how proud she was of his effort. She told him to write to her whenever he wanted. She reminded him of the quote that kept her going when she felt depressed. *Winners are not those who never fail, but those who never quit.*

A couple months later Gina received a letter from Ron. He wanted to thank her for all she had done for him. He vowed to never quit. She had taught him a valuable life lesson. He wrote that St. Johns University was going to honor their full scholarship offer. Whenever he was ready, he was welcome to start his academic career. His choice in field of study was Social Work. He decided he wanted to work with kids who have experienced hardship. He felt, with his experience, he can make a difference in young people's lives. This more than anything gave Gina some closure and allowed her to move on.

One day Gina received a call from an old friend – Jill from St. Helena's hospital. Her and a couple other girls were going out Saturday night and they wanted to meet with her. Gina happily accepted the invitation and they met for drinks at The Ultimate Getaway club near St. Helena's Hospital.

When the four girls met (Jill, Mary Lou Kirkwood, Sue Fleisman, and Gina) they talked about their jobs, their boyfriends, their ex-boyfriends. They looked around the club and talked about every man who walked by – was he married, was he single, was he gay, was he "sponge worthy"? It was a slow night at the club, so they decided to do something different. Jill convinced the other three to go see Francine Quabalah – Tarot Reader and Fortune Teller.

When they arrived at Francine Quabalah's, Gina, Mary Lou and Sue were hesitant. Mary Lou especially was apprehensive. "I don't know Jill. This place looks shady. You know these people are con artists right?"

Sue chimed in. "I'm with you Mary Lou. Are you really going to give somebody twenty bucks to tell you something so generic that it could apply to anyone?"

"Oh come on girls." Jill pleaded. "It's just for fun. It's only twenty bucks. Don't you want to know how your future will turn out?"

"Jill I already know my future - working this dead end job, supporting my two kids until they turn thirty and move out of the house."

"Oh Mary Lou don't be such a party pooper! What do you say Gina?"

"Well, we're already here, so let's throw away twenty bucks for some useless information."

"That's the spirit!"

They opened the front door to a narrow hall. When the door closed behind them, they heard a woman's voice in a Jamaican accent. "Hello ladies, the four of you, please come into my reading room."

Mary Lou whispered. "How did she know there were four of us? I can't even see the room."

"She probably has a buzzer and a camera turned on when the door opens." Sue whispered back.

The four girls walked down the narrow hallway until they came upon a wall of beads. They could see a heavy-set woman sitting behind a table. The woman ushered the girls inside. "Please girls, come sit. Francine will tell you your future. Please, don't be shy, sit. Who is it that wants her future told?"

Jill raised her hand. "I'll go first."

"Please, have a seat." Francine motioned her hand to the chair across the table. "Before we start, may I have something of yours to hold while I look into realm of tomorrow?"

Jill searched through her purse looking for something to give to Francine. She gave Francine a small bear that was given to her by her youngest child. "Thank you dear. Now, let me look at the cards." Francine turned over her first card. "You are a caring parent of three children I see. Yet I don't see a man involved too much."

Jill, taken back glanced to the other girls, then to Francine. "That would be my deadbeat ex."

Francine turned over another card. "I see one of your children is not fully healthy. He seems to have some breathing issues."

"Yes, my middle boy."

Francine turned over another card. "I see a man coming into your life very soon. He is a good man. He will love your children. You will be very happy to have him in your life."

"Is he hot? Can you tell if he has money?"

Francine turned over a card. "I see two children going to college. I see a third child as an artist."

"That's my youngest. He loves to draw."

"I see a long healthy life for you. You are very lucky."

After Jill had ended her reading, Mary Lou was next. Mary Lou had given Francine a bracelet that had been given to her by her husband. Francine told Mary Lou that she too would have a long life. She spoke of Mary Lou's two children and that she would be well off financially. She almost came to tears when Francine mentioned that a woman from the other side was looking after her. She immediately thought of her mother who had passed away less than six months earlier.

Next was Gina. She handed Francine a silver ring. It was a ring that her father gave to her mother when they had first started dating. Francine turned over her first card. "I see a tall man who looks over you from the other side." Naturally Gina thought of her father. "He wants you to know that he is standing tall. He has a woman by his side. She looks very much like you. They want you to know they both are very happy. You carry his words with you."

Gina was startled. *How could she know about the letter from her father?* Francine turned over another card. "I see a lover in your life." Gina thought of Kevin. Would he be the man she spends the rest of her life with?

Francine turned over another card. "I see you will have to make a decision. You will have to decide if a great loss is worth a possible greater gain."

"What decision will I have to make? What will be the loss?"

Francine turned over another card. "I see you helping many people in your life. You will be witness to miracles."

I help people every day. This lady must know I work in a hospital. What miracle will I witness?

Francine turned over another card. She looked up at Gina. "My dear you have been asked to fulfill a promise. You want to fulfill this promise. But I warn you, you cannot force it to happen."

How does she know? How does she know the promise my father asked of me? Gina asked Francine. "Will I fulfill the promise?"

"I'm sorry dear. The cards do not tell me one way or the other."

Gina took out twenty dollars. "If it's more money, here's twenty dollars. Can you tell me now?"

Francine took Gina by the hand. "My dear it is not about the money. Some things in life you have to find out for yourself. All I can tell you is that you cannot force your promise to be fulfilled. If it is fulfilled, you will know. That is all I can tell you."

Gina stood up slowly from the chair. She didn't know whether to feel angry that this lady would lead her on like this. Or should she feel happy that her father is ok and is with her mother. Or should she feel stupid for believing in some psychic tarot reader.

Sue took her turn to hear what Francine had to say about her future.

When they left the room and were back on the street they compared their fortunes. Jill was happy to have a man come into her life. Sue was happy to hear that she would achieve success in her romance novel writing. Mary Lou was happy to hear she would come into money and her two children would be fine. Gina was quiet, and the other three noticed. Sue put her arm around Gina. "What's wrong girl? You're going to witness a miracle."

"That woman, she said things, I didn't think she could know about."

"Oh come on Gina, those people are pros. Why do you think they ask for something personal? So they can get a feel for your situation. She probably saw some of the pictures of Jill's kids when she opened her purse. She probably noticed there wasn't any man in the pictures. With Mary Lou everyone comes into some money sometime. And you're wearing your hospital shoes. No wonder she said you will help a lot of people and witness a miracle. She knows you work in a hospital. Believe me girl those people are nothing but con artists."

"Yeah but isn't it nice to know we're all going to be happy in our lives?" Jill asked.

The girls went back to The Ultimate Getaway for a nightcap. Gina was still shaken.

Chapter 10
A LOT TO LEARN

Brandon Leshing was finishing up his senior year at Althaia University when the NFL draft took place. He had declared that he would not participate in the draft, but that didn't prevent the Atlanta Falcons from selecting him in the seventh round. He graduated from Althaia with top honors.

During the summer, instead of taking a vacation, or celebrating the end of a successful college career, Brandon was preparing for his Medical College Admissions Test or MCAT. He passed on his first attempt and enrolled in Althaia's graduate program of science and medicine. Now that football was no longer in his life, Brandon was able to immerse himself solely into his studies. Shortly after his enrollment, Brandon met Dr. Stephen Bromny, the Dean of the Graduate Program.

Dr. Bromny was an elder statesman at Althaia. His first real practice as a surgeon came while serving in the Vietnam War when Lyndon Johnson escalated the American participation in 1963. Back then he was a 26 year old who had just come out of residency to serve in the army as a medic. Though he was against the war, and seldom, if ever, spoke of his years in the war, he looked back upon those years as the most he had learned about surgery in his life.

After serving his time in the war Dr. Bromny set up a practice in a Texas Veteran's Administration hospital. It was there that he took up training for neurological surgery. He had taken the training after seeing young men and women who had been shot, or suffered from being hit by shrapnel and incurred life altering injuries that he could not treat. Dr. Bromny understood that during war-time there were those who would die on his operating table. But it was the men and women who Dr. Bromny could not help, and sent home, knowing that the patient would never recover, that he questioned his purpose in the war. Because of the helplessness he had felt towards those young patients, he vowed to study neurological surgery.

After working at the Texas VA Hospital for 19 years, he moved his practice to the Philadelphia area. He continued his practice at Pennsylvania Hospital and by 1997, he was considered to be one of the best neurosurgeons in the nation. At the turn of the century he took a seat on the American Board of Neurological Studies. He gave up his position at Pennsylvania Hospital the day he turned seventy. He couldn't handle the hours it took to perform the proper surgical tasks needed for the complex and time staking surgery. Upon his retirement he was offered a seat at Althaia.

Socially Dr. Bromny was a lifelong bachelor. He dated a few women when he was younger but his work was always his top priority. He knew because of his work, he would never be able to provide the commitment he felt was required to make a relationship successful. Now, as a 73 year old man he finally found the time to devote to Lydia, his partner of four years.

Brandon had heard much about Dr. Bromny. He read a number of his publications on neuroscience, and he felt nervous meeting him. "Dr. Bromny, my name is Brandon Leshing. It is an honor to meet you sir. I've studied your journals, and publications regarding your work in neurology."

"Mr. Leshing, I have heard much about you as well, although I am not a big fan of football. I hope you won't hold it against me that I find the sport to be barbaric in nature. I assume that is one of the biggest reasons the American public are fanatical about the sport. I understand that you are quite different. I understand that you were quite good at the game and would have made a lot of money had you pursued it as a professional. Yet you gave it all up to continue your studies. I don't know whether to admire you or take you for a fool. What do you think?"

"I never played the game for money. I don't care to be rich. I know what I want out of life and this is what I need to do in order to achieve it."

"Ah yes, I have seen your speech, your promise to a childhood friend. You feel responsible for his death and you somehow want to make it up to him even though he is no longer here. Is that what you want out of life?"

"With all due respect sir that's something I don't want to discuss. To answer your question, yes, you are correct."

"I admire your integrity. I must warn you. The study of neurology has been around for over a hundred years. We are not much closer to achieving your goal now, than when we started."

"Dr. Bromny, technology has advanced more the past decade than the previous eighty years combined. I believe as technology advances, within a decade, we should be near a solution for neurological disorders like paralysis, Alzheimer's, and MS. I hope to be a part of finding those answers."

Dr. Bromny grinned as a Cheshire cat who knew a secret that no one else knew. As he contemplated, looking back at the days when he was Brandon's age the grin was gone. "I too was full of hope when I was as young as you. I witnessed horrific injuries to young men and women in the Vietnam War. Injuries that I knew would change those young people's lives forever." Dr. Bromny now seemed lost in thought. Brandon didn't know whether to say something or not. Finally Dr. Bromny spoke. "I still sometimes have nightmares of young soldiers no more than eighteen years of age lying on my table asking me to help heal them. I knew then, as I know now that healing them was beyond my, or anyone else's capability. I used to think, just as you think today, that I could learn all I could about neurology. I thought I could find a cure if I dedicated myself. In the seventies, computers were just taking form. They were being used in research, and in hospitals. Many people thought, as I did, and as you do today, that with the help of these wonderful machines that all kinds of cures were just around the corner. All we had to do was feed the machine the right questions and it would tell us the right answers. But, forty years later, we still can't seem to ask the right questions."

"What are you trying to say Dr. Bromny? Are you trying to tell me to forget about my goals? Should I quit without even trying?"

"No, no Mr. Leshing. I am not trying to make you forget about your goals. I am just trying to tell you that you shouldn't throw your life away solely into a pursuit that most likely will not be solved in your lifetime. I want you to go into this pursuit of yours with a full understanding. Though we have never met, I have kept an eye on you, from a distance of course. I don't think there is anything I could say that would alter your goals. And maybe you will attain success in reaching them. It is true that technology has improved much over the last decade. But what you are pursuing is not technological advances. You are looking for answers to the human anatomy, the human brain, the human neurological system. You are looking for answers that only God knows. Mr. Leshing, don't take this as a pleading for you to stop your pursuit. Take this as sound advice from a man who, just like you, wanted to solve mysteries of the human body that only God can solve. Pursue your dreams. Pursue your pledge to keep your promise. But don't do it at the expense of giving up living."

"Dr. Bromny I appreciate your advice. I have to live my life as I see fit. Right now I must do all that I can to keep my promise. I realize that I have given up a lot in my life as you have in yours. However if there is just a sliver of a chance that by giving up those things allows me to keep my promise, then it will be worth the risk of never having lived a full life. Dr. Bromny, if you were me, and you have witnessed the advances in other areas such as developing a vaccine for the AIDS virus, or the advances made in curing various types of cancers, would you make sacrifices in the hope of finding a cure for neurological disorders?" Dr. Bromny didn't answer Brandon. He knew he didn't have to. Both already knew the answer was 'yes'.

While Brandon continued his graduate studies, his father was making advances in his career. Pat was asked to apply for a Sr. Marketing position to help generate revenues in new markets. After doing various television and newspaper interviews, and after being seen hugging his son after the Heisman speech on ESPN, Pat had become a quasi-celebrity. Due to the public's familiarity with Pat, the Directors at Universal Cable thought he would be the ideal spokesman to market their company in new regions across the nation. Pat's base salary doubled and he was given bonuses based upon the number of new cable subscribers. The job involved more traveling but Pat was able to take his wife Cindy with him and treat the travel as working vacations. Pat had never been camera shy and the more commercials he was in, the more he felt like a celebrity. Though Pat would not see any of the millions of dollars his son passed up, he was happy with his new position at Universal Cable.

For the first three years of graduate school, Brandon immersed himself in the classes that were required for him to obtain his degree. He considered a lot of the courses to be more of a nuisance rather than a necessity. Brandon was deeply interested in neuroanatomical studies. However he also had to take classes in physiology, biochemistry, pharmacology and others. He completed every class with top marks.

Dr. Bromny kept an eye on Brandon as he progressed each year. Ever since meeting him face to face when Brandon was a first year graduate student, he saw a lot of himself in Brandon. He saw that Brandon was reclusive-like, only concerned with his work. When there was a break in school, Brandon took up research assignments on the latest treatments for neurological disorders. He wasn't interested in the latest technological advances in wheelchairs or human exoskeletons that were supposed to give more "dignity" to quadriplegics or those inflicted with multiple sclerosis. When Dr. Bromny was in his thirties, he too was only interested in finding a cure not a new piece of machinery. Dr. Bromny noticed more and more that the probability was that Brandon would end up like him – devoting his entire life towards an unattainable goal. Multiple times he had tried to warn Brandon about what he would lose if he continued to focus solely on his work. Brandon listened, appreciated the advice, but was set on his own goal – to find a cure.

"I too had that as my goal. Remember the talk we had about chasing answers only God knows. Many people come into this profession thinking they may become famous, or be successful financially. They see billions of dollars being granted or donated to help find a cure and they think that they are entitled to a piece of that pie once they get their degree. I know you are not like that, but your drive may be just as dangerous. You are blinded by your goal to find a cure, as was I. But I learned that in our profession it may be more prudent and more beneficial to those suffering to find ways of making their lives more tolerable. It is one thing to discover the unknown, but don't lose sight of the benefits of what we already know and improving on that."

"I'm not sure what you mean Dr. Bromny."

"We have made many advances in the medicines, technology, psychology that help make patients' lives more tolerable. Until the complete cure is found, we must work with what is available to us, with what we know. You must learn how to treat patients with the knowledge and understanding we have. As of now you will not be able to help most patients to a full recovery. Try to make their lives more tolerable, more bearable, and more dignified. Help them to become productive members of society so to speak."

Brandon knew what Dr. Bromny was saying. Dr. Bromny had tried to persuade him to be more rounded in life. Now Dr. Bromny's advice was to be more rounded in his medical career. To pin him into one aspect, one branch of science, one that was almost completely unknown, would most likely be a path of despair. It might lead to a life of accomplishing nothing while giving away

238

everything. Brandon was willing to gamble it all for nothing. Brandon felt that dedicating time towards other aspects of science, other than curing spinal cord injuries, would take away time that would be needed to keep his promise. He wasn't willing to compromise. "I understand what you are saying Dr. Bromny. I will give your advice some thought. But I have my priorities and there isn't anything that will change them."

"All I can do is offer. You are different than most students. Most students come into the program with altruistic ideals. They have high hopes of finding cures, helping those who are unfortunate and in need. But most of those people lose those ideals once the tuition loans come due. They lose their ideals once they fall in love, have children or decide that they want that new shiny car or a big new house. You have specific reasons for your ideals. Reasons that I don't think will change for monetary gains. I don't want to see you waste those ideals by chasing something that most likely will never be realized. You have the talent to help a lot of people. I hope you use it."

During Brandon's fourth year of graduate school Dr. Bromny had secured Brandon an internship at a hospital in New Jersey, Burdette Tomlin. It was a rare opportunity which was extremely hard to get for most graduate students. The reason Dr. Bromny had secured the internship was so Brandon could see and work with real patients suffering from neurological injuries. The head surgeon at the hospital was a friend whom he had known for decades, Dr. William Brantly. Though Brandon would be serving a residency for all types of hospital care, there would most likely be opportunities where he could oversee spinal cord surgery. Because Burdette Tomlin is close to the beach, it averaged one spinal cord injury per month due to diving accidents alone.

Fred Arlington was a patient at the hospital when Brandon began his residency. Freddie had broken his back in a surfing accident and was paralyzed from his waist down. Though Freddie couldn't feel pain below his waist, he was given Demerol every 3-4 hours each day. Dr. Brantly said the Demerol was given more for the patient's mental health than physical pain. A few weeks later, Freddie was sent to a rehabilitation facility in New York.

"What happens next? When will you see the Freddie again?"

"I might see the Freddie in a couple months, perhaps. It's more likely however I'll never see him again. As the surgeon, we rarely see the patient after he leaves for rehabilitation. For all I know he could be out running a marathon by next year. Or, and most likely, if he is in a marathon, he will be riding a wheel chair. All we can do is stabilize the patient for transfer to a rehab hospital."

"Don't you want to see the patient all the way through? Don't you at least try to heal him?"

"We can't become attached to the patient. All we can do is what we know – get them stable and to a rehabilitation hospital. With these types of injuries, seeing a patient to the end means caring for the patient for years. We don't know what nature will do or when healing will occur, if at all."

Brandon was extremely upset about this. He didn't want to get into neurosurgery only to ship his patients to a rehab facility, out of his care and control, never seeing and never knowing the end result. "Dr. Brantly isn't that like working half way? Don't you care what happens to the patient?"

"It doesn't mean that I don't care. It's out of my control. No insurance company would pay for a patient to stay here for what may be years at a time. If there was a way to keep them here, we would run out of hospital beds. The patient's care is best being given by professional therapists. I'm a surgeon. I don't have the time or expertise to perform the therapy these patients require."

As Brandon's residency came towards the end, Dr. Brantly wrote to Dr. Bromny saying he wasn't sure Brandon would be cut out as a neurosurgeon. Dr. Brantly believed that Brandon may be best served performing research or perhaps as a doctor at a rehabilitation hospital. He wrote that Brandon didn't seem to have the capacity to distance himself from the patient emotionally. As a surgeon, especially performing surgeries that seldom had the patient recovering fully, that would take a toll on Brandon sooner than later in life. This may eventually cause Brandon to give up his practice altogether, which would be a shame. Brandon did have the acumen, the drive and the intelligence to digest, and analyze the information regarding the spinal cord and other human neuroanatomical that he probably would be best fit in some type of research.

Dr. Bromny never showed Brandon the assessment written by Dr. Brantly. Dr. Bromny's perception of Brandon was concurred by a top neurosurgeon. He also felt that with Brandon's emotional connection created from his childhood, he most likely would become too attached to the patient. Because Brandon would see many failures with little successes, eventually this could destroy him. Dr. Bromny had hoped that after seeing how little time was spent by a surgeon working with patients with neurological injuries, that Brandon would consider opening up more towards other aspects of science. But Brandon held steadfast to his single-minded goal of finding a cure for spinal cord injuries and becoming a neurosurgeon so that he could 'fix it'.

Brandon's thesis was titled: *Molecular Cure to Spinal Cord Injury*. His thesis centered on a theory that if one could remove the frayed, damaged, and dead cells from the area where the injury had occurred, then connect the remaining fibers within the cord, there would be a greater chance of recovery and possibly a cure. He noted in his thesis that the cells within the spinal cord don't normally regenerate like damaged cells elsewhere in the body. This was common knowledge in the medical field. And, in the cases where the cells do regenerate, the process was too slow to depend on for a full recovery. What was needed was somehow to attach the fibers by using some sort of glue. He reasoned that the main deterrent in fiber healing was that when the nerve area is damaged, scar tissue build up prevented the cells from building a connection. If one could remove the scar tissue cleanly, the good or living cells would have a better chance on connecting thus reestablishing the functionality from the brain to the muscle. But Brandon's thesis had three main problems. One, his theory meant removing pieces of fiber within the spinal cord. And, in cases where the fibers were still connected, but damaged, his theory would sever the fibers to remove the scar tissue build up. No medical person in the world would even consider severing a piece of the spinal cord no matter how damaged. Second, there was no proven way to "glue" the fibers back together. Third, fibers are so abundant that figuring out which fiber connected to another was nearly impossible.

Brandon's thesis was looked upon by his professors as insightful, detailed, and imaginative. Most current research for healing the spinal cord focused on injecting the patient with a substance like stem cells that would try to "wake up" the nervous system or become part of the nerve fibers to a point where the nerves would essentially heal themself. Unfortunately not many people, especially the elder statesmen in the neurological field, found Brandon's paper to be valid enough to actually apply funding, research and application, or in other words, taken very seriously.

Prior to his graduation, Dr. Bromny again talked to Brandon regarding his future, both immediate and long term. "Brandon I have given my advice several times. You interned at a hospital and saw first-hand the difficulties a surgeon has trying to repair spinal cord injuries. Whether you adhere to my advice or not is completely up to you. I would like to offer a little more, perhaps for the last time if you don't mind."

"Dr. Bromny anything you wish to tell me I welcome at any time. After hearing of your experiences in life, I respect you all the more. I believe that while our reasons for choosing the path we have chosen may be different, our hopes are the same. You say you may have wasted most of your life working towards your goals, but because of your drive and passion, you have helped a lot of people including myself get closer to finding a cure. I don't think that is a life wasted at all."

"I appreciate your kind words. I see a lot of myself in you. Maybe that is why I have tried to offer what I know to you more than most. Though I don't look back at my life as a complete waste, I do regret not enjoying the finer things in life. I wish I had the ability to have stopped and smell the roses so to speak. I wish I would have fallen in love, had children upon which to pass on my experiences. Those things we have already spoken about. That is not why I have asked to speak with you today."

"What do you wish to discuss?"

"Have you thought about what you will do after you have graduated?"

"My next step is to become board certified for neurosurgery. That will mean finding a residency at a hospital. I appreciate the opportunity you set up for me at Burdette Tomlin. I was hoping that I could apply for a residency there. I will also apply to hospitals in Pittsburgh, Atlanta, Boston and

Minnesota. I never realized how few places actually offered a position of residency for neurosurgeons. I hope to secure a position."

"May I offer an alternative?"

Brandon was hesitant. "Sure."

"All of your work has been in research. Even in your thesis, instead of focusing on a field of surgery that exists today, you focused on new techniques not yet proven much less practiced. If you did get a position of residency, you would be in a position where you would have to observe, and practice under supervision, surgical procedures that for the most part would not have anything to do with spinal cord injury. Any complex surgery related to the spine, or the brain, you would solely be in a position of observation. And, when the time came for you to actually perform neurosurgery, you would have to perform that surgery as it is performed today. You would never have the ability to test your theories. After a few years, maybe a short few years, you may become disillusioned. If not disillusioned, you may become frustrated to the point of giving up or risking your career performing an unaccredited procedure."

Brandon had thought of Dr. Bromny's words. He realized that he could be right. What was the point of all of his study? What was the point of all of the research he had done thus far? What was the point of discovering ideas on how to treat spinal cord injuries if he could never apply them? If he could not perform any research, he would basically be in a position where he would be waiting for someone else to discover a cure. He knew he couldn't live waiting for someone else to find a way to 'fix' things. "I see your point Dr. Bromny but what am I supposed to do? I can't help a patient if I can't perform surgery. But you are right. I can't move on with my ideas if I am never able to apply them."

"Have you thought of moving into research instead of becoming a surgeon? While working in research you would be on the cutting edge of new ideas in spinal cord recovery. Also, working in research you could still become a neurosurgeon. What you would need to find is a hospital that focuses on research, yet also performs surgery. One that would allow you to become board certified. I have a friend that I had served with in the army. We were both young surgeons at the time and when we got out of the army we worked together for many years at a hospital in Texas. He is now on the board of trustees at the Mount Sinai Medical Center in Illinois. If you like, I could write a recommendation for you to join their research staff. The center has begun spinal cord research the last ten years or so. But, the center is within the Accreditation Council for Graduate Medical Education. You would still technically become a resident at the center. But it would take you longer than normal to become board certified for neurosurgery since half of your work would be in research and not actual surgery. Instead of a three year residency, you may be required to be there for five years, maybe six years. The choice is yours of course and I don't need an answer right now. In fact I prefer if you would take a day or two to think about my offer."

"If I accepted your offer, would the residency be guaranteed?"

"No. My recommendation doesn't mean that it is guaranteed. You would still have to go through the application and interview process. But, your ranking is at the top. I have faith that you would perform well in the written test. You have had experiences that other people in your position have never had. I believe you would do well in the interviews. Though many in our field don't have quite the interest in sports as the average person, you have been sort of high profile celebrity and that may serve you well."

"What kind of research would I be doing?"

"That would be up to the center's senior staff. You certainly wouldn't be walking in from day one demanding your own lab equipment and staff. The first couple years would be taking orders from the senior staff. You will have a chance to present your ideas. You may, after a while, even have the chance to head up an assignment and apply your ideas. That is up to you to convince the senior staff that your ideas have merit. No one is going to hand you the keys to the laboratory."

"I see. May I get back to you on Monday?"

"That would be fine. Let's say we meet again Monday at 3?"

"I'll see you here at 3PM sharp."

Walking out of Dr. Bromny's office, Brandon already knew that he would accept his offer to apply for a position at Mount Sinai Hospital. But, he wanted to consider all of his options before stating so. When the two met on Monday, he accepted the offer and sent in his application. Dr. Bromny made a call to his friend from Texas, Dr. Harold Bernstein.

Brandon sent his application to Mount Sinai Medical Center and within three weeks he was granted an opportunity to take an acceptance test and be interviewed by a panel of members of the Mount Sinai Board. He arrived in the Illinois Center at 8AM and was sent to one of the conference rooms. There he took an acceptance test that took four hours to complete. After finishing the test, he was led to a room where he met a three panel interviewing team. The team consisting of two men and one woman, each no younger than fifty years of age, the oldest, Dr. Bernstein, was sixty-six. Both Dr. Bernstein and his colleague, Dr. John Ross had known about Brandon and his college football exploits. The third member of the panel, Dr. Jane Medicci, had never watched a football game in her life. She had no idea of Brandon's success on the gridiron.

The interview lasted three hours with a fifteen minute break in the middle. Brandon left the interview feeling exhausted, but pretty good about how the day went. One month later he was informed that he was accepted to Mount Sinai Medical Center. He had passed the written test easily, and the panel voted two to one for his acceptance. Brandon figured that Dr. Jane Medicci was the lone dissenting vote since she wasn't a football fan. But, it didn't matter, he had been accepted and a new chapter of his life would begin. He was a step closer to keeping his promise to Louie.

Brandon thanked Dr. Bromny for all of his advice and help. Dr. Bromny once again reminded Brandon that he should find the time to enjoy life's pleasures. But he knew his advice would fall on deaf ears. Dr. Bromny told Brandon that it was Dr. Ross who was the dissenting voter at Mount Sinai, though he did not know why.

Brandon was 27 years old when he arrived at Mount Sinai Medical Center to start his residency. Aside from football, all of his life had been classrooms, and performing his own research. Even though Dr. Bromny had tried to temper his vision, Brandon was excited to get closer to keeping his promise to Louie. He had never had the opportunity to apply his work to real life applications. Now procedures, treatments, discoveries found within his research could be applied and tested. This was his first real opportunity to turn thoughts and ideas into tests to prove their validity. Brandon came to Mount Sinai knowing that his own ideas, especially those that he had put to paper in his thesis would most likely be shelved in favor of initiatives brought on by the senior staff. In addition to his research assignments, he would have the opportunity to obtain his accreditation to become a neurosurgeon.

Brandon's first week in Illinois was spent getting to know the staff, his co-workers, and getting familiar with the general area. His living quarters was a dorm like room near the Medical Center that was paid for by Mount Sinai. He roomed with research assistant, Shane Laitner who was also in his mid-twenties. Both were assigned to the research team that looked for ways to stimulate nerve growth. "So you're the famous Brandon Leshing, the Heisman Trophy winner."

Brandon didn't like talking about those days. In his mind that was a different time, a closed chapter, a different life. "That was a few years ago."

"When they told me who I was rooming with I wasn't sure it was really you. I looked you up on the web and found your Heisman speech, pretty touching."

"Those days are behind me now. I'm in the same boat as you. I'm looking forward to the challenges ahead." Shane got the message. His roommate didn't particularly want to talk about his past. Everyone has their reasons. If that was how it was, Shane wouldn't press it. "From what I've heard the next few years will be pretty intense. I hope we can help each other out along the way."

"I've heard the same. I hope we can help each other out as well. Have you heard about our assignments?"

"The only thing I know is that we'll be headed up by Dr. Ross. As to what is expected, I guess we'll find out Monday at orientation."

Brandon was reminded that it was Dr. Ross who had the one dissenting vote when it came to his interview. When orientation began, the team of six assistants, a team leader, Dr. Marion Supek, and Dr. Ross assembled in a class room. Dr. Supek welcomed the team to the Medical Center, and gave a briefing on the assignments, team itinerary, etc. She introduced Dr. Ross.

"Good morning. As Dr. Supek mentioned we will be conducting research regarding the possibilities of stimulating nerve growth by injecting damaged nerve tissue with various elements. With this kind of research and hopeful breakthroughs, we will be developing solutions to real cures for many neurological injuries and diseases. Our goal is to develop a way to aid the nerve cells to regenerate. Our primary focus will consist of the use of stem cells, but we will also be conducting other types of research to regenerate nerve cells."

"What we hope to accomplish is provide a substance that will enable the spinal cord to heal itself. This is the general accepted way to conduct research by the medical community. However we will be using new types of cells and new techniques in addition to common research. The reason we are able to perform this research is that we have been given a multi-million dollar grant by a donor who is suffering from Parkinson's disease."

"One of your colleagues, Mr. Leshing, has written a thesis on the possibilities of gluing damaged spinal tissue back together." Dr. Ross chuckled. "I don't mean to degrade his work. I'm sure he put a lot of time and effort into his publication. Suffice to say, this is nothing more than fairy tale. As most of you know simply attaching the damaged areas within the spinal cord is a fruitless task for a number of reasons. Matching the correct fiber tissue is nearly impossible. Even if you could match the fibers properly you would need some way to hold the fibers in place. To date, there is no such substance that exists. Most important, even if you could match the damaged fibers, even if you came up with a substance that could hold the fibers in place, simply removing the damaged cells, then stretching the remaining fiber is impossible. The fibers are not elastic where you could stretch them together. This is why the accepted practice, and the research we will be conducing, will be to develop a substance that will allow the damaged cells to regenerate, to come alive so to speak."

"Naturally we can't conduct our research on humans. So, we will be using laboratory mice to apply our techniques and procedures. If anyone is queasy when it comes to handling rodents, you have two choices. Apply for a different research assignment, or get used to it. Each of you has been given the tour of the Medical Center and the research you will be conducting. You will also be expected to put in hours of residency within the hospital. You will be expected to observe various operations that will be performed by our senior surgical staff. Occasionally you will assist in some of the operations. Towards the end of your residency you will be required to take the lead in performing procedures while a senior staff member observes. If there are any neurological procedures that will be performed, all of you will be expected to observe."

"You will be paired into three groups. All of your work will be assigned by Dr. Supek, and each week you will turn in your work to her. One word of advice - be very detailed in your reports. Dr. Supek, while a tremendous neurosurgeon, is not a mind reader. If I have to ask Dr. Supek what you meant by something you have written and she is not aware of what is meant it means that you have wasted Dr. Supek's time and more importantly, you have wasted my time. Time is not a commodity we have to waste. If you consistently waste our time, you will be replaced by someone who won't. If I sound harsh it's because I have to report to our donor on our progress. I don't want to tell him that we haven't made progress due to a lack of effort. Do I make myself clear?" All six residents nodded in agreement.

"Good. Ladies and gentlemen we are on the verge of changing the world in a very positive way. We are on the verge of discovering the greatest medical breakthrough since the polio vaccine. To achieve greatness, sacrifices will have to be made. I'm sure all of you realize what those sacrifices are otherwise you would not be here today. All of you have been chosen out of hundreds of candidates because you have shown a willingness to sacrifice. I congratulate you all now for making it this far. Believe me it is an honor to be heading down the road you are about to travel. I look forward to the many successes I know we will achieve."

Dr. Ross left the room without asking if there were any questions. Dr. Supek walked to the front of the room. "Ok everyone that will be all for today. I'll see you tomorrow morning at 8AM sharp in Lab Room C12."

As the students left the room, Shane pulled Brandon aside. "Dr. Ross was pretty hard on you in there. Do you two have any history I should know about? I'm your partner and if there's anything I should know tell me now. "

"Honestly I'm not sure what his issue is. At my interview Dr. Ross seemed like a real nice guy."

"Let's hope he was just trying to make a point. I'm a team player, but this will be hard enough. I don't want to be in the middle of some feud."

The next morning when the team assembled, Dr. Supek handed out the assignments. "As Dr. Ross stated yesterday our research will be conducted using mice. One of the hardest things a resident has to deal with right away is disabling a subject. So, without further ado, let's walk to the table where we have several mice already sedated. I'm going to show you how we disable a mouse, then, I want each of you to do the same."

Once Dr. Supek had completed the incision, and had snapped the spinal cord of a mouse, each resident had to do the same. The first resident, Michelle Brewman, looked down at her specimen and stared before Dr. Supek came by her side. "I know this is tough. You have to remember that this is all for a greater cause. In no way whatsoever can you become emotionally attached to the specimen. You will have to train yourself to think that this is nothing more than an object that will help find a cure. I'll walk you through it."

With the help of Dr. Supek, Michelle was able to complete her assignment. The next three residents, all men, were able to perform their assignment quickly. When it was Brandon's turn to disable his specimen, he immediately he thought of Louie. He didn't think he could do it. He knew at some point in his career that he would need to practice on some type of living being, but now that it was here, he found it harder than he had anticipated.

"Mr. Leshing, the longer you stare at your subject the harder it will be. As I told Michelle, you cannot become emotionally attached. Think of this as a necessary step towards the greater good." Brandon made his incision, and severed the spinal cord of his mouse. When he was done, he continued to stare at the being he had just destroyed.

The type of research that was being conducted on nerve damage was finding a way to inject a substance into the nerves and see if that substance could somehow rejuvenate the damaged cells to the point where they would function. Dr. Ross believed that the best way to a cure was to allow the nerve cells to correct themselves, with a little help. The research that was assigned to Brandon and Shane was to focus on healing damaged nerve cells through incorporating new cells. Brandon and Shane learned everything they could in regard to molecular biology, cellular biology, genetics, immunology, and virology, as well as rapidly rising technologies such as microarray and proteomics. Anything that Dr. Ross and his staff could imagine was injected into the specimen's spinal cord to rejuvenate damaged cells.

Weeks turned into months, then years. The research team headed up by Dr. Ross was no closer to finding a cure then when they had started. Frustration set in among the team especially with Dr. Ross who was beginning to be looked upon as someone with whom millions of dollars had been spent for no return of investment. The teams had tried everything they could think of to "wake up" damaged nerve cells but with no avail. The residents were frustrated, but in their view, they were still obtaining their residency and were closer to obtaining certification to be a neurosurgeon. To them, whether or not the team actually found anything resembling a possible cure was a bonus.

Brandon however, was not in it solely for his certification. He was more interested in the success of the research or rather the lack thereof. Several times he had presented his theories to Dr. Supek, who in turn, presented them to Dr. Ross. While Dr. Supek was willing to listen and suggest part of the team attempt to look into the possibility of Brandon's ideas, Dr. Ross was adamant on sticking to his own agenda. Brandon's frustration was much higher than anyone else on the team.

By the middle of the fourth year, and still no closer to finding any cure, the research was disbanded. Brandon was left in a state of disillusionment. He had applied and had been accepted to Mount Sinai Medical Center and had such high hopes that he would now be in the middle of real research and application towards keeping his promise. Instead he was little closer to achieving his goal than when he started. There was one validation however, he believed more than ever that the only way the nerves would reestablish their functionality was if there was a way to remove the damaged cells and connect the living tissue.

During their years of residency, Brandon and the other residents had observed many surgical procedures. Though they had observed half dozen procedures regarding the spinal cord, they had never been involved in performing surgery to the spinal cord. They had performed dozens of procedures ranging from knee and hip replacements, to appendectomies, to intestinal procedures, but never anything as delicate as the spinal cord.

Dr. Supek had discussed with the team that one resident would be the primary surgeon and another two residents would be assistants the next time a neurological procedure was needed. Both Dr. Ross and Dr. Supek would also be on hand and would take over immediately if any trouble or anything unusual occurred. The residents were asked if any felt that they were not ready to perform such a surgery. Of the six residents, two had stated that they would rather not be the primary surgeon.

After the senior staff conferred as to who would be best to perform as the primary surgeon, they decided that Brandon would be the best choice. This surprised Brandon. He thought for sure that Dr. Ross' input would force him out of any chance to be the primary surgeon. Dr. Supek explained that the senior staff noticed that of all of the residents, Brandon seemed to have the most focus, endurance, and drive. Dr. Supek did confirm to Brandon privately that Dr. Ross was the only one who disagreed with the choice. She didn't why.

"He has had something against me from the start. I don't know why but he doesn't like me. He never listened to any of my suggestions throughout the research. And now that the research funding has dried up, there's no sense in me continuing with my suggestions."

"Honestly Brandon, I don't know why he has that opinion of you. I tried to set aside some time to look into your suggestions. I'm sorry I couldn't convince him otherwise. You have been a model resident and I know that someday you will get your chance. It may not be here, but when you do, I'm sure that you will make the most of it."

"Dr. Supek I know you have tried your best to allow for some of my ideas to be tested and I appreciate that. I'm not sure where I go from here. All I can do is finish out my residency as best I can."

"Well congratulations on the surgery. I hope you don't have to perform it, but be ready."

"Thanks, Dr. Supek."

Anna Regant was brought into the hospital after being involved in an automobile accident. Anna was a passenger driving on Interstate 41 when the front tire blew out sending the car into the guard rail. The driver was able to climb out of the car on her own, but Anna's side of the car spun directly into the rail. Upon impact Anna's head jolted forward injuring her neck. She was rushed into Mt. Sinai Hospital where Brandon, the other residents, Dr. Ross, and Dr. Supek were paged.

After stabilizing Anna, Brandon and the surgical team assessed the injury. Two other senior staff members were on hand to observe. As Brandon read out the damage, a break in the C-4 and C-5 section of the patient's neck,

Dr. Ross began to berate his diagnosis. "Have you checked for any lower extremity lacerations? Have you checked for any possible allergic reactions to any medications?" Everyone looked at Dr. Ross incredulously. The immediate damage, the damage that had to be mitigated as soon as possible was that of her neck. Dr. Supek interjected that the procedure being done by Brandon was the proper one and she asked that Brandon continue. Dr. Ross glared at Dr. Supek who dared questioned his authority.

When the initial diagnosis was complete, the surgical team washed up and prepared for the surgery. The initial surgery would be to remove all loose bone fragments from the damaged area, then take a portion of the patient's hip bone and use that to fuse the neck into place. Titanium rods would be used to fuse the bone. As Brandon cleared out the bone fragments, Dr. Ross continuously pointed out fragments that had to be removed. It wasn't that Brandon didn't see the fragments. He could only remove one at a time and just hadn't had a chance to remove the piece that Dr. Ross had pointed out. When the area was clean, Brandon began to cut out a piece of hip bone to be used to fuse the neck. Brandon measured out the piece of the hip bone to be cut.

"Dr. Leshing, if what you have lined up is where you will be cutting, you are sadly mistaken."

"Dr. Ross I have measured precisely the amount of bone I will need to fuse the neck into place."

"You'll need another centimeter and if you don't do as I say then step aside, I will take over."

Brandon measured out an additional centimeter and cut away the piece of hip bone. Next was the implant of the titanium rods to hold the fused bones in place. Brandon measured precisely the amount of rod needed for the fusion. Once again, Dr. Ross interjected. "Dr. Leshing the amount of rod you have is too small. You need the pieces to cover both the C-4 and C-5 sections and fuse that to the C-3 and C-6 sections. The amount of rod you have will not be enough."

Brandon knew from his last response that telling Dr. Ross that he knew precisely the amount required would only anger him. Thus, he extended his cut of the titanium. When the fusion took place, Brandon had too much hip bone and had to shave off the extra centimeter. The rods as well were too long and had to be shaved. Brandon didn't say a word to Dr. Ross. Everyone in the room knew Brandon had been right all along and that Dr. Ross would have been better off keeping his mouth shut.

Dr. Ross justified his assessment. "It's always best to be too long than to be too short. If you are too short in the amount of hip bone you extract you must then make another extraction from the hip. And if you are too short in the titanium then the rod is of no use, you have to throw it away."

No one cared to listen to Dr. Ross' assessment. After four hours of surgery, Anna was placed in an ICU Unit under critical care. After cleaning up, everyone congratulated the team on a fine job. That is everyone except Dr.

Ross. When Dr. Ross was nowhere to be found, Brandon went looking for him. He wanted answers.

Without knocking, Brandon burst into Dr. Ross' office. "Alright! Let's have it! What exactly is your problem with me?"

"Mr. Leshing I have no idea what you are talking about."

"You don't? Ever since I applied for this assignment you have been against me. I heard from a reliable source that you were the dissenting vote when it came to my acceptance. The first day at orientation you berate me in front of the other residents. All throughout the research when everyone knew there was no progress being made you didn't even consider one idea I had. Dr. Supek herself came to you recommending we try some of my ideas but you were against it. Then all I hear about is how many mistakes I made in the surgery. Even though every correction you made turned out to be wrong."

"Ok Leshing here it is. First of all I felt that there were more qualified candidates when you applied. But, I was overruled. Why? Not because I was wrong, but because the staff felt having a 'celebrity' on board would raise our profile. Second, in regards to your thesis I merely pointed out the holes in your research. The senior staff had already made it clear that I had no say as to whom we would take on for this research, but I'll be damned if I was going to let them have you dictate how the research would be conducted. Therefore I snipped your little thesis in the bud. As for the surgery, I made my point. In cases where bone graph are needed and titanium rods are required it is always better to be wrong on the plus side than on the short side."

"No, I'm sorry Dr. Ross, I'm not buying it. I'm not the only one who had written a thesis regarding nerve regeneration. I'm not the only one who wanted to try some of the ideas I had. And I'm not the only one who looked at you with distain in that surgery room after your constant berating. Now I want to know right now what your problem is with me."

"You just don't know when to quit do you? You want to know why I despise people like you."

"People like me?"

"Yes, people like you. It's because people think you walk on water when all you are is a facade. They see you and they see a celebrity. You don't earn your way through the hardships that every student, every resident, every surgeon must go through. Your way is paved by people wanting to wait on you hand and foot. You play a damn sport and suddenly people can't do enough for you. For every person like you there are hundreds of people getting rejected because they aren't seen as someone with clout. Ok hotshot? Now you know."

"First of all you knew nothing about me prior to my application. Obviously all you saw was some football jock wanting to play doctor. You knew nothing of the sacrifices I have made to get to this point. No one, I mean no one has ever given me a damn thing in regard to the medical profession. Every step I earned. If anything I had to work harder because people like you only saw the football player. Hell, if I wanted to be a celebrity I would have continued with football, made my money and wouldn't have given the medical profession a second thought. Your problem, and people like you, is that you only see what they want to see. They don't take in all of the information around them to analyze and perform the proper action. People like you are the ones in it for the glory. People like you are so afraid that if someone has an idea that works, that you will be shoved to the wayside. So people like you are stuck in their own little world trying to control everything and everybody. People like you are the ones thinking that you have all the answers, when in fact you are the reason why teams such as this fail."

Dr. Ross was enraged. He suspected everyone blamed him for the failures of the research team. And now here was Leshing confirming that. Before Dr. Ross could say a word, Brandon continued. "Now if you will excuse me *I* will talk to that patient's family to let them know that we don't have all the answers. I'm going to be honest and tell them to pray and pray hard because as of now we haven't the slightest clue what kind of recovery she will make." Brandon stormed out of the room.

As Brandon walked to the waiting area his thoughts turned towards Anna. For the first time he would have to be the one to try and console a patient's family. He hadn't the slightest idea of how to do that. His thoughts drifted back to Louie. What did the doctors tell Louie's parents? Did they know, as he knows now, that the prognosis wasn't good? Did they tell Louie's parents that everything would be Ok? Someone told Louie that everything would be Ok didn't they? But it wasn't true, was it. One thing he knew for sure, he wouldn't tell them anything to get their hopes up unrealistically. He had to be honest. As he walked down the hallway to the waiting room he could see Michelle who had served as the anesthesiologist trying to console Anna's parents. When Brandon walked into the room the family immediately approached him. "Doctor, can you tell me anything about Anna? Is she going to be alright?"

"Honestly Mr. Regant we don't know for sure what the prognosis will be. All I can tell you now is that the surgery was a success. There is still a long way until we know for sure what her outcome will be. She is in critical but stable condition. She is resting."

"But she'll live right? There's no danger in that right?"

"There's a very good to excellent chance that she will pull through."

"Oh thank God! When will you know for sure that she will make a complete recovery?"

Brandon looked at both Mr. and Mrs. Regant. Obviously they were not aware that most likely she may not walk again. "Your daughter suffered a broken neck."

"Oh my God!" Anna's mother almost fainted.

"She's going to be fine right? She'll be Ok right? Tell me she'll be Ok!" Mr. Regant pleaded.

"Mr. Regent, right now we are not sure what her outcome will be. What we have done is removed all of the bone fragments from the damaged area. We graphed bone from her hip and fused the area to stabilize her neck. We have given her steroids to help reduce the swelling. Until the swelling has subsided we can't say for sure how damaged the spinal cord is."

"When will you know?"

"It will be two to four days. It depends on how fast the swelling subsides. I can say that we have her stabilized. As far as her life is concerned, there is an excellent chance that she is out of danger. The next 72 hours will be the most crucial. We will be watching her every minute. If she does have any setbacks we will respond immediately."

"Can we see her doctor?"

"I'll have a nurse take you to her. She is sedated and she won't be able to talk. In a day or two you should be able to talk to her."

"Thank you, doctor! Thank you!"

After a few days the swelling in Anna's neck had gone down. The residents, senior staff, including Dr. Ross gathered to go over the MRI that was taken. Upon inspection, there were loose bone fragments that had not been removed. "Damn! It looks like I'll have to go in again. I'm sorry team."

"Don't put too much pressure on yourself Leshing. Most cases the surgeon must go in two maybe three times to ensure that there are no loose fragments. It's nearly impossible to get them all with all of the swelling."

Everyone gave a glance towards Dr. Ross. Everyone had expected him to say something along the lines of "I told you so". However he was genuinely gracious in his assessment. According to the MRI, it looked as though the spinal cord was not severed, but it was damaged. Anna had a chance to make a recovery. Everyone was thankful that at least she had that chance. Brandon wasn't as gracious. He didn't want her to have a chance at a recovery. He wanted her to have a *great* chance at a *full* recovery.

When Brandon met Ana's parents he told them that the surgeries were successful. Everything that needed to be done was performed well. Anna did suffer damage to her spinal cord. Luckily the cord was not severed therefore there was a chance that she would regain functionality in all of her extremities.

Mr. Regant asked. "You're saying she will be Ok? She will be able to walk? She will recover fully?"

Brandon couldn't, and wouldn't build up their hopes. He had to be honest. "There is a chance that Anna will walk again. It may not be for several years. We honestly can't say for sure what her long term prognosis will be. Unfortunately as a science, the brain and nervous system is relatively unknown. The next couple years will be difficult for her. The amount of return she gains will be a correlation to the effort she puts into her rehabilitation. With hard work, and a lot of luck, Anna will be able to live a long productive life."

All of the residents obtained their certification for neurosurgery. They celebrated with a night out on the town. Dr. Supek and a couple other members of the senior staff had come along as well. Several hours into the celebration, Dr. Ross appeared. He bought a bottle of champagne and made a toast to the success of the new doctors. He specifically named Dr. Leshing as one whom he knew great things were to come. It had seemed whatever animosity existed between the two had cleared.

Brandon was happy to have taken his next step in keeping his promise to Louie. He was now 32 years old and contemplated his future. There was a position for him at Mount Sinai Medical Center. But there was no more funding for neurological research. If he was going to stay, it would be solely as a surgeon. Though he would have control over a patient under his care, all procedures he performed would have to be by the book. There would be no opportunity to implement any of his ideas. If a new procedure was to be found, it would have to be found by someone else. Brandon didn't like this at all.

Brandon's roommate Shane accepted a position at a hospital in California. Brandon was now living by himself in the dorm-like building that was still being paid for by Mount Sinai. One day he received an unexpected letter from Althaia University. He hadn't been back to the campus in a long time. He still kept in touch with Dr. Bromny but it was mostly by e-mail. The letter was an invitation to celebrate the ten year anniversary of Althaia's NCAA Championship football team. When Brandon looked at the invitation he immediately wanted to toss it into the trash. Then he thought of the players he had lost touch. He thought of Coach Ringle who had retired two years after Brandon had graduated. He felt guilty that he had been so obsessed in his own career that he cut off all contact with everyone from that championship team. Brandon returned the invitation stating that he would attend.

At the reunion celebration Brandon had a nice time reminiscing with his teammates. He enjoyed talking to his teammates about their Championship season. Coach Ringle was still surprised that Brandon hadn't turned professional as a football player. But, he understood his reasons and as long as he was happy with his life, that was Ok with Buddy Ringle. But Brandon wasn't happy with his life. He had taken big steps in keeping his promise to Louie. Now he was at an impasse. All that would change after meeting Dr. Bromny.

Dr. Bromny knew Brandon was at a crossroads. He also knew that the research he did at Mount Sinai amounted to little more than a complete failure. Dr. Bromny also knew that his old friend at Burdette Tomlin Hospital would be retiring soon. A replacement for head of surgery had not been named. There were three surgeons on staff that had practiced at Burdette Tomlin for over a decade. But none were board certified in neurosurgery as Brandon had recently become. "You're familiar with the hospital. They are familiar with you after your internship several years ago. Why not throw your name into the ring?"

"I don't want to step on anyone's toes by showing up and asking for a head position when I know that there are surgeons who have been there for a long time."

"I understand your apprehension. However none of those surgeons are board certified in neurosurgery. If it isn't you, they will be asking someone else to step in. The surgeons there are too old to become certified. My guess is that they would welcome you with open arms. You wouldn't be walking in and taking over right away. Dr. Brantly won't be retiring for a while. You would be under his wing so to speak until he does retire. Even if you don't become the head surgeon, you will become the hospital's only certified neurosurgeon. Plus, you will have time to conduct your own research. It wouldn't be greatly funded like the research you just concluded."

"You mean the research where nothing was gained?"

"However it ended, my point is that the research you do, will be on your own. You could arrange it that the surgery you put in be primarily neurological. You can ask that the other surgeons be put on call for routine surgery. You will have to perform procedures that aren't neurological but that can be limited. It's up to you."

Brandon knew that this was the best offer he would have. Since Burdette Tomlin was close to the beach, the hospital averaged at least one spinal cord surgery per month from May through September. During fall and winter, only a fraction of the population stayed in town. Thus there was seldom a case where he would be called upon to perform neurosurgery during those months. From October through April he could dedicate his time towards his research. As Dr. Bromny said, he wouldn't be receiving any million dollar grants and his research would be conducted on his own, but there were some advantages. If the lab that he could work in had decent equipment, which due to the number of neurological cases it should, he could perform some valuable tests to apply his theories. There wouldn't be anyone overriding his decisions.

"Dr. Bromny, if you can make it happen, I would like the opportunity. Again I'm in your debt."

"It would be my pleasure. I know that a cure won't be found in my lifetime, I hope that with my help, you will see a cure in your lifetime."

"Dr. Bromny you know that I'll do everything I can to see that happen. I'll never forget the help you have given me, and who knows, maybe you will see a cure in your lifetime."

The next day, Dr. Bromny set the wheels in motion to have Brandon transfer from Mount Sinai to Burdette Tomlin Hospital.

Chapter 11
PLEASED TO MEET YOU

Gina had been working at Macgregor Rehabilitation Hospital for several years, and had become well respected among her peers. She treated patients with neurological injuries ranging in age from eighteen, as was the high school basketball star Ronald Jenkins, to fifty-six. The recovery of each patient varied. Some recovered to a point of being able to perform basic functions, yet remained in need of the help of others. Some had recovered to where the patient was self-dependent. None however, had recovered 100 percent. The emotional recovery of the patients varied as well. Ronald, who married and became a counselor for young adults, kept fighting to thrive in life. Some lost their will only to become more dependent upon friends and family. It was those patients that Gina had the hardest time letting go. Every time she had heard that one of her former patients was having a rough time, she thought of her father. If she had anything to do with it, she would find a way to work with every one of her patients until they made a complete recovery. She didn't want anyone to go through the emotions that her father had gone through. This was the reason she stayed up late at nights. She moved from nursing to therapy so that she could spend more time with her patients. She thought that with more time she would be able to get her patients to a point where she knew that they would be able to carry on with their lives. She found that no matter how much time she had, she could never reach the recovery that she had hoped with her patients.

Finding new techniques in rehabilitation and therapy became an obsession for Gina. Since her father had passed Gina had seen many new inventions and techniques in rehabilitation. She saw new and improved wheel chairs, chairs that raised a person so that they could see 'eye to eye' with whomever they spoke. She saw machines that could lift patients over curbs, ride in rough terrain, or on a sandy beach. The new machines were touted as giving patients more dignity in their lives. These new inventions allowed people to go anywhere they chose, to have more freedom to do the things they wanted. But what every patient wanted was a full recovery. No machine offered that.

Kevin and Gina had become inseparable. People who knew them expected the two to be married sometime soon. As close as they were, Kevin wanted to be closer. However, every time Kevin hinted at the thought of getting married, Gina deflected the proposal. "Why ruin a good thing?" She would tell him. Kevin thought maybe Gina was right. They were getting along a lot better than some of his friends who had been married. So, he didn't press the issue.

Gina deeply cared for Kevin. He was nice. He shared the same career path. He was caring, physically well built, and very good in the bedroom. Gina felt safe and happy with Kevin. Whenever Kevin brought up the idea of taking the next step in their relationship, Gina would think of her father's letter. She felt as though she was doing her best in keeping her promise to find a true love, one that would care for her for the rest of her life. The only problem was that with Kevin, she wasn't fulfilled. It seemed as though something was missing in their relationship, but she just couldn't explain it. Perhaps she saw her father in Kevin and didn't really see Kevin as who he was. Maybe she didn't see enough of her father in Kevin. Whatever it was, it kept her from fully committing to Kevin. This bothered Gina a lot. She wanted so desperately to keep her promise to her father. She wanted to have a relationship with someone as loving as her father had with her mother. But she didn't want to make a commitment unless she was absolutely sure. And she wasn't 100 percent sure with Kevin.

Perhaps her reason for not fully embracing her relationship with Kevin was due to her passion for her work. After a couple hours of passion with Kevin, Gina was searching the internet looking for new advances in the neurological therapy. She should have been resting in his arms dreaming of a perfect life together. Instead she was sitting, staring at her laptop at 4AM Sunday morning. Kevin was awoken by the bright light of her laptop.

"Gina, what are you doing?"

"I'm sorry I woke you hun. I'm looking for new types of treatments."

"Again? Gina, you do this every week. Why don't you come back to bed? The weekend is for fun and relaxation. That stuff will be there Monday."

"Not now, if the light is bothering you I can go to the living room."

Kevin sat up, sighed. "No don't bother. I'm up. If you like I'll put on some coffee."

"Really, you don't mind?"

Kevin was half sarcastic when he made his suggestion. But, Gina took him to be serious. "No, I don't mind." Kevin got up, put some clothes on, and walked out to the kitchen to put on some coffee. When he came back with two cups, he looked over Gina's shoulder to see what she had been reading. Gina was looking at a web site that stated former Althaia University football star and Heisman Trophy winner Dr. Brandon Leshing had accepted a position as a surgeon at Burdette Tomlin Hospital. "I remember him. Everyone thought he was going to be a big NFL football star but he gave it up. It's amazing he did that considering all the money he would have made. What's he doing now?"

"It says that he took a position as the top neurosurgeon in waiting at Burdette Tomlin Hospital in New Jersey. The top guy now is going to retire."

Gina stared at the picture of Dr. Brandon Leshing. That strange feeling she had when she saw him on TV at the bar was coming over her again. It was as if she had known him from somewhere. As was the case the last time, she couldn't explain why she had felt as though she knew him. She knew for certain the two had never met. "I remember seeing him on TV giving a speech when I

256

was at a club. Some guy couldn't believe what you just said, that he gave up a lot of money by becoming a doctor."

"That must have been his Heisman speech. I'm not into football, but I heard he had a childhood friend who died or something after an accident. I think that's why he became a neurosurgeon. I'll tell you, with the money he could have made I would have just donated a couple million instead of giving it up completely. How about you?"

"How about me, what?"

"Would you give away millions of dollars to become a neurosurgeon?"

Gina thought about the question. "I'm not really sure."

"Oh come on, I know you care for your patients more than anyone, but there's no way you would give up all that money. I could see you giving money away for research or to a hospital, but you wouldn't give up all of it."

"Maybe, I guess you never know unless you have the choice."

"Did you find any interesting new advancements or treatments?"

"I haven't found anything concrete. I've read some of Leshing's work. He thinks the way to a full recovery is to cut away the damaged spinal fibers and reattach them."

"Cutting the spinal cord on purpose? That's insane. You could permanently paralyze a person by cutting the spinal cord. You know that."

"His theory hasn't been proven. It is different than most theories. Injecting stem cells into the spinal cord to help regenerate the nerve tissue hasn't proved to work either. Every advance I read about is for a new wheel chair or mechanical suit, or a new medication. There aren't too many I have read that actually deal with giving someone a chance at a full recovery."

"Well stem cell research is in its infancy. Give it time."

"Maybe, his thesis is interesting though."

Kevin massaged Gina's neck. After two hours staring at her laptop, she welcomed the warm smooth coffee and Kevin's warm soft hands. Gina took a sip of her coffee, closed her eyes, and tilted her head back while Kevin's massaging hands reached down to open Gina's robe. He began to gently massage her breast as he bent down to kiss her on the neck. When his lips caressed the lobe of her ear she let out a gentle moan. Kevin whispered. "I know something else that may interest you. How about coming back to bed and I'll try to peek your interest. You've already peeked my, eh, interest."

Gina opened her eyes, put down her coffee and raised her hand to place it on the back of Kevin's neck. Kevin took her hand, and helped her out of her chair. Gina stood up and faced Kevin. She stood on her toes, reached up to kiss Kevin's lips. Kevin opened Gina's robe which fell to the floor, then lifted her and carried her to bed. The next time Gina woke up it was 11AM.

****   ****   ****   ****

"Dr. Brantly it's great to see you. I'm in your debt for this opportunity."

"Certified neurosurgeons, good ones, are hard to find. I spoke to our friend Dr. Bromny. When I decided to retire he was one of the few people I called to get his opinion. He is one of the few people who have truly dedicated their life to their work. When you've practiced something for as many years as he and I, it's hard to give it up. But, we both know it's time to pass the baton onto the next generation. He was the one who recommended you. I don't know if he told you about my report when you interned here, but I told him that I didn't think you would make a good surgeon. I recommended that you continue your career in research."

"Dr. Bromny told me. He recommended that I go into research as well. It was one of the reasons why I took up residency at Mount Sinai. I was able to take a position on a research team as well as obtain my certification."

"Yes, I know. I also placed a few calls into Mount Sinai. They had nothing but high regard for you, both as a researcher and a surgeon. Dr. Ross was particularly high in singing your praises."

Brandon raised his eyebrows at Dr. Brantly's last comment. After the blowup they had, and Dr. Ross' opinion of him, he thought for sure that Dr. Ross would sabotage any chance at gaining a position such as this one. "Does that surprise you Dr. Leshing?"

"Dr. Ross and I hadn't always seen eye to eye."

"Whatever differences you had, he didn't let onto when I talked to him. Let me show you around and introduce you to the staff. Many of the people you already know from your internship."

Dr. Brantly introduced Brandon to the nurses, the doctors, and the staff at Burdette Tomlin, including Michael Murphy. Murphy was the top hospital administrator. All financial, promotional, personnel, and any other hospital decision that wasn't purely medical went through Michael Murphy. He was an African American man who was raised by his mother in the poor section of Atlanta. By the time he was thirteen years old, Michael had seen his older sister die of aids and his older brother shot and killed in a gang fight. Ever since his brother died his mother vowed not to let her only remaining child end up like his siblings. With no husband, she worked two, sometimes three jobs to keep Michael in school. She worked everything from scrubbing toilets during the day to serving drinks at night. Whenever she had any free time she would always spend that time with Michael, or talking to his teachers. She made sure he kept his head in the books and not on the streets.

Hard work wasn't the only trait that Murphy learned from his mother. He was also hard-headed. Just as his mother had said to him many times before, it was his way or the highway. He didn't have time, nor wanted to make time, for anyone who wasn't on the straight and narrow. He was a hard ass, but he was also fair. As long as you gave your best, played by the rules, Michael

Murphy would do anything in his power to help any doctor, nurse, or hospital staff member. As long as the doctor or nurse played by the rules, Michael would spare no expense in hiring lawyers, or investigators to help his staff when it came to medical lawsuits. Dr. Brantly himself had faced two law suits, one of which looked like it might cost him more than just money. It looked as though the lawsuit would cost him his medical profession.

Dr. Brantly was being sued after treating a patient who had broken his neck in a driving accident. The plaintiff had several witnesses who were willing to testify that the patient was able to move all of his limbs freely immediately after the accident. However, after being operated on by Dr. Brantly the plaintiff was no longer able to move his right leg and had limited mobility in his left leg. With the testimony of several witnesses, including the paramedics who arrived on the scene willing to testify the plaintiff's physical state immediately after the accident, the recommendation of many lawyers was to try and settle out of court. When the plaintiff offered to settle out of court, as long as the settlement included the resignation of Dr. Brantly, the hospital lawyers strongly recommended that Michael Murphy take the offer.

Dr. Brantly looked Michael straight in the eye and said he performed his surgery by the book. The anesthesiologist and assisting nurse also had given their word that the procedure performed was by the book. There was no negligence whatsoever in the surgery or post-surgery recovery. This was enough for Michael to hire three high priced neurologists to investigate the plaintiff's injury. How could there be testimony, including the paramedic's, that the patient was able to freely move all of his limbs, but then not be able to after surgery? When the plaintiff arrived at Burdette Tomlin he was unconscious. Therefore there was no way to determine by anyone at the hospital if indeed the plaintiff was able to move all of his limbs freely. Michael also hired a high priced investigator to go over all police and paramedic reports, as well as interrogate all persons who were involved, or near the accident.

It took over five months, but the consensus of the neurosurgeon's analysis indicated that a lesion on the neck was not consistent of what happened at the accident. They determined that the angle of abrasion was not one that would occur in a head on collision, but rather a side impact. The investigator came back with a witness who stated that while on the way to the hospital, the ambulance had to swerve severely out of the way of an on-coming vehicle, then swerve immediately back into the right lane of traffic. Armed with this information, it was determined that the swerving of the ambulance and the fact that the plaintiff was not properly fastened inside may have caused the head to be jolted sideways, and thus was most likely the cause of the loss of movement of the plaintiff's limbs. With the investigator's verified information and the testimony of the surgeons, the plaintiff's lawyers withdrew their lawsuit against Dr. Brantly and Burdette Tomlin Hospital. They instead filed a suit against the ambulance drivers and the company that employed them.

Dr. Brantly knocked on Michael's office door. "Dr. Brantly come in."

"Michael you remember Brandon Leshing don't you?"

"Of course I do. It's Dr. Leshing now, congratulations."

"Thank you, Mr. Murphy. It's great to be back at Burdette Tomlin."

"It's great to have you here. We've heard nothing but rave reviews regarding your work. It must be a great honor to take on the head surgeon position at such a young age."

"I realize the great opportunity I have. I'll work as hard as I can to maintain the high standards already in place."

"Fantastic! I hope you will excuse me. I have to attend a meeting with a bunch of lawyers regarding some libel issues. It would be a wonderful world if doctors could perform their duties without the cloud of a lawsuit hanging over their heads."

"I hope it's nothing serious."

"No, just some auditors looking over our shoulders. We have a tremendous staff that always plays by the book. As long as we play by the rules we have nothing to worry about. Isn't that right Dr. Brantly?"

"That's true. Of course it sometimes comes at the expense of finding new innovations but everyone has to play by the rules put in place I guess."

"That's exactly right. We can choose to play the game, but we can't make up the rules of the game. Now gentlemen if you will excuse me."

"Sure, nice to see you again Mr. Murphy."

Dr. Brantly's plan was to retire at the end of the summer. For the next 8 months he would serve as Brandon's mentor. Brandon, Dr. Leshing, was expected to perform all types of surgeries, when no other surgeon was available, but was the primary surgeon for any neurological procedures. Otherwise, Brandon had time to do research as he saw fit. That is as long as it was legal and wasn't too expensive.

Dr. Brantly found Brandon's theories regarding nerve regeneration fascinating. "I've read your thesis and it is very interesting to say the least. If nothing else, it is a radical way to treat neurological injuries. Cut spinal fiber tissue to heal the nerve damage. The fact that there is no way to attach the fibers makes it hard to digest."

"Dr. Brantly, I've heard it all before. Believe me. It's one of the reasons I was surprised Dr. Ross spoke highly of me. He called my thesis a fairy tale."

"Can you blame him?"

"I know it sounds counterintuitive to cut the nerve tissue to heal it. But I believe that there is no other way to regenerate nerve tissue once the cells are dead. There isn't one iota of life that we can bring back from the dead. I believe nerve cells are the same."

"That's true. I don't know of anything in life that once dead can be revived. But to cut away the tissue, it just seems too dramatic. What about the issue of reattachment? With thousands of fibers to reattach, there is no way of knowing which fibers to attach to which."

"Yes, but if we could work with bruised fibers that are still attached and cut away the dead cells we would know which fibers to reattach. I don't profess that this would be an applicable solution to a completely severed cord."

"That's too bad. You would probably have a better chance of getting approved to apply your theory on a severed cord."

"What do you mean?"

"Let's say you are able to cut away the damaged cells, and attach the fibers through some miracle substance. There is no way you would be approved to cut a partially damaged spinal cord since in most cases the patient will regain some functionality. But a completely severed cord there is almost zero chance that type of patient regains any functionality. With nothing to lose, you would have a better chance for approval to perform your theory on a severed cord."

"You may be right. But if I could prove my theory on a partial, I would have to get approval."

"Maybe so, but it would take years maybe decades before your type of theory would receive applicable approval. Science is guided towards helping what is already there to heal. It isn't easy to cut off a leg to save a body."

"There are times when it is better to cut off a leg to save a body. I can't throw away all I have done because it may take a while for approval. I have to continue my research, I can't give up."

Dr. Brantly looked at his younger replacement. He still believed that Brandon would be better served in research assignments as opposed to being a neurosurgeon. But, Dr. Brantly did his due diligence before giving his approval on his replacement. Everyone he had spoken to regarding Brandon's dedication and skill had nothing but high praises. "At least here you will have time to continue your research. You won't have millions of dollars in funding, but you will have the opportunity to perform your research as you see fit. You will also have the use of the facilities including a small lab facility downstairs. But remember, you're hired to be a surgeon first, not a researcher. The second your priorities change, you will be out of here. Michael Murphy is a nice man, but don't get on his bad side. He runs the team. If he sees that you aren't focused on your responsibilities, he'll take you out of the game and put in a permanent substitute. You know what I mean?"

The reference to his football days wasn't mistaken. If Brandon didn't play by the rules, he would be out of the hospital.

****   ****   ****   ****

A little gift was waiting for Gina on her desk Monday morning. It was a coffee mug with an 'I Love You' logo with a note inside: "*Best 4AM coffee I've ever had! I hoped you liked it too!*" Kevin often left gifts for Gina after spending the weekend with her. There was the Teddy Bear with the 'I ♥ You', the candies with their names, chocolates, and of course flowers. At first Gina was embarrassed with the gifts, but they were usually very small, and everyone knew of their relationship, so she grew to accept them for what they were – tokens of affection. Other girls in the hospital kept telling Gina how lucky she was to have such a thoughtful lover.

Kevin wasn't in the therapy room when Gina arrived to see her gift. He had been in Eleanor Randolph's office discussing an incoming patient. Gina put the coffee mug to the side. She took the note out of the cup and placed it in her pocket. She thought about that Saturday night/Sunday morning spent with Kevin. It wasn't the passion she thought about. It was the question Kevin had asked her. Would she give up millions of dollars to become a surgeon? Would she give up a financially worry-free life in order to dedicate herself towards finding a cure? She sat and thought about that question until an assistant brought in her first patient. Kevin walked in a few minutes later, and came over to greet her. "Well, was it good for you too?"

Gina looked at Kevin, and took his hand. "Was what good for me?"

Kevin was surprised. "The coffee, was the coffee good for you too? Didn't you see my gift?"

"Oh, I'm sorry Kevin. I'm a little out of it today. I guess I didn't sleep enough this weekend." Gina gave Kevin a wink. "Of course, it was great. Thank you." Gina gave Kevin a peck on the cheek.

"Hmmm, something tells me you do have something on your mind. Care to share?"

"No, really, I'm just tired today."

"Ok. If you need any help just give me a yell."

"Thank you, and thank you for the thoughtful gift."

Kevin went to his patient who had just come in for his therapy session. Throughout the week, all Gina could think about was Dr. Brandon Leshing. She had done more research on the internet looking at his biography. She brought up web sites which depicted his college football days at Althaia University. She brought up a U-Tube video of his Heisman Trophy speech. She was brought to tears as this was the first time she had listened to his words. She remembered how she felt when her father had passed. She could only imagine the pain Brandon felt as he blamed himself for his friend's death. She read WEB sites that noted his acceptance to Mount Sinai Medical Center. She read about the research team and how little progress was made in the years he had participated. She read his theories that were published regarding new and innovative ways to aid nerve regeneration. She thought how refreshing his research was to find a cure. Gina also read the abundant backlash from established medical professionals stating that Dr. Leshing's theories were impossible to apply.

During the week, Gina and Kevin stayed at their separate homes as Gina was still reluctant to fully commit to their relationship and move in together. Two, three times each week they would go out to dinner. This week however, Gina stated that she wasn't feeling too well and declined to go out. The real reason was that Gina was drawn more and more towards finding out all she could about Dr. Brandon Leshing. She felt compelled to somehow get to know him. She didn't know why. He was physically attractive, but she wasn't obsessed with him sexually. He was a doctor, but there were many doctors where Gina worked. He was a neurosurgeon of which there weren't too many, but her attraction wasn't to discuss medical procedures. Yet, as she looked at him, albeit through a laptop, she was drawn to him. Maybe it was his life story. When Gina saw Brandon, she saw a big, rugged individual, one who could take care of himself in any physical confrontation. When she looked at his eyes, she saw softness, a kindness, an almost childlike person who was trying to take on the world all by himself. She wanted, no needed, to somehow meet him.

Gina thought up ways she could come in contact with Dr. Leshing. She thought of sending an e-mail introducing herself. She typed a note a dozen times, but she couldn't think of the right words to say. She thought about calling Burdette Tomlin Hospital to ask to speak to Dr. Leshing. She thought of posing as a reporter wanting to place a story in a magazine or newspaper. But she didn't want to lie as a precursor to meeting him. Finally Gina decided that the best thing to do was to make the 100 mile drive to the hospital and ask to see Dr. Leshing in person. At worst, she would be told 'no' and she could spend the weekend at the Jersey shore. That wouldn't be too bad. At best she would be able to meet Dr. Leshing and get to know him. Gina didn't quite know what to say if she was able to meet him, but she would have over an hour to think about it on the drive to the hospital. On Friday Kevin asked Gina what she would like to do during the weekend. "Kevin, I'm sorry, I have to go away this weekend."

"Go away? Where do you have to go?"

"I have to drive to New Jersey."

"New Jersey? What's in New Jersey?"

Gina had spent all week wondering what she would say to Dr. Leshing that she never thought of what she would tell Kevin. Naturally he couldn't go with her. She couldn't tell Kevin the truth either. He would never understand her desire to meet Dr. Leshing. *She* didn't understand her desire to meet him. "I'm meeting a couple girls from the hospital I worked at before here. You know a girls weekend. We haven't seen each other in a long time and one of the girls called to let me know that a few of them were heading down the shore. I thought it would be a kick to meet up with them."

"You just heard this today? How come you haven't said anything?"

"I'm sorry. I wasn't so sure I was going to go until today. You know I haven't been feeling too well this week. But I'm feeling up to it now, so I decided to head down to see them."

Kevin didn't fully buy her story. "You've had your head in the clouds all week. I guess it's the fever or something. First you turn me down all week for dinner, now you're springing this girl's get-away weekend at the last minute. You know some guys might think you're seeing someone behind my back."

"Kevin, you know I care about you. I would never, ever cheat on you. You're everything a girl could want in a man. You're tall, handsome, sexy, caring, and kind." Gina placed her hand on Kevin's cheek, looking at him with her big brown eyes. "Believe me. I would never cheat on you. You know that."

Kevin took the hand that Gina had on his cheek and kissed her palm. If she was lying and was cheating on him she was a damn good liar! He knew there was no way that she was seeing someone behind his back. They spent too much time together for her to hide something like that from him. "So this is a girl's only get-away? I take it no boyfriends or husbands allowed?"

"No boyfriends or husbands allowed. I'm sorry dear."

"It's going to be a lonely weekend without you. I guess I'll survive. Call me when you get back."

"I will Kevin. I'll call you when I get back Sunday night."

Gina awoke early Saturday morning and was on the road heading for New Jersey by 8AM. She stopped at the WAWA to pick up a sandwich and some coffee, and then she stopped for gas. She was on the New Jersey Turnpike by 8:30. She had planned to think of things she wanted to say Dr. Leshing. But she thought of Kevin and the lie she told about the girl's get-away. She had never lied to Kevin before. Was this the beginning of more deceit in their relationship? Should she have told him the truth? It was too late to change things now. She memorized everything she had told him. She didn't want to say anything when she returned that would be different than what she told him.

When Gina started out on the road in the early morning, there was a chill in the air. By the time she arrived at Burdette Tomlin Hospital it was 10:15. The early chill gave way to a warmer late morning and the weekend forecast was for beautiful weather. Gina sat in her car thinking of what to say once she approached the reception desk. She knew that she wanted to ask to meet Dr. Leshing, but she wasn't sure what her reason should be. After sitting in her parked car for fifteen minutes, she decided that if asked, her reason would be simply to discuss his theory of nerve regeneration. Gina checked herself in the mirror, stepped out of the car and walked into the hospital straight to the reception desk. "Hello, I would like to speak to Dr. Leshing."

All ready to give her reason for the meeting, Gina was told something she hadn't expected. "I'm sorry but Dr. Leshing is away this week. He won't be back until next Monday."

Gina stood there dumbfounded. She should have checked to ensure that Dr. Leshing would at least be at the hospital before making the drive from home. She felt so stupid. Now what? Could she drive back next week? How would she explain it to Kevin? Even if she did come back next week, how would she know that she would even see Dr. Leshing? This whole idea was foolhardy. The receptionist looked at Gina, waiting for her to speak. "Would you like to come back in a week miss? Is this in regard to a previous appointment or surgery?"

Gina hadn't realized that she was still standing in front of the receptionist. "Uh, no, no thank you. I'll come back at another time. Thank you for your time."

"You're welcome. Have a nice day."

Gina turned to walk out of the hospital. All she could think about was not only had she driven over 100 miles, but she lied to Kevin. She was no longer feeling stupid. She was now feeling angry to have done so much for absolutely nothing. She was about to walk through the exit doors when she turned around and went back to the receptionist. "Excuse me again."

"Yes miss, can I help you with something?"

"Yes, I would like to put in an application for a nursing position."

"Are you a registered nurse?"

"Yes, I'm currently a physical therapist at Macgregor Rehabilitation Hospital. Previously I was a nurse at St. Helena's Hospital in Philadelphia."

"With the summer season coming we are always looking to fill nursing positions. If you would take a seat, I'll bring you the forms to fill out." Gina took a seat. In a couple minutes the receptionist gave Gina the application forms. When she had completed the application, she handed them back. The receptionist told Gina that it would most likely be one to two weeks until she heard from someone.

Gina walked out of Burdette Tomlin Hospital, got into her car, and wondered what the hell had she just done? She rubbed her eyes not believing what had just happened. She looked into her car mirror and took a deep breath. She felt as though she had just come out of a trance. Realizing what she had done, she opened the car door. She was going to go back into the hospital to pull her application. As she took a step out of the car, the thoughts of meeting Dr. Leshing came to her mind. Instead of getting out of the car, she started the engine and drove off.

Gina rode along Beach Drive with her thoughts racing. When she drove to the jetties, she parked her car, got out and walked out towards the ocean. She spotted a life guard stand that wasn't being used, climbed up and sat facing the sea. She sat for over an hour looking out towards the ocean. Her thoughts raced through her childhood, she thought about her mother and father, she thought about Kevin. She thought about what she wanted, what her father had wanted, what Kevin wanted. She thought about her patients, their pain – both physical and emotional.

Gina eventually walked back to her car and drove to a nearby diner to get something to eat. Afterwards she stopped at a liquor store and bought two bottles of wine. She drove to a motel and checked in. She stepped into her room, walked over to the small refrigerator. On top were a couple glasses of which she took one, and then she went to the bed and lay back. On the side bureau was the remote control to the twenty inch screen TV. She flipped through the channels not looking for anything in particular. She stopped on what looked like a mystery who-dun-it movie that was made in the 1940's. She opened a bottle of wine, poured herself a glass and took two large mouthfuls. She stared at the TV, the sound of which was easy to hear, but she neither saw, nor heard what was going on in the movie. She filled up her glass with more wine. Her thoughts turned to her father's letter, and the promise he wanted her to make. The promise she knew she couldn't keep. She felt as though she had failed her father. Here she had what seemed to be, and what other people had told her, was a great guy that loved her. Gina really did like Kevin. She could see herself being happy living the rest of her life with him. But for some reason, which Gina didn't understand, she was going to give it all away. After a few hours she finished the first bottle. She opened the second and poured another glass. She almost finished the second bottle when she drifted off to sleep.

Just before completely dozing off Gina had a dream in which she could see the tarot card reader Francine Quabalah. This time Gina wasn't there with her friends, she was there alone, sitting at Francine's table. Gina could see Francine reading what looked to be the letter her father had written her. Gina wanted to tell Francine to give the letter back, but she could not speak. Gina tried to reach out to take the letter but she could not move. Francine, seeing Gina trying to reach out looked at her and laughed. Gina didn't understand why Francine was laughing. She wanted to ask her but she still could not speak. Then, Francine's laughter turned to tears. *Why are you crying?* Gina wanted to ask. Francine looked down at the letter. She brought the letter up over her face so that Gina could no longer see her. All Gina could hear was crying. And then, the crying stopped. The letter Francine held was slowly being placed down. Francine's face however was still hard to see. When Francine placed the letter on the table, she lifted her head. It was no longer Francine's face she saw. It was her father's.

Gina woke up early Sunday morning. She didn't bother to shower, or change clothes. She went to the motel desk, dropped off the key to her room and walked out to her car. She made a quick stop for gas, picked up two bottles of ginger ale, some aspirin for her splitting headache and drove back to home. When she returned home she undressed, showered, put on a robe and lay in bed. She thought of what she was going to tell Kevin regarding the changes she was about to make. Should she just come out and say it's over? Should she ask if he wanted to go with her? If she did he would have to live with her in New Jersey. She knew that would be wrong. At 7PM Gina gave Kevin a call to let him know she was home.

"How was your girl's get-away weekend? Did you have a good time?"

"It was nice. We talked, had some dinner, some drinks. It was really good to see some old friends. I hadn't seen them in a while."

"That's great. Would you like some company for a few hours?"

"Kevin I would love to see you. But I have this splitting headache. I think the wine and the long drive home has my head out of whack. I'm afraid I wouldn't be too good of company. I'm just going to go straight to bed."

"Ok, I just thought since I've missed you so much I could at least stop by for a late snack. If you're not feeling up to it I understand."

"I miss you too dear. I'm just not in a good mood right now. I'll see you tomorrow at work."

"Ok, take care of your headache and I'll see you tomorrow. I love you."

"I'll see you tomorrow Kevin, goodnight."

Gina decided to hold off saying anything to Kevin. After all it wasn't a certainty that she would get the job. Why go through all of the drama if she wasn't going anywhere after all? Monday morning Kevin left a gift for Gina on her desk. This time it was small set of seashells in a box of sand. Each shell had a word which spelled out '**I – Love – You**'. When Gina saw the gift she felt embarrassed. She walked up to Kevin, gave him a kiss on the cheek and said thank you. During the week she and Kevin went out to dinner as normal. When the weekend came he asked if he should go to her house, or would she like to stay at his apartment. Gina was hesitant, but said he should come to her house.

Another week went by and still not a word from Burdette Tomlin. Maybe the receptionist hadn't given the application to the right person. Maybe it was still sitting on her desk. Maybe she had thrown it out by mistake. The following Monday Gina had a note from Eleanor asking to stop by her office.

Before Gina knocked on Eleanor's door, Eleanor told her to come in, close the door behind her and have a seat. "I didn't know that you were unhappy here Gina."

"I take it someone from Burdette Tomlin has contacted you."

"Yes, and I must say I was stunned when they told me that you had applied for a position and wanted my opinion of your work. How long have you thought of leaving? If you are having any problems you know you can come to me to discuss it. Is everything alright between you and Kevin?"

"Eleanor it isn't that I'm unhappy here. Kevin and I are getting along fine. I'm sorry that I haven't said anything to you about leaving. It was a spur of the moment decision. It all happened so fast that I didn't think about what to say or who to tell. I didn't even know if I would get the job. So I figured to just go on as normal until I found out for sure."

"It's not like you to do things on the spur of the moment. You are always very meticulous. You always think before acting. It's one of the good qualities that you have. You don't fly off the handle like some people, even when things get hectic."

"I know Eleanor but this time I, I just, I, I don't know how to explain it. I took a ride to the shore. I went to meet someone who worked at Burdette Tomlin. Before I knew it, I put in an application for a nursing position."

"Gina that's very strange not only to apply for a position on the spur of the moment, but to have to pack up and leave everything behind if you take the position. You must have thought this out a little bit. What will you do with your house? What about you and Kevin?"

Gina sat there unable to look Eleanor in the eye. She couldn't explain her actions to herself. How could she explain them to someone else? "As for my house I'll keep it as is. My neighbor Julie lives next door. I'll probably ask her to move in if she likes. I'd rather not sell the house just yet. If I take the job in New Jersey I'll probably rent an apartment for a while."

"Have you told Kevin about your change?"

"I hadn't told him anything yet. I wanted to be sure I had the job before saying anything to him."

"Well you better start thinking of a way to tell him. From what I heard on the call I received, they are anxious to have you start. You'll probably hear from them today or tomorrow."

Gina didn't know what to say. She was embarrassed that she hadn't told anyone of her plan, especially Eleanor whom Gina knew she could trust. "Eleanor, I'm sorry you had to find out like this. I should have said something."

"Gina you know we love you here. You are one of the best therapists we have on staff. If it was a question of money, I would see what I could do to compensate you more. Somehow I don't think this is about money is it?"

"No, it isn't the money. Believe me I love the people here too. I couldn't ask for a better group of people to work with, especially you. It's just that I feel I have to make this move. I can't explain it. I know I'm giving up a lot to do this. Worst of all I know this will crush Kevin."

Eleanor nodded her head in agreement. "Hunny that's something I can't help you with. That's something you'll have to work out for yourself. When they do offer you the job, and if you do decide to accept it, let me know and we'll work out a transition plan of your patients."

"I will. If I take the job I won't leave until you find someone to take over my patients full time."

"Thank you, Gina. I guess that's all for now. I and everyone will be sorry to see you leave. I won't say a word to anyone about this until you have been offered, and accepted the position."

Gina left Eleanor's office. On her mind was what to say to Kevin.

The next day Michael Murphy from Burdette Tomlin called to tell Gina that they would love to have her on staff as soon as possible. Michael discussed Gina's responsibilities, what days and hours she would work, and of course what her salary would be. Gina accepted the position, but she would have to call back later to give a start date. Michael wanted Gina to start as soon as possible with summer, their busy season, fast approaching. But he understood that Gina needed to transition her patients to someone before she could leave her position. After discussing the transitioning with Eleanor, Gina called back to say she could start on June 1st.

Gina still hadn't said anything to Kevin, and hadn't planned to until the weekend at his apartment. She felt that telling him at his place would be better for him. After they had finished dinner, it was time for Gina to tell Kevin the news. She helped put the dishes away and asked Kevin to sit on the couch with her. "Kevin, what I am about to say is probably one of the hardest things I have ever had to say. I don't know how to tell you this."

"What is it Gina? I've sensed that you've had something on your mind for a while. Is everything Ok? Are you pregnant? If you are that's great."

"Kevin, no I'm not pregnant. You're right I have had this on my mind for a while."

Kevin sensed that what he was about to hear, he wasn't going to like.

"Kevin you and I have been together for some time now."

"And I've enjoyed every minute of it."

"I have too. I really have enjoyed it too. That's why what I'm about to say is so difficult."

Gina looked up to Kevin's eyes but instantly looked back down. There was no other way to tell him other than to get it out quickly. "Kevin I've accepted a position at another hospital. I'm going back to being a nurse."

Kevin didn't fully grasp what this news actually meant to him or their relationship. "You're leaving Macgregor? Does Eleanor know about this?"

"Yes, I talked to her about it a couple days ago."

"Why didn't you tell me? Why didn't you tell me first?"

"Kevin I didn't know I was going to have the position until this week. And when I knew I was accepted, and I decided to take the position, I didn't quite know how to tell you."

"Where will you be working?"

And now came the part where Gina knew that Kevin would put two and two together. "I'll be working at Burdette Tomlin Hospital, in New Jersey."

"New Jersey? I *knew* there was no girl's get-away. I knew you were lying when you told me that. I knew it but I didn't want to say anything. I didn't want to believe it. But you did. Didn't you?"

"Kevin I didn't know how to explain it. I didn't go to apply for a job. It just happened."

"Then why *did* you go to New Jersey?"

Even now Gina didn't know why she was doing this. "I honestly don't know. I can't explain it."

"You can't explain it. Does it have to do with that doctor you saw on that web site, that football player? That's it. Isn't it? You went to see that doctor. Have you been seeing him behind my back?"

"Kevin you know I would never do anything like that. I honestly have never met Dr. Leshing before in my life."

"Oh really? Then why the hell would you suddenly quit your job, move to New Jersey just on a whim? You want me to believe that all of the sudden you had the urge to apply for a nursing position all the way in New Jersey?"

"Kevin, look at me, believe me. I would never do anything to intentionally hurt you. You have been my lover, my best friend. This isn't easy for me. You're right I *am* giving up everything. It feels like the right thing to do. I can't make you understand why. I can't make *myself* understand why. It's just something I have to do."

Kevin looked at Gina shaking his head. "I knew it. You know you've said many times that any girl would be lucky to have a guy like me. I guess you meant any girl *except* you. God I love you Gina. I love you more than anyone I've ever known. I want to spend the rest of my *life* with you."

"Kevin, I know. I'm sorry. I am. I'm truly sorry. You are the last person on earth I would hurt."

"I should have known. In all the time we have been together you never once said you loved me. Not once! Every time I tried to suggest that we become closer in our relationship you always got away from the subject. What was I? Was I just a stepping stone until you found someone you truly loved? Did you use me? After all I've done for you? How could you do this to me?"

"Kevin I don't know what to say. I know I've hurt you, and I'm sorry. If there was anything I could say, anything I could do…"

"Gina, just go. Just leave me alone."

"Kevin…"

"Gina, please! Just go!"

The next few weeks were hard. Kevin didn't say a word to Gina unless he absolutely had to. Everyone on the staff was on pins and needles. No one knew what to say. People didn't know the reason why Gina was leaving. Some assumed that Gina and Kevin had a falling out. That was certainly backed up by the chill given off by Kevin whenever Gina was near. The Friday before Memorial Day weekend Gina put in her last hours at Macgregor Rehabilitation Hospital. Her last task was writing a letter to Kevin trying to explain how much he had meant to her. Gina knew the letter would be of little comfort to Kevin.

The next day, while most people were driving to the Jersey shore for holiday, Gina drove there to find a place to live. Julie, Gina's friend next door accepted her offer to stay in her house while Gina was away. If things didn't work out as planned, however little planning Gina actually did, she could return to her home. After finding a place to stay in New Jersey, Gina returned to her home in Philadelphia to pack as much as she could for her new home. Monday morning, with her car fully loaded, Gina headed to her new apartment. She didn't know for sure but she felt that she was leaving Philadelphia for good. As she drove she thought back on everything she left behind, her job, her friends, her ex-boyfriend, her house. She couldn't help but turn her thoughts once again to her family, the mother she hardly knew, the father with whom she had broken her promise, even Oreo, the kitten she found twenty years ago. Gina was saddened by what was left behind, but she couldn't help but feel excited about what was to come in the new chapter in her life.

During the 4th of July weekend, Gina finally met Dr. Brandon Leshing. It was Saturday, around 4PM when a patient, Scott Linehan, was rushed in from an ambulance. Scott was a young male, five foot eleven, around 185 pounds who was drinking with some of friends at a motel. The drinking went from inside the motel room to the balcony when a friend of Scott's decided to jump from the second floor balcony into the motel swimming pool. Seeing that his friend made the jump successfully without harm Scott decided to do the same. Unfortunately, when he jumped from the balcony railing, he lost his footing and missed the pool, landing on the cement. Within the hour he was rushed into Burdette Tomlin Hospital where Gina was working as the admissions nurse.

Upon Scott's arrival, he was immediately treated by two nurses and Dr. Leshing. Gina's responsibilities as the admissions nurse were to get as much personal information as possible from the ambulance medics. She walked along side of the patient, talking to the medics, taking down the information. After getting the required information, name, age, address, she kept walking along with the patient. She wanted to help, but after coming close to the elevator door which led to the operating room, Dr. Leshing yelled at Gina to get out of the way.

Gina asked Dr. Leshing. "Is there anything I can do?"

"Go to your station, contact the patient's family and let us do our job!"

Gina stopped, and watched as the elevator door shut close. She walked back to her station and began dialing the patient's family. Though her shift was done in less than an hour, she was determined to really meet Dr. Leshing now that she knew where he was. When Gina was relieved of her shift, she went to the operating room to wait for Dr. Leshing to finish. After several hours he came out of the room. He looked tired but that didn't stop Gina from approaching him. "How did the procedure go?"

Dr. Leshing looked at Gina. "Are you a relative of the patient?"

"No, remember, I was the one who took down all of his information. I was able to contact his parents who should be here soon."

"I'm sorry nurse, eh," Dr. Leshing noticed Gina's name tag. "Stroit, I can't give out any information. You will be briefed as needed. Now if you will excuse me." Dr. Leshing walked past Gina without waiting for a reply.

Gina returned to the admissions desk where her replacement, Anita Liphon, was going over the status of all patients who were on the floor. "Gina, I thought your shift was over. What are you still doing here?"

"I was here when a young patient was brought in. I contacted his parents who should be here soon. I wanted to wait until they arrived."

"Gina that's very nice of you but you should go home and get some rest. You're coming off a twelve hour shift. You can't give special attention to every patient you see come in. You'll burn out before the summer ends. Don't worry about it. I have all of the information here. You did a great job. Why don't you head on home?"

"I can't Anita. I really want to see his parents when they come in."

"Ok, suit yourself. Why don't you at least grab a cup of coffee?"

Gina went down to the cafeteria, got some coffee and went back to the admissions desk to wait for Scott's parents. When they rushed in asking to see their son, Gina called Dr. Leshing at his office to inform him that Scott's parents were here. "Bring them to my office", was all he said.

Gina took Scott's parents to Dr. Leshing's office. The office door was already open so she walked in with them. Dr. Leshing looked up at Scott's parents, looked to Gina and told her to leave and shut the door behind her. Gina turned to Scott's parents and told them that she would wait outside. She shut the door behind her but stood close enough that she could hear what Dr. Leshing was saying. What she heard surprised her.

After seeing pictures of Dr. Leshing, after hearing his Heisman speech, Gina pictured a caring man who wasn't afraid to show his emotions. What she heard was nothing like she had imagined. He was almost harsh in his words. When Scott's parents asked for his prognosis, Dr. Leshing didn't sugar coat anything. He told them straight out that their son had a very good chance of being physically impaired for the rest of his life. He tempered his bleak prognosis by stating at this point, the prognosis was very uncertain. It would be at least another 48 to 72 hours before any certainty would be known. Gina thought that if there was so much uncertainty, why give the worst case scenario?

Coming out of Dr. Leshing's office, Scott's mother was naturally very emotional as her husband held onto her while she sobbed. When Gina saw them she motioned them towards the elevator doors. "If you'll wait there for me I'll be right with you. I'll take you to see your son."

"Thank you, nurse."

After seeing that Scott's parents had walked towards the elevator, Gina walked into the office. "Dr. Leshing, may I ask you something?"

Dr. Leshing was looking at X-Rays of Scott, he raised his head slowly. "Yes nurse, what is it?"

"I couldn't help but over hear your conversation with Scott's parents. I don't understand why you would give such a grim prognosis, especially as you have stated, there is uncertainty at this time."

"Were you eavesdropping, nurse Strate?"

"It's *Stroit* doctor. No, I wasn't eavesdropping. I couldn't help overhearing your conversation."

Dr. Leshing put down the X-Ray. "First of all it isn't any of your business what I say to my patient's family. Is it, nurse *Stroit*?"

"I guess technically it….."

"Second, nurse *Stroit*, I will never give false hope, to any patient, or his family. I find it to be more devastating to the patient if we paint a rosy picture only to have that outcome destroyed. Third, nurse *Stroit*, whatever I say to a patient or their family is strictly a doctor, patient confidentiality. I don't ever want to explain myself to you again. Am I making myself clear, nurse *Stroit?*"

Dr. Leshing picked up the X-Rays. Gina couldn't believe what she was seeing and hearing. Is this what she gave up her life in Philadelphia for? If it was, she was glad that she didn't sell her house. She wanted to drive back to Philadelphia immediately. It didn't matter if she had been working for over 14 hours straight. She couldn't wait to get away from this unemotional, egotistical, imposter.

"I just thought since there was so much uncertainty at this time that…"

Dr. Leshing put down the X-Rays and cut Gina off in mid-sentence. "Nurse *Stroit*, I believe you have the patient's parents waiting for you at the elevator. I recommend not keeping them waiting any longer to see their son." Dr. Leshing picked up the X-Rays. Gina turned and walked out of his office. Without taking his eyes off of the X-Rays, Dr. Leshing called out, "close the door behind you nurse Stroit." Gina heard Dr. Leshing but was so angry that she left the door wide open.

After showing Mr. and Mrs. Linehan to Scott's room Gina headed for home. After a day off she would return to the hospital for her next shift. While she lay on her bed she thought about returning home to Philadelphia. She decided to give her current position some more time. Maybe she caught Dr. Leshing on a bad day. He must have been extremely exhausted. Trying to get to know someone right after performing surgery surely wasn't the optimal time to do so. She decided that she had to get to know Dr. Leshing before ultimately deciding to return home. Since the only time anyone ever saw Dr. Leshing was during surgery, Gina decided to do whatever she could to position herself to assist Dr. Leshing on a surgical procedure. After all, she was qualified to do so.

After her day off, Gina returned to work. This time she replaced Anita Liphon. One of the first things Gina did at the start of her shift was to check on the status of Scott Linehan. She was told that the swelling had gone down significantly enough that Dr. Leshing would be opening him up to remove bone fragments that were missed in the first operation. This would also be the time when Dr. Leshing would be fusing the neck with a rod and bone taken from Scott's hip. "Anita, did they decide when the operation will be performed?"

"Sometime around 7PM."

"Who will be assisting during the operation?"

"Stacy Weebling."

Stacy arrived at the hospital at 5:45. She was forty-five minutes late. When she approached the administrative desk where Head Nurse Administrator, Theresa Mancleve was seated, she had her hands covering her eyes. "Hi Terry, sorry I'm late. I have a migraine that I can't get rid of."

"Hi, Stacy, did you take anything for it?"

273

"I took an Imitrex but it hasn't kicked in. I'm hoping it does soon."

Gina saw her chance to work with Dr. Leshing. "Stacy you can't go into the operating room in that condition. Why don't I take your place?"

Theresa agreed. "Gina's right Stacy, even if the Imitrex does kick in I don't want you in the operating room in that condition. If Gina is up for it, she can take your place."

"Gina you sure you don't mind? It will probably be a long session. Dr. Leshing is very thorough. He sometimes can be hard to work with in the operating room."

"Stacy I don't mind. I've worked with those types of doctors before. Don't take this the wrong way but right now you look terrible. Why don't you go home to rest?"

"Right now I could use a dark quiet place to lie down. This light is hurting my eyes. Gina, thank you so much. I really appreciate this."

"Stacy, why don't you head on home? Gina, there will be a briefing in the prep room at 6:00. Do whatever you need to do to get ready and meet the team there."

"Thanks Terry. I'll be back in tomorrow. Gina thanks again."

"No problem Stacy. I hope you feel better."

When Dr. Leshing walked into the prep room at first he didn't notice who had already arrived. The anesthesiologist, Dr. Herb Macaw, another young doctor who would be observing the operation, Dr. Benjamin Daniels and nurse Stroit were there waiting for him. Dr. Leshing hung up the MRI so everyone could see. "Ok people as you can see we have a break in the C-4 and C-5 sections. We need to clear out the remaining bone fragments. When I'm satisfied with the removal of all stray fragments, our objective will be to slice out a piece of bone from the hip which we will use for fusion. Herb you've been through this before, I want his vitals every ten minutes or whenever there is a variance that you think I should know about. Dr. Daniels will be observing. Nurse Weebling you… Where is nurse Weebling?"

"Nurse Weebling is under the weather doctor. I will be assisting you."

Dr. Leshing looked to Gina. "I'm used to working with nurse Weebling."

"I'm afraid she can't make it."

Dr. Leshing was resigned to the fact that he would not be working with his regular nurse. "Since this is our first time working together nurse Strate…."

"Stroit"

"Excuse me?"

"Stroit doctor, my name is *Stroit* not Strate. We've been through this before, remember?"

"Nurse Stroit, excuse me. Since this will be our first time working together I'll let you know up front that I expect you to do exactly as I say. I expect you to be quick and I expect you to be accurate. If I ask for a clamp I don't expect to be given forceps. When I ask for suction, I expect the area to be cleared quickly. The area we are working is very delicate. Do you understand?"

"Yes doctor I will do my best."

"Ok team I'll see you in the operating room at seven sharp. Nurse Stroit I expect you to line up all instruments prior to our procedure. Since you don't know the order I like, just do the best you can to make the instruments easily accessible."

"Yes doctor."

Midway through the operation the patient's spinal cord was opened. Brandon could see the damaged fibers within. Luckily the cord wasn't severed which meant that the patient has a chance of regaining some mobility. Brandon stared at the damaged fibers as if he didn't know what to do next. Gina asked. "Some suction doctor?"

"What?"

"Do you need suction in the area? You seem to be hesitant."

"Yes, yes nurse, thank you."

Gina applied suction to the area delicately. When she pulled back, Dr. Leshing resumed clearing out tiny bone fragments. When he was done he began the process to fuse the patient's neck. The surgery took nearly five hours to complete. By the end everyone was exhausted. As they stepped outside the operating room Gina walked up to Dr. Leshing. "You do nice work doctor."

Dr. Leshing, in deep thought didn't appear to hear Gina. "It was no more than routine surgery."

"I beg to differ, doctor. What you did may save that boy's life."

"You think so nurse? What kind of life did I save? If he is lucky he will be out of a wheel chair in five years. All I did was clean him up, zip him up, and in a few weeks he'll be shipped off to a rehab hospital where he'll get to shop around for the best wheelchair technology has to offer."

Gina was astounded. All she was trying to do was pay Dr. Leshing a compliment. However he was too arrogant to accept it. On the other hand he seemed to feel genuinely bad that he couldn't do more for Scott. "Doctor all you can do is the best that…."

Before she could finish her sentence Dr. Leshing retorted. "Nurse I don't have time for chit chat. Once the patient is in ICU make sure he has his monitors set. If any alerts come up I want to be paged immediately understand? If I don't hear from anyone, I'll be in tomorrow morning to check on him."

"Yes doctor, I'll see to it…." Before she could finish her sentence, Dr. Leshing walked away.

A couple days later Dr. Leshing, carrying a box, walked in to check on Scott. Gina was already in the room standing over the patient ensuring that he was as comfortable as possible under the circumstances. When Dr. Leshing approached the bed, Scott asked. "So, how am I doing doc?"

"You're doing as well as expected."

"What's in the box? Did you bring me a present?"

Dr. Leshing put down the box. "In a way, yes, what I have is a halo. This will enable you to sit up a little instead of being tied to that bed. You won't be able to move around much, but when you do move, this will ensure that your neck stays intact."

Dr. Leshing looked to Gina. "Nurse, I'll need you to cut his hair so that we can apply the halo. I'll be back in 15 minutes."

"Scott, it looks like I'll be your barber. How do you want it? High and tight, a little off the ears?"

"I don't care Gina. It's not like I'll be going out to meet anyone."

"I'll do my best to keep you looking good." Gina trimmed around the sides and she cut a little in the front as well as the back. She hadn't given anyone a haircut before, but she didn't do a bad job if she didn't say so herself.

Dr. Leshing came back in a few minutes later. "Nurse, I thought I told you to cut this man's hair for his halo."

"I did doctor, don't you see the clippings on the floor?"

Dr. Leshing mumbled to himself. "I guess if I want something done I'll have to do it myself." He grabbed the electric razor, turned it on and shaved both sides and the back of Scott's head. When he was done all Scott had was a crop of hair on the top of his head. He looked like a punk rocker with a Mohawk. When Dr. Leshing was finished, he gave Scott a shot of Demerol, unpacked the halo kit and fitted the halo onto Scott's head by inserting four screws into his skull. When he was done he took hold of the sides of the halo. He lifted Scott's upper body and began to shake him uncontrollably. Scott said nothing but he was in shock at what Dr. Leshing was doing. Gina's eyes widened, but she said nothing as well. When Dr. Leshing had finished shaking Scott he stated. "This will ensure that your neck is immobile." As Dr. Leshing was about to leave Scott stopped him.

"Hey Doc?"

"Yes?"

"What about my prognosis? When will I be able to walk out of here?"

Without any hesitation, without any condolence or emotion, as if he was asked what the weather will be today Dr. Leshing replied. "Scott you won't be walking out of here. Most likely will be five years before you are able to take a step." Dr. Leshing continued out of the room.

Gina couldn't believe how insensitive Dr. Leshing had been. After seeing him walk out of the room, she quickly turned to Scott who continued to stare at the position where Dr. Leshing stood when he told him of his fate.

"Scott I'll be right back." Gina ran out of the room. She looked left, then right. She caught a glimpse of Dr. Leshing just as he turned down the corridor. "Dr. Leshing! Dr. Leshing, wait!"

Dr. Leshing turned to see nurse Stroit running towards him. "Yes nurse Stroit what is it?"

"What is it? What is it you ask? I'll tell you what it is. What you just did to that boy in there was terrible. He's lying in a hospital bed, unable to move his legs and you tell him he'll never walk out of here? What the hell is wrong with you? Have you no bedside manners at all?"

"What would you have me do nurse, lie to him? Tell him he'll be up and running in no time? Would that make you feel better?"

"I'm not asking you to lie to Scott. But I expect some compassion towards someone whose life has just changed dramatically for the worse."

"Nurse you haven't been here as long as I. Once you have you will understand that it doesn't matter how compassionate you are. All that matters is the truth, and I'm telling him truthfully all that I am able to do for him."

"Doctor you don't know me at all. I've tried to get to know you but you're too damn arrogant to realize that. I've been involved with patients with disabilities from both sides of the table. All you see is your patient during surgery. Once that's done he's sent off to a rehabilitation hospital where you don't have to hear from him again. I've dealt with patients a lot longer after their surgery. Let me tell you something. You have a unique ability to sew someone back together I'll grant you that. But it's a lot harder dealing with the emotional strain the patient will endure after the surgery. I'm not asking you to lie to Scott and tell him everything will be fine. But I expect you to be a little more compassionate and if at all possible give him some hope, because right now he has none. And if he continues to have no hope he will never try to get well. Do you understand what I'm saying to you?"

Brandon stared back at nurse Stroit. What she had said he had thought of many times before. He wanted to see his patients all the way through. But that was out of his control. He did understand what she was saying and he knew that she was right. He thought of the time he questioned Dr. Brantly the same way. He remembered Dr. Brantly's response that all we can do is the best we can do. "Is that all nurse Stroit?"

At that moment all Gina could think was if this could really be the same person she saw give that emotional speech in college? How could a person with so much compassion be so unemotional now? What happened to that person she saw on TV? "Yes doctor that's all I have to say."

Four weeks had gone by and Scott was nearly ready to be transferred to a rehabilitation hospital. Dr. Leshing had been stopping by every day to check on his patient. Every time Dr. Leshing saw Scott he asked the same questions. "Can you feel my hand on your foot? Can you feel this pen touching your foot? Can you feel this pinch on your toes? Can you move your toes?"

At first Scott couldn't feel anything, after two weeks, he felt the touching of his feet. The day before he was to be transferred, Gina stopped in to see Scott as she had been doing whenever she was on duty. As she was talking to Scott, Dr. Leshing walked in to check on him one last time. Again he went through the same questions as Gina watched. For the first time, when Dr.

Leshing asked can you move your toes, Scott wiggled the toes on his left foot. Scott smiled for the first time since coming to Burdette Tomlin. Dr. Leshing replied that maybe that was just a muscle spasm. The smile on Scott's face quickly disappeared. Gina gave Dr. Leshing a look that said: *You better show some compassion!* Dr. Leshing turned to Scott. "Can you do it again Scott?"

Scott closed his eyes, gritted his teeth. Again he wiggled the toes on his left foot. "See Doc it wasn't a spasm. I'm getting better. I'm able to move my toes. Who knows maybe tomorrow I'll be moving my leg. I'm getting better right doc?"

Before Dr. Leshing answered he looked at Gina then back at Scott. "You're doing better than I expected. You're doing very well. The only way you will get better is if you continue to work hard at it."

"You can bet on that. No one will work harder than me. You'll see."

Brandon reached out his hand to shake Scott's. "Best of luck to you, Scott, I hope to see you back here soon, but not as a patient, Ok?"

"I'll be back doc. I'll be back walking. You'll see."

Brandon looked at Gina who gave an approving look back. Then, he walked out of the room to complete his rounds. That was the last time Brandon saw Scott Linehan.

Chapter 12
A BREAKTHROUGH

After completing his rounds, Brandon returned to his lab in the basement of the hospital. Closing the door behind him, he plopped into a chair. He tossed his chart on the desk, leaned back and rubbed his eyes. His thoughts were on Scott Linehan. Once again Brandon felt as if he put a band aid on a broken leg. He knew the hardships that Scott would have to endure and Brandon felt helpless, more to the point, useless. Yet, because of some nurse, he had to give the impression that if Scott worked hard, he would be fine. Who was this nurse? No one else had confronted his bed side manner the way that she did. Who was she to question his attitude when it came to giving a prognosis? Why was she so adamant on painting a rosy picture? Brandon remembered Dr. Brantly telling him that after a while he would become immune to giving patients false hope. Brandon thought that he would never become the hardened surgeon that Dr. Brantly seemed to be. But, here he was, being realistic. He had become what he didn't like in Dr. Brantly.

The rattling of cages behind him awoke Brandon from his thoughts. He looked over to the ten cages, each containing one test subject – a mouse. Five of the subjects were completely healthy. Two subjects had their spinal cord completely severed and were unable to move their hind legs at all. Three had their spinal cord partially cut. One mouse, whose cord was cut eight weeks ago, dragged one of its hind legs. A second mouse, whose cord was cut twelve weeks ago, was able to move all four legs, but the two hind legs were visibly slow. The third mouse, whose cord was cut one week ago, was hardly moving his hind legs at all. Brandon rose from his chair, and walked over to the cages to observe the subjects. He thought of how much his attitude had changed since accepting the research assignment at Mount Sinai. Back then he had difficulty injuring a single mouse. Now, he looked at the mice as nothing more than a bridge to finding a cure. They were a disposable necessity to keep his promise to Louie.

The more Brandon read of other research on spinal cord injury, and their lack of progress, the more he believed in what he was doing. He believed that the way to find a cure was to remove all damaged spinal tissue fibers even if it meant cutting fibers within the cord. But he could not find a way to reattach the Axon fiber tissues within the cord without putting a road block between the neurons. There had to be a substance that could be used as 'glue' that the nerve cells could interact with in order to regenerate until attachment was made. This 'glue' would also have to dissolve without dissolving any of the nerve tissue.

Brandon's latest test subjects had their nerve endings attached using the platelets and fibrin from their own blood to act as the 'glue'. However he couldn't get the right amount of clotting material to work. At times Brandon used too much and the clotting material would interfere with the nerve growth. Other times he used too little and the clotting material would dissolve before the nerve endings had a chance to attach. Maybe this was just another dead-end altogether. Frustrated, he decided to call it a night. He seldom left the hospital without putting in at least twelve hours for the day. Sometimes he spent the night in his lab or in an unused hospital bed. Today he wanted to go home, get away from the hospital and get some rest in his own bed. He locked up the lab, and walked the half mile to his apartment.

There was a cool breeze in the air as Brandon walked home that gave him some renewed energy. Suddenly, instead of undressing and going straight to bed, he felt like doing more research. He made himself a sandwich, put some coffee on, and turned on his laptop. The information Brandon read was little more than what he had previously read dozens of times before. There was little to no advancement in the use of stem cells to aid in nerve regeneration. There was little to no advancement in gene therapy to aid nerve regeneration. Guidance Channels didn't work, applying Growth Factors didn't work. Brandon was about to shut down his laptop when he came across a web site that discussed a new substance that had been created using mitochondria. The substance was a fluid that contained enzymes that was stored in small sacs in the body. This new substance was not only able to surround cells, but it was also able to reproduce and attach itself to other cells nearby. Again, Brandon felt a new energy and spent another two hours immersed into the research that was being done regarding this substance that was called *'Mitochondria Wrap'*.

Brandon thought this substance may provide exactly what he was looking for to act as the 'glue' for his research. If what he was reading were true, it could be the perfect substance he had been trying to develop. The substance was already in the human body so there would be no risk of rejection. The substance seemed to jell among various cells thus holding them together. The substance did not prohibit growth among the cells thus allowing for nerve to regenerate on its own until the nerve tissue could attach. The *'Mitochondria Wrap'* also provided energy to the nerve cells which aided in regeneration. It was 4AM before he forced himself to shut down and get some sleep.

Over the next few months, Brandon had been in constant contact with the team at Martham Medical Research Institute (MMRI) who discovered the *'Mitochondria Wrap'*, or as they called it – *'Mito Wrap'*. Brandon explained that he wasn't interested in profiting from their research. He explained that his research would provide a practical application for their discovery. Once a trust was built between Brandon and those at MMRI, Brandon was able to learn how to reproduce the *'Mito Wrap'*. However, the difference between knowing how to produce the substance and actually producing the substance took one thing –

money, specifically about ten million dollars. For that, he would have to talk to the head administrator, Michal Murphy.

When Brandon was comfortable with what he had learned from the developers at MMRI, he set up a meeting with Michael to discuss a possible breakthrough in his research. Brandon prepared himself for the reasons why asking for ten million dollars-worth of equipment would be a good investment for the hospital. "Come in Dr. Leshing, have a seat."

"Thank you, Mr. Murphy."

"So what is this breakthrough you wanted to talk about? Hopefully it will explain the spike in the overseas calls we are being billed."

"It does Mr. Murphy. I've been trying to develop a substance to act as 'glue', or a bridge between damaged nerve fibers to help in generating a permanent connection between nerve endings."

"Have you developed something?"

"No, I haven't, but a possible substance has been discovered at Martham Medical Research Institute in London. I've been in contact with them the past several months learning of their discovery."

"So that's the reason for the calls overseas?"

"It is."

"Ok, tell me about this discovery."

"It's a substance that is extracted from the patient. It's called *Mitochondria Wrap*. The substance surrounds a group of cells holding them in place but it doesn't prevent the surrounded cells from growing. In fact the substance contains mitochondria which help in the growth of new cells until a connection is made by the nerve endings. Since the substance comes directly from the patient, there is no risk of rejection."

Michael leaned back in his chair. "I see. How does this substance work? How would you use it?"

"I believe that if I can apply this substance to the nerve tissue, allowing for the nerve cells to regenerate and connect, that it could lead to a patient regaining functionality that otherwise would not be attained."

"How do you make this *Mitochondria Wrap*?"

"You extract the substance from the patient."

"Where do you extract the substance from?"

"It can be extracted from a couple places in the body."

"Have you successfully extracted the substance for use in your research?"

"No, and the reason is that while the substance can be extracted from the body, you don't extract the exact substance you need. You need equipment to convert what you extract into the *Mitochondria Wrap*."

Michael leaned forward onto his desk. "Ah and how much would this equipment cost?"

"It would cost approximately eight to ten million dollars."

"That's quite a sum to spend on a *possible* aid to research that hasn't shown any hope of finding a cure."

Brandon looked at Michael knowing that he was right. Even if he had the money and was able to create the *"Mito Wrap"*, it didn't mean that Brandon's work would be any closer to a solution. What Brandon was asking for was money for a possible solution to advance research that wasn't close to providing a cure. "You're right Mr. Murphy. It is a lot of money for something that has no immediate tangible return of investment. But I'm asking anyway. If it will help I'll take a salary cut to help recoup the money."

"Dr. Leshing, you know I can't ask you to do that. You're right. Investors in this hospital want to know what return they will get back. How sure are you that this *"Mito Wrap"* would work?"

"I'm confident I can create the *'Mito Wrap'* using the equipment that I need. As for it being a solution to hold the nerve tissue, I can't say for sure."

"So altogether it's a long-shot that the money spent would have any practical application. If it did work, how much closer would that get you towards finding a cure for neurological disorders?"

"Again, I don't know for sure." Brandon knew the numbers didn't add up to justify the expense. But he had to tell the truth. He couldn't give his patients false hopes, why should he give Michael any?

Michael leaned back in his chair again. "You see my dilemma. I'd have to convince investors of this hospital that it's a long-shot that the money invested would be beneficial. If the investment did work, it would still be a guess as to the progress made to finding a cure for neurological disorders. Dr. Leshing, I like you. You're never late for any appointment, surgery, or call made to you. You always play by the rules and you're one of the best surgeons I've ever had. I would love to help you by getting this money. But I don't think I could convince anyone to pony up that kind of money for a long shot."

"What about donors to the hospital? For them it wouldn't be an investment, they don't care where the money goes."

"No they don't exactly care. However they do assume the money donated goes towards helping patients and running this hospital, not bet on slim hopes. Plus, the problem with donations is that we don't get enough of them. The money we do get from donors mostly goes to maintaining the building, paying salaries, or paying those damn overpriced lawyers we have to keep. We just don't get the kind of donated money that you need."

The excitement Brandon had when he learned about the *'Mito Wrap'* was being crushed by the inability to produce the substance. He was at a loss at what to do. Michael couldn't help but see the onset of despair beginning to show on Brandon's face. Michael did have one idea. "I'll tell you what. We have our banquet coming up in three weeks. It's our way of attracting donors, and investors. Some big-wigs will be there. We present the current state of the hospital, what our plans for the hospital are, what we expect costs to be. We have a presentation to go over our needs for donations and investments. What I can do, if you're up to it, is allow you to make a presentation on what your research is about. You can talk about this '*Mitochondria Wrap*' discovery and why you need it. If some of the people take a liking to it and decide to donate then more power to you. All I ask is that you be honest in your presentation. Don't sell them something that isn't true. I shouldn't even do his because I can't let people ask for money for their own causes. That would take away money that would go towards keeping this hospital afloat. That's the best I can do."

"Mr. Murphy, thank you. I appreciate this offer. I'll be honest, and to the point when I make my presentation. Thank you. You won't regret it."

"I'm not guaranteeing that you'll raise enough money. All I'm giving you is a chance to ask people to help."

"Mr. Murphy when I came in here all I hoped for was a chance and you're giving me one."

Over the next few weeks, Brandon developed his presentation. He had to present it to the seventy plus people sitting in a banquet hall who had just finished their dinner and dessert. His presentation was honest. He stated why he needed the equipment, what the '*Mitochondria Wrap*' would be used for, and that it *possibly* would help him discover new treatments for neurological disorders. When he ended his presentation he received polite applause. He thanked the audience for their time and stepped down from the podium. He went to his seat and listened to Michael give his own presentation on the current state of Burdette Tomlin Hospital. Brandon could hear Michael, but didn't listen to a word he was saying. All he could think about was did he do enough to impress anyone to help him with a donation?

When all of the speakers had finished, Brandon had some immediate responses. One was from a 77 year old woman, Helda Vanderstan. She was the widow of Frank Vanderstan, a wealthy businessman who had passed away several years ago. Helda and her son Richard ran the philanthropic ventures that Frank had started after his retirement. Burdette Tomlin was one of the recipients of the philanthropy and this year was no exception. "That was a wonderful presentation you gave Dr. Leshing."

"Thank you, Mrs. Vanderstan. I hope it will persuade some people to help purchase the equipment I need."

"You have persuaded me. My brother had lost the use of his legs as a result of a motor cycle accident many years ago. He was my older brother and when we were growing up he sort of protected me. He was funny, charming and very athletic. After his accident he became reclusive. He lived with my parents but only for another ten years. I've often wondered what he would have become had he not been in that accident."

"I'm sorry to hear that. My goal is to give people such as your brother hope to regain the life he had before such accidents."

"Yes, I see that. I'd like to help you with your goal. While I can't give you all of the funds that you need, I'll discuss it with my son Richard. We'll see what we can do."

Brandon shook the hands of over thirty other people before heading home. While he lay in bed all he could think about was did he do enough to keep his promise?

He received his answer a week later when he received an e-mail from Michael asking to meet him regarding the equipment needed to continue his research. Brandon knocked firmly on Michael's door. "Come in." Michael shouted with his hand on the phone speaker.

When Brandon walked into the office, Michael waved his hand towards a chair. When Michael hung up the phone he looked and smiled at Brandon. "You wanted to see me Mr. Murphy?"

"Yes, the call I was on was another person asking how he could contribute towards your project. I've had about a dozen other calls similar to that one. One of those calls was from Richard Vanderstan. Apparently you made a big impression on his mother, Helda."

"Yes I remember talking to both of them."

"They have made a sizeable donation towards your research. All told, you have convinced enough people to secure close to seven million dollars. Congratulations."

"Are you serious? I hope the contributions didn't take from the money ear-marked for the hospital."

"Some of it was, but the money from the Vanderstan's is above their annual contribution. So it wasn't too bad. I hope this equipment gets put to good use and some return is shown in a couple years."

"I don't know what to say. This is one of the best days I've ever had. I want to thank you personally for giving me the opportunity to reach out to people. I won't let you or those donors down."

"I know you won't. The Vanderstan money has already arrived. The rest should clear by the end of the month."

Within three months Brandon had the equipment needed to generate the 'Mito Wrap. Try as he might though, he couldn't generate the substance quite the same as it was being generated at MMRI. He kept in touch with people from the Institute constantly. However no matter how meticulous he was in following their instructions, he could not duplicate what their research studies had produced. Frustrated, he began to doubt that this substance really existed, maybe it was a scam, a publicity stunt. No matter what he tried, he could not generate a substance that wrapped itself around cells and allowed those cells to regenerate to the point of connecting to the other tissue. Slamming down his notebook, after another failed attempt, he heard a knock on the door. No one ever knocked on the door to his lab. If anyone ever needed him he either received a phone call, or his pager would ring. The person at the door knocked again. No doubt the person knew he was in the lab after hearing the notebook slam to the floor. "Yes!" Brandon shouted.

"Dr. Leshing?" A female voice replied.

"Yes!" Brandon shouted again.

"May I come in?"

Brandon opened the door. "May I help you nurse Stroit?"

Gina was nervous. She questioned to herself if she had made a mistake coming unannounced. "I was wondering if I might come in. I've been interested in your work for a long time."

"Excuse me?" Dr. Leshing was in no mood for a social visit. Especially from a nurse who thought of him as some unemotional, pragmatist.

"I just finished my shift and I had been interested in your work for a long time. I wanted to stop by and see what you were doing. A lot of people up stairs think of you as some recluse who only comes out for surgery. Some people have been here for months and have never seen you. So I thought I'd stop down to see what all of the excitement was down here."

Dr. Leshing looked at nurse Stroit thinking, *who was this person?* "So you thought you would stop down to see what all the excitement was about?"

"Excitement may be the wrong word. But I want to get to know you. You only come out when you're needed for surgery or making rounds. I wanted to see what it is that keeps you locked up in here."

"Look, nurse Stroit…"

"Call me Gina."

"What?"

"My name is Gina. I'm off duty and you're not on duty. May I call you Brandon?"

"Uh, I guess since we're both off duty. But, what I…"

"How come you didn't play football?"

"What?"

"How come you didn't play football? Why did you give up all that money? My boyfriend at the time, we're no longer seeing each other, asked if I had a choice to make millions of dollars or become a surgeon, what I would do. He told me he would take the money and donate a portion towards research. I thought about it and at the time I probably would have done the same. But thinking about what you would do versus actually having to make that choice are two different things. So what was it that made you give up all that money?"

"That's why you came down here? To talk about something that happened years ago? That was another time, another life. I didn't play football to make money."

"Why did you play football?"

How could Brandon explain the real reason he played football? "My father wanted me to play. I found that I happened to be good at it. After high school I was good enough to gain a scholarship to college. So I played football."

285

"I see. Why give up millions of dollars to become a surgeon? With all that money, you could have been retired by now and financially well off."

"It's complicated. Let's just say I made a promise I needed to keep."

"The promise to your childhood friend who passed away."

"Yes."

"That's very admirable of you. I don't think I could have kept a promise like that. In fact I know I couldn't." Gina thought of the letter her father had written and the promise he had asked of her.

Brandon noticed Gina had fallen silent. "So what brought you here?"

"Huh? Oh, I wanted to get to know you. See what makes you tick."

"No, I mean how did you end up at Burdette Tomlin?"

Gina brightened up a bit. "Promise not to laugh or get mad?"

"Laugh or get mad? That's a pretty wide range of emotion."

"Honestly, the reason I ended up at Burdette is because of you."

"Me?"

"Yes, you. I told you I've been interested in your work for a while."

"Why is that?"

Gina told Brandon about her father. She told him how much her father meant to her especially since she had lost her mother at such an early age. She told Brandon how big and strong she had always thought her father was. Her father was the world to her. In the end her father didn't want to become a burden to her. She spoke for over ten minutes straight without realizing it. It felt good to Gina to let out everything she had felt about her father and the end of her father's life. The only part of her father's life she didn't let out was the letter he had written to her. "I'm sorry. I seem to be dominating the conversation. I didn't mean to go on for so long. It's just that I haven't really spoken to anyone who might understand how I feel. Someone who kind of went through the same thing you know?"

After listening to Gina, Brandon saw her in a completely different light. "Yes, I know what you mean. I'm sorry to hear about your loss. That's what drives me to find a cure. I want people like your father to be healed, not just given devices to make their lives better."

"That's why I've been interested in your work. That's why I wanted to see you in person, why I wanted to meet you. To give up what would have been a financially secure life to become a surgeon is very admirable. It's obvious you aren't doing this for the money. I've also read your thesis regarding the healing of nerves. Have you made any progress? I heard you were awarded a grant for your research."

"I was lucky enough to have met some people who were kind enough to allow me to continue some new advancements, however I haven't had too good of progress lately."

Gina looked around the lab. She saw the cages where the subjects were. She noticed there was only one desk in the lab. "Do you have any assistants?"

"No, I work alone. We don't have the funds for a research staff. Besides, I prefer to work alone."

"Why? Don't you need someone to bounce ideas or talk things over?"

"Most of the people I talk to about my ideas think they won't work. I tried working on a research team. It didn't go so well. At least this way if I fail, it's all on me."

"Were you always like that?"

"Like what?"

"A loner, always doing things yourself?"

Brandon thought of Gina's question. It was true ever since Louie had passed away he had been a loner. "I guess."

"How sad."

"Yes, well, if you will excuse me, I have some work to do."

"Do you think you will succeed?"

"Not if I keep talking to you instead of getting back to work."

"What are you working on?"

"Nurse Stroit, if you please…"

"Gina."

"What?"

"Gina, we're off duty, please call me Gina. Ok Brandon?"

"Gina, if you will please let me get back to my work. I'm not in the mood for conversation."

"Humor me, please. Tell me what you're working on and I'll leave. I'm really interested, please."

"If you must know, I'm trying to create a substance from test subjects." Brandon pointed to the mice in the cages. "It's a substance that I hope will serve as 'glue' to connecting nerve fibers. I'm hoping that if I can get the substance to hold the nerve endings that nerve cells will regenerate and connect on their own. If I can do that, I'm hoping that signals from the brain will make its way to the muscle."

"Interesting, has anyone been able to create this substance?"

"Yes, a team in London has been able to do it. It is where I got the idea. It's the reason for the donations I received, to help pay for the equipment needed to convert the substance."

"So they can produce this substance but you can't?"

Brandon was frustrated at the question, more accurately the failure Gina pointed out. "Correct."

"What are they doing that's different from what you are doing?"

If Brandon's frustration wasn't shown with the last question, he was showing it now. "If I knew that, I would be able to correct the errors and produce the substance, now wouldn't I?"

"Don't get mad at me Brandon. I'm just making sure I understand. Have you spoken to anyone on the London team?"

"No, I'm going to keep trying by myself until I figure it out, or I die. I'm a loner, remember?"

"Well you should call someone from the London team."

"I have been calling the London team! I was being sarcastic!"

"Ok, you don't have to yell. How am I to know what you did or didn't do? Why don't you invite one of them here? Maybe they can spot something that you're doing wrong if they see you in person."

Brandon was taken back at the thought. Gina was actually right. He had spent so much money on the new equipment, but what good was it if he couldn't get it to work? Maybe one or two people from the London team could come to the hospital. If he packaged it up to an all-expense paid trip, put them up at a nice hotel, gave them an expense card to some nice restaurants, some shows, who knows maybe he could get someone to observe what he was doing. It was a good idea, but he didn't want nurse Stroit to know that. "We'll see. I'm sure they are busy with their work. And speaking of work, I really must be getting back to my own. So if you will excuse me nurse…"

"Gina."

"Yes, if you will excuse me Gina."

"Ok. If you ever want to get away from all of this, maybe we could go out to dinner sometime. From all of the time you spend here I'm sure you're getting sick of the hospital food."

"Maybe, we'll see. Now if you will excuse me."

"Alright, alright. Thanks for taking some of your valuable time to talk to me." Gina stepped closer to Brandon, she grabbed his forearm and gently squeezed. "I hope you do come up with some type of cure. If there is anything I can do to help, please don't hesitate to ask, ok?"

Brandon once again saw the girl who lost her father. "Of course, thank you Gina."

As soon as Gina closed the door behind her, Brandon was on the phone calling the London team to see if he could persuade any of them to come to visit America.

Weeks went by and Brandon still could not produce the 'Mito Wrap' that was created, at least it was published that it was created, in London. The coming weekend two members of the London team were visiting Burdette Tomlin. They were going to see Brandon's work in person. Brandon personally was there to greet Rachel and Paul Rawling, husband and wife, at the airport.

"How was your flight?"

"Fantastic! It was a real thrill to ride the Sonic Star. The flight from London to New York took an amazing three and a half hours. The flight alone was worth the trip. It was so fast that Paul didn't have time to get air sick." Rachel said with a poke at her husband.

"If you ever get the chance to come to London I recommend the flight. I started eating my meal when we were airborne and before I could finish my desert we were asked to buckle up for the landing."

"Glad to hear the flight went well. We should be in Cape May in about 20 minutes. Do you need to make a stop before we go?"

"No I'm fine. Rachel?"

"Yes we should be fine. Let's go."

After the 20 minute ride Brandon stopped in front of the General Washington hotel. "Well, here we are."

"General Washington, you sure know how to rub it into us Brits?"

"Oh, I didn't think anything of it. I…"

"My husband is joking Dr. Leshing. It's that dry British humor I suppose may take a while to get used to. This will be fine."

"Great, I'll have a car pick you up at 9AM tomorrow. Is that Ok?"

"That will be fine. We'll see you tomorrow."

The next morning, Brandon showed the Rawlings his entire lab which took a whole ten minutes to do since the lab was the size of home living room. "Here is where the frustration takes place. I've been extracting the mitochondria from the eukaryotic cells that are within the skin tissue but as you can see, the amount of mitochondria per cell is nowhere near the amount I need to create the proper substance. The other problem I have is that once the substance is extracted, the mitochondria die off in a matter of hours. I need to be able to extract enough to apply to hundreds of spinal microfibers and I need the extract to remain active for at least 24 hours."

"I believe my wife and I can help. The amount of mitochondria contained within different tissue areas varies greatly. Instead of extracting the substance from the skin area, the best place to do the extract is from the liver, lung, or heart. The least invasive would be an extract from the liver. Mind if my wife performs an extract from one of your test subjects?"

"No please do."

"You shouldn't need much just a half of a vial should be enough. Within each eukaryotic cell in the liver are plenty of mitochondria. You must place the needle just under the base of the liver to get the best results like so. Also you need to extract a small amount from different areas around the liver."

Brandon observed as Rachel extracted the substance. "And now, onto the next step." Paul continued.

"This next step is the most frustrating part. How do I store the mitochondria so that I can have it readily available when I perform my procedures? It takes hours for the mitochondria to separate from the eukaryotic cells. It will take hours for me to apply my procedure to the spinal microtubules. That's too long of a delay."

"I take it that after you have your samples that you have been putting them through the binary fission module."

"Yes according to your papers, that is the only way to get the right mixture of mitochondria that will attach to nerve endings."

"Yes that is true. What we have found is that if you keep some of the eukaryotic cells intact, that the mitochondria can feed off of the remaining cells and stay alive for longer periods of time, within reason of course. The more eukaryotic cells you leave, the longer the mitochondria stay alive."

"You're saying if I put the extract through the binary fission module for say four hours instead of five, leaving some of the eukaryotic cells, that the mitochondria would remain useful for a longer period of time. Then, when I'm ready to actually perform my procedure, all I would need to do is put the substance through the binary fission module again to get the right mixture of mitochondria I need."

"Basically, yes. The amount of eukaryotic cells that need to remain in order to keep the mitochondria alive is not concrete." Rachel replied. "We can't give you a specific formula to say if you put the substance through the binary fission module for four hours that the mitochondria would remain alive for four hours and if you run the module for three hours the mitochondria would remain alive for ten hours. We have been conducting these types of tests ourselves and we haven't found a conclusive formula. Our research does show that you can keep the mitochondria alive longer with more eukaryotic cells for them to live off of." The three continued to test out different ratios of eukaryotic cells to amounts of mitochondria. Brandon saw that his frustration wasn't so much his lack of understanding as it was an unproven theory of how to producer the proper 'Mito Wrap' and keep it ready when needed to apply to spinal microtubules.

"I'm glad you two were able to visit. I have learned more these last few days than I have in the last several weeks combined."

"Glad we could help." Rachel said.

"We'll be here for the remaining week if you need help." Paul stated.

"You have helped more than enough. I don't want you to work the whole time you're here."

"We have some entertainment plans as well. We can't wait to see your Atlantic City casinos and shows." Rachel replied.

For the rest of the week, Brandon, Paul and Rachel worked on trying to come up with a formula to achieve maximum mitochondria storage with minimal eukaryotic cells. By the end of the week they still had not come up with an exact formula, but they were able to extract an amount that allowed for the substance to be processed within the binary fission module and have the mitochondria remain alive for 16 hours. When ready, the substance would be put through the binary fission module again until the right "Mito Wrap" mixture would be obtained.

When the week was over, Brandon drove the Rawlings back to the airport. "Thank you again for your help. We accomplished more this week than I had accomplished in months."

"We were happy to help. Good luck on your research. Keep in touch if you need any assistance. At the very least we hope you will keep us apprised on how your research is coming along."

"I certainly will. Have a safe trip home."

Back at Burdette Tomlin, Brandon took great joy in filling in Michael Murphy on the progress in his research. Brandon also sent a letter to the Vanderstan's noting that the money they had donated had produced results. When Gina saw Brandon while making his rounds, she congratulated him on his recent success. "I guess my suggestion worked."

"Your suggestion?"

"Yes, I believe I was the one who suggested you bring some of the London team in to help you."

"I don't recall. The people who stopped by were a married couple who wanted to see the states."

"And of all the places in the country, they chose New Jersey?"

"Why not, there's a great deal to see and do here, the beaches, the casinos, and the shows in Atlantic City."

"So it was pure coincidence that a married couple who work on the London research team that was developing a substance that you need, happened to book a vacation to New Jersey just when you were at your wits end on creating the same substance?"

Brandon didn't want to give Gina the satisfaction. "Something like that, now if you'll excuse me nurse Stroit, I need to finish my rounds."

"Sure Dr. Leshing, I need to get back to my station as well. At least you've learned something."

"Yes, with their help I've learned how to create the substance I need."

"I wasn't talking about that."

"What do you mean?"

"You've learned that sometimes a little help will go a long way. Instead of hibernating in that cell you call a lab thinking you need to do everything yourself, it's Ok to ask for a little help now and then."

"I think you said you were needed back at your station nurse."

"Yes, of course Dr. Leshing. I hope to see you later."

Brandon completed his rounds and as always went straight to his lab. Since being able to create the *"Mito Wrap"* Brandon had a renewed vigor in his work. He was one step closer to keeping his promise to Louie. The next step was far from easy. Brandon now had to try to take damaged nerve tissue, remove the dead or damaged cells, and then apply enough of the '*Mito Wrap*' to hold the ends of the microfibers in place but not too much to saturate the endings. Not only that, there were thousands of microfibers within the spinal cord that needed to be mended. The work to apply the '*Mito Wrap*' was tedious and long. For each test subject, Brandon would spend five hours on average applying the substance to as many microtubules as possible before complete exhaustion set in. Even with meticulous work and care there would be no way for Brandon to determine if he was connecting the right fibers. For all he knew the work he was doing may have been a complete waste of time.

Weeks turned into months. More and more mice subjects were being tested. The euphoric feeling Brandon had when he was able to create the 'Mito Wrap' was gone. It was replaced once again by frustration. Only this time there was no one to call for help. No one was available to ask what procedures to take. No one had done what Brandon wanted to do. This time, whether he wanted it or not, he *was* all alone.

After another long day at the hospital, Brandon went home to his apartment. He stripped down, took a shower, put on some sweat pants and a t-shirt and decided to make something to eat. Upon opening the refrigerator a terrible odor overcame him. There weren't too many items in the fridge so it wasn't too long before he realized that the milk had passed its expiration date by more than a couple weeks. He drained out the milk, threw away the carton, but realized that the milk wasn't the only culprit for the terrible smell. Next were the boxes of leftover Chinese food. Brandon quickly emptied the remains down the garbage disposal. Relatively sure he had removed the offending odors, he looked to see what was left that he could eat. There was some lunch meat, but that didn't look all too appetizing. Brandon tried the freezer. There he found some mint chocolate chip ice cream, a lone box of Momma Leone's pizza, and two trays of ice cubes. Nothing appealed to him. He sat down on the couch, clicked on the television and surfed through the channels. His mind went back to his work. Had he reached an impasse? Would he ever be able to keep his promise to Louie? Were the millions in donated money all for nothing? He realized the longer he sat alone the more he would torture himself over the failures of the past couple months. He needed someone, anyone to talk to. Only one person came to mind.

Nurse Stroit did say that whenever he needed someone to talk to that he could reach out to her. Oh but she was so annoying. She tried so hard to get personal. He certainly didn't want to spend a rare night off answering dumb questions about why he had chosen the life that he had. She had such a condescending tone whenever she felt that she was right. Could he make it through a dinner with her? He decided that it was too much for him to handle. He couldn't make it through 15 minutes with her, let alone a whole meal. He continued surfing through the TV channels. He stopped on the History Channel where they were showing 'The History of Mankind'. After watching for a few minutes he heard his stomach growling. He knew he had to get something to eat. Nurse Stroit did have her good qualities. She was extremely kind to her patients. She did have a genuine interest in his work. There were moments when she was nice to talk to. Maybe he could make it through one meal with her. Brandon called the hospital. "Hello, this is Dr. Leshing. I'm calling to see if nurse Stroit is on duty."

"Hello, Dr. Leshing. Gina is on duty tonight. Would you like me to have her paged?"

This was his last chance to change his mind. "Yes, thank you."

A couple minutes later Gina spoke on the phone. "Hello, Dr. Leshing. Is there something wrong? Do you need me to check on a patient?"

"No, I uh, well that is, I was wondering what time you got off duty."

"My shift ends at 8:00."

"Oh, good, that's a little over an hour. In that case I was wondering if maybe since you would be getting off, uh, I mean since your shift would be ending maybe, if you hadn't eaten, maybe you would want to grab a bite to eat."

Gina lowered her voice so no one could hear. "Dr. Leshing, are you asking me out on a date?"

"No, not a date, I finished work a little while ago. I realized that I don't have much here to eat so I was going to go out to get something. I thought if you were hungry you may want to eat too that's all."

"You figured I may want to eat too. Hmmm, well I actually do eat, and I am a bit peckish."

Brandon thought this was a mistake. He could picture her with that smirk on her face and definitely picked up that condescending attitude. "Well if you are going to have a bite to eat, and I'm going to have a bite to eat, then we may as well eat with each other, I mean we may as well have a bite with each other, I mean we may as well...."

"Dr. Leshing I think that would be a great idea. How about we meet at The Grill at 9:00?"

"Ok I'll see you there at nine." Brandon hung up the phone and realized that a bead of sweat was coming down his left eyebrow. He couldn't believe how nervous he was talking to this woman. He hated the fact that he was so nervous. He hated even more knowing that nurse Stroit was not nervous at all, she was her usual condescending self. Why the hell was he so nervous? He was a prominent doctor. He was well respected, at least he thought so. Who was she to make him so nervous? Then he realized that she would be the first date he had in a long, long time. He couldn't help but think of the advice Dr. Bromny gave him when he said that dedicating his life solely to the medical profession was a mistake. Dr. Bromny regretted not to have led a more rounded life and finding someone to love and care for. Brandon wondered if he would have the same regret later in his life.

When Brandon walked into The Grill, he saw nurse Stroit sitting at the bar. She was talking to a young male nurse who also worked at Burdette Tomlin. Did he come in with her? When Brandon called he assumed that he didn't have to say that she come alone. But, when nurse Stroit asked if this was a date, he specifically said no. I guess she took him literally and figured she could invite the man. Suddenly he found himself hating the young man. He gathered himself, walked up to nurse Stroit and tapped her on the shoulder.

293

"Hello Brandon, you know Ryan Wardly. He is a nurse at the hospital."

"Yes I believe I've seen you on the floor, how are you?"

"I'm fine Dr. Leshing. I didn't know you came to The Grill."

"I don't come in too often but nurse Stroit and I were…"

"Gina, you mean Gina and I, we're off duty, remember?"

Brandon gave Gina a quick glance. "Yes, Gina and I were just…"

"We were just going to order some dinner. Would you like to join us Ryan?" Gina turned to see Brandon's expression. "You don't mind do you Brandon? It's not like we're on a date."

Ryan, looking puzzled, replied. "No, I have to get back to my friends at the table. We're all heading out to the concert at the Pavilion."

"Oh that's too bad. Well Brandon looks like it's just you and me. Should we find a table?"

Brandon was visibly relieved. "Yes, I'm starving. Let's get a table. It was nice meeting you Ryan."

"You too Dr. Leshing, I'll see you at the hospital. See ya Gina."

"See ya Ryan."

Ryan went back to his table of friends while Brandon and Gina made their way to an empty booth. "What made you call me for dinner? I must admit I was surprised by the invitation."

"I kind of had been burned out with my work. I just needed to get out and do something. Even though I've been working at the hospital for several years, I really didn't know who to call. You did say if I ever wanted to go out that I could call, so I called."

"Oh, I see. Well, it doesn't surprise me."

"What doesn't surprise you?"

"It doesn't surprise me that you couldn't think of too many people to call. I've been here for over a year and I have seen you less than a dozen times in all. I've worked different shifts, I've worked different areas, and I still rarely see you. In fact no one sees you. You're always cooped up in that lab of yours doing whatever it is that you do. People are starting to wonder about you."

"And what exactly do they wonder about?"

"They think you're either a mad genius concocting some wonder drug, or you're some sort of serial maniac who keeps bodies down there."

"You've seen me in my lab. I'm certainly no serial maniac."

"No, but you're bordering on being a mad genius trying to develop some kind of wonder drug."

The waitress came to the table bringing menus. "Can I start you off with a drink? I see you have a drink ma'am. Sir, can I get you something?"

"I'll have a bottle of Bud. Gina would you like another?"

"I'm fine for now, thanks."

"One bottle of Budweiser it is. Just to let you know we have a linguini and seafood special that is out of this world. It comes with two sides and a salad. We also have veal parmesan that is also incredible. That comes with a side of pasta, or baked potato, and a salad. Here are your menus and I'll be right back with your drink."

"Do you see anything that you like, Gina? Have you been here before?"

"Actually I have. They have a nice porterhouse steak. If you like steaks, I would recommend it."

"That sounds good. I think I'll have the same then."

"Once again you're taking my advice. I'll have to start charging."

"Taking your advice again?"

"You know. You never would have brought those people from London if I hadn't suggested it."

"I told you they were on vacation."

"Uh huh." Gina rolled her eyes making sure Brandon noticed. "Have you made any progress on your wonder drug?"

"It's not really a drug, more of an aid to the nerve cells. But no, honestly I haven't. Sometimes I wonder if what I'm doing is a complete waste of time. Almost everyone who has read my thesis has criticized it, some calling it a fantasy. Maybe they're right."

Gina could see how dejected Brandon had become. Once again she saw the grown man with the helpless childlike eyes. If she could, she would have reached across the table placed her hands on his face and told him that everything would be alright.

The waitress brought back Brandon's beer. "Are you ready to order?"

"Yes we'll both have the porterhouse steak. I'd like mine cooked medium with a baked potato and French dressing on my salad."

"Excellent choice sir, ma'am?"

"I'd like mine medium rare. I'll have fries and on my salad I'll have blue cheese dressing."

"Another excellent choice. I'll put the order in and I'll be back in a jiff."

When the waitress left to put in their orders, Gina looked to Brandon. "Well that was rude."

"What do you mean? I thought she was fine."

"Not her, you."

"Me?"

"Yes you. Always let the woman order first. You really don't know how to act on a date do you?"

"This isn't a date."

"Oh, that's right, I forgot. Speaking of the waitress, if someone did make a bad meal choice, do you think she would say that's a terrible choice sir?" Gina's attempt at levity didn't seem to hit. Brandon seemed to have his mind on something else. "Penny for your thoughts?"

Brandon snapped out of what he was thinking. "Sorry. So are you happy that you moved here from Philadelphia?"

"Honestly I wasn't at first. I seriously thought that I had made a mistake. Like you I made a promise to someone years ago. When I left to come here I broke that promise. But, now that I'm talking to the main reason why I came here, things are getting better."

"What promise did you make? Who did you make it to?"

"The promise I made was to my father. As to what that promise was, I'd rather not get into it. Like I said, I broke that promise when I left Philadelphia. Sometimes I can't help but think I let my father down. If he was sitting here now, what would he say to me?"

"I'm sure your father would be very proud. I certainly don't want your ego getting any bigger but you are an exceptional nurse. I've seen how you handle your patients. You really care and your patients know that."

"Well thank you, Dr. Leshing. That's nice of you to say."

"That's Brandon remember? When we're off duty, it's, Gina and Brandon."

"Yes, of course." Gina liked the sound of *Gina and Brandon*.

The two talked about places they have been in the Philadelphia area. They talked about people they both may know, restaurants, stores, movies they had seen. It was normal small talk. Gina came back to Brandon's work. "Not to beat a dead horse but what seems to be the problem with your work?"

"I can't get the right amount of '*Mito Wrap*' to work. I spend hours at a time trying to repair the spinal fiber tissue by applying a certain amount to each test case. But I can't get the right amount to work. At times it seems as though I don't use enough and the substance wears away before the nerve cells have a chance to regenerate and connect on their own. Other times I seem to be applying too much and it interferes with the passageway between the nerve endings. I don't know if there *is* a right amount to use. I don't know if what I'm doing will actually work.

The waitress came back with their meals. Gina and Brandon continued chatting while enjoying their dinner. When they had finished their meal, Brandon paid the check and both he and Gina left to go home. Brandon walked Gina to her car. When they arrived Brandon said to Gina, in the accent of the waitress − "That was an excellent choice ma'am. I really enjoyed that. It has been a while since I've had a good steak."

"Once again I'm happy to be giving this great free advice. You know the toll is running and you are going to have to pay me back at some point for all of my words of wisdom."

"I'd be happy to pay you in spades if you could give me some advice on my research."

"Lucky for you I do have some advice."

Brandon was shocked. "You do? Were you going to tell me tonight? Or were you going to let me stew in my own frustration?"

"I can't tell you what to actually do in terms of what amount of '*Mito Wrap*' to use or how to get the nerves to regenerate. My advice is to get your mind off of your work. I know you spend almost every waking hour that is not spent on your patients, thinking about your research."

"That's true. But I can't help myself. When I try to think, or do something else I almost immediately come back to my work. That's why I asked you out to dinner. I couldn't stand being alone. What do you suggest I do?"

Gina looked up into Brandon's face. She reached out to hold his hand and when she took hold she gave a little squeeze. Noticing Brandon hadn't rejected or had taken a step back, she drew her face close to his. She could smell the mixture of Budweiser beer and steak. As she drew nearer she looked into his sullen childlike eyes. He was looking back into her eyes not resisting her advances. Gina closed her eyes as her lips touched his. Brandon took his open hand and caressed Gina's hair. *This wasn't a mistake!* Gina thought. *I knew he was the one!*

As quickly as they started, Brandon pulled away. "Gina I can't. I'm sorry. I can't get involved in that way. I know the cliché - 'it isn't you it's me'. You have to know that in this case it's true. I can't get involved with you or any other woman. It wouldn't be fair to you. You said it yourself I spend almost every waking hour thinking about my work and you're right. Tonight was the first time in a while that I thought of something besides work. I just can't make this a regular thing."

"It's Ok, really. I went too far. I apologize. I shouldn't have done that."

"No, please don't apologize. Nothing would please me more than to take this to another level. But we both know tomorrow my mind will be right back in my lab. Until I fulfill my promise I can't get involved with anyone."

"Brandon it's Ok. Look, you know how I feel about you. I'm not going to make a scene or become some kind of insane jealous school girl who tries to make your life miserable because I was rejected. I know your work comes first. Oddly enough that is what drove me to want to meet you in the first place. If you are willing to give up millions of dollars playing football in order to pursue your work, than I guess putting your work aside for me isn't going to happen either."

"So we're Ok here then?"

"Sure, we're Ok here."

"If I could put my work aside to give my attention to someone, I couldn't think of anyone else I would give my attention to than you."

Gina took Brandon's hand and placed it upon her cheek. She kissed his hand. "Try a shower."

Brandon was confused. He tugged on his shirt, looked down to smell himself. "I need a shower?"

"I do my best thinking in the shower. Whenever I have a tough decision or I'm uncertain on how to proceed, I sometimes stand in the shower and think. It usually works for me. It might work for you."

"I'll try that. It couldn't hurt. I've tried everything else. Thanks Gina. Thanks for everything."

"You're welcome. Now if you'll excuse me I'm going to sit in my car and see if I can find a radio station that's playing the blues."

Brandon didn't know what to say. He knew he broke Gina's heart. What's worse is that he knew Gina was probably the best thing to happen to him in his life. In Gina he had found someone who could be his best friend, a lover who could understand him. They shared a common bond. He said nothing as he helped Gina into her car. He walked away without saying a word.

Watching Brandon walk away, Gina sat motionless in her car. She kept watching Brandon, hoping he would change his mind and come running back to her saying he had made a mistake. But he didn't. Instead she watched as Brandon pulled out of the parking lot. When he made the right hand turn onto Cyprus Street a tear streamed down her face. She *had* made a mistake. She had let her father down. She felt like such a fool. She gave up a chance to love a man in Kevin back in Philadelphia. Maybe it wasn't too late to go back. She still had her house. But when she thought about Kevin she didn't have those same feelings that she had when she thought of Brandon. But Brandon made it clear that there was no room in his life as long as he continued his work. Gina looked at herself in the rear view mirror. "What the hell am I gonna do? Maybe I'm the one who needs a long shower." She started the car and drove to her apartment.

Brandon lay in bed thinking about Gina. Was he wrong? Should he have accepted her advances and try to build a relationship? Could he take himself away from his work enough to give Gina the attention she deserves? What if he did take himself away from his work to build a relationship? If no progress was made, would be blame Gina? It was 3AM before he finally was able to drift off to sleep. His final thought was with a smile. At least he wasn't thinking about the failures of his research.

Brandon woke up at 10AM. With still so much on his mind he decided to take a drive to the beach in hopes of clearing his thoughts. He walked along the shore for hours yet he was unable to clear his head. His thoughts constantly went from Gina to his research and back to Gina. He decided that he did the right thing. There was no way he could have a lasting, fulfilling, loving relationship with someone if he couldn't give her the time needed. A relationship doesn't work on its own. Both people had to work to keep the relationship alive and healthy. Brandon knew he hadn't the time to keep a relationship healthy.

Brandon's thoughts returned to the recent failures of his research. He hadn't anything new to report since creating the '*Mito Wrap*' substance. Worse, he was out of ideas on what to do next. He drove home, and plopped onto the couch. He knew putting the television on would do no good so he didn't bother. What was it that Gina said? Whenever she had to think about something she took a long shower. Brandon decided to take a long shower.

As he stood under the water as it streamed down upon his body he envisioned each water stream as a separate nerve microtubule with signals coming from the brain, or in this case the shower head. He felt each individual pulse of water hitting his body, some pulses was heavy, and some were light.

Then it dawned on him. Up until now he has applied the same amount of 'Mito Wrap' to each microtubule in the subject's spinal cord. In some subjects he applied a heavier amount, in other subjects a lighter amount. What if he were to apply a different amount to each microtubule? In one subject, with hundreds of microtubules to apply the 'Mito Wrap', he could vary the amount. In some microtubules the substance would wear off too soon, in other microtubules it would be too much and it would interfere with nerve cell regeneration. But in some microtubules the amount could be just right and the nerve endings might be repaired as hoped. Instead of testing different amounts of 'Mito Wrap' by the subject, of which there were dozens, he could test the amount of 'Mito Wrap' by microtubules, of which there were thousands.

Once again Gina's advice worked. He couldn't wait for Monday to run his new tests, so he decided to go to his lab and begin his work immediately. For this experiment Brandon took three mice with different levels of spinal injury. The first had a severe injury that left its hind legs completely immobile. The second had moderate damage to its spinal cord which left the mouse with limited use of its hind legs. The third had light damage to its spinal cord where the mouse was able to use its hind legs, but only for short distances as they were very weak. All three mice were injured over three months ago. All three mice had a majority of their returned mobility come within the second month after being injured. All three mice had a limited amount of mobility returned during the third month. The last two weeks saw no gain of mobility in all three mice.

Brandon extracted the eukaryotic cells from the first mouse. He put the substance in the binary fission module and converted the cells into 75 percent 'Mito Wrap' mixture. The next morning he put the modified substance through the binary fission module again, this time he converted the substance into the pure 'Mito Wrap' needed. He then began working on mending the mouse's spinal injury. He spent over six hours operating on the mouse, the longest amount of time he had spent on a single session since he had started the procedures. He applied different amounts of the 'Mito Wrap' on hundreds of microtubules within the subject's spinal tissue. He documented as best he could the different amounts as he went along. The only reason why he stopped the procedure was his hands could hardly grasp the instruments.

When he was finished with the surgery, he stabilized the mouse's neck and placed the subject back into its cage. The next day he performed the same process on the second mouse. Two days later he applied the procedure on the third mouse. With all three mice carrying various degrees of the 'Mito Wrap' within the damaged spinal area, all that was left to do was to wait to see if any of the subjects would heal. Hopefully, Brandon would see some of the nerve cells regenerating to the point where the microtubules would fully connect.

After Saturday's dinner with Brandon, Gina did not have to return to work until the following Tuesday. When Tuesday came she felt like calling in sick. Though she hardly ever saw Brandon while at work except for a chance meeting while on rounds, or being called upon to assist in a surgical procedure, she didn't want to take the chance on seeing him. She told Brandon that she was Ok with how things ended, but she wasn't Ok. She wasn't quite sure how she would react. Would she break down? Would she become angry? Would she ignore him? She had the phone in her hands as she dialed the hospital to call in sick. Just as she was about to punch the last digit she slammed the phone down. Sure she could call in sick today, but she would have to show up for work at some point. And who was he to dictate how she led her life? If she had to work, she had to work. If she had to work with Dr. Leshing she would work with Dr. Leshing. She could control her emotions. If it was strictly a working relationship he wanted, then strictly a working relationship it would be.

As Gina approached her work station, Stacy, waved to her holding a note. "Hey, Gina."

"Hi, Stacy."

"Dr. Leshing stopped by. He gave me a note to give to you."

"Did he say what it was about?"

"No, he just asked for me to give it to you when you came in." Stacy handed the note to Gina. *'Gina, you were right. When you can, stop down to see me. Please. Brandon.'*

I was right. Gina thought. *I was right! I knew it! I knew we were meant to be!*

"Is everything Ok Gina?" Stacy asked.

"Everything is great Stacy. Thanks for the note."

"No problem."

Now came the hard part. Gina couldn't go straight down to the lab to see Brandon. She had to go over the patients that were in her care with Stacy whom she was replacing. It would be at least three hours before she could take a break. Every minute that passed seemed like an hour. Finally she was able take her 15 minute break. Instead of heading straight to the lab, Gina ran to the ladies room. She wanted to look as best she could when Brandon would tell her that she was right all along. Finally she was at the door to Brandon's lab. She took a deep breath and knocked.

"Yes?" Brandon shouted back.

"It's me, Gina."

Brandon opened the door. "Come in, come in." Brandon seemed as excited as Gina felt. As Gina walked in, Brandon had his hand on her shoulder almost shoving her into the room. "You wanted to see me Brandon?"

"Yes, yes I wanted to tell you that you were right once again."

"I was. I'm so happy you were able to see that. What made you change your mind?"

"Change my mind? If you mean what helped me figure out how to proceed with my research it was the shower you suggested."

"Huh?" It was as if someone had just cold-cocked her right in her gut. "The shower?"

"Yes, you said that when you were at a loss or needed to make a big decision that you would stand under the shower and the answer would come to you. Well that's what happened to me."

"What happened to you?"

"I took your advice. I was at my wits end. I was walking the beach, nothing came to me. I decided to think while in the shower and it came to me. Instead of trying to determine the right amount of '*Mito Wrap*' to use per subject, I should use different amounts per microtubule. I can get the results I need in one subject."

Gina was still trying to recover from the knockout punch to the gut. "I don't understand."

"Remember at dinner when I said I was testing different amounts of '*Mito Wrap*' on each subject but I couldn't get it right?"

"Yes, I remember."

"At the rate I was going, I probably would never develop the right amount of '*Mito Wrap*' to apply because I was using the same amount on all damaged nerve cells for each subject. While in the shower it occurred to me that instead of the same amount per subject, use different amounts per microtubule. You follow?"

"Not really but…"

"This way, instead of observing one subject at a time, I can observe hundreds of microtubules at a time. Of course it also means that the right amount of substance won't be used on the entire area, but once I find the right amount to apply, I can use that amount on the entire injury. If all goes as planned, I'll have my next step solved and I owe it all to you. Once again you were right and I'm not too proud to say so." Brandon stood there smiling like a kid in a candy store.

All Gina could think of saying was, *I was right about a lot of things Saturday night you idiot!* She composed herself. "That's wonderful Dr. Leshing. I'm glad that I could help."

"That's all? No I told you so? I'm admitting you were right."

"No gloating. I'm glad you were able to get to the next step."

"Even with this strategy it doesn't mean that what I'm doing will work. All it means is that my tests can be done at an accelerated pace. In a few weeks I'll be able to see if my theory holds any water. At least now I have an end in sight. I'll know soon if I can continue with my theory, or if I need to go in a completely different direction. I wanted to thank you again Gina for listening to me Saturday and offering me some advice."

"Nurse Stroit."

"What?"

"It's nurse Stroit. I'm on duty. Remember while we are on duty we have to keep it professional?"

"Oh, yes, of course, nurse Stroit."

"I need to get back to my station Dr. Leshing."

"Yes, of course Gin… nurse Stroit. Perhaps we can have dinner when we are both off duty?"

"I'll have to check my schedule. I'll get back to you." Gina walked out of the lab, closed the door and again felt like calling in sick. But she was already at work. The worst was over. She had not only seen, but talked to Dr. Leshing. She took a deep breath, mumbled to herself *keep it together Gina*, and headed back to her station to complete her shift.

Over the next few weeks Gina never did get back to Dr. Leshing on a night they could have dinner. She hadn't seen too much of him at all. Whenever Dr. Leshing was near, Gina tried her best to keep her distance, though there were times when they needed to talk about patients in their care.

Brandon noticed a change in Gina's behavior. But he didn't press her on it. He was right to not start a relationship with her. Had he done so, it would have been an injustice to her. His research came first.

After a few weeks, Brandon could see some of the microtubules within the test subjects mending slightly. He noticed some damaged nerve endings actually nearing the point of connection. Some of the 'Mito Wrap' seemed to be interfering with nerve cell regeneration and with other microtubules the substance had dissolved to a point where the nerve endings had stopped regenerating altogether. The fact that some of the nerve damage was healing was miraculous.

A couple weeks later Brandon could see more damaged nerve cells healing and not only did he see a difference in the nerve tissue, he saw a difference in all three subjects. Each of the three mice had made progress regaining a little mobility in their paralyzed limbs. The mobility wasn't much, but each had regained more mobility over the past two weeks than they had in the previous month. The only conclusion was that the 'Mito Wrap' was working for some of the nerve fibers. Even if it was just a couple dozen microtubules that were restored it was enough for the brain to reconnect to the muscles that had previously been dormant. Knowing that his procedure was working, he couldn't wait to file his report to Michael Murphy.

After reading Dr. Leshing's report Murphy wanted to discuss the findings to ensure what he was reading was truly what was written.

When Brandon arrived in Michael's office he was ecstatic. "Mr. Murphy, I have great news!"

"With your research I see?"

"Yes, yes! I've made a breakthrough! I've been able to determine the right amount of 'Mito Wrap' to use in healing damaged nerve tissue. I have three subjects who had varying degrees of spinal damage. With the right amount of 'Mito Wrap' substance, some of the damaged microtubules have regenerated enough cells to establish connections."

"Dr. Leshing, that is wonderful news, congratulations!"

"That's not all, each subject was able to regain more mobility over the past couple weeks than they had over the previous month."

"Dr. Leshing I know how much time and effort you have out into this. Are you at a point where you can publish your results?"

"I don't want to publish my results just yet. I need to do more tests. I need to apply the proper amount of 'Mito Wrap' to a subject's entire injured area. All I had done was apply various amounts to individual microtubules within each subject. I had hoped to see some nerve cells regenerate in order to better gauge a proper amount of substance to use. I never dreamed that the process would have this much success!"

Murphy looked pensive before replying. "Be sure to keep me updated on your progress. This could put us at the forefront of spinal research. It could mean additional funding for the hospital, and of course additional funding for you, and your research, perhaps with an actual staff and an actual lab."

"Mr. Murphy I don't care about that. All I know is that this means I'm on the right track to finding a cure!"

"Congratulations, again Dr. Leshing. Please, keep me informed of any progress. Now, if you will excuse me I need to get ready for my next call."

"Sure, sure Mr. Murphy, I'll be sure to let you know of any progress."

When Brandon closed the door he couldn't help but wonder why Michael wasn't more excited with the news. Then again Michael hadn't put as much time in as Brandon. Brandon had dedicated his life to find the result he had just discovered, Michael had not.

The next person he needed to tell was Gina. Brandon hadn't seen much of her recently, and when he had, she was always too busy. She still had not gotten back to him regarding dinner. He knew perfectly well the reason why she had been avoiding him. It wasn't hard for Brandon to find Gina. He just checked the work schedule. "Gina, I have to talk to you. I have terrific news."

"It's Nurse Stroit, Dr. Leshing. And I'm afraid I will be starting my rounds in a couple minutes."

Brandon stepped closer to Gina. He spoke in a low, demanding voice. "Dammit Gina, I need to talk to you. It will only take a minute of your time."

Gina had never seen Brandon this irate. She had seen him frustrated, but never like this. "Fine, let's go over here." Gina led Brandon down the hall. "What do you want to tell me?"

"First, I have always been straight with you. I know you're pissed off at me but there's nothing I can do about that. Besides, I didn't do anything wrong. I was upfront and honest with you. Second I made a breakthrough with my research. I have been able to create the proper amount of 'Mito Wrap' to apply to each microtubule within the nerve tissue. I have seen nerve endings that had been damaged heal to the point where brain signals can get through to the muscle. This is the best news, the subjects that I have applied this to have been able to regain motor functions in their limbs."

Gina stood there, straight faced, not a smile, not in anger, looking at Brandon as if she were looking at paint dry. "That's fantastic news doctor. I hope that your research continues to be successful. Now if you will excuse me I have to check on my patients."

"With this new success, I was hoping maybe we could celebrate."

"I'll get back to you." Before Brandon could answer Gina walked back to her station.

Chapter 13
STUCK IN THE MIDDLE

Brandon had found what appeared to be a procedure that enabled nerve regeneration within the spinal cord. But he still was not able to help a single human being. Before he could publish his findings he had to ensure his tests were accurate. He had to improve upon his procedure. The more test cases he performed, the more accurate he became in determining the proper amount of *'Mito Wrap'* to use on damaged nerve tissue. Brandon performed his procedure as before, extracting eukaryotic cells from each subject's liver. He transformed the eukaryotic cells into mixture of mitochondria by putting the cells through the binary fission module. He performed his surgical procedure on each subject first removing damaged and dead nerve cells. This meant severing parts of the spinal cord. A procedure every medical professional was against doing. Then he applied the *'Mito Wrap'* on the damaged area.

After a week of going through this procedure with the next set of subjects, all that remained was to observe. Brandon didn't know how long he would have to wait until he saw results, but based upon the previous the subjects, he hoped it would be two to three weeks until he would see some progress. His prognosis turned out to be pretty accurate. Within twenty days he began to see nerve cell regeneration. Days later he saw several microtubules connected. The healing process was progressing faster than he had anticipated. After four weeks, and more nerve endings connecting, the mice began to show improvement in their mobility. Brandon was ecstatic with the results. However he tempered his enthusiasm in that regaining some mobility was great, but he was looking for complete recovery.

In most spinal cord injury cases, major improvements stopped after five to eight weeks. However Brandon's subjects were still improving as much in weeks ten and eleven as they had in any week prior. After three months the mice were still regaining mobility. In the mouse that was slightly injured, it was hardly noticeable that it had suffered any nerve damage at all. The other two mice had not made a full recovery, but were still showing signs of improvement. With each set of subjects, the improvement in the *'Mito Wrap'* procedure enabled them to regain more mobility than the test cases prior. Brandon wanted to tell the world. First, he needed to tell Michael Murphy. After several dozen test cases, he was ready to publish his research.

"Mr. Murphy I've conducted the *'Mito Wrap'* procedures on dozens of subjects. All have had recoveries far and above what I had hoped."

"That's great news. Are you ready to publish your findings?"

"I am."

"Ok, get to work on your papers and I'll set the wheels in motion on submitting your work to various Medical Journals and Publications. When do you think you will have your material ready?"

"If all goes well and we don't have a rush in-coming patients I should be ready in two months."

"Fantastic. This could mean a lot of publicity for the hospital, as well as new sources of income and investments."

"All I care about is getting the word out and taking the next step towards applying my procedure on patients."

"Whoa, hold on Dr. Leshing. I'm as enthusiastic as you are about your findings. But it will be a dozen, maybe twenty years before you can apply your work on a patient."

"Twenty years? Why is that?"

"You didn't think that after applying your procedure on mice that you could go straight to applying the same to people?"

"No, not right away, but I didn't think it would take twenty years. What I'm doing is working. It's no longer just a theory."

"It's working on mice Dr. Leshing. Before you were able to get the procedure to work, how many times had you failed?" Before Brandon could answer, Murphy continued. "The subjects you have been working on are disposable. If your procedure fails you simply do away with the subject and try again. The same can't be done on human beings."

"I see your point Mr. Murphy, but twenty years?"

"I'm saying twenty years at most. I know how much time and effort you have put into this. I realize the sacrifices you have made. But look at how far you have come. Up to this point you haven't taken any shortcuts. You're excited at the possibilities. Hell I'm excited at the possibilities. You can't start taking shortcuts now; especially when you are this close. You have to play by the rules or you risk malpractice suits and losing everything. All of the work you have done will be for nothing."

Brandon knew Murphy was right. He had come so far. He worked nearly his whole life to get to this point. He couldn't do anything irrational now, not when he was so close. "What do I do now?"

"You write your findings. We publish your work and you get opinions from the medical field. If enough professionals agree, you may apply for accreditation of your procedure. Your procedure will be presented among a Medical Board and they can decide if your procedure is within the best interests of the patient without jeopardizing the patient's health. First things first, let's get your research published."

The number of patients that had come to Burdette Tomlin was pretty light with nothing but routine surgeries. All that changed when Kristy Matthews was brought into the hospital. Kristy had been involved in an accident in which she was a passenger in a car that was hit by a driver that went through a red light directly hitting the passenger door where Kristy was sitting. The driver had been texting a friend and never saw the light change to red. Kristy's head snapped to its side, breaking the C-5 section of her vertebrae. She never lost consciousness, and never felt any pain. Almost immediately she was unable to move any part of her body below her neck. When she was rushed into Burdette Tomlin, Dr. Leshing was paged immediately. Nurse Stroit was the scheduled O.R. nurse. She had still been keeping her distance from Brandon. However, on this night, working side by side with him would be unavoidable.

Dr. Leshing briefed the operating team prior to performing the surgery. Dr. Macaw, the anesthesiologist was first to walk into the operating room. Nurse Stroit followed right behind setting up the instruments required for the operation. Dr. Leshing walked in shortly after to perform the operation. The first step was to clear out all of the broken bone fragments.

After successfully removing all fragments he could see, right before closing up the damaged area, Brandon thought of his procedure. Could he possibly perform his *"Mito Wrap"* procedure on Kristy? Who would know other than the three people in the operating room?

"Dr. Leshing, are you ready to close?" Gin asked. Brandon continued to stare at the open area. "Doctor?" Still no response, Gina looked over to Dr. Macaw who looked back with raised eyebrows. She gave Brandon a nudge with her elbow. "Dr. Leshing, are you ready to close? That was the last fragments."

Brandon snapped out of his trance. "Yes, I'm ready to close, sutures."

When the operation was over Brandon walked out of the operating room. Gina cleaned up as quickly as she could. She realized that she had been a fool to act as she had. She couldn't blame Brandon for choosing not to start a relationship. Seeing him operate emphasized how dedicated he was towards his work. She wanted to say how sorry she was for avoiding him. She also wanted to see if she could help with whatever seemed to be bothering him. But by the time she was out of the operating room, Brandon had already left. Gina knew exactly where to find him. She went to the lab to speak to him.

After knocking on the door, Gina heard a faint "Come in".

"Hi, Brandon, are you Ok? You seemed to have your mind elsewhere in the operating room."

"Nurse Stroit, I'm fine. Is everything Ok with the patient?"

"Yes, everything went well. She is resting. I wanted to say I'm sorry for the way I've been acting recently. I guess I took your rejection a little harder than I expected."

"It's Ok. I knew you were avoiding me but I didn't want to press it. I knew eventually we would talk." Brandon gave Gina a wink.

"How is your research going?"

"Actually it's going great. I have seen great results. In fact those three subjects there have had their spinal cord injured to various degrees and now to look at them. You wouldn't know that they had an injury at all."

"That's amazing!" Gina walked over to the mice that Brandon had referenced. "You're right the way they are running around, you would never tell that they were injured. You must be excited."

"I am, rather I was until I met with Murphy."

"Why? What does Murphy have to do with this?"

"He runs the show here. When I told him of my success he seemed excited as well. But when I mentioned taking this to the next step he really dealt me a blow."

"What did he say?"

"That it could be ten to twenty years before I could apply my procedure to a patient. And looking at it from his perspective, I realize that he could be right."

"Oh, that is disheartening. You had to know it would take some time before you could go from practicing your procedures on mice to performing it on people."

"I guess I never thought about it. I have something that works. It actually works! This could be a cure for neurological injuries. This could be a cure for paralysis, MS, Alzheimer's, and so many more."

"Like Kristy. I see why you were apprehensive before closing."

"I couldn't help but think I could do something to actually help her. The way she is and the surgery I performed will do nothing more than leave it up to chance. And it's a slim to no chance that she will fully recover. But I couldn't risk it. I couldn't risk losing my license or putting this hospital as risk. I *know* what I have learned would have helped her. If nothing else it would have given her a much greater chance of a full recovery."

"Maybe she will recover."

"I'm sure she'll recover some. But we both know her chances of a full recovery are slim."

"What can you do now?"

"All I can do is write up my findings and submit them to Medical Journals and other publications and hope my procedures are accepted among the medical field."

"Why wouldn't they be accepted? At least when it applies towards your subjects, you have proof that what you are doing is working."

"I don't know. Every other paper I've put out has been met with skepticism. I have hardly ever received a good review of my theories."

"That was before you had actual cases where your theories have been put to practice. The medical community has to accept your procedures now."

"We'll see. Judging from past experience most of the Medical community know nothing about the spinal cord. They are more interested in developing a new body suit."

"Well then, make them understand. Try me for instance."

"Try you for what?"

"Tell me what your research revealed. I know a little about what you've been doing but I don't fully understand. Make me understand."

"You want to go through this now? I'm tired after performing surgery."

"Then let's do it over dinner. I did say I would get back to you when I was free. How does Saturday night sound?"

Brandon, who was dead tired after the surgery, perked up. "That sounds great."

Gina met Brandon at The Grill. They had the same waitress as before. Both ordered the Prime Rib again. "So tell me about your latest breakthrough."

"You already know about the *"Mito Wrap"* that I needed to extract."

"Yes, you need that to be some sort of 'glue' to mend broken microtubules in spinal tissue."

"Yes but it does more than that. I've discovered something else."

"What is that?"

"My initial understanding was that the microtubules within the spinal tissue needed to be connected to the sibling in order for brain signals to get through to the muscle. The general understanding was that paths from the brain to a specific muscle within a limb were unique. We thought that you couldn't send signals from the brain through nerve tissue designated for an arm let's say, and then connect that tissue with nerve endings designated for a leg. What I've found is that it doesn't matter which microtubules are connected. As long as there is a pathway, the signal will find a way."

"Are you saying that it doesn't matter which microtubules you connect? It doesn't matter if the pathway of nerve tissue from the brain to an arm is then connected to nerve tissue used by a leg?"

"It's something like that. Let me try to explain this way. Say you're driving from Philadelphia to the Jersey shore. And in this case, Philadelphia is the brain, and the Jersey shore is the body. There are many ways you can get from Philadelphia to the Jersey shore. You can go over the Walt Whitman Bridge, or you could take the Northeast Extension and drive the Jersey Turnpike, or you could take any number of back roads. All of those routes act like the nerve tissue from the brain to the body."

"Ok I'm with you so far."

"Now let's say you want to take the Walt Whitman Bridge, but when you get there, the bridge is out. In fact all main routes are out. Only the back roads are available. The connection from Philadelphia to New Jersey, or the nerve, has been damaged. The regular routes are cut off. What would you do?"

"I would take the back roads. It would take longer but I would make my way around it."

"Exactly, the brain, nerve tissue and muscle work the same way. Just because a connection is cut off, doesn't mean that there is no hope. It may take longer but signals from the brain to the muscle can be made as long as there is a pathway to connect. There aren't microtubules or nerve tissue specifically used for brain to leg functionality or brain to arm functionality. As long as there is a pathway for the brain, the signal will find a way. We just have to open up a pathway, and I have been able to do that with the *"Mito Wrap"*.

"I see. But why cut away nerve tissue? If a nerve tissue or microtubule is already connected, but has been damaged, why can't the *"Mito Wrap"* still work? Why need the *"Mito Wrap"* at all if the connection is still intact?"

"Nerve cells are extremely fragile, if a nerve cell is damaged, it's pretty much dead. The problem is that those dead cells create a roadblock. Most, if not all research is looking to rejuvenate the damaged cells. But once the cells are dead, they are dead, and they block any neurological activity from the brain. The only way to open up that activity is to remove the dead cells and reconnect the living cells. The only way to do that is to remove the nerve tissue."

"I see, so write that. Write what you explained to me. You have to make them understand."

"I've been working on some papers for a couple weeks now. I should have something to publish by the end of the month. The only drawback to my work so far is that I can't get it to work on completely severed spinal cords. It's as if once all contact has been cut, there is no going back. In these cases it would be like all of New Jersey floating off into the ocean with no way of getting there. As long as you can get there some way, you can repair what has been damaged."

"If you can get partially damaged spinal injuries to recover, that's far more than anything that we have today."

"Yes but as someone told me years ago, it would be easier to get approval to perform this type of procedure on a completely severed spine than a partially damaged one."

"Why is that?"

"Because the medical community agrees that a completely severed spine has virtually no chance of regaining mobility. Because they have no chance, the risk would be a lot less than someone who does have limited mobility. Someone with a partially damaged spine who regains some mobility runs the risk of losing everything, because my procedure cuts the spinal tissue."

"Some people would take the risk. I know my father would."

"Even if I did get volunteers, the procedure would be illegal. I'm afraid all I can do now, is publish what I have and hope for the best."

"I'm sure given the proof of your work that people will take notice."

The dinner ended less dramatic this time. Gina didn't give any indication of anything more than just a dinner. When they had finished dinner Gina and Brandon drove to their separate apartments.

When Brandon finished his papers he handed them to Murphy. After receiving the work, Michael made a call. "Hello George, its Murphy. I have the papers. No I haven't gone through them. They were just handed to me."

George was a man that Michael Murphy had never met. He didn't know George's last name nor if George was the man's real first name. George hesitated, thinking about the ramifications of what Murphy had in his possession. "We knew this day would come. Here's what you do." George explained to Murphy who to contact to have the papers published in the journals George had chosen.

The papers meticulously detailed the process Brandon took to injure, then heal the mice he had performed his *"Mito Wrap"* procedure. He left nothing to chance. He didn't care if anyone took his ideas and tried to make them their own. All he wanted was his procedure to be accepted by the medical community. As detailed as he was, with as much documented proof he had, he didn't see how anyone could not at least consider that what he had performed was accurate, honest, and most of all, a procedure that could be used to cure neurological injures. The responses received however were quite different.

Murphy had managed to get Brandon's papers published in four medical magazines and three medical journals that were highly regarded among the medical community. The papers were highly publicized, and highly criticized. The responses were no different, and in some cases worse than what Brandon had heard before. Responses ranged from asking why there were little to no other people performing the procedures. Others had noted that while the procedures provided some insight to the uses of mitochondria, the use of such a substance in the healing of spinal cord injuries was ideological at best. Other medical professionals responded that while there may have been regeneration of nerve cells in mice, the same could not be certain in humans. Others wrote that the healing of the injured spinal cord with mitochondria showed no proof that the healing would not have occurred without the substance. The highest criticism was in regard to the cutting of the spinal cord to remove damaged cells. Not one medical professional agreed that this was a proper procedure to even consider applying to a human being.

Brandon couldn't believe what he was reading. He didn't know whether to be angry, embarrassed, or dismiss all of the criticism. "Mr. Murphy, I've shown you the proof. My procedure works. Why am I being discredited like this? What am I supposed to do? If I can't be accepted by the medical community, how am I supposed to get my procedure accredited?"

"Dr. Leshing I know you're upset. But you have to consider that what you're proposing will have a dramatic impact on the medical community. Up until now, no one has been successful in healing the nerves within the spine. Now you're suggesting that all you need to do is extract some substance found in the body, inject it into the spine and Walla! It isn't that easy."

"I'm not suggesting that it is that easy."

"To many it sounds as if what you are doing *is* that easy. You have to give it time. It's like suggesting that the earth revolved around the sun in

Copernicus' time. He was chastised, ostracized by society for suggesting such a thing. Now, it's common knowledge."

"Yes but Copernicus wasn't chastised by the scientific community. He was chastised by the religious community. A lot of the scientific community accepted his theories but were afraid to admit it."

"Maybe there is some of that today. There are so many people who don't agree, that those who do are afraid to say so."

"What do you suggest I do?"

"My suggestion is to continue your work. Keep documenting what you are doing. Perhaps invite people to witness your procedure. Your work has just begun. Practice your procedure. Improve on what you have done so far. If you keep giving me new papers, I'll keep getting them published. Before you know it, you'll have a couple people step up in your defense. Soon, the number of people supporting you will outnumber those who don't."

Brandon thought about what Murphy was saying. Since he didn't have any other options, all he could do, was agree. "Ok, I'll keep working on my procedure. As I make improvements I'll document them for publication. If possible, I'll give demonstrations. I'll keep telling people my procedure works until they believe me."

Murphy walked over and placed his hand upon Brandon's shoulder. "I believe in your work. You're still young and with your persistence, luck, and patience, you will see the day when your procedure helps people."

Brandon stood up, thanked Murphy for his support. After Brandon left his office, Murphy made a call to the man he never met. "George, its Murphy. Leshing just left my office."

"How is he doing?"

"He's naturally very upset."

"He should be. I've read his work. It will only be a matter of time before it's completely out."

"What should I do?"

"Keep him under wraps. He can't apply this to any patient any time soon. Once he does, billions of dollars will be lost."

"I've told him that. Sometime soon we'll have to make him an offer."

"We're aware of that. Let's hold out until we absolutely have to. Maybe he'll do something stupid before that day comes. What's he doing now?"

"I've told him to keep working on his procedure. I told him to keep improving the process, keep documenting what he's doing and eventually the medical community will accept his work."

"Excellent. If anything changes we want to know about it. As long as you keep him under wraps we'll continue to make donations to you and your hospital. If things get too hot, we'll step in and make an offer he won't refuse."

Murphy hung up the phone. He genuinely felt bad for Dr. Leshing. Brandon had no idea what he was really up against. But as long as George's group continued with donations, there was nothing Murphy could do to help.

When Brandon got back to his lab all he could think about was the negativity within the Medical community towards his publication. How could everyone be so blind? Were they jealous of his findings? He wished he knew the true reason why he was being chastised. For now, all he could do was continue to improve his procedure. He would film, document, and do whatever it took to get people to believe that what he had was a valid treatment.

He was getting more precise at applying the right amount of *"Mito Wrap"* to the damaged nerves. He was getting better at removing the damaged nerve cells in order to provide a clearer pathway for the brain signal to the muscle.

Brandon performed his procedure on video. He had Murphy put the videos on various medical web sites. Even there he was met by critical responses. He was a magician, not a surgeon. And every magician had a secret why their act worked. When a magician sawed a girl in half it was because there was a girl in each half of the box. In Brandon's miracle cure there must have been a reason why it appeared to be so.

Brandon had perfected his procedure to a success of nearly 98 percent recovery rate on his test subjects. The two percent that did not regain full functionality had developed an infection or had an unexplained anomaly that prevented any recovery. Still, with this rate of success, and given the alternative that the patient would have in their future, Brandon was sure applying the procedure was worth the risk to the patient. But was it worth the risk to him and the hospital? For now, the answer was no. For now, all he could do was perform assembly line surgery where he would clean out the damaged area, stabilize the damaged area, sew up the damaged area, and send the patient to a rehabilitation hospital where the amount of mobility regained by the patient relied mostly on luck.

Gina hadn't seen Brandon too often the past couple weeks. When she did it was to assist on a surgical procedure. There hadn't been any major or critically injured patients coming into the hospital so the number of procedures performed by Brandon was low. When Gina had seen Brandon she could tell that he was depressed and frustrated. They hadn't seen each other outside of the hospital since their last dinner together. She decided to pay him a visit.

When Gina walked into the lab Brandon was sitting at his desk, his head resting on his left hand, his right hand tapping documents with a pen. "I haven't seen you much lately. How have you been?"

"Here I sit, on the brink of actually helping people and I can't do a thing about it. I sit here performing the same procedure on mice. I can help 98 percent of the mice who suffer, but I can't help one single person."

"Someday you will. I know it. I guarantee it."

"How can you be so sure?"

"Someone told me you would years ago, before I ever met you."

"And who was that?"

"Francine."

"Francine? Francine who?"

"Francine Quabalah. She was a tarot reader in Philadelphia."

Brandon laughed. "Thanks Gina I really needed that, a tarot reader."

"Yes and a very good one."

"Maybe she should publish my work and I'll finally be accepted."

There was a knock on the door. Michael Murphy stepped in. "Hello, nurse Stroit don't tell me Dr. Leshing has recruited you for his research."

"No sir, I just stopped down to brief Dr. Leshing on a patient."

"Ah, I was hoping you could steer him away from hospital business. I've never seen a more dedicated surgeon. Don't get me wrong, we love that about the good doctor. But at this rate I'm afraid he'll end up a spinster. He's at this hospital so much I don't think he has a place of his own." Murphy smiled as if he just told a joke, Brandon was in no mood, and Gina just gave an awkward laugh.

"Can I help you with something Mr. Murphy?" Brandon asked.

"I just stopped by to see how things were coming along."

"It's coming along fine. I've improved my process to where the cases have a 98 percent chance of a full recovery. But I'm still stuck in the middle of all of the negativity from the Medical community. I fear I'll never get to the next step. You have presented my work to medical journals, and other publications. You have placed video on medical web sites. You've even brought in medical professionals to see for themselves the work that I'm doing. Yet none of that has gotten me any closer to being accepted. I honestly don't know what to do."

"Dr. Leshing you just keep refining your procedure. We'll keep knocking on the medical community's door. Eventually they'll have to let you in. Trust me your time will come. For now, continue your procedure on your test subjects. Do you understand?"

"I do."

"The medical process may be slow, but they'll eventually come around. When they do you'll be more famous as a surgeon than you were as a football player." Murphy looked to Gina. "Has Dr. Leshing told you of his football exploits, nurse Stroit?"

"I am aware he was an excellent player Mr. Murphy."

"That he was. Why he never became a professional is beyond my comprehension." Murphy shook his head. "With his talent he could have been the next Jim Brown or Walter Payton. Well I'm off to do battle with some lawyers, every one of them looking to make a fast buck off this hospital. But as long as we play by the rules, we have nothing to worry about." Murphy gave a wink to Brandon. "I'll talk to you later."

Once Murphy left, Gina said the same. "I have to get back to my station. Don't worry what other people think of your work. You know what you are doing is right. Sooner or later everyone will realize that as well." Gina wanted to hold Brandon close and let him know that everything would be alright, that she was there for him. All she could give him was a look of understanding and a smile.

"Thank you, Gina."

Chapter 14
WHO AM I TO PLAY GOD

Michael Murphy sent Brandon's research papers describing the '*Mito Wrap*' procedure to several carefully selected medical publications. Most of the feedback was highly skeptical, as Murphy knew it would be. With each passing week, and month, Brandon became more frustrated, distant, and isolated. If it weren't for the need to treat patients in the hospital, he would be hibernating in his lab. Gina had noticed how isolated, how depressed Brandon had become. She even went to talk to Murphy about Brandon's condition. All Murphy could say was that he had spoken to Dr. Leshing several times. There was nothing he could do as long as Dr. Leshing performed his responsibilities without incident.

Summer arrived and with it came the tourists and beach goers from Philadelphia, Delaware, New York, and people all the way from Canada. With the influx of people, came an influx of people who needed medical attention. Most were treated and let go. It wasn't until Senior Week, when high school seniors came to party at the jersey shore that more serious injuries had to be treated. The cause of those injuries was mainly due to underage drinking. Some injuries resulted from fights, and accidents. Other injuries occurred while performing acts of stupidity or as the boys called it acts of dare, as they tried to impress the female friends. These types of injuries usually required a cast, a brace, with one to two nights stay. Occasionally there was a more serious injury that required special attention.

Bruce Hopkins, who had recently graduated from Lincoln High School, was with friends on the boardwalk when he got involved in a contest of dare with a fellow classmate. Each had dared the other to perform a tight-rope act and walk along the top rail along the boardwalk. Bruce took the challenge without hesitation. He needed to walk fifty yards, from one pole to another to complete the dare.

Bruce jumped onto the rail then steadied himself holding onto the starting pole. Once he gained his balance he began walking along the rail. He walked half way when he looked to see how far he had left. He gave his friends a look of confidence, and then looked down at the other side of the rail. Once he did, he saw how high up he actually was. The rail was only four feet above the boardwalk, but the boardwalk itself was fifteen feet above the beach. With the change in depth perception, Bruce quickly lost his balance. Knowing he was about to fall, he turned facing the boardwalk and tried to push his weight forward for the short fall. But he fell backwards onto the beach where he hit a discarded log. His classmates looked over, seeing him on what they thought was nothing but sand, and laughed. His friend who dared him wanted Bruce to pay up. Soon they discovered that Bruce wasn't as fine as they thought. Within an hour Bruce was in an ambulance on the way to Burdette Tomlin Hospital.

Dr. Leshing was called upon immediately as the paramedics wheeled Bruce into the hospital. Nurse Stroit was also on call and supported the staff by getting Bruce's vital signs, and taking as much personal information as possible. Bruce was immediately wheeled into the X-Ray room where it was determined that the C-6 section of Bruce's neck was completely shattered. The C-5 section was also fractured, but was intact well enough that it did not need to be replaced. Bruce was transferred into the operating room where Dr. Leshing, Nurse Stroit, and Dr. Macaw began the preparation for clearing out the bone fragments of the C-6 section. It took five hours for the team to clear away all of the fragments. Once completed Bruce's neck was stabilized and he was wheeled to the intensive care unit. It would be 24 to 48 hours for the swelling subsided enough to gauge the amount of damage done.

When an MRI was taken two days later, it revealed that additional bone fragments needed to be removed. The spinal cord was not severed, but there was enough damage to indicate that Bruce would have less than a five percent chance of complete recovery. The plan was to wait another 24 hours to give the swelling more time to subside, then Dr. Leshing would remove the remaining bone fragments, and fuse the C-7 through C-5 section of the neck.

It had been over a year since Brandon perfected his *"Mito Wrap"* procedure that gave 98 percent of his test subjects a near complete recovery. He came to the realization that it would be another five to ten years at best before he could gain accreditation to apply his procedure on someone in Bruce's condition. If Brandon played by the rules, there would be a slim chance that Bruce would be able to function as he had just two days ago. He felt in his heart that if given the chance, based upon the hundreds of tests he had run, he would be able to give Bruce a real hope of regaining close to, if not a complete recovery. But what if Brandon failed? What if his *"Mito Wrap"* procedure made things worse? By cutting away nerve tissue to rid the spinal cord of damaged cells, he risked turning Bruce's condition from an incomplete to a complete spinal sever. He ran the risk of Bruce regaining *zero* functionality as was the case in two percent of his test subjects.

If Bruce's injury had happened to one of Brandon's test subjects, he could perform the *"Mito Wrap"* procedure blindfolded. But, as Murphy had said, human beings can't be discarded if mistakes are made. Brandon knew that if his procedure went as planned, Bruce would have a reasonably high percentage chance of regaining most, if not all mobility. But in doing so, Brandon wouldn't be playing by the rules. If there was any setback, whether it was due to his procedure, or any unrelated reason, Brandon's medical practice would come to an end. He stood the chance of serving jail time for purposely putting a patient at risk of further injury. All of his life's work would be thrown away. If his procedure didn't work, Brandon would be the cause for destroying another life. Could he live with himself with the guilt he would feel for the rest of his life?

It was 3AM and Brandon still had not made up his mind. He decided to make rounds to check in on his patients to help take the dilemma off of his mind, if for only a few minutes. He was able to concentrate on the conditions of those patients in the hospital as he stopped by each room not disturbing those who were sleeping. Eventually he came to Bruce's room. He was surprised to see Gina standing by Bruce's side. "How is he doing?"

"He is resting. His vitals are fine. What are you doing here at this hour?"

"I was checking on patients. How about you? I thought your shift would be over by now."

"I have one more hour. I'll be back on duty at 8PM. I'll be assisting you during the operation tomorrow night. You should go home, get some rest."

Brandon stared at Bruce looking as if he hadn't heard a word Gina said. Finally he replied. "I will. Bruce is my last patient."

Gina sensed something was on Brandon's mind and she knew precisely what that was. "You're thinking what his chances would be if you could apply your procedure aren't you?"

"I can help him. I know I can. I've been applying my procedure on hundreds of test subjects. I've written papers, produced videos, and asked those who doubt me to watch me apply my procedure. Still it isn't enough to get them to listen."

"In time people will come around. We both know what you are doing is right. You can't risk everything now."

"If not now when? It's been almost two years since I discovered a way to help someone in Bruce's condition. Murphy says to play by the rules. By the time the rules change I'll be too old to play. I can't stand by any longer sending people in Bruce's condition to a rehab hospital knowing his chances of walking again are slim."

"You can't risk your future over something that is out of your control."

"Gina I'm not worried about my future."

"Then think about Bruce's future. What if something does go wrong? What if you make things worse? At least now he has a chance. What if you do something to take away any chance?"

"Don't you think I've thought about that? I've already ruined one life. I can hardly live with myself now. I've been thinking about my work, Bruce's life, the hospital's reputation. I've been thinking about all of that. What I come to in the end is that I can really help this person. I know I can. And knowing that, shouldn't I do it?" Brandon then took out the needle used to extract the eukaryotic cells. "Nurse Stroit. I want you to leave the room."

"Why?"

"You know why. I don't want you to have any part in what I'm about to do. I don't want you implicated in any way. You've done your checkup on the patient. I'm finishing up my rounds. Before I do, I would like you go back to your station while I finish up here."

Gina knew exactly what that meant. Deep down she believed Brandon really could help Bruce. Looking at Bruce she thought of her father. Given the chance she knew that her father would have taken the risk in a heartbeat. Most of all Gina loved Brandon and didn't want to stand in his way. As she walked past him, she grabbed his arm. She stood so close to him she could clearly see the wrinkles in his eyes due to lack of sleep. "Brandon, I know you truly believe in your work. I believe in your work. Ultimately what you decide to do is completely up to you. But if something goes wrong, anything, think how hard it will be to live knowing you gave up everything because you couldn't wait."

Gina opened the door to let herself out. Before she was fully out of the room Brandon replied. "I don't know how much longer I can live with myself sending another kid to a life of hardship knowing I can help him." Gina closed the door behind her. She hesitated, wanting to say more, to say something that could ease Brandon's mind. She walked back to her station.

After seeing Bruce, the last patient on his rounds, Brandon went back to his lab. He placed the eukaryotic cells he extracted in the fission module. Once the mitochondria was mostly separated from the rest of the cells Brandon placed the substance in the refrigerator, turned out the lights and went back to his apartment where he would try to get some much needed sleep. Still thinking about how to perform his upcoming surgery, and the consequences of applying his "*Mito Wrap*" procedure, Brandon found it hard to sleep.

The team of Dr. Leshing, nurse Stroit, and Dr. Sheldon Crane, a young anesthesiologist who had been working at Burdette Tomlin less than one year, met to go over Bruce's MRI. By the looks of the photos of Bruce's neck, they had seen that the swelling had gone down well enough to see all of the remaining bone fragments that had to be removed. Brandon went over the game plan with the team. "If all goes well, we should be done in five hours." Gina hadn't said a word, instead nodding in approval. In her mind she felt some relief since Brandon hadn't mentioned a word about applying his "*Mito Wrap*" procedure. Dr. Crane hadn't assisted in too many procedures like this. This was only his third time assisting in a spinal cord surgery. Yet he seemed calm, and ready to go.

The operation started off as planned. Brandon had removed all bone fragments that the team had seen from the MRI. Gina had the hip bone extract and titanium rods ready knowing that it was time to fuse the area. Dr. Crane gave one more assessment that Bruce's vital signs were well within normal parameters. It should be smooth sailing from here.

Beads of sweat began to appear on Brandon's forehead. Gina noticed and wiped the sweat from his brow. Brandon hadn't moved, staring straight at the spinal cord. Dr. Crane began to notice that Dr. Leshing was more hesitant than normal. "Is everything Ok doctor? Do you see something?"

Brandon didn't answer. The pupils in his eyes began to widen. Beads of sweat continued to form on his forehead. Gina again wiped his brow. "Doctor, are you Ok? He gave no response. Gina looked at Dr. Crane who looked back with a shrug. Gina gave Brandon a nudge with her elbow. "Are you Ok doctor?" She asked louder.

Brandon gave no reply. He moved his right hand into his pocket and pulled out the vial of 'Mito Wrap'. Gina knew exactly what was on Brandon's mind. Dr. Crane on the other hand had no idea what was going on. Finally, Brandon spoke. "Nurse I'll need the loupe glasses, highest magnification." This time Gina didn't move, nor offer any reply. "Nurse Stroit! I'll need the loupe glasses, highest magnification, now!"

"Doctor, are you sure?"

"Yes, now get them, stat!"

Dr. Crane had no clue what was happening. "What is going on doctor? What is in that vial?"

"Dr. Crane I need you to keep an eye on the patient's vitals. We're going to be here for a while."

"Dr. Leshing you didn't answer my question. What's in the vial?"

"I'm saving this patient's life. Please do as you are told and keep a close eye on his vitals. The minute anything goes awry, I want to know about it."

"All that's left is for you to fuse the area and we're home free. What is in the vial?"

"Dr. Crane! I know what I'm doing. I'm going to give this patient a chance to recover, completely. All I want you to do is keep a close eye on the patient. Can you do that?" Dr. Leshing was hollering at the young assistant.

"Yes Dr. Leshing, but I don't understand. Isn't then next step to…."

"Dr. Crane, for the last time, all I need you to do, is to administer the anesthesia properly and monitor the patient's vitals. If anything starts to go awry I want to know about it. Do you understand?"

Dr. Crane still had no idea what Brandon was about to do. But he couldn't get up and leave. And he wasn't about to argue with the head surgeon. "Yes doctor".

"Nurse Stroit, glasses please."

The team spent another four hours in surgery as Brandon cut away dead nerve tissue and applied the "Mito Wrap" to the microtubules within Bruce's spinal cord. Gina watched in awe at Brandon's skill working with such minute pieces of tissue. She kept a close eye on him, wiping away sweat every few minutes, getting the surgical tools he needed in an instant. Working so close, for so long, it was as if she became a part of him as he performed his procedure. After a few hours Brandon didn't need to ask for a wipe or a surgical tool, Gina was already performing the task without being asked.

Dr. Crane looked on in half horror, half amazement. He was horrified to see Dr. Leshing cut away pieces of nerve tissue. But he too was amazed at the precision in which Dr. Leshing worked. He seemed to never tire, not one bit. It was only every twenty minutes that he lifted his head for nurse Stroit to wipe away the perspiration. It was only once or twice per hour that Dr. Leshing took a sip of water.

All Brandon could think about was finding microtubules to connect using the "*Mito Wrap*". For him time had stood still. He didn't know how many hours had passed when he realized that he had run out of the '*Mito Wrap*' substance. Now it was time to fuse the bones and close the wound. This took another hour before the team was finally finished. Brandon asked the team to meet in the post-op area to discuss what they had just done. "Nurse Stroit, Dr. Crane I want to thank you both for an outstanding job in there. Thanks to you, this boy now has a good chance of a full recovery."

Dr. Crane was tired, as were the other two, but still questioned what had just happened. "Dr. Leshing I don't understand. I know you have been working on a way to cure nerve damage for several years. I didn't know you had received approval to apply your procedure."

Brandon looked at Gina before answering. "I haven't received full approval as of yet. However the procedure has been tested for over two years with nearly 100 percent success. The patient was the perfect case to apply the procedure to give him the best chance at a full recovery."

"You mean what we just did is not approved?"

Brandon hesitated before answering. "As of now, no."

"What the hell do you mean 'as of now no'. You mean we just performed a procedure on a patient that hasn't been approved? What are you trying to do get me to lose my license before I even have a career? Why didn't you tell me you were going to do that? If I had known, there would be no way in hell I would have participated." Dr. Crane looked at Gina who hadn't said a word since leaving the operating table. "Did you know about this?"

Before Gina could answer Brandon jumped in. "She didn't know. I didn't know until I saw how much the swelling had subsided. What we did was give that boy a chance for a full recovery. Do you know what that means? He won't have to spend the rest of his life in a wheel chair. He won't have to wonder what his life might have been like if he weren't disabled. If I had fused his neck, closed the wound and shipped him off to some rehab he would have less than a five percent chance of being able to walk on his own. And now, if all goes well, he'll have a 98 percent chance of not only walking, but running on his own just as he did less than a week ago."

Brandon let that thought sink in a bit before continuing. He was about to continue when Dr. Crane beat him to it. "And what if all doesn't go as planned? I saw what you did in there. You cut away at his spinal cord. What if instead of a five percent chance to recover, he now has a zero percent chance? Did you think about that?"

"Ever since he came into this hospital I thought about that. Ever since I started to develop this procedure I thought about that. Every time I applied my procedure on hundreds of test cases I thought about that. I know what we have done will work."

"Not *we* Dr. Leshing, *you*. I don't want any part of this."

For the first time Gina spoke. "Dr. Crane if I may, I have worked with Dr. Leshing for several years. I've seen his work. I've seen the miraculous recoveries that have happened. I believe in his work. I know this is hard to accept. But what is done is done. We don't want to get you into any trouble. We don't want you to lose your medical license. Before we do anything, let's give the procedure time. Let's see if what we have done will give the patient his life back."

"What are you saying nurse Stroit? You want me to turn a blind eye to what I just witnessed?"

"All I'm asking is to give the patient time to heal. If Dr. Leshing's procedure is correct, we may have found a way to cure neurological injuries. Think about that. We may have found a way to cure paralysis, Parkinson's syndrome, or MS. There's no telling what can be accomplished."

"Sheldon, all I'm asking is to give it a chance. I will take full responsibility. It's my procedure, Murphy knows that. If anything bad happens, it will all fall on my shoulders. I take no one with me on this, not you nor nurse Stroit. I know this will work. Can you give me a couple weeks?"

Dr. Crane was tired. He could hardly think after so many hours in the operating room. Though he was younger than Dr. Leshing, he wasn't used to the strain put on by having someone's life in the palm of his hands for so many hours. He knew Dr. Leshing was sincere when he said that he would take full responsibility if anything did go wrong. He also had truth on his side that he had no idea what Dr. Leshing was going to perform prior to the operation. As for nurse Stroit he didn't know what to think. Dr. Leshing said she also had no idea about the procedure prior to the operation. She seemed more than willing to go along once Dr. Leshing had begun. Finally, Dr. Crane responded. "Ok, I won't say anything about what happened in there. But I'm only giving it a couple weeks. If anything starts to go wrong I have to come clean. I can't knowingly participate in a scheme of malpractice surgery. I won't say a word, but if I'm asked what happened in there, I won't lie."

Brandon looked at Gina, then at Dr. Crane. "That's all I'm asking. Everything that went on in there falls on my shoulders. I won't put either one of your careers in jeopardy."

The next day Murphy asked Brandon to meet. "You wanted to see me Mr. Murphy?"

"Yes, Dr. Leshing, have a seat." Murphy pointed to the chair right in front of his desk. "I wanted to ask about the patient, Bruce Hopkins. How did the surgery go?"

Brandon didn't know if Murphy knew that he had applied his "*Mito Wrap*" procedure. Dr. Crane may have gone to Murphy right after the surgery

322

and told him what had taken place. Still, Brandon didn't want to offer up anything he didn't have to. "The operation took longer than expected."

"I can see that from the logs. A procedure that should have taken four, five hours max, took eight hours to perform. Why the delay?"

Brandon took his time to answer. Was Murphy toying with him? Did he already know what had gone on in the operating room? Was Murphy giving him a chance to come clean? Brandon still didn't know for sure. "There were more fragments found than what showed on the MRI. Some of which were extremely hard to get, some of which were in extremely delicate areas. We felt that rather than hurry through the procedure we should take our time to clean the area as best as we could without risking the patient of further injury."

Murphy sat in his chair looking straight into Dr. Leshing's eyes. It was as if he was playing a game of poker waiting for his opponent to show weakness. Brandon didn't flinch. "Unforeseen fragments, that was the reason for the longer than expected time in surgery?"

"Yes, that and some of those fragments were in very delicate areas. We had to take extra care in removing them so as to give the patient the best possible chance of recovery."

Murphy had a feeling that there was more to the procedure than what Dr. Leshing was letting on. For now, he had to take his word for it. "How is the patient doing?"

"He's resting comfortably. We'll know more in a couple days."

"Ok, that's all. Keep me informed of the patient's progress."

"If there is any change, good or bad, I'll let you know right away." Brandon stood up and headed for the door. As he opened the door, ready to step outside he began to feel tremendous relief, until Murphy spoke. "Oh, Dr. Leshing."

Brandon stopped, closed his eyes, he could feel Murphy upon him, not quite ready to let him off so easily. "Yes Mr. Murphy?"

"How is your research going?"

"I'm at a 98 percent recovery rate. I've performed and perfected my procedure on over two hundred cases. However as you know I have hardly been accepted for accreditation."

"Keep perfecting your craft. We'll put out another publication soon. I'm sure if we keep knocking on the door the community will let us in. Try not to get too frustrated. You're still young and I'm sure eventually your procedure will be accepted. I know it seems as though the rest of the world doesn't want to listen, but eventually they will. Stay the course and don't do anything rash that will put your work, your career, and this hospital in jeopardy."

Brandon nodded and once again made his way out of the office. When he closed the door behind him, he let out a sigh of relief. But he knew the eyes of Murphy wouldn't go away that easily. Brandon had to speak to Gina and Dr. Crane. He had to know if Murphy had spoken to either one of them.

As Gina came in to start her shift, she was given a note to see Dr. Leshing at once concerning the patient Bruce Hopkins. Knowing it was too soon for any progress to have been made Gina immediately thought Bruce had taken a turn for the worse. Before checking her schedule Gina excused herself and headed straight to see Dr. Leshing.

"Come in Gina, close the door behind you."

"I got your note. Is everything Ok with Bruce?"

"He's doing fine. I had a meeting earlier today with Murphy. He asked why the operation took so long. Did he meet with you?"

"No, this is the first I've been in the hospital since the surgery."

"Did he call you? Did he leave a message to meet with him?"

"No, he didn't call and as far as I know he didn't leave any messages. As soon as I saw your message I came straight here."

"Ok, good. When we met he asked why the surgery took so long."

"What did you tell him?"

"I told him there were more bone fragments than what the MRI had shown. I told him that some of those fragments were in particularly delicate areas and we didn't want to rush."

"Did he buy it? Do you think he knows you tried your procedure?"

"I'm not sure. Murphy didn't come out and say anything directly. But, as I was about to leave he asked how my research was going. He told me not to do anything rash that might jeopardize my work, my career, and the hospital."

"Do you think he spoke to Dr. Crane?"

"I'm not sure. Dr. Crane isn't due back in the hospital until tomorrow. I don't know whether to call him at home or wait until he comes into the hospital. What do you think?"

"Knowing Murphy, if he did know you applied your procedure he would have come out and said so. He's not the type to dangle something like that on a string. He's more of the direct face to face let's get it out in the open kind of person."

"You're right about that. He's not one to be coy."

"And by calling Crane at home you might set him on edge. He wasn't too cooperative when we asked to give the patient time to recover. Calling him now might set him off to go to Murphy. I would wait until he comes in tomorrow. Then feel him out."

"You're right. Maybe I'm reading too much into Murphy's meeting. I'll wait to talk to Dr. Crane until he comes into the hospital. I'll set it up so that one of the first items on his list is to check in on Bruce. Thanks Gina." For the first time all day, he was able to relax. Brandon knew Gina was a damn good nurse. He also knew she was a damn good friend.

"You're welcome Brandon. If Murphy wants to discuss the surgery with me, I'll let you know. Why don't you get some rest? You look tired."

"I will." Gina went back to her station and checked to see if anyone else had left any messages. There weren't any.

324

Brandon locked up his lab and headed home. He was dead tired. Gina was right again. With his mind at relative ease, he fell asleep immediately waking up nine hours later. He was in the hospital the next day by 1PM. The first thing he did was to ensure that when Dr. Crane came in his first responsibility was to check on Bruce Hopkins.

Dr. Crane arrived at the hospital at 3:30, got the message to check on Hopkins and was in the ICU checking Bruce's vitals at precisely 4:00. Brandon came into the room immediately after him. "How is our patient doing?"

"Oh, Dr. Leshing I didn't hear you come in. He's doing fine. The chart says he slept all through the night. He awoke this morning at 9AM. He was alert, relatively comfortable. He has a slight fever but nothing to worry about at the moment. His family came in at eleven and stayed until two."

"That's fine, fine. How are you holding up?"

"Me? I'm fine. After the surgery I went and had a couple drinks with my girlfriend to wind down. With the day off yesterday I'm feeling fine."

Brandon didn't quite know how to ask Dr. Crane if Murphy had spoken to him. He couldn't think of a way to ask in a casual way, so he asked straight up. "Have you spoken to Murphy recently?"

"Murphy? No why? Is anything wrong?"

"No, nothing is wrong. He did meet with me to go over the surgery. Specifically he wanted to know why the procedure took so long to complete."

"Did you tell him you applied your procedure?"

Brandon took a few seconds to respond. "No, I didn't tell him that. I told him there were some bone fragments that weren't shown in the MRI. I told him that some of those fragments were in very delicate positions which took a while to extract. I told him the reason it took longer than normal was to give the patient the best chance of recovery."

"And you're worried Murphy will come asking me why the surgery took so long?"

"Well, it did cross my mind."

"Look, I'm not happy with what went down in the operating room. What you did is a classic case of negligence, bordering on pre-meditated criminal activity. I told you then that I won't lie about what happened. There is no way in hell I'm throwing my career away before it even gets started just for you. But I also told you I wouldn't do or say anything for a couple weeks. I'm giving you the benefit of the doubt that you truly believe you have the patient's best interest in mind. That what you did wasn't to satisfy some egotistical curiosity. If Murphy does ask me directly, did you perform your procedure I'm going to tell him the truth. If he asks why the procedure took so long I'll tell him it was due to an unexpected complexity and we needed to take extra care to give the patient the best chance of recovery. If Murphy doesn't ask, I won't tell. If I'm asked, I won't lie."

"Thank you, Sheldon. I appreciate your help in this case."

"It's Dr. Crane, and I don't need your thanks. Don't ever put me in this position again with any other patient. Do you understand me? Do I make myself clear?"

"Yes, yes of course."

"Now if you will excuse me I have other patients to check."

For the first time since the surgery Brandon didn't have to worry about Murphy, for now at least. Bruce was resting comfortably. It would be at least another two weeks before any noticeable improvement would be seen. Brandon couldn't do anything about that. He simply had to wait. He had waited all his life for this moment. He could certainly wait another two weeks.

After the first week Bruce was able to feel general touch in his feet. Though he couldn't tell the difference between a pin and a sponge, the fact that he could feel anything at all was a positive sign. So far Murphy was none the wiser. Brandon knew Gina wouldn't say a word to Murphy, Dr. Crane was another story. So far he had kept his promise to not come out and say what had gone on in the operating room. After another week, Bruce was taken out of the ICU room and placed in a single bed room. His progress during the past week was hardly any better than the first week. Bruce was still unable to move anything below his waist. He was able to move his arms and hands, but he did not have nearly the strength he had before the operation. Another week went by and still there was no improvement, Brandon became visibly stressed.

Brandon sat in his lab going over MRIs, other X-Rays, and the process of extracting the eukaryotic cells. He went over the process of extrapolating the mitochondria from the eukaryotic cells. Everything he had done was by the book. Well, his book anyway. Yet no visible improvement was shown in Bruce. He heard a knock on the door. He fully expected it to be Murphy. In the previous staff meeting Brandon had to explain why there was no improvement at all over the past nearly three weeks in Bruce's recovery. No one expected Bruce to be up and walking around, but normally in cases like these, where there was no severing of the spinal cord, a patient usually showed some signs of improvement, even if it was just a slight movement of the toes. Brandon explained that no two spinal cord injuries are alike. A patient showing no improvement was certainly possible. Murphy seemed to take the response in stride. He certainly couldn't refute Brandon's claim. During the staff meeting Brandon could sense the uneasiness in Dr. Crane. As each day passed, and no improvement was seen in Bruce, Brandon began to feel the world caving in on him. The person at the door knocked once more. This is it. Brandon would have to give a full confession to Murphy. "Come in."

When the door opened Brandon was relieved to see it was Gina. "Just thought I'd come down to see how you were doing. No one has seen you much the past few days."

"Hello Gina."

Gina saw how despondent Brandon was. "Are things that bad?"

"You tell me. Have you checked Bruce today?"

"Yes."

"And?"

"Still the same, there hasn't been any progress."

"Exactly, he hasn't improved at all. By now my test subjects were moving their limbs. I didn't expect Bruce to be standing, but I expected some kind of movement in his legs. What's worse, his injury shouldn't have affected his upper body. He could hardly grasp my hand when I shook it. He should have been able to fully grasp my hand even if he hadn't had *any* surgery at all. I don't understand it. I've been going over every step of the procedure. I didn't do anything wrong. It should be working by now."

"Give it time. There is no exact timetable for these injuries."

"There should have been some improvement. What if I was wrong? What if everyone else was right?"

"You did what you thought was right."

"It doesn't matter what I thought was right! I should have listened. I should have done what *was* right, not what I *thought* was right. And now it may be over, all over, all my work, all my research, my career. I should have listened but I didn't. What was I thinking?"

"Brandon calm down. It's still early. You thought you could give Bruce a chance at a full recovery. Your procedure has worked, hundreds of times. Just give it more time. It's not over yet."

"Dr. Crane looks ready to burst out stating what I had done. I can tell it may be a day, maybe two before he goes to Murphy, if he hasn't already. What about Bruce? What do I tell him? Sorry son I tried to help you but it looks like I fucked up any chance you had at any recovery."

"Brandon I realize that you are under a tremendous amount of stress."

"No you don't realize what I'm under. I've already ruined one life. I made a promise to fix it. Now I've ruined another life. I'm not going to get another chance. My life is done."

"Don't say that." Gina walked up close to Brandon. She wanted to hold him as strong as she could. But she could only put her hand on his shoulder. "Your life is not over. You are incredibly smart, dedicated. You don't have a bad bone in your body. You have developed something that can help hundreds of thousands of people. You can't give up now. Just give it a little more time."

"How much more time do I have? Dr. Crane looked ready to tell Murphy everything. Once he does, Murphy will have my head. He specifically warned me not to do anything rash. You know what he says - everyone must play by the rules. But I didn't play by the rules? I made up my own rules."

Gina could think of nothing to say to make Brandon feel any better. She wanted to let him know that no matter what, she would be there for him. She wanted most of all to tell him that she loved him and that everything would be alright. But she couldn't. She had been down that road before and she knew Brandon didn't feel the same way.

Brandon knew that if there was no improvement soon, the jig would be up. After over four weeks since the surgery, and no improvement from Bruce, Brandon was surprised Murphy hadn't come down hard on him yet. It was 11:30 in the morning. Brandon had seen all of his patients, only Bruce remained. He walked to Bruce's door and noticed Bruce had some family members with him. Gina was there as well making sure Bruce was comfortable. Brandon knocked on the door. "May I come in?"

"Hi doctor." A man, who looked to be Bruce's father, replied.

Brandon approached the bed. He looked at Bruce's chart, then grabbed Bruce's left ankle to see if any swelling had occurred. He grabbed Bruce's right ankle again checking for swelling. "I can feel that doc. I can feel your hands. That's a good sign right doc?"

"Yes, that's a good sign. You were able to feel my hand three weeks ago. How about some movement? Can you move your toes?"

Bruce's family members, his mom, dad and sister each prayed for movement in Bruce's toes. Bruce closed his eyes, his cheeks puffed up with air, tried. "Am I moving them doc? Are they moving?"

Bruce's family, Gina all saw that nothing was moving. No one said a word. No one wanted to be the one to say a discouraging word to Bruce. Brandon stared at Bruce's toes. If he had performed the procedure on one of his test subjects, the mouse would be moving around on its own by now. However this wasn't a mouse. This wasn't a test subject. This was a human being. This was another kid whose life was ruined. How could he have done this?

"Are my toes moving doc?"

"Try again."

"Ok doc." Bruce relaxed. He took a deep breath, and then tried again. "How about now doc? Are they moving?"

Again, everyone saw that there was no movement. No one told him his efforts were in vain. Brandon stared at Bruce's feet. How could this be? He had done everything right. He had perfected his procedure on hundreds of mice. Nearly every one of them made a recovery. Even the ones that didn't fully recover showed *some* sign of improvement. How could this not work at all on this kid?

"Doc, are my feet moving?"

Brandon didn't answer. Still no one wanted to be the bearer of bad news. Everyone waited for Dr. Leshing to say something.

"Doc?"

Brandon looked up from Bruce's feet. "No son, nothing moved." Brandon said in a matter of fact tone. His voice had risen at his next question. "Are you even trying?"

At this second everyone turned from deep sorrow to shock at Dr. Leshing's words.

"I am trying…"

"I don't think you are! You're not trying hard enough! You should be moving your legs by now. Every test case I had was able to move by now!"

Bruce's father tried to jump in. "Doctor!"

Brandon kept going. "We'll have no choice but to move you out of here in a few days. Do you want to remain an invalid for the rest of your life?"

Bruce's father again tried to interject. Bruce's mother and sister stared at Dr. Leshing, their eyes and mouths wide open. "You know it's completely up to you to walk. I can't do any more for you. If you don't want to remain a cripple you have to try. You have to try!"

Now it was Gina trying to interject. "Doctor Leshing!"

Brandon was about to continue when Gina grabbed him by the arm and pulled him aside. "Doctor Leshing may I have a word outside!"

It was as if Brandon was in a trance, staring at Bruce. Bruce had tears streaming down his face. "I am trying. I don't want to be a cripple. I am trying. I'm trying as hard as I can."

Gina finally managed to turn Brandon around to face her. "Doctor Leshing may I have a word with you outside!" Without waiting for an answer Gina pulled Brandon out of the room. Bruce was in tears, saying over and over - "I am trying. I don't want to be a cripple." Bruce's mom tried to calm her son down. Bruce's father stood there not knowing what to do. He didn't know whether to stay with his son, or beat the hell out of Dr. Leshing.

Outside Bruce's room Gina started in on Brandon. "What the hell was that in there? What were you thinking? I know you put your life's work on the line. I know the stress you are under. You may take it out on yourself, you may take it out on me, but you *damn* sure cannot take it out on that patient. You don't think that kid was trying his best to move? What were you *thinking* saying those terrible things in there? I've never seen you like this before."

Brandon was still seemingly in his trance. Gina was so angry she wanted to slap the shit out Brandon. Before another word was said, Nurse Stacy Weebling came running down the hall. "Dr. Leshing, Mr. Murphy wants to see you in his office right away." Neither Gina nor Brandon acknowledged Stacy's instructions. Stacy waited until she was right next to Gina and Brandon. "Is everything Ok here?"

Gina turned to Stacy. "Yes."

Stacy reiterated. "Dr. Leshing, Mr. Murphy wants to see you in his office right away."

Brandon came out of his trance-like state. "Thank you, nurse."

Gina walked back into Bruce's room to try and console him. When she stepped in, Bruce's father asked. "What the hell is wrong with that man?"

"He's been under a lot of stress. He's not normally like that."

"It's not normally like him? It's not normally like me to beat the shit out of someone either." Bruce's father walked out of the room hoping to meet Dr. Leshing. When he stepped outside, Dr. Leshing was gone.

Chapter 15
LOST AND IN LOVE

Brandon walked straight to Michal Murphy's office. As he walked the halls, a couple of people said 'hello', but he didn't hear a word. All he could think about was why his procedure failed. He didn't even realize what he had said back in Bruce Hopkins's room. Just before knocking on Murphy's door he realized exactly where he was and what was about to happen. Before he could get off the second knock, Murphy hollered for him to come inside. As soon as Brandon stepped inside, he knew his day would go from bad to worse.

"Have a seat Dr. Leshing." Before drawing back the chair Brandon gave Dr. Crane a quick glance. The second he looked over, Dr. Crane looked away. "Dr. Leshing I specifically asked a few weeks ago, why the operation on Bruce Hopkins had taken so long. Your reply was something to the affect that there were complications due to bone fragments not picked up by the MRI. That some of those fragments were in extremely delicate areas. That the reason the operation took so long was to give the patient the best chance of recovery. Have I paraphrased what you told me accurately?"

Brandon kept his answers short and succinct. "Yes."

"However you didn't tell me the whole story did you Dr. Leshing?"

"No."

"You said you wanted to give the patient the best chance of recovery. Tell me, how is Mr. Hopkins' recovery going? He has been here for over four weeks. Normally we would be contacting the rehabilitation hospital. Yet we haven't done that. Is the recovery going as planned?"

Brandon wanted to somehow explain why the patient hadn't made any recovery. But he couldn't explain it. The patient should be on his way to a full recovery. All Brandon could say was – "No."

"No. In fact Hopkins hasn't made any recovery at all. Has he Dr. Leshing?"

"No."

Murphy waited for Brandon to continue. Seeing none was forthcoming, Murphy continued. "Dr. Crane has given me a different account of what took place in the operating room. I'm hoping, praying to God that his version is incorrect. I'm going to give you one last chance to come clean. What the hell went on in that operating room?"

For the third time Brandon looked to Dr. Crane. And for the third time Dr. Crane looked away. Brandon wasn't angry. He asked Dr. Crane to keep what had happened at surgery to within the group, for a couple weeks. After four weeks, he couldn't blame Dr. Crane for coming clean.

"Dr. Leshing, what happened during the surgery performed on Bruce Hopkins?"

"I, eh, I performed my *"Mito Wrap"* procedure. After looking at the X-rays, seeing how his spinal cord was bruised not severed. He was the perfect patient to apply the procedure. Dr. Crane had nothing to do with the decision. He had no idea I was going to apply the procedure. In fact he tried to talk me out of it. But I went ahead anyway. I had extracted eukaryotic cells the night before. When the operation took place I had enough *'Mito Wrap'* to apply to several hundred microtubules. When I began the operation I still wasn't sure I would go through with it. The operation was going as planned. All of the bone fragments were removed. I could see how damaged his spinal cord was. I knew that if I had just followed normal procedure, he would have less than a five percent chance of a full recovery. Almost every test case with the same injury that I had treated for two years had made a full recovery. I thought I, I *knew* I could help Bruce make a full recovery. So I and I alone, decided to apply my procedure." Brandon again tried to make eye contact with Dr. Crane. "Mr. Murphy you shouldn't put any blame on Dr. Crane." It was at this moment that Dr. Crane finally was able to look Brandon in the eye.

"I told you not to rush into applying that damn procedure on a patient! Didn't I? I specifically said you can't throw away a person like you can a test case! But you decided to apply your procedure anyway. And by cutting away the nerve tissue you turned an incomplete spinal injury with a chance of recovery, even if it was just five percent, into a complete spinal injury with zero percent chance of recovery. God damn it Leshing do you realize what you have done! Because of your rash judgment, because of your impatience you have now ruined your practice. You have put this entire hospital and every person who works here at risk of losing their job. At the very least, if this gets out we're liable for millions, tens of millions of dollars because you decided to be a hero instead of what you are supposed to be, and that is a surgeon."

"Damn it Murphy it should have worked! I don't know what went wrong. I did everything by the book. He should be well on his way to a full recovery by now."

"You didn't perform by the book. You performed by your *own* book. Whether it should have worked or not, doesn't matter. Your procedure hasn't been accredited. I can't go to the lawyers and say well according to our book it should have worked. This is why it takes ten to twenty years for procedure to become accredited. Just because the procedure worked on mice doesn't mean it will work on a human being. And now, from what I've been told, that kid hasn't moved at all. God-damn-it Leshing, you hung this whole hospital out to dry."

After more hollering, Murphy finally calmed down. He looked at Dr. Crane who still hadn't said a word. "Who all knows about this?"

Dr. Crane glanced at Brandon. He cleared his throat. "As far as I know, Dr. Leshing, myself and nurse Stroit."

"That's it? Are you sure?"

"I haven't told anyone."

"Dr. Leshing what about you, have you mentioned this to anyone? Dr. Leshing? Leshing!"

Without moving a muscle, staring into his empty hands, Brandon softly replied – "No one."

"Ok, maybe we can keep this under wraps. Where is nurse Stroit now?"

"She's on duty." Dr. Crane replied.

Murphy pushed a button on his phone. "Theresa, get me nurse Stroit. Tell her to come to my office immediately."

Within ten minutes Gina knocked on Murphy's door. "Come in."

As soon as Gina stepped into Murphy's office she knew something bad had taken place. She quickly glanced to Dr. Crane and gave a polite nod. Then she looked at Brandon who still hadn't budged.

"Nurse Stroit, please have a seat." Gina sat next to Brandon who hadn't yet acknowledged her presence. "What I'm about to ask you is very important. It's important I hear the truth. I already know about the procedure Dr. Leshing applied to Bruce Hopkins. I'm aware that he hasn't made any progress in the four weeks he's been here. Dr. Leshing has already told me that the procedure was his idea alone. You are not in any kind of danger or in any way responsible for what had taken place. I can't stress this enough, the next question I am about to ask must be answered truthfully and thoughtfully."

Gina looked at Brandon who still hadn't moved.

"Nurse Stroit, have you told anyone about the surgery performed on Hopkins? Before you answer think about it. Take your time."

"Mr. Murphy I don't have to think about it. I haven't told anyone about the surgery."

"Are you sure? You haven't mentioned a word to anyone? Not even in casual conversation?"

"No Mr. Murphy, I haven't said a word to anyone."

"Have you been intoxicated in the past few weeks at any time, and if so was there the slightest chance that it could have been mentioned?"

"Mr. Murphy I'm going to have to take exception to your questioning! I have not been intoxicated in the past few weeks. I have not told anyone about the surgery."

"Nurse Stroit I don't mean to insinuate anything or insult you. Unfortunately the surgery performed on Hopkins has put you, me, Dr. Crane, this entire hospital at a tremendous risk. This hospital has it's ass out on a sling waiting to be wacked. That cowboy surgery that was performed has made us liable for God knows what. Jobs, careers could be lost. So again, I'm going to ask everyone. There's no reason to lie, what's done is done. It's now a matter of control. Has anyone mentioned the surgery to anyone outside this room?"

Murphy first looked at Dr. Crane who answered – "No."

Murphy looked at Gina who also answered – "No."

Murphy looked at Dr. Leshing who didn't say a word. "Leshing, did you mention this to anyone outside this room?"

Brandon answered softly – "No."

"Ok, maybe we have a chance. Everything that went on in that operating room has to stay in the operating room. We need to get Hopkins shipped to a rehabilitation hospital as soon as possible. How is he doing?"

Gina didn't like where this was going. "You mean aside from the fact he can't move his legs?"

"Nurse Stroit I am aware of his condition. Is he stable enough to be sent to a rehab?"

Gina just stared at Murphy. *How callous can he be?* She thought.

Dr. Crane spoke. "I would say that he could be sent within a week."

"Nurse Stroit I'm putting you in charge of making it happen. Work with his insurance company, work with his case manager, work out the transfer details, the rehabilitation hospital, everything. Barring any physical setbacks I need him in another hospital's care within the week."

No one said a word. Murphy knew the others looked at him as a callous bean counter. "Look I don't like this any more than you. The fact of the matter is if anyone, especially anyone associated to Hopkins' family hears about what happened we could be done as a hospital. So don't give me some sob story about how we owe something to somebody. Think about every employee in this hospital who unknowingly and undeservedly could lose their job. If anyone has any suggestions let's hear them now."

Gina immediately spoke. "We could keep Bruce here until he shows signs of improvement."

"As much as I would like to do that, we simply can't. What if there is no improvement? After a couple weeks the questions start coming in. Why is he still here? Why isn't he in a hospital closer to his home in Delaware? Why hasn't there been any improvement? Then the insurance company starts with their questions. Then they start an investigation because they think we're trying to milk the insurance money. The last thing we need is for someone outside this office asking questions. The best thing to do for this hospital is to send Hopkins to a rehab as soon as we can."

"Is that the best thing for Bruce?"

"Nurse Stroit, Dr. Leshing is the one who put us in this predicament, not me. My job is to look out for what's best for this hospital. Even if it means making decisions that may not be in the best interest of the patient. And it's not like I'm sending him home to fend for himself. There are at least two rehabilitation hospitals near Hopkins' home that are very highly rated. He will continue to receive excellent care. It just can't be here. Now, does anyone have anything else they want to get off their chest?"

No one said a word.

"Ok, you all know what to do. I don't need to remind any of you to keep what happened in that operating room to yourself. If you won't do it for yourself, do it for the people we have on staff. I've dealt with many lawyers when it comes to protecting this hospital and the doctors and nurses who work here. However there is no way in hell I would be able to protect anyone if this gets out. Do you understand?"

Gina and Dr. Crane slightly nodded yes. Dr. Leshing continued to stare into his empty hands.

"I want a status given to me every day on Hopkins' health and his placement in a rehabilitation hospital. Now let's get back to work."

Dr. Crane was the first one out of Murphy's office. He didn't want to face nurse Stroit or Dr. Leshing for fear they saw him as a snitch. Gina hesitated, waiting for Brandon to stand up. When she saw him begin to get up, she started towards the door. As Brandon turned to walk behind Gina, Murphy told him to stay. Gina continued out of the office.

When Gina closed the door behind her, Murphy began to speak. "Dr. Leshing you put this hospital at great risk. Right now I could strip you of your medical license for what you have done. Hell, stripping you of your license would be the right thing to do. But that would bring unwanted questions to the hospital. Questions I don't want to answer. So as of now, I am relieving you of your duties indefinitely. I want you to pack up whatever personal belongings you have and head straight out of the door. I don't want you to stop and chat with anyone. I want you to walk out the door and don't come back until I say so. Do you understand?"

Brandon slowly nodded he understood.

"If asked why you are taking an extended leave we'll say it is due to burnout. Since you have worked so hard for so long, you need an indefinite amount of time away. You keep your license, and we keep any unwanted questions away from this hospital."

Brandon nodded his head again understanding.

"Leshing you brought all of this onto yourself. You could have had it easy. Money for your research was coming in. You could have helped build a modernized technological nerve research center. Yet you had to risk it all. You had to jump the gun. I don't understand why. Why risk your job, your career, everything, all for one patient?"

Brandon stood at the door until Murphy was about to tell him to leave. Brandon finally replied. "I could have fixed it. I could have saved him. It should have worked. *It should have worked!*"

"But it didn't work did it? And now your entire life's work may amount to nothing. My advice to you is this, not that you have listened before, take a vacation. Take a long vacation. Honestly I don't think I can ever have you work here again. I can't trust you. Maybe in six months, maybe a year from now you can start looking for a position in another hospital or research facility. Perhaps pick up where you have left off. You're smart and you are dedicated. When you played by the rules you were a damn fine surgeon. But I can't have you work in a hospital for which I am responsible. It isn't anything personal I have towards you. I have to look out for an entire hospital. This is the only solution I have that will keep this hospital intact as well as give you a chance to continue your work at some point in the future."

Brandon turned to walk out of the office.

"One more thing Dr. Leshing, and for now you are still *Doctor* Leshing. If you tell anyone of what happened during that surgery, I'll personally see to it that not only will your medical license be revoked, but you will be pressed with criminal charges of gross negligence putting a patient at an unnecessary risk. Do I make myself clear?"

Brandon hesitated until Murphy finished speaking, and then continued out of the office. After Brandon closed the door Murphy got on the phone. "Hello, George, it's Murphy. Leshing's done it."

"What has he done?"

"He's performed his procedure on a patient."

"What? I specifically told you to keep him under wraps. What the hell were you thinking?"

"Wait, I didn't know until after the surgery. I had no idea. Believe me had I known I would have put a stop to it."

"What's the status of the patient?"

"Actually he hasn't had any progress in four weeks. Leshing's procedure may have done more harm than good."

George thought for a few seconds. "We may have gotten lucky."

"Lucky? How the hell is that lucky? If anyone finds out about this the hospital would be liable."

"How many people know about it?"

"Five people, you, me, Leshing, the anesthesiologist and a nurse."

"Where is Leshing?"

"I've basically fired him. I told him to take a vacation, never to return. I told him if he mentions a word of this to anyone I'd see to it that his license is revoked and he be put away for a long time."

"Did he buy it?"

"I believe so. He's smart enough to know if this gets out I won't have to do anything. He'd be sued up the ass and would most likely face criminal charges of gross negligence."

"Good work. Putting Leshing away delays his cure and we didn't have to buy him out. I'll mention your efforts to the board. You'll see a nice bonus coming your way. Keep me informed if word gets out or if there is any change in Leshing's status." Before Murphy could reply, George hung up the phone.

When Gina left Murphy's office she knew she couldn't wait outside the door and listen in on Murphy's conversation with Brandon. Murphy's secretary was sitting two feet away. So Gina walked down the hall and waited for

Brandon to come out of the office. When she saw him she ran to him. "What did Murphy say? You're not fired are you?" Brandon kept walking. "Brandon! Talk to me! What did Murphy say?"

Still walking at a quick pace, looking straight ahead, Brandon replied. "He told me to take a long vacation. My time here is done."

"What are you going to do? We can appeal. You didn't *mean* to harm Bruce. You tried to do what was best for him. I'll testify on your behalf. I'll..."

"You'll do nothing of the kind. It was my decision to try the procedure. I failed. Because of me, another kid's life as he knew it is over."

"It wasn't your fault. You tried your best to help him. You meant no harm. You...."

"Gina, it's over. I was wrong. I had no right to do what I had done. Murphy was right. I jumped the gun. Whatever my reasons, I was wrong. There's no going back now. I don't want you to do anything. I don't want you to risk your job too."

"What are you going to do?"

"Right now I'm going to get my belongings and head home."

"I'll come with you. I can have someone cover for the rest of my shift."

"No, I told you I don't want you to do anything. It's over. Go back to work. Please!"

After collecting what personal belongings he could, Brandon headed back to his apartment. Not knowing what to do, where to go, he plopped onto his couch. He leaned forward, and put his head in his hands. All he could think about was what he had promised Louie – '*I'll fix it*'. But he didn't fix anything. Instead, he ruined another person's life. He looked over to his bookshelf and saw a gift he had received from a friend upon graduating from Althaia. It was a bottle of Tullamore Dew that had never been open. Today would be the day. He went to the kitchen brought out a glass, opened the bottle and poured himself a small amount. He slammed the drink back grimacing after he swallowed. He felt the warmth of the Irish whiskey go through his body. He sat down on the couch and poured himself more. In a couple gulps, that was gone.

Gina had three more hours to go until her shift was done. She couldn't keep her mind on her work. All she could think about was Brandon. With one hour to go she asked if it was Ok if she left early due to having an upset stomach. Gina clocked out and headed straight for Brandon's apartment. She knocked on the door, hoping Brandon hadn't gone anywhere or done anything rash, but she got no reply. Gina knocked harder. This time she heard a faint "Who is it".

"Brandon it's Gina, is it ok if I come in?" Gina heard a low grumble and couldn't make out what Brandon said. She opened the door and saw Brandon lying on the couch. Throughout the apartment, papers, books were thrown all over. It was as if a small tornado had come through scattering everything about. On the table she noticed the half bottle of Tullamore Dew. She rushed over and sat next to Brandon placing her hands on his face, and brushed aside his hair. She noticed his eyes swelled with tears. She smelled the whiskey on his breath.

Brandon looked up to Gina. "What have I done? I failed. I'll never fix it. I've ruined them."

Gina tried her best to console Brandon. "You're a brilliant, selfless, honest, good hearted person. You are so close to doing great things. You can't give up now. I know you think you have failed. You haven't given yourself enough time. I believe in you. You will do this."

"You don't understand. I've ruined two people's lives. I killed a seven year old kid. I've ruined an eighteen year olds life. Because of me neither one will ever have a chance at a normal life."

Gina took the empty glass out of Brandon's hands. "Brandon this isn't the answer. This won't help you now or ever." She continued to try to console him. "Brandon, look at me." Gina took both of her hands, and gently placed them on both sides of Brandon's face to get him to look into her eyes. "Brandon I believe in you. I don't know why, I don't know how, but I believe that one day you will make this work. It's why I came to Burdette Tomlin. When I first saw you, I, I don't know what it was. Something told me to go to you. Something, or someone, maybe it was my father, I don't know, but I knew I had to come to you. Maybe it was for this moment right here, right now. You *will* make a difference in people's lives. I know you are determined to make it right. You *will* be successful."

The sun was going down and there were no lights on in the apartment. Brandon could still see the soulful look in Gina's brown eyes. All of his life he had never needed anyone, until now. Though he wasn't sober, he wasn't too drunk to feel a wanting to kiss Gina, to hold Gina, to make love to Gina. He lifted his head to get his lips closer to hers.

Gina wiped away a tear from Brandon's cheek. From the minute she saw him she wanted to see that look in his eyes. The look she had given him before. The room was dimly lit by the fading sun but the look she longed for was now in his eyes. Seeing that he wanted to get closer, Gina leaned down to touch his lips with hers. It was a slow, soft gentle kiss. Gina had longed for this moment ever since she first saw Brandon on TV. Brandon had always denied himself of this moment because of his work. Now that his work was gone, he wanted to feel something besides the pain and guilt he felt for destroying two lives.

Brandon stood up, took Gina by the hand, and led her into his bedroom. He stopped at the bed, looking at Gina. Until this point in his life Brandon had been a college football Heisman trophy winner, he was a successful neurosurgeon. He was big, strong, intelligent, and self-reliant. He was also inexperienced when it came to women. He had dedicated his life to his work. He denied himself any intimacy with any woman. Standing next to Gina, not knowing exactly what to do, he wished he had done things differently in life.

It had only been a few seconds standing in front of Gina, but to Brandon it had seemed like an eternity. Surely Gina now knew how limited his experience was when it came to women. When he finally stopped thinking of what to do next, staring into Gina's eyes, he slowly drew his face closer to hers. He touched her lips with his own. The softness of her lips, the warmth of her body, the scent of her hair made Brandon want more. He pulled back to again look into Gina's eyes. He wanted to be sure this was what they both wanted.

Brandon placed his right hand upon Gina's left cheek. She placed her right hand on the back of Brandon's neck and drew him closer for another kiss. This time their lips parted, their tongues slowly mingled, softly touching. There was no turning back. Brandon wrapped his arms around Gina, holding her tight. He picked her up and placed her upon his bed. As Gina lay there staring into Brandon's eyes she unbuttoned her shirt, Brandon removed his. He bent down to kiss Gina on her forehead, then her lips. He moved slowly to her chin, to the nape of her neck. As he was kissing Gina, making his way down he removed his trousers. Gina slid off her slacks.

From kissing her neck, Brandon began playing with Gina's breast with his mouth as he gently tugged at her nipple. Gina let out a slight gasp, her nipples becoming hard. She had her hands on the back of Brandon's head, pushing his head down. Brandon was happy to oblige. He went down further, until he reached Gina's panties. Brandon parted Gina's legs, and began to massage Gina with his tongue until her panties were soaking wet. As good as she felt, Gina wanted more. She lifted Brandon's head. He looked up at Gina. Gina looked back with a smile. She brought her legs together to remove her panties. When they were down to her kneecaps Brandon took over and removed them entirely. He kissed the inside of Gina's thighs and moved once again to the moistest part of her body. Brandon continued to play with Gina with his tongue. After several minutes of pleasure Gina arched her back, let out a low groan as goose pimples covered her body. Her hands clasped the back of Brandon's head, her legs on Brandon's shoulders.

Gina wanted Brandon close to her. She pulled his head up towards her own. Brandon kissed every inch of her body until he was face to face with her. He realized that Gina was the most beautiful woman he had ever seen. Why had he denied himself all these years? They lied naked together, Brandon on top of Gina. They kissed. Gina wanted Brandon more than ever and Brandon was all too happy to let her have her way. Brandon wrapped his arms around Gina, holding her tight. Although she was lying on her back, Gina felt as though she was in the air with nothing but Brandon's arms holding her afloat. She wrapped her legs around Brandon's waist as he gently worked his way inside her. Slowly inch by inch rhythmically inserting, pulling, inserting a bit more and more until he was completely inside her. He raised his head, and let out a groan as he worked faster. Gina took a quick gasp of air. Brandon stiffened his back, he closed his eyes and, and, and, just like that, he was done.

This intelligent, strong, confident, self-controlled man was done in less than a minute. Brandon was embarrassed. He wanted to bury his face in the pillow but that would mean looking at Gina who obviously would be disappointed at his performance. Maybe he could blame it on the alcohol. Maybe he could blame it on her beauty. She was so beautiful that he couldn't control himself. Ultimately he didn't know what to do or what to say.

Gina stroked away Brandon's hair from his face. She looked at him, then, as if she couldn't be any more perfect for Brandon she said – "I'm not going anywhere. I'll be here all night. We have plenty of time." This made Brandon love her even more. He held her, kissed her, gently nibbled on her ear lobe. He loved how Gina sounded, how soft her skin felt, how pleasant the scent of her body. After several minutes of kissing and touching, Brandon was ready for more.

This time he was in greater control. He made love to Gina for what seemed like hours. This time it was Gina to finish first. A few minutes after Gina, Brandon was satisfied as well. They lay next to each other, holding each other's hand. Brandon took Gina's hand to his lips kissing her fingers. "I have spent my whole life on a mission. I have deprived myself the pleasures that people enjoy for the sake of my work. I never socialized in high school or college. I've never had a girlfriend. I've never taken a vacation. My whole life has been dedicated to one purpose." Brandon hesitated. He squeezed Gina's hand tighter. The pain of recent events began to come back. "And now I've thrown it all away. I've sacrificed everything for nothing."

"Brandon, don't think like that. You had a setback. Everything you have set your mind to you have succeeded – in football, school, work, you have always come out on top. For the first time in your life you have had a setback. Maybe you have made a mistake. It happens."

"A mistake? Gina I've done worse than just made a mistake. I've ruined two people's lives."

"Brandon I know, and you know as well, that you didn't harm your childhood friend on purpose. You were just a kid playing a prank. You never meant any harm. As for Bruce you truly thought you could give him a good chance at a full recovery. You thought you were doing the right thing for Bruce, not for yourself. Maybe there is still a chance Bruce will pull through."

"I acted selfishly. I put his life, my career, your career, the entire hospital in jeopardy. I only saw the reward. I never saw risk. Or worse, I did see the risk. But I ignored it and went ahead anyway."

"You did what you believed to be what was right. Now you are at a crossroad. You have to decide what you want to do from here. Do you quit? Or do you learn from this and continue?"

"Continue where? I'm banned from the hospital. I've been told to take an extended vacation. No hospital or research facility is going to hire me now.

Even if they considered taking me on, they will ask questions as to why I left Burdette. They'll ask questions that I won't be able to answer."

"Brandon you can't quit. You're so close. I know what you are doing is right. I know you will succeed in your work. You have to keep going."

"How do you know so much? How do you know I'll succeed?"

"The first time I saw you, was when you made your football speech in college. I didn't even know your name but when I saw you on TV, I, I don't know, at that moment, I knew you were special. Not because you decided to continue your education instead of making money playing football. There was just something about you that I knew was unique. I didn't think too much about it at that time. Then, one night some friends and I went to see the taro reader I told you about. She told me that I would be part of something that would change the world. I didn't know what it was. She never told me specifically what that something was. Later on I thought of you again. It was when you first took the job here at the hospital. I had to know more about you. I don't know why, maybe it was due to what my father went through, but I had to know. For some reason when I think about what that taro reader said about changing the world I think of you. I believe in you. You need to continue your work. And if you will let me, I want to be there by your side. I want to be part of something great. I know you are the one I need to be with to make that happen."

Brandon had always gone through life alone. He had classmates, he had friends, he had family, and he had colleagues. Yet he still went through life alone. Gina was right. He had always been successful at whatever he had set his mind to do. Because of his success Brandon had always been regarded, even praised as a strong, resourceful man. He never experienced failure, true failure. Maybe that was why he believed he didn't need anyone close in his life. There were too many things he needed to do. He had too much to learn in too little time. He never had time to devote to someone. Now he knew that kind of thinking had been a mistake. He did need someone close. He needed someone who believed in him even when he failed.

Brandon sat up and turned to Gina. "Trying to take on the world like I have is hard. It's too hard to do alone. I've been a fool to think I could take it all on by myself." At that very second Gina couldn't help but think those same words were written to her by her father.

"Ok Gina, we'll take on the world together." Brandon rolled onto his back. He swung Gina on top of him. Gina felt Brandon between her legs. Her eyes widened. "Again?"

"You did say that you would be here all night right?"

"I did say that."

They made love until Gina collapsed unto Brandon who was happy to let Gina lay upon his chest. Within minutes both were sound asleep.

Chapter 16
PROMISES KEPT

It was 10AM when Brandon rolled over on his bed wanting to hold Gina. He squeezed gently, then more firmly. He reached to give her a kiss, but when he thought he was close, he was still kissing air. He awoke to find that he was holding a pillow. Gina was nowhere on the bed. Maybe she was in the kitchen or maybe the bathroom. Or maybe what he experienced during the night was nothing more than a dream. Brandon rubbed his eyes, shook his head to become more awake. He remembered distinctly cracking open the Tullamore Dew and for the first time in his life wanting to get drunk. He also remembered, though not as distinctly Gina knocking on the door. It couldn't have been a dream. Was he that drunk? There was no sign of her anywhere. Brandon hollered out – "Gina! Gina, are you in the kitchen?" There was no reply. He rolled over to the edge of the bed and sat, still needing to shake some of the cobwebs. He grabbed his robe that was hung on the bed stand and covered his naked body. He walked to the living room where he saw the half empty bottle he distinctly remembered opening. He saw the books and papers thrown carelessly about the room. How they got there he did not remember so well.

From the living room Brandon went to the bathroom where he looked at himself in the mirror. He looked more disheveled than he had ever seen himself look in his life. He took off his robe, grabbed a towel and took a shower. While in the shower his thoughts went immediately to the surgery he performed on Bruce Hopkins. The streams of water from the showerhead reminded him of the breakthrough idea he had about the microtubules within the spinal cord. He pounded his fist on the wall. "Damn it! It should have worked!" But he had to resign himself to the fact that his procedure had failed. He thought about what he could do, what he *should* do, now that he had ruined two lives. Brandon stayed in the shower for so long that the hot water began to fade. Finally he turned off the water, dried himself off and went back to the bedroom to put on some clothes. It was there he saw the letter from Gina. It hadn't been a dream after all.

Hello my love. I have to head to work and wanted to stop home to shower and change clothes. I was going to wake you but you look so cute cuddling that pillow. ☺.
– Gina.

Gina was the only bright spot in Brandon's life. She was the only person who could take some of his pain away. He smiled as he recalled the night they had spent together. Still a little embarrassed about their first time, he was able to laugh about it now. The passion they shared, the love they shared would stay with him no matter what for the rest of his life. But Gina could not take away the pain entirely. She believed in him and that was enough to continue. He didn't know how, he didn't know where, he didn't know when, but he made a vow to continue his work until he could fix it.

It was 8AM when Gina awoke next to Brandon. Knowing that she had to be back in work by noon, she realized that she would have to leave soon. For now, for a few minutes, she watched her lover as he lay sound asleep cuddling a pillow. She had always known that he was the man she was destined to love. Even though Brandon didn't realize at first that they were meant to be together, she knew. When Brandon first rejected her advances, she didn't give up. Though there were times when she thought she might. There were times when her heart was broken. There were times when she thought it better to go back to Philadelphia. But deep down, she knew. She just knew. And now it had come to fruition. Gina felt a happiness she never felt before in her life.

Gina debated waking Brandon to spend another hour awake in each other's arms. However he seemed to be at such peace that she didn't want to disturb him. She quietly got out of bed and put on the clothes that she wore the night before. She walked into the living room, picked up a piece of paper that was strewn on the floor. She found a pen and wrote Brandon a note. When she finished, she placed the note on his bedroom bureau, then quietly, without waking Brandon, left his apartment.

When she got home she put on some coffee, took a shower and changed her clothes. After dressing she poured herself a cup, toasted a bagel, and then headed to work. When she got to her station she discussed the patients that were on her watch. Most of the patients had relatively peaceful nights. However, Bruce Hopkins got little sleep and complained of cramp-like symptoms in his legs. This was odd because up until now Bruce had very little, if any feeling of pain in any part of his body below his chest. When Dr. Crane observed Bruce he attributed the symptoms to a lack of hydration so he ordered additional fluids. Gina made it a priority to check on him.

It was 1:30PM. Gina knew Bruce's lunch was over. She also knew it would be another half hour before Bruce's family and friends would visit. She decided now would be a good time to check on him. She knocked on Bruce's door, opening it at the same time. She noticed that the TV was on. A music video was playing, but Bruce paid no attention. He stared into the ceiling.

"Hello Bruce. I heard you had a rough night last night."

"Hi nurse Gina. My legs had weird feeling in them. Doctor says I need to drink more fluids."

Gina walked up to Bruce and placed her hand upon his forehead to feel for any sign of fever. "That's what I've been told as well, so I'm here to see that your water is filled. Would you like me to get you some juice, or maybe a coke?"

"No, the water's fine. Where has that asshole Dr. Leshing been? I haven't seen him in a couple days. You know he thinks I'm some sort of punk ass kid just laying here not trying. I swear to God I'm gonna…."

Gina could see Bruce's eyes begin to swell. In two days he would be transferred to a rehabilitation hospital. "Dr. Leshing has been under a lot of stress lately. He didn't mean what he said. Believe me, aside from you and your family, no one wants to see you get better more than him." Gina held Bruce's hand. She gave a gentle squeeze to let Bruce know she was here for him.

"Yeah, well I'm gonna get better. I'm gonna walk. And when I do, I'm gonna walk right up to that asshole and shove it in his face. He doesn't know me. He doesn't know what kind of man I am. I ain't no punk. I ain't just gonna lay here and let it be the end."

"I know Bruce. I know how much of a fighter you are." As Gina said this she noticed how strong Bruce was gripping her hand. Gina had asked Bruce many times before to grasp her hand to test his hand strength. Up until now Bruce could hardly muster a squeeze. Now however, Gina's hand was turning red from the strength of Bruce's grip. "Bruce, would you mind if I check your legs? I want to see if there is any swelling."

"No, go ahead." Gina removed Bruce's blankets. Then she removed the stocking from each leg. She couldn't see any signs of swelling. "While I'm here why don't we try to wiggle the toes?"

"Ok." Bruce closed his eyes. He looked as though he was about to lift a thousand pounds. Suddenly the toes on each foot moved as if it were spasms.

Gina was shocked to see the sudden movement. "Bruce, your toes moved. Was that you?"

"I'm trying nurse Gina." Bruce's toes remained curled. It was as if a cramp set in locking them tight. "Can you release them? They're locked."

"I can't. It's like a muscle spasm."

"Ok relax, try to relax." Gina began to massage Bruce's feet until the locked toes were free. "Ok, let's try that again. Try to wiggle your toes."

Bruce closed his eyes again. Immediately the toes on his feet locked in a spastic state. "Alright, alright, that's good Bruce. Try to relax again." Gina again massaged Bruce's toes until they were free. "Let's do that one more time. Show me this isn't a fluke."

For the third time, Bruce moved his toes. This time he was able to release his curled toes on his own. "Bruce this is amazing. I've never seen you do this before."

"You mean its working?"

"Yes! Yes, I think so. And when you held my hand, it was like a vice grip. I've never felt your hand grip so strong." For the first time since he was brought into the hospital Bruce had something to smile about. "Ok, not to push things but see if you can move your left foot. Now relax your body. Concentrate on your foot. Try to push it towards me."

Bruce took a deep breath. He tried to relax. "Ok, here goes." Bruce's face turned red as he pushed his foot. It wasn't much, but Gina felt the pressure. "That's great Bruce! Now bring it back towards you."

As Bruce tried to pull his foot back towards him, his entire leg shot up as if he stepped on an electrical wire. In an instant his left leg was up at his chest. "Bruce what are you doing! I just wanted you to move your foot. You moved your entire leg!"

"Nurse Gina I know. I just tried to, I don't know. It just happened."

"Ok bring your leg down."

As Bruce tried to lower his leg, it began to shake uncontrollably in spasm. It took almost Gina's entire body weight to bring the shaking to a halt. Seeing how Gina had practically hopped onto his leg, Bruce began to laugh. Gina couldn't help but laugh as well. "Bruce, you're too strong for me."

"Can I try it again?"

"Bruce I don't know. I'm afraid the spasms are too strong."

"I got to keep trying. This is the first time I've moved my legs. I have to keep trying. Let me try again. Please. I have to keep trying."

Gina knew if she asked Bruce to hold off that Bruce would be trying to move his legs anyway as soon as she left his room. And seeing how upbeat he was for the first time, she agreed to keep working. "Ok, let's try again."

Bruce pushed his foot towards Gina who stood at the end of the bed. Bruce's toes again curled but he was able to release them more easily. "Nice, that's very nice Bruce. Ok, now try to bring your foot back towards you." Again Bruce's foot moved back towards his body. Uncontrollably his leg was up on his chest. "Bruce this is amazing! I've never seen an improvement come so quickly. Ok, lower your leg slowly." Gina took hold of Bruce's leg and helped guide it until it was resting on the bed.

Bruce was able to do this exercise three more times before his leg and foot tired. Even though he was barely able to move his foot after the fourth try, Bruce was ecstatic. "I knew it! I knew I would get better! I can't wait to show Dr. Leshing. When is he coming back in to see me?"

Lost in the excitement of seeing Bruce move his leg was the fact that Brandon could be vindicated. This brief explosion of movement could be just a start towards a full recovery. Gina couldn't wait to tell Brandon. This meant he didn't have to leave the hospital. Brandon's surgery didn't take away all hope of Bruce's recovery. The surgery may have given Bruce a real chance. "I have to check the schedule Bruce. I'm not sure when his next shift is. I'm sure as soon as he gets here you will be his first visit. You rest up. I have to go see other patients. You've been through quite a workout, besides your family will be here soon. Maybe you can show them a thing or two."

"Ok nurse Gina. If you see Dr. Leshing, tell him to come and see me."

"I will."

Gina left Bruce's room and headed back to her station. She couldn't wait to tell Brandon. But every time she tried to call, she got the same message:

I am not available now. Please leave a message. There was no way to get a hold of Brandon, at least not until her dinner break at 4:30. Unable to get a hold of Brandon, Gina met Dr. Crane to tell him the good news. After that she headed for Murphy's office. His assistant, Betty was at her desk. "Hi Betty, is Mr. Murphy available? I need to speak to him."

"Hello Gina, I'm afraid he is on a conference call right now. I can tell him you stopped by and that you need to see him."

"I'm afraid I have to speak to him now. You know I would never disturb him if it wasn't important. But this cannot wait. It's regarding a patient."

"Oh, if it is a matter with a patient, I'll see if he can talk to you now."

"Thank you, Betty."

A minute later Betty came out of the office. "He asked for you to wait here. As soon as he is finished he will let us know."

Gina waited for 10 minutes when Betty's phone buzzed. When Betty put down the receiver she notified Gina that she could go into Murphy's office. Gina practically jumped from her chair straight into the office. "Nurse Stroit, Betty tells me you wanted to see me regarding a patient."

"I do Mr. Murphy. It is regarding Bruce Hopkins."

Murphy put his pen down and looked up at Gina. His interest peaked. "Well, what is it?"

"Mr. Murphy, Bruce has had some improvement this morning. He seems to be getting stronger."

"What kind of improvement?"

"His hand grip is a lot stronger. He was able to bring his leg up to his chest."

"That's great news. Have you informed the doctors on staff?"

"Yes, I have. I've informed Dr. Crane."

Murphy played with his pen. He seemed to be in deep thought. "That's great news Gina. I'm glad you came here to tell me. What day is his transfer?"

Gina expected more excitement from Murphy. She knew he wasn't the most outgoing or excitable person, but still she expected more than *thank you, when is he leaving.* "I believe his transfer is scheduled for Thursday."

"Very well, thank you again for keeping me informed."

"You're welcome. May I ask if this means Dr. Leshing is welcomed back from his suspension?"

"I asked Dr. Leshing to take some time off. He obviously has been under a lot of stress lately. I'll have to take it up with some people as to when he may return."

"But he will be able to…"

"Nurse Stroit, I appreciate you keeping me informed about our patient's well-being. As to the personnel of this staff, that's something not under your job description. Please return to your station."

Gina watched Murphy pick up some paperwork that he began to read. Not knowing what to say, Gina turned and walked out of his office.

Immediately after Gina shut the door behind her, Murphy picked up his phone. "George? It's Murphy. I have an update on the Leshing patient....."

It was 2:30. Gina had two more hours before her dinner break. She tried calling Brandon several more times, but she kept getting the same voice message. *Why won't he pick up the phone!* The time was passing excruciatingly slow. At 4:10 she asked if she could break early for dinner. When she was told she would be covered, Gina headed straight for Brandon's apartment.

After showering and getting dressed, Brandon began cleaning up the books, papers, and everything else he had thrown about the living room floor. He put the cap on the half empty bottle of Tullamore Dew and placed it back in its original box. After cleaning up he contemplated his situation. For all intents and purposes he could not go back to practicing medicine. If he had applied for a position anywhere, he would have to explain why he left Burdette Tomlin. Even if he could explain why he left, Murphy was sure to get a call from his possible new employer. No way would Murphy give Brandon a ringing endorsement. And if it was ever found out that he had taken an untested risk, he may lose the ability to ever practice medicine again for the rest of his life. Maybe Murphy was right that it was time to take a vacation. Brandon never took one before. Maybe a few months in Cost Rica would benefit him. Maybe it would invigorate him. He didn't have to worry about money. As a neurosurgeon he was paid extremely well. He had no major expenses. The biggest expense Brandon had was paying his parents back the money they spent taking out the insurance policy his senior year at Althaia.

What would Gina think about going away with him? He knew she loved him, and he knew that he loved her. Would she love him enough to pack up everything, quit her job and go away? Could she do that even if she wanted to? As long as he had known Gina, he really didn't know her personally too well. He knew that her parents had passed away. He knew that she was originally from Philadelphia. But that was about it. After sitting and thinking for another hour, he decided to head out to the beach and take a walk. He was back home by 4:00. A half hour later he heard a pounding on the door. Then he heard Gina yell – "Brandon are you here?"

Brandon opened the door, Gina walked past him into his apartment. She was out of breath as if she had just finished a quarter mile sprint. "Brandon I've been trying to call you all day. What's wrong with your phone?"

"Nothing I..." Brandon took out his cell phone and immediately noticed that it was turned off. "I must have turned it off last night. I didn't realize. Why? What's wrong?"

"Nothing is wrong, everything is right. He moved today. He was able to move today."

"What are you talking about? Who moved?"

"Bruce! He was able to lift his leg up to his chest! It's a miracle! He can move! Do you know what this means? It means...."

"Gina, Gina, slow down. Hold on for a minute. Take a deep breath. Tell me from the beginning. Before you get too excited, are you sure he wasn't having muscle spasms. It happens in almost every case. A patient mistakes muscle spasms for the ability to move on his own. Tell me from the beginning what happened?"

Gina finally caught her breath. "When I got to my station I was given updates on all of my patients. Everyone had a peaceful night except Bruce. He complained that he was feeling cramp-like symptoms in his legs. Dr. Crane thought it was a lack of fluids that was causing the cramping. I went to Bruce's room and looked at his chart. I made sure he had plenty of fluids. Then we started talking and he got a little emotional. That's when I held his hand and as he was talking he began squeezing my hand. It was a stronger grip than he ever had since his post-op. So I asked if he would mind if I took a look at his legs to check for any swelling. I took down his bed sheets and I didn't notice anything unusual."

"I asked him to try to move his toes. He braced himself and tried as hard as he could to move them and he did! His toes curled and cramped so I thought maybe it was the sudden coldness that hit his legs. I asked him to try to relax but he couldn't on his own so I massaged his toes back to a relaxed state. Then I asked him to try to move his toes again, and again his toes curled up and cramped."

"Ok so what you saw were spasms. That's perfectly normal Gina."

"Brandon will you shut up and let me finish!"

"Ok, sorry, please continue."

"I was able to get his toes back to a normal state and for the third time I asked him to try to move them again. This time he was able to move them on his own. This time he was able to move them back to a relaxed state on his own. I asked him to try to push his feet towards me. And damn it Brandon he did! He did it a couple times. On his own! Then, when I asked him to bring his foot back towards him, instead of just moving his left foot back, his whole leg lifted towards his chest. After I helped bring his leg back down to the bed, he lifted his leg again, and then again. He did this three times on his own. Then he started to get tired and couldn't lift his leg as much so I told him to rest. This wasn't a spasm Brandon. He moved his toes, his feet and was able to lift his left leg! Brandon it was incredible! I've never seen anything like it before in all of my years as a nurse. I've never seen such a dramatic improvement in such a short time. Have you seen anything like it in your tests?"

Brandon didn't know what to say. Taking Gina at her word, and there was no reason not to, it seems as though Bruce's chances of recovery went up dramatically. "Well, in my tests, the advances were in shorter bursts than what is normally seen. Usually it's a slow process for the patient. But, with my tests, it was more of a burst where the test subjects had improvement in a shorter period of time. After a few days they would have another burst of improvement. After that it was a matter of building strength back." Before

Brandon could let himself be overtaken with excitement he had to know more. He had to see for himself.

"Brandon, do you know what this means? This means you don't have to leave the hospital. This means Bruce may be on his way to a full recovery like you predicted. I spoke to Murphy today and…"

"You spoke to Murphy? What did he say?"

Gina's enthusiasm suddenly dropped. "I told him about the progress Bruce had made."

"And?"

"And he thanked me for keeping him informed."

"Did he say anything else?"

"He asked me when Bruce's transfer to his rehab would be."

"That's it?"

"I asked if this meant that you could come back to the hospital."

"What did he say to that?"

Gina hesitated. "He didn't say no. He said it wasn't in my job description to decide on staffing."

"He isn't going to allow me back in Gina. I'm black-balled. There's something going on with him. I don't know what it is but ever since I made a breakthrough with my work he's seemed really strange. Maybe he doesn't trust me. Lord knows I've given him plenty of reasons not to."

"You don't know that for sure. Murphy can be a real hard-ass but he isn't blind to all the good work you've done. Maybe he won't allow you back right away. Maybe after Bruce is transferred Murphy will calm down. You have to go back if only to see Bruce. You're the reason he was able to move his legs."

"Maybe, maybe not, he may have had this progress even if I didn't apply my procedure."

"I'm not talking about that. I'm talking about the last time you spoke to him. You really made a terrible impression on him. All he talked about was how he was going to show you that he isn't the lazy kid that you think he is. He really wants to shove it in your face."

Brandon smiled. It was the first smile he had regarding Bruce. "He's going to need all the motivation he can muster. Alright, let's head back to the hospital. I'll try to stop by his room to see him. But I have to see Murphy first. The last thing I want is to be escorted out by security in handcuffs. Why don't you head back now? I have to get a few things before I go. I'll see to you there." Gina went back to the hospital. Brandon picked up some of his research documentation to compare with the results he was about to see with Bruce.

Brandon walked into the hospital and went straight to Murphy's office. Instead of asking Betty if Murphy was available, he walked past her and into his office. Murphy was going through monthly expenses when he was caught by surprise. "Leshing! What are you doing here? I thought I made myself perfectly clear. You are forbidden to come back into the hospital."

"I heard Hopkins has had some improvement since the last time I was here. I wanted to see for myself. I wanted to come here first to not cause a scene."

"That was very thoughtful of you, but my order still stands, improvements or not. You are not to set foot in this hospital."

"Mr. Murphy with all due respect, Bruce's improvements may mean the hospital is off the hook as far as any possible litigation. It means my procedure may be working. It just may have taken longer. I need to see for myself what kinds of improvements have been made. I need to run some tests."

"Dr. Leshing, and I say doctor tentatively, what this means is that we may have gotten lucky. The fact of the matter remains that what you have done is still considered to be negligent, careless and possibly criminal. It is out of the question that I let you in this hospital, let alone near that patient. He has two more days until he is transferred. At that point his case is out of our hands. Until then I don't want you observing the patient, I don't want you near that patient. I don't want you in this hospital period! Now if you don't walk out of this hospital this instant, I will be forced to call security to escort you out."

Brandon knew Murphy wasn't going to move an inch on letting him see Bruce. Yet he pleaded his case one last time. "Mr. Murphy, Michael, we might be on the brink of something miraculous. If my theory is correct, within a few more weeks Bruce should expect to see some more major improvements in his recovery. If we monitor, document his recovery, we can learn so much. When the next patient comes in we will be better prepared. Not only that, my procedure would be more acceptable to the medical community. It would be one step closer to accreditation."

"You don't get it do you? One word about you applying your procedure to anyone outside this office opens this hospital up to litigation. Whether that patient fully recovers or not, what you did was negligent. We can't let it out to the medical community that you went ahead and applied your procedure. If that patient does make a full recovery what would be next? Brain surgery on those with autism because you have a theory about a cure? You are really trying my patience Leshing. Leave now or I will be forced to call security."

Brandon's last stand didn't move Murphy one bit. "Can I at least see Bruce before I leave?"

Murphy looked at Brandon for several seconds. He seemed to be on the verge of allowing Brandon's last request. Then, Murphy pushed the button on his phone. "Betty, call security please."

Brandon knew it was over. Without saying a word, he turned to leave Murphy's office before security arrived. "Oh, Leshing, one last thing, if I hear that you have gone to Hopkins' rehab hospital, I'll have your license revoked. Stay away from that kid. Understood?"

Gina rushed back to her station after meeting Brandon. She expected to see him stop by, but it had been an hour since she returned to the hospital

349

and she still had not seen, or heard from him. She had to make rounds to check on her patients and decided that Bruce would be her last stop to give Brandon more time. She wanted Brandon with her to see Bruce together.

When she got to Bruce's room she saw that one of his friends had already stopped by to see him. Gina knocked on the door. "Hi nurse Gina. I was telling Jason how much improvement I've made. Do you think we can take the bed covers off and I can show him?"

"Why don't you wait until your family stops by? Dr. Crane wants to see you as well."

"Ok. Speaking of doctors, have you heard from Dr. Leshing? I want to show him too."

"Dr. Leshing knows about your progress. He is very impressed. He said he will stop by when he can. Is there anything I can get you? Do you have enough water?"

"I'm fine nurse Gina. The only thing you can get me is Dr. Leshing."

"I'll see what I can do. I'll be back when Dr. Crane stops by. I'll leave you and your friend alone. If you need anything just hit the buzzer."

"Ok, I'll see you later."

Gina went back to her station to update her logs. It was obvious that Brandon wasn't going to see Bruce. When she had her fifteen minute break at 7:30 she called to see what had happened. This time Brandon answered his phone. "Brandon what happened? Why haven't you stopped by to see Bruce?"

"I'll tell you why, Murphy, that's why. He won't let me in the hospital let alone near Bruce."

"Why? I don't understand."

"I don't know Gina. Something isn't right."

"I'll be done my shift at nine. Can I stop by after?"

"Sure, I'd like that."

Gina was back in Bruce's room with Dr. Crane. A couple more friends and family had gathered. "Bruce it is show time. Let's show everyone what you showed me this afternoon."

"I'm ready nurse Gina."

"If you people will excuse us for a second. I need to get Bruce prepared. I don't want him showing too much."

Gina closed the curtain around Bruce's bed. She pulled off the bed sheets and placed a blanket over Bruce's hips. "Ok Bruce, just relax. We're going to do the same exercises we did earlier. No pressure. Whatever happens, happens, ok?"

"I'm ready."

Gina opened the curtains and everyone gathered around with much anticipation to see what Bruce had been telling his friends and family. Gina stood by Bruce's side, Dr. Crane stood at the bottom of the bed. "Gina tells me you were able to move your toes today Bruce. Can you show me?"

Bruce gave a quick glance to Gina who gave a wink in return. Just like earlier in the day his toes curled and he was unable to relax them. "Try and release them Bruce." Dr. Crane asked. It took a couple minutes until Bruce's toes were back normal. "Good Bruce. Can you try that again?" Bruce pushed his toes forward again. Again they curled up but this time Bruce was able to bring them back to normal. "Great, Bruce, great! One more time, let's see that one more time." For the third time Bruce pushed his toes forward. In seconds he was able to bring them back to normal. "Ok Bruce, let's see you move your feet. Try and push forward." Bruce was able to push his feet forward. "Great Bruce, ok, relax." Dr. Crane waited. He could see that Bruce was getting tired. "One more time, I want you to push as hard as you can with your feet. I'm going to put my hands in front to measure the force, ok?" Bruce nodded. "Ok, when you are ready." Bruce pushed his feet as hard as he could. Dr. Crane noticed he was pushing with a force that wasn't enough to uphold a lot of weight. But the force was noticeable. He waited a couple minutes before asking Bruce for his last test. "Bruce this is very good. I'm very impressed with your progress. I can see why Gina was so excited when she told me this afternoon." Bruce again gave a quick glance to Gina, who smiled back. "Alright, now for the big test, let me see you raise your leg like you did earlier today." Bruce braced himself. He closed his eyes and just as he had done earlier, he brought his left leg up to his chest which came up like a shot. Gina had to help ease the leg back into place. Bruce's friends and family were astonished.

Bruce was able to lift his leg two more times before tiring out. "Bruce this is a very good sign. I'm sure you are going to do great things when you get to rehab on Thursday. Ok people the show is over. Let's give our star a hand."

Gina began clapping as did Bruce's friends and family. Gina closed the curtain and put back Bruce's bed covers. She said in a voice that only Bruce could hear. "Bruce that was really good. You're getting better. It's going to take time but I know you're going to fight all the way through."

"Thank you nurse Gina. I got to be honest. I was having my doubts but no more. You're right. I'm not giving up until I'm back all the way. I just wish Dr. Leshing was here to see me. Do you think he will be back before I leave?"

"I'm sure if he is able to see you before you go, he will. Don't worry about Dr. Leshing. You just worry about getting better, ok?"

Gina pulled back the curtain. Bruce's friends and family couldn't wait to show Bruce how happy they were to see his progress. Gina and Dr. Crane left the room. Dr. Crane was very surprised how much improvement had been made in a day. Though he hadn't worked on too many spinal injuries, he had never seen, or even had heard of a case where so much improvement was made in such a short time.

Immediately after finishing her shift Gina went to Brandon's apartment. When she came in, she saw him sitting on the couch. He hadn't been drinking. He hadn't made a mess. He just sat there. "As you can see I'm not off the hook. I'm as suspended as always."

"I don't understand why would he act that way if Bruce is getting better?"

"I don't understand it either Gina. He said he still can't trust me. He doesn't want me near that kid. He said if I go near Bruce while he is in rehab he'll have my license revoked."

"That jackass! Why is he acting this way?"

"I don't know!" Brandon realized he was yelling. "I'm sorry. I don't mean to take it out on you."

"That's Ok I understand. I would be pissed off too if I was in your position. What are you going to do? He hasn't taken away your license. You can still do your research."

"We've been through this before. Right now I'm toxic. I can't open myself up to anyone about this. As much as I would love to show the world that my procedure has hope, I can't tell a sole without jeopardizing everything I have done."

"Well what then? You can't just sit here until it is a good time."

"Last night I asked you something but you never gave me an answer."

"Last night we both had our minds on other things." Gina gave Brandon a wry smile. "What was it that you asked?"

"It wasn't really a question, but more like a statement. I said that the world is too hard to take on alone. It's easier if you have someone who believes in you standing by your side."

"That's true. If you're asking me to stand by you, the answer is yes."

"Before you answer you have to realize what I'm about to ask."

"Ok what is it?"

"I was thinking about going away. I can't do anything regarding research or being a surgeon without having to answer a lot of questions that I can't answer at this time. As much as I would love to work with Bruce to see his rehabilitation, Murphy hasn't made that possible."

"Where would you like to go?"

"Some place far away from everything. I was thinking going to Costa Rica for a while."

"Costa Rica? Why there?"

"I've heard from a few people that it is a beautiful place. You can live right on the beach all year round. The people are nice, most speak English. You don't have to answer to anyone. It's a place where you can go without being disturbed by people, or politics, or even the weather. No one will know we are there. We can learn about each other. I'm not saying that we live there forever, but maybe just for a while."

Brandon wanted to let what he had proposed sink in. Gina wanted to stay by Brandon's side but she didn't expect to pack up everything once again, this time move to out of the country. She thought about what she would be leaving behind. The more she thought about it, the more she realized that there wasn't too much that she had that held her back from leaving. She still had her home in Philadelphia, but she wasn't living there. She could continue to let Julie stay there and look after the house. Other than that she had no ties except for the only one that truly mattered. He was sitting next to her now. She didn't want to sever that tie.

"Of course I'll go with you Brandon. I made a promise too and I intend to keep it."

"Gina, are you sure? You haven't promised me anything. You owe me nothing. I would love for you to come with me but I don't want you to do it for the sole reason that you think you would be breaking a promise to me."

"It isn't you whom I made the promise. I want to go with you because I love you. I just need to tie up some things here, but whenever you want to leave I'm willing to go."

Brandon didn't know what promises Gina meant, but he was too happy to ask. For the first time in his life he was going to do something other than devote his time towards his work. He thought about what Dr. Bromny had told him while he was at Althaia about the regrets he had for not living a more rounded life. Brandon was on the same path as Dr. Bromny, and he realized that he didn't want to have the same regret. Brandon would do whatever it took to build a life with Gina.

The following day Gina put in her resignation at Burdette Tomlin Hospital. After two weeks, when Gina completed her last shift, she and Brandon drove to Philadelphia. Gina met with Julie to make arrangements on her house. Those arrangements were basically the same as they already had. She met her friends from St. Helena's hospital and Macgregor Rehabilitation including Kevin.

Gina wanted to try to mend any hard feelings that Kevin may have had. Kevin never fully accepted that Gina had moved on, and he still loved her. He hadn't dated once since Gina had left him. He held out hope that she would return some day. When Gina met Kevin to say goodbye for good, Kevin realized that it didn't hurt as much as before. He realized that he was living in the past. The fact that Gina had moved on and seemed to be happy with her life was Ok. He finally had closure for himself.

Brandon stayed with his parents while Gina tied up the loose ends. Brandon didn't have any loose ends to tie up, except to explain to his parents what he was doing. His mother was happy to have her son home, if only for a few weeks. She was extremely happy to see her son in love with someone. His father, now semi-retired, was able to secure a spot on Universal's board as a voting member. Although Pat didn't have any real power other than being able to cast a vote.

Brandon explained what he was doing and why he was moving to Costa Rica. He didn't tell his parents anything about his research other to say that he had come to a road block and needed to get away to revitalize himself. He didn't say a word about the procedure he had performed on Bruce Hopkins. Brandon's parents didn't quite fully understand why their son had to move so far away. But if that is what would make him happy, and he had found someone to share his life, then they weren't going to question their son's decision.

Gina and Brandon left Philadelphia behind and had settled into a nice little bungalow on the beaches of Costa Rica. Though it was more rustic than what they had been used to living, the place was big enough for the both of them. The weather was always beautiful. The people were extremely nice. They had been there for almost a year. Neither had wanted anything but to stay by each other's side. Gina was happy, and Brandon had found a peace he never felt since he was a child.

One day a package arrived addressed to Brandon. It was an envelope the size of which seemed to contain business letters. The return address said *Pat and Cindy Leshing*. When Brandon came home Gina showed him the package. Brandon thought nothing of it when he began to open it. Inside was a disk to be inserted into a computer. There was also a letter, written by Brandon's mom.

Dear Brandon,

I hope you and Gina are well. A package containing this computer disk arrived yesterday. It is from a patient you had cared for while at Burdette Tomlin Hospital. The man's name on the package is Bruce Hopkins. He said he had been trying to locate you for some time. No one at Burdette was able to give him your forwarding address. Somehow he was able to find our address and phone number. He called and asked if we could forward this to you. Your father and I told him we would be more than happy to do so and, well, here it is.

Love, mom and dad.

Seeing that the package was from Bruce Hopkins both Brandon and Gina wondered if Bruce had somehow found out that Brandon had performed his *"Mito Wrap"* procedure. There was some trepidation that the disk in the package was some sort of legal dissertation. But, there were no letters, nothing to indicate a lawyer was involved. The disk simply had the title – *"To Dr. Leshing"*.

"What do you think is on the disk?" Brandon asked.

"There's only one way to find out. I'll get the lap top."

Brandon inserted the disk into the lap top and immediately saw that the disk contained one file – **DrLeshing.mpg**. Evidently it was a video. Brandon opened up the MPG player and clicked the play button. The first image was that of Bruce sitting in the bleachers. Bruce began to speak.

"Hello, Dr. Leshing. I hope this video makes its way to you. After my rehab ended I tried to get a hold of you. I called people at Burdette Tomlin Hospital but all they could tell me was that you were no longer working there. I hope the reason you had to leave had nothing to do with me. I'm not gonna lie to you. The last time you spoke to me you were harsh to say the least. I don't know why you acted the way you did, not knowing me and all. Nurse Gina said you were under a lot of stress."

"Speaking of nurse Gina I heard she left the hospital too. I tried to get her address but again no one was able to help. If you see her tell her I said thanks for all she did for me. Out of all the people at that hospital she was the one who truly believed in me."

Gina, looking over Brandon's shoulder gave him a slight squeeze with her hand. Brandon smiled back but quickly turned his attention back to the video. Bruce continued.

"I never forgot what you had said to me back then. I don't know if you really thought of me as some lazy kid looking for an easy way out, or if you said those things to get me mad, to motivate me. All I know is that I never forgot that day. I wanted to tell you, to show you that I wasn't some punk kid who gives up easily. I wanted to someday shove it in your face. So I worked, and every day I worked, I thought about you. It took me almost a year to get to this point. It took me almost a year to show you who I really am. When I was finally ready to show you, I couldn't find you."

"I remembered from your college days that you lived in the Philadelphia area. So I contacted every Leshing in the phone book until I found your parents. At least they said they were your parents. I asked them to forward this video I made and they said they would. I'm hoping you're watching this."

"Are you ready hun?" A female voice could be heard in the video – "I'm ready Bruce." Until now Bruce had been sitting in the bleacher. What happened next made both Brandon and Gina wide-eyed. Bruce stood up and walked down the two steps onto a running track. Bruce continued.

"Before I show you doc, I want to introduce you to my fiancé. Lori, step in front of the camera and say hi." Lori put the video camera on the bleacher, stepped to the front and waved hello. "Lori and I met while I was at rehab. From day one she believed in me. If it's one thing I've learned it's that life is hard enough to go through alone. If you find someone who believes in you, don't let her go."

Gina kissed Brandon on his cheek and whispered in his ear – "It only took him a couple months to figure that one out. How come it took you years?"

"I guess some guys are slower than others."

"Doc, I hope you're ready for this. Like I said, I ain't the lazy kid you think I am. I've worked my ass off. I hope you're watching. Let me know when you're ready Lori."

"I'm ready Bruce."

Bruce walked up to the starting line on the track. He got into a runner's stance. Lori shouted out. "Ready. Set. Go!" And with that Bruce began sprinting around the track. Gina and Brandon were amazed at how well Bruce was running. If they hadn't known any better neither would have guessed that a year ago Bruce was completely unable to move his legs. Yet there he was, sprinting around the track as fast as he could. Lori was filming him the whole way. When he crossed the finish line after running a quarter mile, Bruce was completely out of breath.

"Lori." Bruce gasped. "What was my time?"

"Fifty-nine seconds!"

Bruce pumped his fist. "Yes!" He exclaimed. "That's a new personal best." He finally caught his breath well enough to speak. He walked closer to the camera. "I looked you up Dr. Leshing. I didn't know it at the time I saw you but you were a pretty good football player in your day, a Heisman Trophy winner. Any time you want a crack at me on the track you just let me know. I'll show you who the punk is." Bruce's menacing look was replaced by a smile. "And doctor, one more thing, thank you. I know the odds of coming back from the injury I had sustained. I know that the percentages of a complete recovery are minimal at best. I wanted to show you this not to shove it in your face, but to show you that you did it. You fixed it. Thank you."

The video ended. Brandon stared at the lap top. Gina had tears in her eyes. "How about that Gina it worked. I fixed it." For the first time since the day he made a promise to Louie he was at total peace with himself. The promise he had made to his childhood friend had been kept.

Gina wrapped her arms around the love of her life. She sensed the pure satisfaction that her lover was feeling. She now knew exactly what her father meant when he wrote that success was nothing unless you could share it. The promise her father had asked of her was kept.

THE END

Bobby Hellings is a graduate of William Penn Charter High School in Philadelphia, PA

He obtained his B.A. in Computer Science degree from La Salle University.

He currently resides in East Norriton, PA.

If you wish to contact the author you may do so by sending an e-mail to:
BobHellings22@GMail.com

Or on Facebook at:
https://www.facebook.com/bobby.hellings